Bloody Piracy!

The French patrol copters tried hailing the Danish cargo carrier *Dolphin*, but to no avail.

When the helicopter reached the *Dolphin*, it found the vessel still afloat but obviously not under control. Three armed crewmen rappelled down to the ship. One of them lost his footing and fell. Pulling himself to his feet he realized to his horror that the slick substance covering the deck was blood. Walking more carefully now, he and the other French sailors searched high and low but could find no sign of the ship's crew.

The cargo of cheap furniture and electronics was intact. There was a large empty space in the hold, as if *something* had been taken. Also, the ship's bridge had been stripped of its GPS system, its satellite phones, its fax machine and its weather computer.

After the men finished their fruitless, dispiriting search they returned to the helicopter and flew back to their ship in dazed silence. The French had been doing anti-pirate duty in these waters for more than a year, and while they'd seen their share of incidents, those incidents were *always* just hijacking attempts—not willful killings or the intentional sinking of ships.

In just one night, the pirate problem in the Gulf of Aden had become a lot more dangerous.

The Pirate Hunters

Mack Maloney

FORGE®

A TOM DOHERTY ASSOCIATES BOOK
New York

This is a work of fiction. All of the characters, organizations, and events portrayed in this novel are either products of the author's imagination or are used fictitiously.

THE PIRATE HUNTERS

Copyright © 2010 by Mack Maloney

All rights reserved.

Edited by James Frenkel

A Forge Book
Published by Tom Doherty Associates, LLC
175 Fifth Avenue
New York, NY 10010

www.tor-forge.com

Forge® is a registered trademark of Tom Doherty Associates, LLC.

ISBN 978-0-7653-6521-7

First Edition: May 2010

Printed in the United States of America

0   9   8   7   6   5   4   3   2   1

For brave soldiers everywhere

ACKNOWLEDGMENTS

Many thanks to Jim Frenkel, Dominick Abel, Peter Calandra, Sgt. David Graves, Captain Randy Lynch, Walt Boyne, Phil Motoike, J. L. Brown, Tom Howley, Joe Kelleher, Rod Webber, Doug Bolick, Larry Stone, Sgt. Luke Hartmetz, Brian Malone, "Snake" Jackson, Dmitry and Oleg Gurtovoy, Clancy Miller, Jim Cook, John Daniels, Bill Kellan, Jack Shane, Buzz Summers, Gil Gillis, James Beam, Sgt. Tony Pluger, Gene Smith, Chip Bruynell, Mark Conley, Bob Messia, Seth Lerner, Ed Chapman, George Ebersole, Ron Elkin, Steve Minar, Richard Kennedy, Sr., Robert Buonfiglio, and especially, Doug Newman. Very special thanks to my wife, Doreen.

PART ONE

Team Whiskey

1

THREE SMALL FLAGS flew above Team Whiskey's base camp.

One bore the insignia of the New York City Police Department; another, the Fire Department of New York. The third was the American flag. They fluttered in the stiff breeze blowing down from the nearby mountains, their makeshift flagpoles bending but not breaking in the cold Afghani wind.

Huddled inside a tent nearby was Delta Force Unit 606, code-named Team Whiskey. They were wearing oxygen masks and struggling to keep warm.

Their tiny camp was situated about 500 feet up the side of Hill 3434A. In the valley below, three T-55 tanks belonging to the Eastern Alliance were lazily firing at al Qaeda positions on the opposite side of the next mountain over. A half-mile to the north, another squad of Delta operators, Team India, was climbing Hill 3438 in a convoy of lime-green Toyota pickups. Two larger trucks carrying more Eastern Alliance fighters trailed behind.

High above them all, a B-52 Stratofortress circled endlessly, leaving doughnut-ring contrails across the blue winter sky.

Team Whiskey, one of the most experienced Delta Force units in the Afghanistan theater, was part of the final push in the two-week battle to destroy the nearby al Qaeda stronghold at Tora Bora.

Yet they remained in place, crowded together in their Black Diamond mountain tent, sucking in oxygen and waiting.

* * *

THEY WERE TYPICAL Delta, tough guys with comic-book names—Twitch, Batman, Crash, Gunner and Snake. They were a tight-knit group, closer than brothers and unrelenting in their dedication to team and country. They'd fought together in Croatia and Kosovo, and in the rout of the Taliban in northern Afghanistan a month earlier. They'd made a dozen forays into Tora Bora in the past two weeks, performing behind-the-lines interdiction raids and guiding in air-support missions.

But today, the fifteenth day of the battle, they were sitting tight, waiting for a local contact code-named "Real Deal." *His* nickname was a little dubious, because like most of the Eastern Alliance fighters, he was a liar, a thief, and had close relatives fighting for the enemy on the other side of the mountain.

Yet he claimed to have a piece of information so explosive that it would not only win the battle of Tora Bora, but could turn the whole world upside down.

REAL DEAL ARRIVED at the base camp at 0710 hours. He was of indeterminate age, skinny and perpetually dirty. He squeezed into the tent, taking a seat among the uneasy Delta operators. He reeked of hashish.

He was dressed as they were—or more accurately, they were dressed like him. Each team member wore a mix of Afghani clothing and American-made North Face gear. They didn't look much different from Real Deal, either. They were all bearded and unkempt, with long hair and faces darkened either by heritage or bronzing cream. This was Whiskey's way of fitting in.

In working with Real Deal, the team was going against the conventional wisdom of how to win at Tora Bora. The Eastern Alliance *mujahedeen,* their ranks so highly touted after beating the Russians back in the 1980s, were actually more looters than soldiers. They fought ineffectively during the day and went home before nightfall, giving back any territory they'd won to the hundreds of al Qaeda fighters trapped inside the notorious ten-square-mile valley, allowing the terrorists to fight on.

That was the dirty little secret of Tora Bora. Instead of committing conventional forces to the battle, the politicians in Washington had decided to outsource the job to the local Afghani warlords, to avoid taking too many American casualties. But what had worked with the Northern Alliance in sweeping the Taliban from most of Afghanistan a month before was not working here with the Eastern Alliance. The problem was, from the White House on down, everyone was convinced Osama bin Laden was going to fight to the death at Tora Bora, cementing his status as a martyr. So the strategy was to use B-52s to bomb the crap out of him and then send in the Eastern Alliance and the Delta operators to look for his body. The battle plan was no more complicated than that.

But Team Whiskey thought otherwise. They believed bin Laden was a coward and would run the first chance he got. So they bought information, not from the warlords and their fighters, but from local civilians—the shopkeepers, taxi drivers, moneychangers and shepherds. People who'd done business with the al Qaeda fighters before the Americans arrived and, due to the porous frontlines, were doing business with some of them still.

This had led Whiskey to Real Deal. He drove a taxi; his father ran a spice shop. One of his uncles was a shepherd and another uncle a moneychanger, and they all lived in villages within five miles of Tora Bora. No one had an ear to the ground as much as these guys did.

For $500, Real Deal was going to lead Team Whiskey to a place they'd dubbed Looking Glass. Supposedly it was a secret tunnel that led to a blind canyon that bin Laden and his entourage would use this very morning to make their escape. Looking Glass was located on the side of Hill 3014, an unlikely place as it was far south of the current fighting. But it also made sense. While everyone was concentrating on battles to the north, the al Qaeda leadership would go out the back door to the south.

In other words, with Real Deal's help, Team Whiskey was going to do what all the Afghani fighters and other Delta teams could not: They were going to find Osama bin Laden and kill him.

Before he got away.

* * *

MAJOR PHILLIP "SNAKE" Nolan was Whiskey's commanding officer. West Point, 82nd Airborne, Green Berets and now Delta, at just thirty-three years old, he'd done so many black ops, he'd lost count. Rugged and smart, with hard eyes and a jaw to match, he was nicknamed for his ability to fly below the radar, stay invisible, and get things done with a minimum of bullshit from above. Conversely, he was so photogenic that when he was a junior officer, the Army had used his image on its recruitment posters, something his team never let him forget. But in many ways, the poster-boy image fit.

Nolan took off his oxygen mask now and checked the time. It was 0715. He pulled out a small transistor radio.

According to Real Deal, the signal that bin Laden's escape was imminent would come in code during his daily radio broadcast to his fighters.

The radio crackled to life. A voice came on, one they all knew by now. Strangely calm. Clear. Articulate. It was the Sheik himself.

"Here we go," Nolan said. "Showtime. . . ."

"Batman" Bob Graves was Whiskey's air combat controller. He was a captain in the Air Force, a fighter pilot, well-trained, well-educated, a no-nonsense guy with the slicked-back look of a card shark. A bat had bitten him during basic training, earning him a nickname that would stick forever. Graves's job within the team was to call in air strikes. He also spoke Pashto and Dari, the languages of the region, as well as Arabic. So when the broadcast started, he translated.

"Things are not well, my friends . . ." the voice began. "Our world might have been different if our Muslim brothers in other countries had helped us in our time of need, but our prayers have not been answered."

"That's it," Real Deal said excitedly, tapping his chest in triumph. "'Our prayers have not been answered.' *That* is the code phrase. He is escaping today."

Nolan eyed the other team members. They all questioned Real Deal's trustworthiness. His price had gone up twice since they'd first met him, and he seemed stoned pretty much all the time. But at this point, he was the only game in town.

Nolan flipped open his satellite phone and called their division commanding officer up at Bagram Air Base. He told the DCO what they'd just heard. The DCO already knew what Whiskey was planning. All they needed now was his clearance to move out.

The superior officer responded in such a booming voice, everyone in the tent could hear him. "I don't know how you talked me into this, but you've got exactly two hours. What you're doing is so against the grain, I've bypassed everyone right on up to CENTCOM itself—and if it doesn't work out I'm disavowing any knowledge of it, which means you'll all be looking for new jobs."

"What about air support?" Nolan asked him.

"Just as long as they don't declare this party over today, there'll be a Buff in your general area at all times. Tell your air controller his code sign will be Nail 22."

Nolan asked, "Will the blocking force be in place when we need them?" This was the most important question.

"They're already loaded onto TF-160's Chinooks," was the reply. "They should be in place in time."

"Will there be enough of them?" Nolan pressed. But the DCO was running out of patience.

"You said you needed two companies of Marines and that's what you're getting," came the terse reply. "I don't know how big this pass is that you want them to seal, but they're on the way. Now get going while I still have my commission—and remember, for this one, you're on your own. So don't let the other teams see you."

Click.

End of phone call.

TORA BORA WAS one of the toughest battlefields Delta Force had ever faced. Nestled in the towering White Mountains close to the Pakistan border, it was a dizzying complex of tunnels and caves, some natural, some built during the war against the Soviets and now taken over by al Qaeda. Thick with weapons bunkers, antiaircraft positions and ammo dumps, it was not far from parts of Pakistan where bin Laden was considered a hero. With peaks as high as 14,000 feet and lots of fir trees, dry creeks and blind canyons, it also had an abundance of places to hide.

It snowed in Tora Bora every day, usually in the morning. Fortunately these mini-storms rarely lasted more than fifteen minutes, because it was when the sky was clear that the alliance forces felt most secure on the ground. That's when the doughnut rings could be seen overhead, contrails of big B-52 bombers—the Buffs—constantly circling, their bomb bays full of JDAMs, laser-guided weapons that could be dropped on the head of a dime.

But whenever the contrails weren't there, the al Qaeda fighters came out of their holes and started firing huge 122mm Chinese mortars. And if there was one thing bin Laden's fighters were good at, it was firing mortars.

They could put a mortar round down your shorts from just about anywhere.

BOARDING THEIR PAIR of Toyota trucks, Whiskey drove at top speed up the steep face of Hill 3434A.

Kenny "Twitch" Kapula, the team's demolition man, was behind the wheel of the first truck. Small and muscular, he was a *kanaka,* a native Hawaiian. His dark skin and Polynesian features allowed him to blend-in in many parts of the world, a great asset for the team. It made him perfect for extended undercover missions, too, of which he'd done many. A man of few words, he'd been an elementary school teacher before joining the military, which was funny because when it came to combat, he was absolutely cold and ruthless. He had a distinctive head twitch that grew worse the angrier he got, thus his nickname. He also routinely fired off twice as much ammunition as anyone else in the squad during combat. No one could imagine him molding young minds.

Driving the second Toyota was Huey "Gunner" Lapook, Whiskey's weapons expert. A product of the Louisiana bayous, at 6'3", 260, Gunner took up a lot of space. He carried the team's Striker Street Sweeper, a massive shotgun that fired like an automatic weapon. He was also the squad's door-kicker. During forced entries, Gunner always went in first.

It was a tough climb up 3434A and the air grew thin rapidly, which is why the team had been taking in oxygen before they left. They carried no rucksacks, no food, no Kevlar helmets, body armor or heavy clothing. They had to move fast and travel light. Weapons, ammo, their sat phones and their three lucky flags. Just about everything else stayed behind.

They had to reach the opposite end of Tora Bora quickly, but the higher they drove, the more enemy positions they could see arrayed across the nearby mountains. Dozens of gun emplacements, dugouts and bunkers, some with smoke coming out of them, others displaying the telltale flash of weapons fire. In the thinning air, the noise was deafening. So far, at least, no one was shooting in their direction.

It took thirty minutes, but they finally reached the pass between Hill 3434A and 3433. Real Deal directed them across a ridgeline that served as a bridge all the way over to Hill 3014. It was in a small valley next to this mountain that he claimed Looking Glass could be found.

They reached a frozen stream that ran down the side of Hill 3013, the next mountain over. Here they found four burned-out al Qaeda T-62 tanks, each victim of a direct hit from a JDAM earlier in the fighting. There was little left of them or their crews; still, it was amazing that bin Laden's fighters had somehow gotten the four tanks up to such a high elevation.

Nolan ordered the trucks to stop and called out: "Crash, front and center. . . ."

Jack "Crash" Stacks was the team's SEAL sniper. A surfer dude from LA, he was also known as "Nun Killer," because shortly before making Delta, he'd been involved in a car accident with a minivan full of nuns. Crash was an outstanding marksman. He rated at an astounding 6,800 meters on the Barrett M107 sniper rifle, meaning he could shoot out someone's eyeball from almost four miles away. He was also the team's medic.

Crash was quickly beside Nolan. The team CO pointed to the area below and said, "Take a look."

Crash adjusted the high-powered scope on his weapon and scanned the terrain at the bottom of the hill. He saw lots of bomb craters, lots of ice, lots of trees blown apart, but no signs of life.

"I doubt anything is breathing down there," he told Nolan. "My guess is the battle passed this place by at least a week ago."

The team left the trucks and, one by one, slid down the frozen streambed to the foot of 3013. Once at the bottom, they took cover in a tree line on the stream's eastern bank. Real Deal pointed to a cave opening on the side of the next mountain over, Hill 3014. From their position 100 yards away, the opening didn't look any different from the dozens of similar caves that dotted Tora Bora, except this one had bales of hay stacked around its entrance.

But Real Deal was insistent.

"That is it," he told Nolan. "Your Looking Glass."

Real Deal already had his hand out—he was expecting Whiskey to pay him on the spot. But just as Nolan was reaching for the money, the air erupted with heavy-weapons fire. The team hit the ground as a long, noisy fusillade went over their heads and crashed into the ice sheets behind them, shattering them like panes of glass.

The barrage was coming from the entrance of the cave; some weapon normally used to shoot down aircraft or destroy armored vehicles was firing on them. Nolan didn't have to yell any orders. The team immediately returned fire, trying to zero in on the cave's entrance. But it was like shooting BBs at a battleship. This was a *huge* gun they were up against, and they were absolutely pinned down.

Nolan had taken cover behind a large boulder. Twitch was jammed in beside him; Real Deal was on Nolan's other side. Twitch wasn't firing his weapon, but instead was looking directly at Nolan and making the knife-across-the-throat gesture. Nolan got the message: Real Deal had set them up, walked them into an ambush—and Twitch was going to make him pay, here and now.

But Nolan waved him off. Real Deal was so badly shaken by the gunfire he'd wet himself. He'd been as surprised as they were.

"This is a good thing," Nolan told Twitch instead, yelling to be heard above the noise. "No one else around—but someone operating a big gun like that? Someone high profile *must* be nearby."

Twitch finally opened up with his M4, firing madly as usual. "Always the optimist," he yelled back at Nolan.

The one-sided battle was frightening—for about thirty seconds. Then the gunfire from the cave mouth suddenly stopped. Whiskey hadn't killed any of their attackers; instead, the enemy had mysteriously abandoned its big weapon. Through the smoke and swirling snow they saw a handful of al Qaeda fighters rush to the cave opening and disappear inside. They were all wearing black clothes.

"Fucking Egyptians!" Nolan exclaimed.

This was significant—and it also explained the bales of hay. Bin Laden's most-trusted troops were from Egypt. There were at least a dozen of them around him at all times, and they always dressed in black. Whenever bin Laden was on the move for long distances, he was accompanied by several dozen of these black-clad Egyptians. Many times he rode a horse with this small army running alongside, trying to keep up.

It was beginning to add up. The deserted part of the battlefield. The heavy weapons in evidence. The huge gun fired at them and then abandoned. The Egyptians. Even the hay . . .

He *is* running, Nolan thought. And we're right behind him. . . .

The team moved quickly. Protecting one another with covering fire, they made their way up to the cave, the still-shaking Real Deal in tow. But there was no further opposition; whoever had fired at them was gone.

Besides the hay, the team also found a stack of cut firewood outside the cave opening. It was wrapped in plastic and covered by fir limbs and branches for camouflage from above. There were lots of empty ammo canisters scattered about, too, and every tree within 100 feet of the cave was riddled with shrapnel. But most telling, hidden in the brush on one side of the opening was a massive 122mm antiaircraft gun.

Team Whiskey had seen many of these caves before, mostly through night-vision goggles or the scopes of their M4 rifles. But a big AA gun, so well-hidden, protecting a single cave? That was a first.

They checked the opening for tripwires, then threw in two flash grenades. Both exploded with a loud *pop!* They waited ten seconds, and, receiving no return fire, turned on their gun lights and rushed inside. They were ready for anything—booby traps, mines or even suicide bombers hiding in the dark. But the front part of the cave was empty—except for a lot of trash.

Discarded clothing, bloody bandages, used-up water bottles and dirty socks were strewn everywhere. A woodstove in one corner was still hot, a pan of water on it still boiling. Boxes full of Chinese-made ammunition were piled high in every corner.

"They're running so fast they're leaving their ammo behind," Nolan said.

Most telling, dozens of empty vials and used hypodermic needles littered the cave's floor.

Batman picked up one vial and sniffed it. "Adrenalin," he said. "Whoever was here left hopped up like supermen."

Nolan got the team running, but 200 feet into the cave, they came to a dead stop. Two wooden beams the size of railroad ties were locked firmly in place on the wall, marking the end of the cavern.

But under the glow of Nolan's gun light, Real Deal pointed to the bottom timber. "Help me move this," he said.

Nolan and Twitch complied, and the three shifted the beam, causing a huge brick door to swing open. Beyond was a hidden tunnel, at least twelve feet in diameter, which ran straight for as far as their gun lights allowed them to see. On its floor were more discarded ammo boxes and empty Adrenalin vials.

The team froze and listened. In the distance they could hear the unmistakable sound of footsteps running away.

"We're right behind them," Nolan said. "Let's go!"

The team charged into the tunnel and started running full out. Nolan and Batman, in the lead, fired their weapons every few seconds, knowing they probably wouldn't hit anything, but firing anyway, just to add fuel to their excitement.

But suddenly, Batman went down hard. Everyone skidded to a stop, weapons up, their gun lights pointing in all directions. Nolan was sure the Air Force officer had been shot, but looking over at him he could see he wasn't bleeding. Instead, he was scraping something off the bottom of his boots. He'd slipped—on horse manure.

"God damn," Batman said. "He *is* on a horse."

They ran for the next ten minutes; finally a faint light appeared ahead. It was the outside world again. They'd reached the end of the tunnel.

They spilled out of the opening. Just as Real Deal had promised, it led into a narrow canyon that ran east to west. It was snowing fiercely here, and they could see footprints in the newly fallen snow. At least three dozen people were heading east. And there was something else: another clump of fresh horse manure.

The team began running again, staying close to the sides of the canyon, which was only fifty feet across at its widest. Its sheer walls went up about twenty feet to where the tree line began and continued to the tops of the north and south peaks. The trees were thick, with so much overhang in some places that parts of the canyon would have been almost impossible to see from the air.

And looming over the eastern horizon, a dark, foreboding mountain.

"Pakistan," Real Deal said, pointing to it. "Where the dogs are running to."

The canyon twisted sharply left and then fell off about fifty feet before becoming straight and level again. When Whiskey reached this sharp bend, they could see the bare, elongated shadows of several dozen people cast against the canyon wall about 800 feet ahead of them. They were moving fast. In the lead was the silhouette of a galloping horse and a rider, a man of substantial height wearing robes and a turban.

"Son of a bitch," Nolan swore. "That's *got* to be him."

He screamed for Crash; the SEAL sniper was soon running alongside him.

"First chance you get," Nolan yelled over to him.

Crash got the message. He leapt on the first high rock they came to, went into his sniper stance and looked for the fleeing group farther down the canyon. He spotted them, now about 1,000 feet away, took aim and squeezed off a shot—all in one motion. Then he let out a halfhearted whoop.

He jumped down from the rock and was soon running alongside Nolan again.

"I missed him, sir," Crash told him. "But I might have got the horse."

They ran on and on and on. It was a chase now, which was OK with Nolan. As long as the fleeing group stayed in the canyon and thought someone was in pursuit, then they would eventually run right into the blocking force of Marines waiting at the other end. It was called a hammer-and-anvil play. And Team Whiskey was the hammer.

They were soon down to the spot where Crash had fired on the fleeing party. A long trail of blood brought them around the next bend. That's where they found him. Not the rider—but his horse.

Crash had shot it in the head.

The team stopped to examine the dead animal, hoping to find any kind of definitive clue as to who'd been riding it. Suddenly four mortar rounds landed not sixty feet in front of them. In such a confined space, it was like four 2,000-pound bombs going off. The floor of the canyon rose and fell with each explosion. Smoke and dust were everywhere.

Everyone hit the deck, taking cover next to the bloody horse. Behind some rocks down on the canyon floor, not 200 feet away, a rear guard of black-clad fighters had hastily set up four heavy mortars. There were at least twelve gunmen jammed into a small space, trying to work the weapons while the rest of their party continued to flee.

Four more mortar rounds came crashing down, exploding

just fifty feet in front of the team, showering them with rock and debris. Then four more shells exploded about fifty feet behind them. Nolan gave his ears a sharp snap, hoping to clear them. It worked just enough for him to hear another series of *whomps!*—signaling that more mortar rounds were on the way.

This time the four shells landed not thirty feet behind them, again in a perfect row. The people firing at them had both ends of the team in their sights and were zeroing in.

The book said the best way out of this kind of situation was to go back the way you came in, retreating and getting out of range as quickly as possible. But that wasn't going to happen here.

Nolan turned to Batman, but the Air Force controller already had his sat phone out. A JDAM here would solve this problem very quickly.

Batman started calling for Nail 22, the code name for the B-52 bomber that was supposed to be up there, somewhere. But he got no response. He tried different frequencies, different hailing patterns; he even called for any available U.S. aircraft in the area, B-52 or not. But to no avail.

His face went taut with frustration. He'd guided smart bombs onto dozens of al Qaeda positions in the past two weeks. Now, when they needed just one more JDAM, there were no more planes, no more comforting doughnut trails overhead.

"I can't hook up with anyone," he told Nolan in disgust. "It's like no one's home."

Nolan shook his head. "Like the DCO said, everyone thinks this party is over."

Another four mortar rounds came crashing down in front of them, even closer than the last. Batman was pissed. He jammed the sat phone back in his pocket. "What the fuck am I doing here then?" he said bitterly.

With no air support, Nolan told the team to lay on the counterfire. This got the black-uniformed fighters ducking for cover. Then he grabbed Gunner and they crawled down the right side of the canyon, getting to within 100 feet of the enemy's unprotected left flank.

On Nolan's call, Gunner opened up with his massive Street Sweeper. This started an intense twenty-second gun battle that saw hundreds of rounds from both sides pinging off rocks and ricocheting wildly around the narrow canyon. But in the end it was Gunner's firing that tipped the balance. Even the promise of heavenly paradise was not enough to overwhelm the fear brought on by his automatic shotgun. After one particularly long burst fired directly into their formation, the men in black finally turned and ran.

Lucky to be unscathed, Team Whiskey was quickly in pursuit again—but the battle had been costly. They were down to their last clips of ammunition. But they knew the Marine blocking force was waiting for the escaping al Qaeda fighters at the far end of the canyon. All Whiskey had to do was keep chasing them, keep the pressure on, and the enemy would run right into 200 jarheads.

They hastily checked the rocks where the al Qaeda fighters had set up their mortar line. Six of them had been killed, but their colleagues had taken their weapons with them.

Looking deeper into the twisting, turning canyon, the team could see the survivors of the gun battle running full tilt, indeed like hopped-up sprinters. And off in the distance, maybe a quarter mile away, they spotted the main party itself, now with the tall man in robes moving on foot, still heading eastward, but at a much slower pace.

"This time we got him *for sure*," Nolan said.

That's when his sat phone came to life. It was division headquarters at Bagram.

From the moment the DCO started talking, he didn't sound right. The piss and vinegar was just not there. Nolan could barely hear his voice.

"What's your location?" he asked Nolan.

Nolan had no idea and said as much. "Somewhere near the Paki border."

"OK," the DCO said. "You've got to come back. We've got to end this one."

Nolan froze on the spot, sat phone in hand.

"Please repeat, sir," he said "We're seconds away from driving them into the anvil. . . ."

The DCO interrupted him. "The Marine blocking force isn't coming,"

"But you said they were already on the choppers, already on their way."

"They've been recalled," the DCO said starkly.

Nolan was livid. *"Recalled?"* he shouted into the phone. "By who? Why? We're as close as anyone has gotten in this whole thing. We're seconds away!"

"Washington recalled them," the senior officer said. "They got wind of all this and decided if 200 Marines suddenly landed on the Pakistan side of the border it might upset the locals. Or at least that's the excuse. Either way, this came right from the top. From the top of the DoD himself. So start back, return to your IP and we'll deal with the fallout later."

Nolan began pleading with him. "Do you realize we have these guys in sight?"

"Get back to your IP," the DCO repeated. "That's an order. Conversation over."

Click.

Nolan didn't even think about it, didn't hesitate for even a moment. He just threw away the sat phone, smashing it on the rocks nearby, and said: "Fuck that. I'll go kill the bastard myself."

Then he picked up his weapon and started running down the canyon alone.

A second later, the rest of the team was right behind him.

THEY RAN A half-mile farther, slipping in the snow, gashing knees and elbows, but never slowing down. The canyon began to twist and turn again, and more than once they got fleeting glimpses of some of the enemy fighters as they were going around the next corner, just up ahead.

All the while the large, dark mountain across the Pakistani border loomed over them. It kept getting closer. And Nolan knew that without the Marine blocking force in place, the mountain was the end of the line.

They arrived at one particularly sharp turn, too sharp to go around blindly. The team stopped and Nolan stuck his head around the corner.

He found twenty of the black-clad gunmen standing behind a flimsy wooden barricade, all aiming their weapons at him.

Beyond them all was an ancient gate and an elderly sign hand-printed in Pashto and English. It read: THIS SIDE IS PAKISTAN.

Now a second gun battle began. Nolan and the others took turns firing their weapons around the rocks and ducking away from the counter fusillades. After five minutes, Team Whiskey ran out of ammunition. But the fire from the other side died down, too.

When Nolan looked around the corner again, he saw a pile of dead bodies lying on the path and the rest of the al Qaeda group running headlong across the border, carrying their dead companions' weapons with them.

They were escaping across a snowy field, the same one where the Marine force would have landed had D.C. not lost its balls at the last minute. After another fifty feet, they disappeared for good into the thick black forests of Pakistan.

Whiskey just stood there and watched them go, exhausted and furious. With not a bullet among them to fire.

"So much for this football game," Crash said.

But as Nolan was still processing all this, a stream of gunfire erupted from across the border. Real Deal took the first two bullets right through his heart. He collapsed in Nolan's arms, looked up at the Delta CO and tried to speak but couldn't. He coughed once and died.

The same barrage caught Twitch just above the knees, nearly cutting him in half. He, too, fell over at Nolan's feet.

As the others blindly dove for cover, Nolan bent down to help Twitch. That's when a single mortar round came in. It hit the canyon wall off to Nolan's left, exploding in a haze of shrapnel and rock shards.

One of these shards hit Nolan with such velocity that it broke through his goggles and went deep into his left eye.

He fell backward, bleeding profusely.

Crash was soon at his side, a bandage pack ready to be applied. But he couldn't staunch the blood gushing from Nolan's gaping wound. The bandage just fell away, as did two more. Even applying the team's three lucky flags could not stop the bleeding.

Though he was aware of much confusion and shouting going on around him, Nolan was also slipping away. Everything was fading from red to yellow to black.

Finally, he grabbed Crash's collar with the last of his strength and said: "Just get me to the water . . ."

2

The Gulf of Aden
Nine years later

THE CREW OF the fishing boat *Mindanao Star* spotted the first flare just after midnight.

The 200-foot trawler of Filipino registry was one hundred and ten miles off the coast of Yemen, fishing for big-eye tuna. The flare appeared off the ship's port bow, arcing across the clear, calm night. Thirty seconds later, a second, and then a third flare streaked into the sky, coming from the same direction.

The ship's captain was woken and apprised of the situation. He ordered the forward searchlight directed to the spot of the flares' origin. The powerful light revealed a small motorboat carrying four men. Three were waving their arms frantically; the fourth was holding a gasoline can upside-down to indicate the boat was out of fuel. The men looked emaciated, their clothes little more than rags. They were shaky on their feet and seemed confused and seasick—signs they'd been adrift for some time.

The captain ordered the ship to port and told his deck crew to ready a ladder to take the men aboard. The *Mindanao Star* reached the small craft in short order and found the four young black men, fishermen themselves, yelling "Thanks to you!" to the Filipino crew.

Each man needed help coming up the trawler's ladder. Once the last was aboard, the captain ordered that they be taken below and fed. Their boat was taken under tow and the *Mindanao Star* was put back on course to its next destination, the Port of Aden, where it was to take on ice.

This done, the captain looked away to turn off the searchlight. When he looked back again, he saw his chief engineer lying on the deck. One of the men they'd just taken aboard was holding a gun to his head.

Then the other rescued men pulled submachine guns from under their shirts and started firing in the air. All the crewmen up on deck immediately fell to their knees, putting their hands over their heads.

Still up on the bridge, the captain realized what was happening. How could he have been so foolish? These men were pirates. His ship was being hijacked.

He reached for the radio and punched into the IDF, the international distress frequency. He hurriedly identified himself and his position. Then he started saying firmly in English: "Mayday, Mayday—we have been boarded by pirates."

The radio crackled in response. There was a French warship on anti-piracy patrol just ten miles away, and its communications officer began speaking to the Filipino captain.

"Remain calm," the French officer told him. "Our helicopter is refueling and is about to launch. It will reach you as quickly as possible, and we will be close behind. But don't worry. The pirates will not harm you. Just give them what they want. If they hijack you, you will be taken to a spot off Somalia and they will ransom you and your ship. At worst, you will have a couple weeks off in the sun. This happens all of the time."

By the time the Filipino captain got off the radio, all ten members of his deck crew had been subdued. They were made to kneel against the starboard railing, hands on their heads, facing out to sea.

One pirate appeared on the bridge. He began waving his gun around, making it clear that he wanted the captain to open the ship's safe. The *Mindanao Star* had just offloaded twenty tons of tuna in Oman and had been paid in cash: $46,000 that was soon in the pirates' hands.

The pirate then led the captain down to the main deck to join the other crewmen. Speaking in Filipino, the captain repeated to his men what the French naval officer had told him. Stay calm. We won't get hurt. Let them do what they want. He added an apology for not knowing better than to fall for the hijackers' simple ruse.

As two of the pirates kept the crew under guard, two others went below to the ship's hold. It was full of freshly caught big-eye waiting to be rough filleted, a process in which the heads and tails were chopped off with long machete-type knives, and their bodies placed on large industrial-size cutting machines.

The eight-man cutting crew, involved in the noisy operation, was not aware of what was happening up on deck. They were surprised to see the two black men climb down into the cutting room waving machine guns at them.

The pirates made the cutting crew stand along the bulkhead and proceeded to rob them of their valuables. Then one pirate demanded to see their footlockers, located at the far end of the cutting room. The pirates thoroughly searched the lockers, finally coming away with a heavy white plastic bag.

The pirates found an empty crate and started filling it with the long tuna knives. They also took the cutting crew's supply of industrial earmuffs. The cutting crew was led up onto the deck and lined up with the others.

There was a long discussion among the four gunmen. It was as if they were waiting for something. That's when another vessel suddenly appeared out of the night and came alongside the *Mindanao Star.*

At first the Filipino captain thought it was the French warship, improbably arriving even before its helicopter, and much sooner than expected. But as the vessel drew closer, he realized it was actually a large sea-going tug, newly painted black and red. The pirates waved to people on the tug, and they waved back. Collaborators . . .

This made sense in a way, the captain thought. Maybe the pirates planned to use the tug to tow them back to Somalia, just as the French officer had told him. And while he had no desire to take the next two weeks off waiting for his company to ransom back the ship, he supposed there were worse things to do in the world.

He was about to relay these feelings to his men when, without warning, the pirates began firing their guns into the backs of the crew. Some of the victims fell over the railing and others slumped to the deck, bleeding.

The captain, who was at the end of the line, got up and started running.

Two pirates gave chase. The terrified captain scrambled up the foredeck ladder, quickly reaching the bridge, where he grabbed the radio microphone, pushed the IDF button, and started screaming: *"Mayday! Mayday!"*

The same French naval officer came on the line. He asked the captain for his position—but the captain ignored him.

Instead he began yelling: "They are killing us!"

As this was happening, the other pirates waved the tug closer. One of the gunmen held up the crate containing the knives and a dozen industrial earmuffs and shook it like it was a prize of war, causing the people on the tug to cheer. The other did the same with the white plastic bag, getting more cheers from the tug. They passed their booty over to people on the tug and then found the gas can the trawler crew had filled for their motorboat. After splashing the gas around the trawler, they lit a Bic lighter and threw it on the deck. The gas exploded instantly. In seconds, flames were spreading around the ship.

That's when the two other pirates finally caught up to the captain. They fired at him through the bridge window. An explosion of glass and bullets hit the officer like a broadside. He fell to the deck, bleeding profusely from multiple wounds as the two pirates joined their colleagues in jumping off the burning ship to the waiting tug.

The captain still held on to the microphone.

"They've killed us," he gasped into it, using his last breath. "We are all dead. . . ."

THE CAPTAIN OF the Danish cargo ship *Dolphin* had been following the *Mindanao Star* drama on his ship-to-ship radio.

He was ninety miles off the Yemeni coast, heading toward the Suez, and only about twenty miles from where the Filipino fishing boat had been attacked.

His 255-foot ship was bound from South Africa to Malta, its hold filled mostly with cheap furniture and off-brand computers and TVs. The seas had been growing around them, as a weather front was moving in. Waves were cresting at six feet, and every few minutes, the freighter was drenched by a rain squall.

The captain had hoped the unsettled conditions would give him protection against pirates known to frequent this area, but thirty minutes after the last broadcast from the Filipino trawler, one of the *Dolphin*'s crew members spotted two small speedboats fast approaching from the starboard side.

Counting on bad weather to deter the pirates had been a foolish decision. But unlike the crew on the *Mindanao Star,* the *Dolphin*'s captain was prepared.

He blew the ship's fire alarm four times. This was the predetermined signal for his crew that a pirate attack was in the offing.

The twenty-two men on board went to their trouble stations. Eight reported to the engine room, the most important place on any ship in an emergency. Four more reported to the bridge, charged with turning the freighter around and laying on speed in an effort to outrun the pirates. The rest manned the fire hoses.

Of these, the captain took his five best men and went down to the foredeck. Here, wrapped in a cotton bag and sealed inside a life raft trunk, was his secret weapon.

It was called an LRAD, for long-range acoustic device. It was a round piece of hardware, similar in appearance to a large black frying pan. When activated it could produce a noise similar to that of a smoke detector, but at 145 decibels— enough to cause permanent ear-damage. This sound could be directed at targets up to 900 feet away.

The captain and crew set the LRAD on its tripod and attached its power cable. By this time the speedboats were within a quarter mile of the ship. Even though the *Dolphin* had turned 180 degrees and poured on the speed, the pirates continued to gain—fast.

On the captain's signal, the crew put their fingers in their ears and he turned on the LRAD. Its sound was instantly loud and painful, even though the majority of it was being directed at the oncoming pirates. The captain put on his night-vision goggles, focusing them on the pair of speedboats. But he was puzzled to see that the men driving the speedboats didn't seem disoriented. Nor had they slowed their approach one bit.

He zoomed in and was disheartened to see the pirates were wearing industrial earmuffs.

"Why are they picking on us?" one of the crewmen asked the captain anxiously. "We got nothing in our hold but junk."

The captain ignored his question. He pushed the man out of the way, ran up to the bridge, and finally sent out a Mayday. The same French warship that had communicated with the *Mindanao Star* received his call. It was approximately twenty-eight miles from the *Dolphin*'s position but was adjusting its course and coming to the ship's aid. It also had just launched its helicopter.

"Just stay calm," the French officer said. "The pirates will not harm you. Just give them what they want. If they hijack you, you will be taken . . ."

But the *Dolphin*'s captain cut him off. "That's what you told the Filipinos," he said. "And look where it got them."

He threw the radio mic across the room and ran back down to the deck. The speedboats were just 100 feet off his starboard bow and still coming fast. He ordered two crewmen to ready the nearest fire hose, the anti-pirate weapon of last resort.

He turned to say something to one of these men when he saw a bubble of blood shoot out of the man's nose. Another bloody bubble was gurgling from his mouth. The captain's first thought was that the LRAD had burst something inside the crewman's head.

Only when the man pitched forward and landed face first on the cold, hard deck did the captain realize what was happening. Behind him were four young black men with machine guns. They had stolen aboard the ship from the stern while everyone's attention had been drawn to the pair of speedboats threatening from the front.

All four pirates were wearing industrial earmuffs.

The two original speedboats then pulled around to the back of the ship and fired rocket-propelled grenades directly at the rudder, blowing it off the ship and damaging the propellers in the process.

At this point, about half of the *Dolphin*'s crew jumped over the side, either to swim or drown. There was no other choice.

The pirates rounded up the rest of the crew and lined them up on the railing. There were soon eight armed men on the *Dolphin*'s deck. While two held guns on the crew, two others ransacked the captain's quarters, taking $4,000 from the ship's safe along with the captain's personal valuables.

The other four pirates went below. One soon reappeared with a handful of large-caliber bullets, causing the other pirates to let out a whoop of triumph.

One of the pirates walked up to the captain. He was holding a long machete-type knife. He stood nose to nose with the ship's commanding officer, looking him up and down. He commented on the captain's massive gold ring, worn on his right pinky finger. Then he took the captain's night-vision goggles from around his neck.

In thickly accented English, the pirate said: "Your things will fit me just fine."

BY THE TIME the French warship launched its refueled helicopter and reached the last reported position of the *Mindanao Star,* all that was left of the trawler was a smoky oil slick and some bobbing wreckage. The copter circled the area for five minutes, but spotted no bodies, no survivors.

It had turned back to its ship and landed—but no sooner was it down when the news arrived that a Danish ship close by also was being attacked by pirates. Not hijacked. *Attacked.*

The helicopter took off again and headed for the *Dolphin.* The copter's crew tried hailing the Danish cargo carrier many times on the way, but to no avail.

When the helicopter reached the *Dolphin,* it found the vessel still afloat but obviously not under control. Three armed crewmen rappelled down to the ship and searched it thoroughly. They discovered that while the cargo of cheap furniture and electronics was intact, there was a large empty space in the hold, as if *something* had been taken. Also, the ship's bridge had been stripped of its GPS system, its satellite phones, its fax machine and its weather computer.

Blood just about covered the foredeck, but the French sailors could find no sign of the crew.

Retrieving its men, the helicopter once again turned back to its ship. The French had been doing anti-pirate duty in these waters for more than a year, and while they'd seen their share of incidents, they were *always* just hijacking attempts—not willful killings or the intentional sinking of ships. These things were firsts.

In just one night, the pirate problem in the Gulf of Aden had become a lot more dangerous.

3

The next night
0100 hours

THE *GLOBAL WARRIOR* was way off course.

It was sailing 425 miles east of Somalia, heading for the Gulf of Aden. One of its engines had been disabled, so it was moving at barely half speed and drifting more with each passing hour.

The immense, 720-foot cargo carrier had sent a message to officials of the Suez Canal Authority earlier in the night. Its scheduled transit of the waterway in two days would have to be delayed due to its propulsion problems. This was troubling news.

An Italian Navy frigate on anti-piracy patrol had contacted the ship around midnight to inform the crew that it would be without protection from pirates for at least five hours; that's how far off the normal shipping lanes the cargo carrier had drifted. The Italian warship advised the *Global Warrior* that the closest vessel of any consequence was the sea-going tugboat *Yabu*. It suggested that if the big freighter needed any assistance, it should contact the tug.

IN FACT, THE *Yabu* had been stalking the *Global Warrior* for hours, trailing fifteen miles behind it, just over the horizon. Big, powerful and fast, the *Yabu* was one of many sea-going tugs plying the waters of the Indian Ocean and the Gulf of Aden—the perfect disguise for a pirate mother ship. Its crew was made up of Somali and Kenyan fishermen, handpicked from the myriad seafaring gangs along the East African coast. They'd spent the night up on deck chewing *qat,* the stimulant plant that grew rampant in Somalia. It was their way of getting ready for what lay ahead.

Certain it was the only other vessel within fifty miles of the *Global Warrior*, by 0200 hours, the tug had drawn to within 3,000 feet of the crippled freighter. Five speedboats were lowered over the side. Two armed pirates climbed aboard each and set out toward the big cargo ship. A few of them still had blood on their clothes from the attacks the night before. The seas were calm and the moon was near full.

Joseph Mdoobi was the chief of this small navy. A Kenyan with extensive experience on the water, he maneuvered his speedboat in front of the others and led them toward the *Global Warrior*. Once they were within 1,000 feet of the ship, Mdoobi signaled his men to put on their earmuffs. Seconds later, they heard, just barely, the bleating sound of an LRAD being aimed in their direction. It had no effect on them.

Mdoobi's speedboat was the first to reach the *Global Warrior*, which was limping along at barely five knots. This, too, worked to Mdoobi's favor, as it would make it that much easier to climb onboard.

His speedboat circled the ship once. As planned, two of his other boats shot to the front of the ship, where a gangway was partially retracted in an attempt to draw the pirates in. As the two boats approached, they were hit with spray from two fire hoses.

Meanwhile, Mdoobi and the two other boats went around to the back of the ship and threw a grappling hook with a rope ladder attached up to the stern handrail. In seconds, his men were clambering up to the ship's main deck.

Mdoobi was the last to climb the rope ladder. On reaching the top, he found all his men were onboard and the crew had fled belowdecks. Three of his men were already securing the main deck; four more were ready to go below to search the cargo hold. One pirate had disconnected the LRAD, ending the annoying sound for good and allowing the others to take off their earmuffs. Another was waving to him from the bridge. Mdoobi immediately took out his sat phone and dialed his boss back on the tug.

"All is OK," he reported. "No problems at all."

THE PIRATE CAPTAIN, Turk Kurjan, sat a quarter-mile away in the tug's wheelhouse, watching the *Global Warrior* through night-vision goggles. A middle-aged Indonesian with a long scar splitting his nose in two, he wore his years at sea on his weathered face. He didn't dress like the Somali pirates, who favored American-style ghetto chic once they had some money in their pockets. Turk always dressed in puffy rayon shirts, tight leather pants and combat boots. He wore earrings in both lobes and his head was shaved, except for a long, braided ponytail in back.

He'd been a pirate all his adult life, not in the Gulf of Aden or off Somalia, but in and around the Java Sea. Born of a long line of pirates, he and his brother had spent years attacking ships moving through the Strait of Malacca, stealing everything from

SUVs to iPods to food aid meant for tsunami victims. It had made them wealthy men.

But with the number of ships transiting the waters of the Gulf of Aden increasing every day, Turk, the older brother, had decided to move his operations westward. He stole the tug, gathered a crew and quickly went to work. Now, flush from his deadly attacks the night before, he was ready to go for a bigger prize.

But the *Global Warrior* was not just any victim. Turk had selected tonight's prey very carefully. In his hold were the spoils from the previous night. From the Danish ship, not cheap furniture and brand-x computers, but five tons of 7.62mm ammunition being smuggled to Hamas on the Gaza Strip. From the Filipino fishing trawler, not tuna or fish bones, but fifty pounds of pure China White heroin, found secreted in one of the cutting crew's footlockers.

Turk had known about these things prior to attacking the ships because, before moving his operations to this part of the world, he had set up a network of spies that stretched from Mumbai to the Suez. Eyes and ears in just about every major port reported which ships were going where and which vessels were carrying things they shouldn't—which, truth be told, was the majority of flagged vessels sailing these waters. Smuggling by sea was as old as seafaring itself. And so was stealing from the smugglers.

Turk was not interested in hijacking tankers or cargo ships and becoming entangled in lengthy negotiations with their owners, just to squeeze a two-million dollar ransom out of them. He'd leave that to the Somalis. He could get twice that amount selling the valuable ammunition to the highest bidder, and probably three or four times more than that by selling the heroin to his contacts in Sicily.

Turk was a real pirate. He didn't hijack ships, he attacked them. He took booty, not hostages. He had just one hard-and-fast rule: Leave no witnesses in your wake.

A slew of stolen electronics surrounded him in the wheelhouse. Sat phones, a GPS system, a ship-to-shore shortwave radio, a long-range portable radar. One supreme piece of eavesdropping equipment was the military-issue communications suite known as the ANQ-202, which could monitor the shipboard communications of just about any vessel anywhere on the globe.

But again Turk counted on HUMINT—his human intelligence-gathering network—and this had paid off for him tonight. According to his spies, the *Global Warrior*'s manifest listed 202 used BMWs on board; they were being taken from Dubai back to Germany, where they would be reconditioned and sold again. Perhaps some of these cars were stolen and on their way to chop shops, but that isn't what interested Turk. His informants reported that shortly before the *Global Warrior*'s departure from Dubai, a section of its loading pier had been cordoned off and a number of mysterious crates put aboard.

Turk was guessing that, just like the smack on the trawler and the bullets on the Danish ship, there was something more valuable than dinged-up BMWs in the *Global Warrior*'s hold.

He was intent on stealing it.

BACK ON THE deck of the cargo ship, all was still going well for Mdoobi and his men. They were in complete control of the vessel and the crew would be found and snuffed out in due time. Meanwhile, the pirates had thrown the LRAD overboard, along with all of the ship's radios. And four of them had already gone below to search the cargo hold.

So far, so good.

Mdoobi flipped open his sat phone, intending to update Turk on all this, when he felt something cold against his back. He turned just enough to see the silhouette of a man standing behind him. Mdoobi froze. Then he heard the sound of a trigger being squeezed. A moment later, he was looking down at a gigantic hole in his chest.

The gun blast echoed across the deck, startling the other pirates up top. They saw Mdoobi go over, but couldn't see what had happened to him. The pirate who'd raced up to the bridge came out to investigate. He was killed by a shotgun blast to the back of his head.

The pirate who had thrown the LRAD and the radios overboard ran to see if Mdoobi was really dead. As he was checking on his boss, a pistol came out of the darkness and shot him point-blank in the temple.

The pirate fell backward and was suddenly looking up at the stars. He never saw the person who shot him.

His last thought was: *I've been killed by a ghost.*

THE FOUR PIRATES who went below to search the *Global Warrior*'s cargo hold had found the place unexpectedly dark and creepy.

The ship was not only moving at half speed, its electrical systems were working at half power, too. The light in the vast cargo hold was so dim, the pirates could barely see their way around. Making matters worse, a steam line had broken somewhere, and it had filled the hold with a weird kind of fog. Otherworldly sounds were coming from the deepest parts of the huge steel cavern, emanating from places where it was pitch black and the pirates could not see at all.

Displaying a lot less verve than when they first climbed down, they'd started to move into the hold itself when they heard three loud gun blasts come from up top. The pirates froze in place, their hands shaking as they tried to hold their Uzis steady.

A minute passed—but they heard nothing more from above. They had no sat phones, no way to talk to Mdoobi, so they decided one man would turn around, climb back up to the main deck and see what had happened. As this man disappeared into the mist, the three other pirates timidly forged ahead.

The fog became thicker the deeper they went into the cargo hold, a canyon of shrink-wrapped BMWs stacked five high and forty rows deep, creaking and groaning with the rolling of the ship.

Because there was almost no light down here, the pirates were forced to feel their way along the outer stack of cars. The unsettling ethereal noises grew louder as they crept forward. They sounded like the noise a ship's engine would make, only amplified. At the same time, the foggy air was also filled with electronic squeals and the sounds of people wailing in the background.

The pirates moved slowly. Walking in a line, they gingerly poked their rifles up under the shrink-wraps, but found nothing except chrome rims and the occasional flat tire. They became frustrated and scared. Where was the great treasure Turk had promised they'd find here?

At one point, the first two pirates turned to discover that the third pirate was missing. They whispered his name as loud as they dared, but got no response. He'd vanished.

This didn't make sense—he'd been out of their sight for ten seconds at the most. They began backtracking, wondering if the man had lost his nerve and had decided to return up top.

But they soon found him, between two stacks of cars, fifteen feet away. He was crumpled on the oily deck, bleeding profusely from a stab wound to the neck. A nine-inch dagger had pierced his throat just below the Adam's apple and exited behind his left ear, severing his vocal chords and his windpipe—preventing him from screaming. His eyes were still open, an expression of horror on his face. He'd been killed, silently, in less than ten seconds.

The two pirates dropped their weapons and started running. All thoughts of looking for Turk's magical booty were now gone. They headed straight for the ladder they'd used to climb down into the belly of the beast. But just two steps up they found their way blocked by the body of the man who'd turned back to investigate the noise up top. He was hanging upside down on the ladder rungs, his torso grotesquely contorted, holes from two bullets shot at close range puncturing his forehead.

The two pirates fell back to the cargo deck, terrified. They were in full panic now, trapped among the creaking BMWs, the steam almost enveloping them, the weird noises coming at them from all sides.

They began running for their lives. They could hear footsteps chasing them—but any time they dared look behind them, no one was there.

"They are hunting us!" one man yelled to the other. "They will kill us both!"

They reached the far end of the hold and found themselves in the propulsion area, a series of dark, narrow passageways with fading lights and a blanket of even thicker fog. The strange noises were almost deafening here.

Spotting the refrigerator room ahead, one of the pirates bolted for it, thinking it was a good place to hide. Just as he was about to reach for its door, though, the butt of a rifle slammed him in the face. He fell backward, smashing his head. When his vision cleared, he found himself looking up through the mist into the barrel of a shotgun. It was the last thing he ever saw. The weapon was lowered to the pirate's chest and the trigger was pulled. There was a moment of tremendous pain, but then everything went black.

Only one pirate was left below now. He stumbled on to the engine room but realized it was not a refuge but a trap. He ran farther down the foggy passageway, spotting a bulkhead door ajar up ahead. He darted up to it, looked inside—and was astonished to find the ship's crew, Eastern Europeans most of them, sitting around a table, drinking coffee.

They didn't seem too surprised to see him. He was terrified, and they were strangely calm. When he spewed out some Somali curse words, the crewmen laughed at him. One man stood up, forced him back out into the passageway, and slammed the door in his face.

The pirate turned and started running back through the cargo hold, trying to find another access ladder. Unseen pursuers previously hidden in the shadows began chasing him. As he pleaded with them not to shoot him, their footsteps grew closer.

He began weaving his way around the shrink-wrapped cars, hoping to elude the phantoms, but then two shots rang out at close range. Both hit the pirate in the back. Another bullet got him in the buttocks. He staggered to a nearby ladder and tried to climb up, but two more rounds, fired from just a few feet away, hit him in the legs. With all the strength he could muster, he hauled himself up to the next deck only to find a man in black camouflage waiting for him.

"No need to waste a bullet on you," the man in black said, kicking the pirate in the face instead. The pirate fell down the ladder, cracking his skull on the deck below.

THERE WERE ONLY three pirates left alive aboard the ship now, all on the main deck. Two managed to make it down one of the rope ladders to a speedboat tied up below. But in the rush, one man pushed the other, causing him to fall headfirst into the water. He was soon churned up by the huge ship's wake.

The pirate who made it into speedboat tried to start the engine. But before he could turn the key, a torrent of bullets came raining down on him. Some kind of massive weapon put twenty large holes in both boat and pirate, blowing them to pieces.

Now only one pirate remained. He found himself running around the expansive main deck, being chased by at least four ghostly figures who were trying their best to take him down with one careful, fatal shot. He'd thrown away his gun and his knife by this time and yelled in surrender, but his pursuers were relentless.

In his terror, the pirate passed an odd sight: a small helicopter parked on a makeshift metal pad on the bow of the ship. Its engine was running, its rotors were turning, but no one was in it.

If only I could fly that thing, he thought.

He continued running, dodging bullets by ducking behind crates and various pieces of equipment on the deck. He made one entire circuit of the ship this way, out of breath and in a complete panic, somehow finding himself on the stern again.

And here he finally stopped, collapsing to his knees, unable to go on.

He turned slowly to find a tall man dressed in black had appeared above him.

The man was holding a gigantic .45 automatic. He also had a black patch over his left eye.

He pressed the pistol against the pirate's mouth and said: "Suck on this."

Then he pulled the trigger.

* * *

TURK HEARD THE helicopter coming.

The high-pitched whirring cut like a knife above the deceptively calm sea, sounding eerie and mechanical at the same time.

He was still in the wheelhouse, watching the *Global Warrior* and feeling uneasy. All of the ship's lights were still on; it was dimly lit from bow to stern. It was still moving north, slowly. He could even see his speedboats, or at least three of them, tied up to its side.

He just couldn't tell what was happening onboard.

It had been ten minutes since he'd received a message from his men—their orders were to call him every two minutes. He'd been trying to raise Mdoobi or anyone else on the ship for the past eight minutes, with no response.

The only explanation was that Mdoobi's sat phone must have gone on the blink—and at the worst possible time. Turk had two men and one motorboat left on the tugboat with him. He was about to send these men over to the *Global Warrior* with another sat phone when he first heard the whirring noise.

A few seconds later he saw it: a tiny helicopter coming out of the darkness just to the left of the cargo ship. It was a work aircraft, something usually found servicing offshore drilling platforms or oil fields. But this one had four men hanging out of its open bay, two on each side. They were carrying weapons on their laps. And they were coming right for him.

What was going on here?

He got his answer a moment later.

The four men hanging off the copter turned their weapons toward him. Turk froze. The helicopter whooshed over the bow and the men began strafing his tug with machine guns.

He hit the deck just as a massive barrage crashed into the wheelhouse, covering him with burning glass. The volley took out all the bridge windows, the outer deck rails, the bridge ladder and the safety buoys.

Turk scrambled back to his cabin behind the wheelhouse. He looked for a weapon—a pistol, anything—but found none. The copter doubled back and went into a hover over the tug's bridge. The four men fired directly into the wheelhouse. Turk could hear all of his newly acquired electronics being shot to pieces. Then he heard the main mast fall, taking the Morse lamp, the shortwave antenna and the funnel with it.

The copter began flying figure eights around the tug, allowing each pair of gunmen to fire on the vessel at close range. They blew away the aft propulsion hatch, which allowed them to shoot down into the engine room, striking power cables and hydraulic lines. They severed the boat's steering controls and demolished the tug's long-range communications antenna and its navigation cone. The tug was now deaf and blind.

Turk hugged the deck, hands over his ears, screaming for the noise to stop. The helicopter was now hovering right outside his cabin's porthole, letting the gunmen pour fire directly into his quarters. The cabin was systematically torn to shreds. All the furnishings, all his belongings, even the walls were reduced to sizzling metallic splinters.

He crawled to the far corner of the room just as a huge explosion rocked the tug. Its power plants had blown up, lifting the *Yabu* right out of the water. It came back down, hard, and immediately went over on its starboard side. That's when Turk heard his two remaining crewmen jump ship and try to swim away.

The copter returned outside his cabin, firing more intensely than before. A fire started in the head. Another was blazing out of control in the wheelhouse. A weapon that sounded like a small artillery piece was relentlessly firing at the tug's lower hull. It finally punched a large hole just below the water line, allowing the sea to rush in. The tug went over, turning completely upside down.

Turk's cabin flooded quickly, smashing him against the far bulkhead. Suddenly he was under water, looking up at his cabin floor. There was no way out.

Though completely submerged, he could still hear the gunmen crazily firing into the crippled tugboat, using way too much ammunition.

In his last conscious moment, as the water flowed into his lungs, Turk couldn't help but think: "Who *are* these people?"

4

THE PORT WAS huge.

Almost five miles of docks, tie-ups and harbor slips; massive cranes gliding like dinosaurs in the mist; armies of dockworkers moving nonstop, loading and unloading ships. Forty or more vessels were in process here on any given night, all under a canopy of ghostly sodium light.

This place spanned history itself. To the east, up in the hills, Cain and Abel were said to be buried. To the west, off the place called Steamer Point, the *USS Cole* had its hull blasted open by al Qaeda bombers. Located exactly halfway between India and Egypt, the Port of Aden had been a crossroads of civilization for thousands of years.

Towering over the docks stood a building that looked out of place. Made of ultramodern gray glass and steel, soaring thirty stories above structures built by Cain and Abel's ancestors, this was the district office of Kilos Shipping.

THE MD-600 HELICOPTER circled the building twice before landing on its roof. The luxurious copter's doors opened, and four men dressed in identical suits stepped out. Each held a Steyr machine pistol.

It was close to midnight, yet the four were wearing sunglasses. They scanned the helipad and the roofs of the nearby buildings; they also gave the once over to a smaller, far less opulent helicopter parked on the edge of the helipad. They signaled a fifth man still sitting in the MD-600, and he climbed out. He was Mikos Kilos, shipping magnate and number 201 on the Forbes list of the world's richest men.

He lit a cigarette and began puffing like mad. "My own goddamn helicopter," he grumbled, "and I can't even smoke in it."

Sixty-two years old with a shock of jet-black hair, Kilos had made his fortune as a young man in the 1970s building cargo ships that could transport dry goods such as grain, electronics and automobiles to the Middle East—then, after being thoroughly washed and cleaned, carry oil back to Europe on the return trip.

During the Iran-Iraq War of the 1980s, Kilos's ships were the only vessels that dared take on oil from Iran's vast Kharg Island loading facility. Even though they were easy targets for Iraqi aircraft carrying anti-ship missiles, in eight years of war, none of Kilos's vessels received so much as a scratch—and every gallon of oil they carried was delivered. His profits soared. When he later expanded into container ships and port management, Kilos's millions became billions. These days, his company operated more than one hundred ships.

One of them was the *Global Warrior*.

HIS BODYGUARDS HUSTLED him off the roof, throwing away his cigarette for him. They escorted him down two flights of stairs to a dark corridor on the twenty-eighth floor.

Only one of the dozens of offices here still had its lights on. A bodyguard opened its door and Kilos walked in. Covered with wall charts and maps, the office was not at all like the palatial suite in London where he usually did his business. In fact, his servants' closets were bigger and better appointed than this. Yet here he was.

The forty-ish man sitting behind the office desk jumped to his feet at the first sight of him. He was Mark Conley, ex-NYPD detective and now Middle East security manager for Kilos Shipping.

"Relax," Kilos told him. "It's only me."

One of Kilos's security men retrieved a chair and let his boss sit down. The four bodyguards then took up positions near the closed office door.

"Where are they?" Kilos asked Conley plainly, loosening his tie.

Conley indicated a door that led to an adjacent inner office. "Waiting, in there," he said.

"And the news is still all good?" Kilos asked him.

Conley nodded. "The *Global Warrior* and its cargo are safe and sound."

Kilos relaxed considerably. He signaled his bodyguards that they could now wait outside.

"This was a close-run thing, wasn't it?" he asked Conley once his goons were gone.

"That's because our opponents were not typical Somali pirates," the hard-nosed ex-detective told him. "They were a gang run by a guy named Turk Kurjan. He'd been able to take some of that Somali rabble and organize them, and for a very short while, he'd been doing a hell of a job at it. Even the other pirates were afraid of him. Until last night, when our new employees took care of the problem, no muss, no fuss."

"Who are these guys?" Kilos asked. "Where did you find them?"

"They're all ex-Delta Force," Conley said, acknowledging the gravity of his words. "I found them working as rent-a-cops in Saudi Arabia. I heard they were looking to get into maritime security, so I gave them a shot."

Kilos was immediately wary. "But why would ex-Delta operators be working as rent-a-cops? The world grows more dangerous every day, yet these people were barely employed? You mean, even Blackwater wouldn't hire them—or whatever it is called these days?"

"They told me they were considered too 'disruptive' for Blackwater," Conley replied. "Or any other private security company."

"An odd word, 'disruptive,' " Kilos said.

"It has to do with why they were bounced from Delta," Conley told him. "I did some checking. They went on an unauthorized mission—to kill bin Laden himself. But just when he was in their grasp, Washington told them to let him go."

Kilos was amazed. "Really?"

Conley nodded. "They were victims of the politics, I guess. An ugly severance from the U.S. military followed, and because all their old friends now work for Blackwater, they wanted nothing to do with them."

Conley paused, then asked: "Want to meet them?"

"I do," Kilos said. "I'd like to thank the people who just saved us a hundred million dollars."

Conley grabbed his laptop and a briefcase and they walked into the adjacent office. Here they found the five men, dressed in black camouflage uniforms, lounging on the office's three couches. Their exotic weaponry was scattered around the room.

Cowboys. That was the first word to come to Kilos's mind. All five were undeniably American in their looks and demeanor. But he could tell they were also hard-bitten, hard-drinking, cynical, bitter—and very tough. They made his bodyguards look like choirboys.

They were all in their late thirties or so, he guessed, but each man appeared old beyond his years. All of them had scars on their hands and faces. One wore a black patch over his left eye. Another had a prosthetic leg.

When Kilos walked in, they slowly got to their feet. He embraced each man, kissing them on both cheeks. They were less than warm in returning the gesture—but it didn't matter. These men had just done Kilos an enormous favor.

"It is my good fortune that you were available when we needed you," he told them. "It would have been disastrous if those pirates actually got away with our ship."

There was only a token amount of mumbled acknowledgment from the five men.

Kilos went on: "I'm also told you kept the gunplay down to a minimum while dealing with those animals—again, just as we had hoped."

One man spoke up. He had spiked, bleached blond hair, though he seemed a little old for such a style.

"Sure didn't want to pop any windshields on those BMWs," he said. "That glass must go for at least a grand, right?"

Both Kilos and Conley laughed. "It was not the BMWs we were worried about," Conley said. Then he asked, "How much do you know about the pirate gang you squashed last night?"

"Just what you told us," the man with the eye patch said. "That they attacked a Filipino trawler and a Danish freighter the night before."

"Well, those ships were carrying stuff off the manifest, too," Conley revealed. "The Filipino ship had fifty pounds of heroin on board. The Danish ship was carrying illegal ammunition for delivery to Hamas."

"Did you just say 'too?'" the man with the eye patch asked. "You mean there was something else on your ship besides BMWs?"

Conley contemplated them for a moment, then looked at Kilos. The shipping magnate nodded once and said: "They're big boys. They can take it."

Conley opened his laptop and put it on the table in front of the men. "We want to show you something," he said.

The laptop's screen came to life and they were soon taking a virtual tour of the *Global Warrior*'s cargo hold, the same place where the men had hunted down and killed four of the pirates the night before.

Though it still looked like a vast forest of stacked BMWs, a digital overlay revealed something else: a cache of large military weapons including rocket launchers, crates of air-to-air missiles, several large antiaircraft guns, armored cars and smart bombs, all shrink-wrapped, all hidden among the used luxury cars.

"*This* is what you saved for me," Kilos said. "Shall we call it 'secondhand military hardware?' In any case, there's more value there than in a thousand used BMWs, especially to the people we're moving it for. However, if one stray bullet had hit one of those air-to-air missiles, or a smart bomb? The whole ship would have gone up—and you along with it. That's why we requested you keep the gunplay to a minimum. And *that's* why we are so appreciative."

He nodded to Conley, and the security manager opened his briefcase. Inside were several packs of crisp $500 bills held together by rubber bands. Kilos counted out $10,000 for each man and handed it to him.

"We heard the leader of that pirate gang was bad news," Kilos told them as Conley distributed the money. "Apparently he was nothing like the Somalis who hijack ships using canoes and knives. May I ask you just how you did it?"

The man with the eye patch shrugged. "As soon as we got

on board, we asked your crew to stop one of the engines," he said, still studying the screen showing the hidden weapons. "We figured at the very least these guys would spot us traveling slow, and so far off the shipping lanes, we'd be too good of a target to pass up. And once they came on board, well . . ."

He let his voice trail off. Kilos knew that was all the explanation he was going to get.

"Look, we're not angels," Kilos told them, lowering his voice. "In this business, few people are. So I'll tell you a little secret: Black-market weapons are among the most profitable cargoes to carry these days. They are easy to handle, easy to ship, easy to sell. Just as long as the anti-piracy patrols don't find you, or the pirates themselves, it's a quick way to make a lot of money, off the books.

"Now we have some important shipments coming up. We have to protect them, without bringing any attention to ourselves. We don't want any of the NATO naval ships to be involved. If any of them got a real look at our cargo holds, it would not be good."

Conley spoke now: "This guy you greased, Turk Kurjan. He might be gone, but we've learned he has a brother, over in Indonesia, who could follow in his footsteps. Turk had informants in some key places—he probably even had a clue what we were carrying on the *Global Warrior*. If his brother decides to pick up where he left off, and is half as good as Turk was, it could make things difficult for us."

"This is why it would be in our best interest to deal with this brother right now," Kilos said. "Before he becomes a problem. And of course, do so as quietly as possible."

An uneasy silence fell on the room.

Conley said: "So—are you guys interested in more work?"

PART TWO

Reunion—One Year Earlier

5

Lost Limb Ward
Building 18
Walter Reed Army Medical Center

IT WASN'T THE cockroaches that finally got to Twitch.

Nor was it the chronic infection above his severed knee, the perpetual phantom pain, the paint chips falling on and into everything, or the drug dealers who roamed the halls of Building 18 at will.

It was the mouse shit. It was everywhere—around his bed, on his sheets, on his meal tray, on his clothes. In his only shoe.

He never saw the little bastards, only their droppings. And they made him sick to his stomach, especially in the morning, when he was usually in the bathroom puking anyway. In the perpetually humid LLW—the Lost Limb Ward—the mouse shit produced a smell of its own. A package of rancid hamburger left rotting in the sun offered a good comparison.

Twitch had been stuck in the same boxlike, four-bed room for three years, his fifth hospitalization since 2001, when he left most of his right leg back in Tora Bora. Besides the unsanitary conditions, Building 18 was a nightmare of Army bureaucracy. Every patient needed a case manager, but it took twenty-two documents, filed with eight separate Army commands, just to arrange an initial sit-down with one. Every time Twitch got close to getting all twenty-two documents approved, they would inevitably get lost, in a computer crash or through a misplaced file, or simply into the ether. No case manager meant Twitch had no contact with the outside world, no way to get things he needed, no way to complain. No way to get out.

It didn't end there. His physical therapist was so incompetent, Twitch suspected he was on drugs or perhaps brain-damaged. Sometimes Twitch would wear his prosthetic leg; other times he'd get around in a wheelchair, if one was available. Because of this, his physical therapist came to believe he was *two* different people and demanded the proper paperwork from him every time he arrived for a session, which was infrequently.

The last straw came during a ceremony marking the anniversary of 9/11. Twitch had never gotten a replacement for the uniform they'd torn off him that horrible day in Tora Bora. When he finally tracked down the clerk responsible for issuing new uniforms to those who had lost them in combat, the man demanded Twitch *prove* his fellow soldiers had destroyed his old uniform in the course of treating him. Twitch had no idea how to do that. Later that day, at the 9/11 observance, a soldier who had lost both legs, an arm and an eye in Iraq was being presented with his Purple Heart. The officer in charge of Building 18 had ordered all patients who could get out of bed to attend the ceremony. Twitch went in the only clothes he had—his gym clothes. The officer in charge chewed him out in front of the entire ward for being out of uniform.

Returning to his bed, he found it again covered with mouse droppings. And that was it, the final straw. That's when he decided to just end it all. He had no wife, no kids, no real family other than a few distant relatives back in Hawaii to whom he hadn't spoken in years. Even if he ever were released from here, he had nowhere to go, no place to live, no prospects for employment. Not many demolition companies would hire a one-legged charge setter. He didn't want to do it, but he just couldn't take it anymore.

That day, he set about hoarding his codeine painkillers, and after three weeks had fifty-six in all. With high irony, he'd bought a bottle of paregoric and 100 aspirins from one of the coke dealers he saw regularly walking the halls. On the day before his thirty-seventh birthday, Twitch crushed the codeine pills and the aspirins into a powder and mixed them with the paregoric. The result was a cocktail that he was sure would end his life peacefully.

He waited until the lights went out in the LLW that night, then retrieved the potent concoction from beneath his bed. He put the plastic cup up to his lips, tried to remember a prayer, couldn't, and started to drink.

That's when the man in doctor's scrubs and mask strolled into his room, turned on the light, and told Twitch that he was being moved.

"Moved? Where?" Twitch asked him, stunned and confused. It was the middle of the night.

"Back to the real world," was the reply.

The man lowered his mask and Twitch realized it was his old friend, Crash.

He'd never forget what his former Delta mate said to him next: "You're too good to be wasting away in here, buddy. So I'm breaking you out."

Twitch had already swallowed a bit of his suicide cocktail, so all this was like a dream. Yet, he didn't question how Crash was going to do it; he didn't care. What did he have to lose? So he climbed into his gym clothes, put his leg on, and then flushed the rest of his deadly drink down the toilet.

Then he hobbled outside, with Crash leading the way. A couple of orderlies challenged them outside the main door, but his old teammate growled them away.

By now, Twitch felt like he was floating. It didn't seem real. One second he was about to end it all, and the next, he was sitting in the front seat of Crash's rental car, speeding out the front gates of Hell.

The Bahamas
The next day

THE NIGHT IT happened, Batman Bob Graves thought he was having a nervous breakdown.

He'd been living in paradise for the past year. A ten-room

waterfront villa, perched on one of the highest elevations in the Bahamas, surrounded by plant life that seemed sprung from heaven. The ocean water he looked out on every day was the most amazing shade of blue, and the stars at night were absolutely brilliant. Whenever he wanted to, he could break out his telescope and look northeast, into the heart of the Bermuda Triangle, and wonder what exactly was happening out there.

This life was everything he thought he'd ever need. He had money. He had privacy. He wanted for nothing.

But he was miserable.

Even worse, he was paranoid. He lived alone, but was always looking over his shoulder. His nearest neighbor was two miles away, a light year in terms of Bahamian real estate. Yet he always heard voices at night, or thought he saw someone sneaking through the bushes during the day. Did he really lock that door, or unlock that second-floor window? Who turned on the lawn sprinkler the other morning? Was his rental car's interior sky blue when he first got it? He thought it had been red. These sorts of things had been happening with much frequency lately, and it was scarier than any kind of combat he'd ever been in.

As with every other night, this night he'd called for a dinner delivery at 8 P.M. He had a deal with a restaurant farther up the beach, and usually these things took a matter of minutes from phone call to drop-off. He'd been on Xuila for a year, and never had a food delivery been more than a twenty-minute wait. But by 10 P.M., he'd still seen nothing of it.

He sat on the front porch waiting, praying to see the headlights of the delivery Mini bumping along the beach road. To his mind, if his meal didn't come, that meant something was *really* wrong. But he saw nothing, not even the darkened car coming from the other direction, creeping up his steep gravel driveway.

But the sound of his front gate being opened? *That* he'd heard clearly. It sent him into a full-fledged panic attack. Someone *had* sneaked up on him, his worst fear come true. And he had no way to protect himself. Not for the first time since coming here, he cursed himself for not bringing a gun.

When he heard the front door squeak open, and then the sound of footsteps in the hallway, he knew it was the end of him. He sensed two dark figures standing behind him, saw their scrambled reflections in the porch window. He froze, unable to move, unable to even reach for the phone and call for help. There was no way he could call in a JDAM this time. He was unarmed and had made himself too many enemies.

So he turned to face the music, only to find it was Crash and Twitch standing behind him.

He barely recognized them; he hadn't seen them in eight years. Crash looked older, a more-sophisticated surfer dude. Twitch? Well, he looked a mess.

He almost threw his chair at them.

"What the fuck?" he kept saying over and over.

"You're getting nervous in your old age," Crash said calmly.

He pulled them both into the porch and closed the front door behind them, furious but immeasurably relieved. "What the hell are you guys doing here? How did you find me?"

Both collapsed on a long divan.

"It's 2009," Crash replied nonchalantly. "Anyone can find anyone these days. What do you have to drink?"

Batman sprinted into the kitchen and returned with a six-pack of Red Stripe beer. Crash drank one bottle in a long, noisy gulp. Twitch could barely twist the cap off his.

Batman checked the locks on the front door again.

"What's your problem?" Crash asked him. "I thought you'd be thrilled to see us."

Batman calmed down. He opened a beer. "It's hard to be thrilled about anything when half the fucking world is looking for you."

"So I heard," Crash said, taking another beer. "Who's worse? SEC? FTC? FBI?"

"All of them and ones I don't even know about," Batman replied. "You think bin Laden and his crew were bad? These Wall Street cops make them look like fairies."

"Hey, can you blame them?" Crash said. "Your name is right up there with Bernie Madoff. I mean, I thought you were doing the best out of all of us. I saw you in *BusinessWeek,*

Forbes. Caught you on CNBC a bunch of times. So what happened?"

Batman's relief turned to defiance. "I *wasn't* involved with Madoff. Let's get that straight. I was just doing side deals on what he was into."

"Like what?"

Batman shrugged. "I was selling Madoff shares to people who knew it was a Ponzi scheme but still wanted in."

"There are people *that* stupid?"

"It wasn't as stupid as it sounds," Batman told him. "They wanted in because it was quick money and they thought the government would bail out Madoff's investors once the whole thing came crashing down—just like they bailed out those assholes at AIG and the others. But they didn't. And so here I am. Trying my best to stay out of sight, and feeling like shit day and night."

Batman drank more of his beer. "So really—why are *you* here, after all these years?"

"I got a call from Gunner," Crash said. "He wanted to know if we were interested in work overseas."

"What kind of work?"

"Security work for the Saudis. That's all he could tell me. But he said it would be good pay if I could get the whole gang back together. Of course, it might not be the kind of money you're used to."

Batman took another swig of his beer. "At this point, don't assume anything."

"Well, if you're interested, there's something we got to do first," Crash told him.

"Snake?"

"Did you hear what happened at his trial?"

Batman stopped in mid-sip. "I didn't even know he had a trial."

Crash produced a DVD. "I was freelancing as a shooter in Southeast Asia earlier this year; I saved a guy's ass on Sri Lanka during their last big battle against the Tamils. This guy was another ex-Delta operator, and he's like an octopus, he has so many connections. He owed me the favor, so when we got out of there, I asked him to track down Snake. He gave me this."

They walked to the living room where Crash stuck the DVD into Batman's Sony player. The big screen came alive with a burst of static, then the image cleared to a black-and-white scene of a spare military courtroom. There were only four people in attendance. The judge was an Army officer dressed in plain unmarked fatigues with black bands covering his rank and name plate. A PFC was serving as the stenographer. Another Army officer, also in plain, unmarked fatigues, was reading off a long list of questions. And on the stand, looking beaten and exhausted, was Snake Nolan.

A bandage covered his left eye, a cane was nearby. Most alarming, he was wearing the uniform of a private; he'd been busted down that far. A time stamp in the corner indicated the video was shot five weeks after the disastrous mission in Tora Bora. Nolan was so gaunt and pale, he looked like a ghost.

The prosecuting officer was in the middle of questioning him. It was clear the former Team Whiskey CO was on trial for insubordination and disobeying a direct order. Yet there was no defense attorney present.

"Those assholes in Rummy's office wanted their pound of flesh," Crash said. "And this is them getting it."

There were no histrionics. This was not Nuremberg or The Hague they were watching. Everything was calm. Everything was deliberate. A sham trial on Xanax.

That is, until the prosecuting officer asked Nolan if he considered himself a traitor—and Nolan finally exploded.

"I was doing what I was told to do!" he roared, ignoring the judge's orders to lower his voice. "And when I had the chance to finally kill this son-of-a-bitch mass murderer, I took it, like any American would have. Like any American would have *wanted* me to. Except these people running the Department of Defense, for reasons I still can't fathom, determined that our high-priority target was more valuable to them alive than dead. A little more than a year later, we invade Iraq on a lie. You want me to explain things to you? Well, someone please explain that to me."

The judge was then heard saying: "The U.S. government wants you to . . ."

But Nolan loudly interrupted him: "Screw the U.S. government. And screw all of you."

The three ex-Delta mates were stunned, not so much at what Nolan had said, but by his condition. They'd been under enemy fire with him. Dodging artillery and mortar rounds. Charging machine-gun positions. Blowing up high-priority targets in the middle of the night. Every time, he had ice water in the veins, with never a hint of lost resolve, never coming close to losing his cool.

Seeing their hero reduced to this was hard to take. But what came next shocked them even more.

The video jumped to another edit point with more static. When it cleared again, the judge was announcing his verdict.

Again, the audio was poor, but they heard the judge find Nolan guilty of all counts. His punishment was a dishonorable discharge, loss of pension, and six years hard labor in an Army prison somewhere outside the U.S. Nolan sat frozen as the sentence was read.

But just as it seemed the farce was over, the judge dispensed another ruling: Once his prison time was served, the judge said, Nolan would be banned from ever entering the United States again. If he did, he'd be arrested for treason.

The pronouncement seemed to astonish even the prosecuting officer. It didn't make sense, even to him.

The prosecutor began to say something, but the judge simply raised his hand, indicating that nothing more should be said. Then he looked directly at the camera and gave the "cut" sign.

That's where the video ended.

Crash ejected the DVD and the three of them just stood there. It took a while before anyone could talk again.

"What happened after that?" Batman finally asked.

"They held him down in Gitmo, in solitary, away from the detainees," Crash said. "But he kept trying to escape and was always fighting with the guards. He was just too hot to handle, so they shipped him to a Navy maximum-security brig on Sardinia—but he caused problems there, too, always trying to escape. Finally, they sent him to a military prison just outside Baghdad. He escaped from there for real. They caught him walking in the Iraqi desert, heading east."

"Jesuszz—what was he doing?" Batman asked.

"He told them he was trying to get back to Afghanistan," Crash replied gravely. "To finish the job."

"'To *finish* the *job*?'" Batman whispered. "He really *did* lose his mind. And I thought *I* was nuts."

"When he completed his six years, they just tossed him out on the street in Baghdad," Crash explained. "He was picked up in the desert twice more, both times walking east."

Batman asked: "So, where is he now?"

"My guy says he's locked up in Kuwait," Crash said. "For 'terrorist activities.' But my guess is, they locked him up as a favor to the U.S. military."

Another long silence.

Crash finally said, "He took the fall for us—and look what it did to him. Those bastards broke him in two. Now it's up to us to do right by him."

"Are you suggesting we break him out?" Batman asked.

"If a bribe doesn't work, then yes," Crash said firmly. "So—are you in?"

Batman looked around his lavish retreat and spontaneously gave Crash a bear hug.

"Give me ten minutes to pack," he said.

Outside Kuwait City
Three days later

THEY DIDN'T RECOGNIZE Nolan.

His tiny jail cell was made of mud bricks and dirt. There was no window, no bunk. A sink the size of a water fountain served as both bathtub and toilet. A single light bulb dangling from the clay ceiling provided the only illumination. Scorpions and spiderwebs were everywhere.

On the other side of the bars, sat a man who was a dead ringer for Jethro Tull's Aqualung: greasy hair falling on his shoulders, a matted beard reaching his chest, a filthy sack-cloth shirt and burlap pants his only clothes. His hands were scraped down to the nails, his face dark and sunken. A bandage that looked months old covered his left eye. He seemed to be shaking uncontrollably.

More disturbing was the writing on the cell walls. It was everywhere. Numbers, letters, maps, diagrams, hundreds of arrows connecting all of it and none of it. The scribbling, as if drawn by a caveman who had gone mad, seemed to go on forever.

A Kuwaiti lawyer had brought the three Team Whiskey members here, to the basement of al-Kabat Prison, twenty miles west of Kuwait City. Just for this, his fee was $3,000. To actually arrange bail for Nolan—if this man was, in fact, Whiskey's former CO—would be $4,000 more, and the accompanying bribe, somewhere north of $5,000.

Luckily, between them, Crash and Batman had the money. The question was, did they have the right madman?

"Are we sure it's even him?" Crash asked, peering through the bars at the motionless figure in the corner.

"It's him," the lawyer insisted. He showed them a laminated ID card. Ragged around the edges and stained with blood, it bore a military ID photo of the man they had once known.

"You have five minutes with him," the lawyer said. "Make up your minds quickly. This is a one-time offer. I can't guarantee that I can arrange this for you ever again."

The lawyer unlocked the cell door long enough for the three men to step inside, then locked it behind them.

"Five minutes," he said before departing.

Batman approached the prisoner first. He wasn't sure what to say exactly.

But the prisoner beat him to it.

"Is he gone?" The voice came out almost impishly, each word moving the hairs hanging over his cracked lips. "The shyster. Is he gone?"

"Yes—he is," Batman replied.

The man looked up at them—and only then were they sure it was their former CO. But it was an uncomfortable meeting.

"Bad timing," Nolan said, his voice agitated. "Very bad timing."

There was something wrong here. Instead of being overwhelmed to see them, Nolan almost seemed upset they were there.

"What terrorist activities were you involved in?" Batman asked him.

Nolan laughed crazily. "Is that what they say I'm in for?"

"What were you doing?"

He got an even crazier glint in his eye. "I was looking for *him,*" he barked at them.

"Who?" Crash asked. "God?"

"No," Nolan said, throwing a handful of dirt against the wall. "Our high-value target. Remember? I was following leads that he was living here—I was tracking him down."

"By yourself?"

Nolan went silent, and just pulled on his dirty beard.

"Dude," Crash said. "You're in *Kuwait*. They're on our side. Why would he be here?"

"Why are *you* here?" Nolan asked them.

They were surprised by the question. "To get you out," Crash told him. "We're bailing you out."

"No," Nolan repeated. "It's bad timing."

"But it's all set," Batman insisted. "We got the money. And you can't stay here. You'll die."

"Oh, I'm not staying here," Nolan told them. "If you had come an hour later, you would have found this place empty."

Batman glanced at the others; they looked as worried as he. Nolan seemed to have gone so far around the bend, he wasn't coming back.

Batman tried to reason with him. "Look, Snake, we're laying out a total of twelve grand to spring you. We got a safe room nearby, where you can get cleaned up, get some strength back, and then we're out of here. Do you understand what I'm saying?"

"And can you understand what *I'm* saying?" he spit back at them. "Save your money—I'm out of here in an hour anyway. I'll meet you—outside."

This was going nowhere. Once again, Batman looked to the others, not knowing what to do.

"Do we carry him out of here?" he asked. "We got about two minutes to make up our minds."

"That's if they don't just leave us here locked up with him," Crash observed.

Nolan started cackling. "Enough bullshit," he said.

He crept over to the section of the cell farthest from the door. He put his hands up on the wall and started moving them in a circular fashion.

"Damn, he *is* nuts," Crash whispered.

"Hey—maybe not," Twitch said.

He pointed to the wall where Nolan was moving his hands. Like magic, the dirt was sliding away. Beyond it was a crude screen mesh, and beyond that, a long tunnel.

Batman couldn't believe it.

"Jesuszz, how did you do that?"

"I dug it," Nolan said with no small amount of glee.

"But how?"

Nolan held up his cracked and bleeding hands.

"With these."

Crash looked into the tunnel. It was about four feet around, seemed solid, and went so far, he could not see the end.

"Where does it go?" he asked Nolan.

"It ends one foot from the edge of the wadi on the north side of this place," Nolan said. He pointed to a nonsensical-looking diagram on the wall next to the tunnel. "All the calculations are right here, I just wrote them backwards. I memorized the distances when they were bringing me in. The wadi leads to the road. I hear a lot of trucks on the road, and hitchhiking is very popular in this part of the world—no matter what you look like."

He glanced up at them and smiled. "I'm serious. I would have been out of here in another hour."

The three men were speechless, until Crash said, "You know, that wadi also leads to the parking lot, where our rental car is."

* * *

THE KUWAITI LAWYER was two minutes late in returning to the cell.

"Let us decide," he moaned. "Time to make up your mind. Does he stay or does he go?"

Only then did he look in the cell and find it empty.

Near Yanbu, Saudi Arabia

THE NEWLY PAVED two-lane road looked oddly out of place.

Located near a rare bend in national Route 40, the strange side road ran deep into the Saudi desert, disappearing behind two shallow mountains many miles off the highway. An elaborate white gate stood at its entrance; a large air-conditioned gatehouse was located close by. Inside the gatehouse were six Saudi district policemen each wearing a crisp, new uniform.

Gunner was waiting for the rental car when it arrived at the gate. It had been two days since the reunited Team Whiskey had left Kuwait City, in a hurry, their bribe money still intact. A long drive across the burning interior of Saudi Arabia followed, the rented Mercedes's air conditioning crapping out about halfway through the trip.

But no problem. Bigger than ever, Gunner greeted them warmly, then ushered them into a stretch Range Rover waiting nearby. Two Saudi policemen were sitting in the truck's backseat, waiting for a lift. Before the team climbed in, Gunner subtly indicated that they should talk carefully in their company.

Gunner drove them down the long private road, confirming that it went more than thirty miles into the desert. As they roared along, they pretended to update him on their travels, making it sound like they'd all just jumped on an airliner and flown to the Middle East for this reunion. Despite the cops' presence, Gunner couldn't hide his excitement. He told them that when he'd first gotten in touch with Crash, he never thought it would all work out and that Whiskey would be together again. They, in turn, were genuinely glad to see him.

He spoke in very general terms about the security job he'd

arranged for them. They would need uniforms and firearms, of course. And he'd arranged for lodging for them. He also mentioned their employers had just leased a helicopter for their use.

"They were looking for people who knew their way around weapons and could keep their mouths shut," Gunner told them. "I figured one out of two ain't bad."

Thirty-two miles into the desert, they finally reached their destination. But it was not an oil or gas field, the type of place the others had expected they'd be protecting.

Instead, it was a man-made oasis with a huge resort area built up around it. Casinos, swimming pools, water parks, restaurants, all under a half-dozen immense glass domes. The place looked like Monte Carlo, Las Vegas and Disneyland, all rolled into one—if such a place had been built on another planet, in a galaxy far, far away.

"What kind of security force does *this* place need?" Batman asked, authentically puzzled. "They expecting an attack from Mars or something?"

Gunner had stopped at another guardhouse by this time. He turned to the pair of cops riding in the back.

"Thanks, guys," he said. "I can take it from here."

The two policemen left without saying a word.

Only after they'd gone did Gunner fess up.

"This place is called Al Zakkar," he began. "It's a secret resort, shopping mall, whatever you want to call it. Only the richest of the rich even know it exists, and only their top earners are allowed to come here or shop here."

"It's a *fucking shopping mall?*" Batman roared.

"It's a very high-end resort," Gunner replied, defending himself. "With places to shop, yes."

"It's a *top-secret shopping* mall?" Batman roared again.

"Hey, these Saudis got money to burn," Gunner explained. "And this sort of stuff really turns them on."

Batman scanned the futuristic layout.

"But again, what do they need a security force for?" he asked. "Are some Muslim hotheads threatening to blow this place up?"

"No," Gunner said, his voice falling low now. "And actually they don't want us to be a security force so much as they want us to be, well . . . security guards."

"You mean like prison guards?" Crash asked.

"No, I mean security guards," Gunner replied. "Like mall cops?"

The four team members groaned as one—even Nolan, who, now clean and shaven, was slowly coming back to life.

"Mall cops?" he said. "Jesuszz . . ."

Crash said: "Gunny—you didn't tell me this on the phone."

Gunner was mortified. "I know—but would you have come if I had?"

"*No,*" Crash, Batman and Twitch all answered at once.

Gunner shot back: "Hey, I said it pays good, and it does. And there's no heavy lifting. They just need us to be visible, in the casino, in the stores. In the restaurants."

Another groan, especially from Crash, the designated wrangler of this reunion. Nothing was unfolding as he'd imagined it.

"But if all they want us to do is walk around and look awake," he asked Gunner, "what the hell is the helicopter for? Chasing shoplifters?"

"Not exactly," Gunner replied, again awkwardly. "The thing is, this place is so big, we might need it to fly some of the better customers from one end to the other."

Batman slumped down in his seat.

"Just shoot me now," he said.

PART THREE

The Ghosts of Happy-Happy

6

SINGAPORE.

More ships were loaded and unloaded here than anywhere else in the world. Half the globe's oil supply passed through its waters. Thousands of tons of raw goods, from sneakers to SUVs, arrived in its harbor every day. At any given hour, upwards of fifty ships could be in berth taking on or offloading cargo, with three times as many anchored offshore, waiting for their turn at the dock.

On this early morning, three of those vessels belonged to Kilos Shipping. Two tankers and a container ship, they'd been loitering offshore since the previous afternoon. Singapore was the largest port in the world—so busy, ships sometimes had to wait a day or more to be unloaded.

The Kilos ships had arrived here from three different points of the globe. This was not unusual. There were dozens of Kilos vessels traversing the oceans at any given time. For a few of them to wind up in Singapore on the same day was not uncommon.

By 5 A.M., a berth had opened up for the first Kilos tanker. The harbormaster radioed the ship's crew with the news. A harbor pilot was dispatched to help guide the vessel in. With any luck, the ship would be empty and on its way by noon.

Oddly, though, no one on the tanker answered the harbormaster's radio message. He sent another, to no avail. A call was placed to the tanker captain's personal cell phone. Still no reply.

This was strange. If anything, ship captains waited anxiously for the call to come into berth. Every minute spent at anchor was a minute they weren't making money.

By this time, the harbor pilot had arrived at the tanker. Warned by the harbormaster that he was getting no response from the ship, the harbor pilot climbed up to the tanker's bridge and made a grisly discovery: The captain and the six-member crew were all dead. They'd been stripped naked, their throats slashed.

The pilot immediately informed the harbormaster, who called the harbor police. Murders in the Port of Singapore, while not unheard of, were rare. But no one had ever heard of an entire crew being killed while their ship was waiting to dock.

While the harbor police raced to the scene, the harbormaster had no choice but to continue unloading ships. They still had an open berth and many ships were waiting to dock. So the harbormaster went down to the next vessel on his list of loitering ships. It happened to be the container ship owned by Kilos.

The harbormaster radioed the ship to tell them they were next in berth. But there was no reply. He tried again—still nothing.

This time the harbormaster called the police directly. The cops boarded the container ship and made another gruesome find: The entire crew had been killed in the same way as those on their brother tanker ship: stripped naked, their throats slit.

The harbormaster immediately called every ship waiting at anchor, asking for a status check. Every vessel replied, except the remaining Kilos tanker. The harbormaster got no answer from them—but by now he had a good idea what had happened.

He had a hasty phone conversation with the chief of the harbor police.

"Only one person could have done this," the harbormaster said, his voice a whisper. "Someone who is 'invisible,' if you get my meaning. My inclination is not to pursue this any further, because I certainly don't want those kinds of ghosts knocking at my bedroom door."

"Nor is it my desire to investigate it," the harbor police chief admitted. "Or even report it to higher authorities. I don't need any trouble with those spirits, either."

There was a long, uncomfortable silence.

Then the harbormaster asked the chief, "What can we arrange for it to look like?"

The chief was stumped. "Three simultaneous murder-suicides?" he said finally.

The harbormaster was silent for a few more moments, then said: "Well, it's nonsense, of course. But believe me, the alternative would be worse."

7

Tang Island
Indonesia
The next night

THE MAGICIAN WAS getting tired.

He checked his watch.

"How many more?" he asked his assistant wearily.

"Just four," was the reply. "They've been waiting the longest."

The magician adjusted his fez and straightened his long flowing robes. "I'm getting too old for this," he muttered.

His hut was built on stilts just like every other hut on the tiny, picturesque island. It was located close to the beach and looked out on the Strait of Malacca to the west and the Phillip Channel to the east.

This island was one of literally thousands in the area, each its own little Bali Hai. Off in the distance, dominating the northern horizon, was the shimmering city-state of Singapore. On a night like this, with clear skies and calm seas, it looked like a real-life Shangri-La.

The magician's hut was cluttered with shelves that held the

tools of his trade: potions, flash powder, a few skulls, empty bottles of many shapes and sizes. On the floor by his feet was a basket where he kept his money.

"Let them in," he finally told his assistant, not hiding his annoyance. "But after these four, I must go to sleep."

The four men climbed into the hut. The magician almost laughed when he saw them. The first two were twins, so big, they just about took up all the extra space in the hut. The third man, heavily tattooed, was more average size, as was the fourth, who was wearing a pair of ancient 501 jeans.

The tattooed man was their spokesman.

"Many thanks for seeing us," he told the magician.

"You brought money, I hope?" the magician asked.

"Yes, we did."

"The correct amount?"

"Yes, for sure."

The magician settled back down and fumbled for a cigarette.

"What do you need my help for?" he asked them. "What is it that you want to accomplish?"

"We want to become part of Zeek Kurjan's pirate crew," was the reply.

The magician immediately blew some magic powder into the tattooed man's face. Suddenly, the man couldn't talk.

"You cannot *ever* speak that name here or anywhere else," the magician growled as the tattooed man's face turned red and he began to choke. "Did you hear about those fools over in Singapore—those murdered crews? The police tried to hush it up, but that just guaranteed everyone would be buzzing about it. Those people who were killed were probably speaking that name carelessly, as you just did. That brings bad luck from which even I can't save you."

The magician blew more powder into the man's face and he recovered. The rest of the group shifted uneasily.

"Our friend is a fool," one of the large twins said. "But he speaks the truth. That is our dream. To make some real money."

The magician finally lit his cigarette. "This dream won't

come easy," he told them. "You must prove yourself—all of you."

"That's why we're here," the tattooed man said, though his tongue was still thick and aching. "We want to make our bones—and be noticed."

"So then go get noticed," the magician replied through a cloud of smoke. "Why are you bothering me?"

"Because we need your magic," the man said. "This is what everyone has told us."

The magician took a long drag on his cigarette and sighed. He held out his hand. "Pay up first. Twenty dollars and no less."

The tattooed man collected five American dollars from each man and passed them to the magician. The bills were wet and ragged.

The magician counted them out, then studied the line of bottles on the shelf behind him. He checked the money again, then selected an old quart-size juice bottle.

He blew into the bottle then sealed it with a twist cap. He handed the bottle to the tattooed man.

"When you go to make your bones," the magician said, "open this first, pour it on your boat, and your boat will become invisible."

The tattooed man took the empty juice bottle, studied it, and then looked back at the magician.

"But what about us?" he asked. "We want to be invisible, too."

The magician was perturbed. He took down a much smaller plastic Coke bottle, hastily blew into it, capped it and flipped it to the spokesman.

"Here you go," he said. "Open it, pour it on yourselves and you will become invisible, too—until you want to be seen, that is. Simple as that."

The magician yawned and crushed out his cigarette. The meeting was over.

The four men got up to go, but the magician stopped them.

"But don't forget: Do not speak that name recklessly," he told them, seriously. "Because if you do, that dream of yours will go up in smoke—and you'll all go up with it."

* * *

THE SHIP APPEARED right on schedule.

It was slowing down, as all ships did when leaving the Malacca Strait and entering the Phillip Channel, its engines reducing their sound from a dull roar to a low groan.

Hiding in the reeds on the southern shore, the four fledgling pirates watched it go by. It was a small freighter, 120 feet long, just the type of game they wanted to take down first, to get their feet wet.

By the time its bow light cut through some low fog, the freighter had slowed to barely five knots. The tattooed man started the engine on their motorboat and steered it out into the strait. It was midnight and a slight wind blowing off the islands had caused most of the thin mist to disappear.

"Now?" one of the twins asked.

The tattooed man took out the empty juice bottle the magician had given him, uncorked it and pretended to spill the air all over the boat.

"We are now invisible," he said. "I hope . . ."

They allowed the ship to pass, and then the tattooed man opened the motorboat's throttle and they were quickly roaring up to the back of the freighter.

He turned the steering of the boat over to the other twin, and they almost capsized while changing places. Then the tattooed man took the long bamboo pole from the bottom of the motorboat and attached a hooked knife to one end.

"You're sure you are better with this than with a hook and rope?" one twin asked the tattooed man.

"I'm sure," he replied. "I have the magic."

They were now right up against the ship's stern. The twins were doing their best to keep the boat out of the vessel's wake, but it was becoming a rough ride.

Nevertheless, the tattooed man stood on the motorboat's bow and launched the bamboo stick up toward the ship's railing. He missed. He tried again—another miss. A third time not only missed, but it was only by sheer good luck that he was able to catch the pole as it fell away from the freighter.

This was not going well.

The fourth man silently made his way to the front of the motorboat. He took the bamboo stick from the tattooed man and heaved it up toward the stern of the freighter. It caught the railing on the first try. Then he took the plastic Coke bottle from the tattooed man's pocket, uncapped it and let the air within pour all over him. Then he yanked on the pole to make sure it was secure, put a big knife between his teeth, and started to climb.

The tattooed man and the twins were astonished at their colleague's actions. They weren't even sure of his name. He was just the water taxi driver—the *haki*—they'd hired to take them to the magician's hut, and he joined their band only because he had the last five dollars they needed to buy the magician's bottle of air.

He was about halfway up the side of the freighter when he looked back to see the tattooed man hesitating at the other end of the pole. He was losing his nerve.

He called up to the haki. "Can you do this on your own?"

"Rob the ship—*by myself?*" the haki yelled back.

The tattooed man sucked it up, hastily poured some of the magician's breath on himself, then grabbed the pole and started to climb unsteadily.

The haki had reached the railing by this time. The ship's deck was dark and slippery; the only light to be seen was coming from the bridge.

The tattooed man arrived and the haki helped him over the railing.

"It's too dark," the tattooed man complained.

"But darkness helps," the haki told him.

Again the tattooed man asked him: "Can you do this alone?"

He nodded impatiently. "OK—just watch my back." The haki limped down the deck and climbed the ladder to the freighter's bridge. He knocked hard on the door, causing it to swing open.

The satchel full of money was sitting on the map table, right next to the door. The four people on the bridge didn't say a word; they didn't even look at him. The haki took the money and went back down the ladder.

He made his way back to the railing to find the tattooed man already on the other side, ready to go down the pole. He was surprised the haki had returned so quickly. His eyes went wide when he saw the sack full of money.

"The magician was right," the haki told him. "They couldn't see me."

The next night

ONCE AGAIN, THE ship appeared right on time.

It was small, a coastal freighter, identical to the vessel the night before. This type of ship was common in this region, delivering goods to the thousands of islands in the Java Sea and beyond.

The twins were excited to no end.

"Two ships in two nights," one of them said. "Certain people will definitely take notice if we pull this off."

There were only three of them tonight. The tattooed man did not show up at the appointed time at their prearranged meeting place. He had taken his portion of the money from the night before and headed off to spend it on the Happy-Happy, local slang for "booze and women." This was where a lot of would-be pirates floundered in their careers; the tattooed man had made himself $1,000 the night before, more money than he'd ever seen in his life. The temptation to blow it had been too much for him.

So now it was just three.

The trio had agreed to hang onto their booty. They'd splurged on only one thing: an ancient five-shot revolver they'd bought from a drug dealer on Goat Island. The weapon came with only three bullets, so they would have to be economical in how they used it.

They waited for the freighter to go by. Then, as before, they emptied the magician's breath onto the boat and themselves and started out into the channel.

They were soon right up against the rear of the freighter. The haki used the bamboo stick and hook again. As before, he caught the rail on his first try. The twins held the boat steady as he shimmied up the pole and grasped on to the stern railing. With great athletic ability, he swung up and over the railing, landing square on his feet. He had the weapon up and ready.

As before, he was gone for under a minute. When he reappeared at the railing, the twins thought something had gone wrong. But again, he was holding a bag that appeared to be full of cash. He slid down the pole and into the boat. The twins quickly motored away.

"That was so easy," one of the twins told him.

"It's that magician," the haki replied. "His stuff *really* works."

THE FOLLOWING NIGHT the trio were in their same hiding spot. This time, the target ship was sailing westward. The two times before, their victims had been heading east.

By now, they were accomplished at moving into position. Roaring out of the reeds, they were soon riding along the freighter's stern. The haki did his thing with the empty bottles and his bamboo pole, and soon was standing on the railing again.

Then one of the twins noticed something.

"Isn't this the ship we hit two nights ago?" he asked.

The other twin studied the vessel's stern. It did look the same—and its name appeared to have been painted over recently.

"Lots of ships like this go through here," he said. "But it does seem familiar."

They dropped the subject when they saw their colleague reappear on the railing, once again, waving a bag of money.

"How does he do it?" one twin asked the other excitedly.

"It's magic," his brother replied.

The man came down the pole and off they went.

THEY RETURNED TO their hideout—a shack at the edge of their home island—and for the third time, counted their loot.

Each time it equaled $4,000. On the button.

"We were lucky," the haki told the twins as they examined the money. "We got all three ships just before they had to make their payrolls. That magician is a genius."

The twins contemplated the situation. The haki was a weird one. But it was hard to argue with what he'd done.

Three nights, three attempts, three successes?

The twins had never heard of anyone being such a good pirate.

8

The next night

THE TWINS STAGGERED up the long set of steps to the hut where the haki said he lived.

They found him in a room empty of everything except a bucket of rainwater. No mattress, no blanket to keep the centipedes off. Just the hard wooden floor. He was asleep, still fully clothed, wearing his 501 jeans as always.

The twins were amazed he could sleep with all the noise around him: the water splashing up against the hut's stilts, the grunts and groans of sex coming from the shack next door, the bad disco music blasting over the water from Goat Island just 100 yards away. The sound of money being spent twenty-six miles across the channel in Singapore.

They roused him by gently nudging his behind. He woke with a start. They laughed and handed him a bottle filled with an amber liquid.

"Is this gasoline?" he asked them, still groggy. "And are we going hunting tonight?"

"No, it's whiskey," one twin told him. "And no—tonight we're going to make Happy-Happy."

"But we shouldn't spend our money," the haki told them, wiping his bleary eyes. "That was the agreement."

"We don't need to spend our money," the other twin said. "Word has gotten around about us. We have made some new friends. They want to pay our way."

"Who are these 'new friends?'" the haki asked.

Both twins put their fingers to their lips, and then smiled drunkenly.

"We can not say their names," one replied. "Not yet . . ."

FIVE MINUTES LATER, they were on a large *sekoci*, heading past Goat Island. A man wearing black pajamas and a red bandana steered the twenty-foot-long motorboat. None of them knew his name. He was one of their "new friends."

It was almost midnight, and the water was lit up in many colors. There were so many lights, it was hard to tell if they belonged to passing ships or if they were coming from the hundreds of islands around them.

After a half-hour journey, during which they finished the bottle of whiskey, they arrived at an island none of them had ever been to before. It was surrounded by wooden buildings all resting on stilts about ten feet off the water. Some of the buildings seemed as large as the island itself.

The buildings, bars and lounges mostly, were covered with Christmas lights and tacky Chinese lanterns. Lots of sekocis, rubber rafts and water taxis were either moving around them or tied up nearby. Altogether, the island looked like an incredibly low-rent version of a city in the sky, something from a Grade-D *Star Wars* movie. But the music here was loud and the lights were bright. And they were much closer to the Shangri-La city of Singapore.

They climbed off the sekoci and staggered up a gangplank to a place called the Great Fortune Lounge & Karaoke. In this part of the world, "karaoke" was a euphemism for brothel.

The lounge part was huge and crowded. There were at least 300 people jammed into the place, probably more. It took the trio a while to realize they were actually inside the remains of a large wooden sailing ship that had been converted into a massive dance hall and bar. And though it was dark inside, it was soon apparent the place was filled with two kinds of people: "happy girls"—traveling prostitutes—and the area's criminal element.

The hall reeked of spilled beer, cigarette smoke, bad perfume and sweat. The men outnumbered the happy girls by at least three to one. And all of the men looked like escaped prisoners, hustlers, or worse: real pirates.

The man in the black pajamas led the twins and the haki across the dance floor to a particularly dark corner of the club. Here was a large rectangular table, bigger than any other piece of furniture in the place. Sitting at this table were twelve men all wearing the same style clothes: new jeans, white sneakers, black T-shirts and red bandanas. A thirteenth man, older than the rest, wore his bandana tied around his neck, allowing him to show off his long, snow-white hair.

"Zeek's crew," one of the twins whispered. "This means they want to meet us."

The other twin punched his brother hard on the arm. "Do not speak that name, you fool," he growled. "Or these people will make spare ribs of us."

They sat at the end of the table and the men in red bandanas ignored them. A waitress appeared. The men in red bandanas ordered two bottles of whiskey and five pitchers of beer—and told the waitress to bring glasses for their three new friends. Then they called over a group of happy girls and signaled that the twins and the haki dance with them.

So dance they did.

Though none of them could move around very well—the beer and whiskey were kicking in—the happy girls they were dancing with not only looked beautiful, they were getting more beautiful with every beat of the music.

So they danced and drank, and danced some more and drank some more. And the hall got more crowded, and the stink of perfume and sweat and beer became like a fog. It got to the point where they almost forgot why they were there.

That ended when the men in the bandanas all rose as one and swept across the dance floor. The crowd parted for them like the Red Sea. The last man in the group, the pirate with the white hair, indicated that the haki should go with them. When the twins tried to go too, one look from this man discouraged them on the spot.

The last time the haki saw the twins, they were standing side by side, waving meekly, as he was led out of the club.

* * *

"MY NAME IS Bantang," the man with the white hair told the haki, slurring his words. "I've lived on these islands my entire life."

They were walking down a gangplank that led away from the lounge and to another boat. But this boat was not a sekoci. It was a yacht, a long, stiletto-shaped vessel sixty feet in length and pimped out like something from an action movie.

"Our boss heard you can really handle yourself," Bantang told him. "If that's true, you can make big money with us. Does that sound good?"

The haki nodded. His jaw was too numb to move.

"Our boss said you should make the rounds with me tonight," Bantang went on. "You can see how we operate. It's a privilege not afforded to many. It means he almost considers you part of the crew already."

They climbed aboard the yacht and went below to a cabin that appeared almost the same size as the dance hall at the Great Fortune Lounge. The cabin was dark and the music was mellower, more European. There were couches lining the walls and, in a reversal from the last place they were in, the ratio of happy girls to guys was about three to one. Indeed, the yacht was overflowing with beautiful women.

The haki was led to one long couch, and now he sat with the main group of men wearing red bandanas. Bantang sat next to him. The haki noticed all of the men had pistols stuck in their waistbands.

Bantang whispered to him: "You're among *real* pirates now."

The haki also noticed some of the pirates were now wearing T-shirts that seemed to be from the same shipping company.

"Those are the clothes of their enemies who have passed on," Bantang explained. "You heard about what happened over in Singapore Harbor recently? Those people are dead, but their clothes have come to good use."

One of the pirates produced a paper bag and dumped its contents out on the table. The others cheered and drunkenly applauded him.

What he'd spilled out was a load of large blue capsules. They looked like cold medication except they were the size of horse tranquilizers.

"We do drugs now," Bantang said to the haki. "The night just begins here."

The pirates fell upon the small mountain of blue capsules and started gobbling them up.

"These are Ecstasy," Bantang explained. "Big favorite of the Boss."

In most parts of the world Ecstasy meant MDMA, a drug that made the user feel not only high, but also in love with the rest of humanity, at least until the effects wore off. In Indonesia, though, Ecstasy meant something different. Here, it was a hodge-podge of heroin, cocaine, methamphetamine, and usually two or three hallucinogens all mixed together in one capsule. Under Indonesia's harsh drug laws, possession of any of these substances would mean life in prison. But getting caught by law enforcement was obviously not the pirates' concern.

"Take one," Bantang urged the haki. "Big Boss is in love with Ecstasy. He wants all his men to be, too."

The haki recognized this for what it was. A test.

So, he took what looked to be the biggest capsule in the bunch. Then, snatching the beer out of Bantang's hand, he popped the capsule into his mouth and swallowed it by draining the beer.

The pirates cheered wildly. They started comically imitating the haki's action. In just a few seconds, the party atmosphere on the yacht skyrocketed.

The happy girls on hand also indulged—and soon they were stripping off their clothes and doing lap dances. The haki jumped up and began dancing frenziedly with two Chinese girls. The large cabin began to spin. He drank more beer. The cabin began spinning faster.

It was only when the two Chinese girls fell over that the haki realized the yacht was moving. He was able to grab onto Bantang for support. He looked up at him as if to say: Where are we going now?

Bantang's eyes were so red it was hard to make out his pupils.

"Wait and see," he replied with a wink.

WHAT FOLLOWED WAS a high-speed boat trip in and out of the inlets of the Talua Islands. It went by so fast, the intoxicated people on the yacht felt like they were flying. It ended near a place called Pootan, another narrow strip of water connecting the Strait of Malacca to the Phillip Channel.

This was an especially dangerous place for ships in transit, as they had to slow down due to the narrow waterway and shallow depth. It was a prime place for pirate attacks.

And that's what had just happened here. The speeding yacht came up on a midsized oil tanker that had been seized by more members of the Red Bandana pirate gang.

The yacht tied up next to the dead-in-the-water ship. Bantang took the haki up with him along with several other pirates.

"As you are my helper tonight," Bantang told the haki, "I will need your muscles to help me carry some money."

As they reached the deck of the tanker, several different things were happening at once. There were at least two dozen pirates systematically going through the ship, looting and taking anything not bolted down. Seven hapless crewmembers of the tanker were on their knees next to the starboard railing, blindfolded, their hands tied behind them. Showing not the slightest hesitation, two pirates came up behind them and nonchalantly shot each prisoner in the back of the head.

Two smaller tankers had tied up on the other side of the hijacked ship, and their crews were in the process of off-loading oil from the big tanker into their smaller holds. Another group of pirates was painting the bridge and changing the hijacked ship's name and registration numbers.

Most surprising, an Indonesian Navy patrol boat was motoring back and forth nearby, its crew watching the whole thing. Every once in a while, they would wave to the pirates and the pirates would wave back.

"We are like ants taking over a hive," Bantang said to the

haki. "There will be nothing left when we are done. No clues. No witnesses. Everything is covered."

A pirate approached Bantang and gave him a cardboard box. It was full of money, at least $40,000 American.

"You know what to do with this," the pirate told him.

At the same time, he handed Bantang a bulky, ancient-looking mobile phone. It was one of many the haki could see the pirates using. While he couldn't pick out individual conversations, he was sure that this was how the pirates communicated with their Indonesian coconspirators.

"Old these days means more secure," Bantang told the haki, showing him the 1980s-era mobile phone. "Anyone can listen in on cell phones, but no one tracks the old stuff. One big rule for us? Owning a cell phone is punishable by death. Cell phones mean detection by people who are not under our pay. Always remember that."

Bantang held up the old phone.

"When our boss puts out a call on his old phone network," he explained, "his allies act immediately. Other pirates, police, military people we've bought off. If he ever needs help, he calls on this and they all come running."

But truth was, the haki could barely hear Bantang anymore, because at this point the Ecstasy began kicking in. His head was suddenly spinning with colors. His hands were covered in gold dust; what he imagined was the happy girls' perfume was suddenly visible to his naked eyes. The stars above him were moving, creating intricate patterns and twirling circles. The night was folding and then refolding itself into one long hallucinatory play, and the haki was just one more actor in it.

The next thing he knew, he was on another sekoci, speeding along with Bantang, heading for a new destination.

IT WAS A twenty-minute trip to Skull Island.

This place was similar to the island where the Great Fortune Lounge was located: lots of shacks on stilts by the waterside, a few dance halls and many places to buy liquor and drugs.

But this island also had a small downtown and main street, and the most prominent business here was a place called the Red Skull bar.

Run by a woman named Miss Aloo, it looked like something out of a 1930s movie, especially to someone under the influence of Indonesian Ecstasy. Old, in disrepair, and surrounded by dreary palm trees, it was adorned on the outside with cracked stained-glass windows and pieces of ancient nautical trash like old wooden anchors and the main mast of an eighteenth-century sailing ship. Customers went through squeaky swinging doors to enter the smoky, smelly, vile saloon within, complete with a piano player, an untethered brass-colored macaque monkey, a rope-and-teak bar, hundreds of bottles of exotic liquor and—because of the frequency of fights—a soggy, filthy mop and a bucket that, on some nights, could be filled with both water and diluted blood.

Bantang and the haki made their way through the mob of customers, ducking and dodging punches thrown randomly in the drunken throng, continuously sending off the monkey, which seemed intent on picking their pockets, and the small army of happy girls who were trying to do the same.

"Be careful," Bantang yelled back ominously to the haki as they waded through the madhouse. "Some of those girls aren't girls at all."

They eventually reached their destination, the bar's kitchen, which, the haki learned, also served as the unofficial bank for the red bandana pirates.

They were greeted with much respect and fear by the kitchen staff. One bowed and scraped as he opened a door that appeared to lead into a food storage cabinet but actually revealed a huge set of steel doors bound by a combination lock.

This was Zeek's local depository. Bantang astutely worked the lock's tumblers, and soon swung the massive doors open. A vault the size of a walk-in closet was on the other side.

Sitting in the corner of the kitchen was a man who looked more Middle Eastern than Indonesian. He rose from his seat as soon as the vault door opened. Bantang gave the box of money to him.

"We wait while he counts it," Bantang explained. "Then we'll lock it up and be on our way to our next stop."

The Middle-Eastern man counted the money with the dexterity of a casino pit boss. It took him just three minutes to declare the box held $47,522. Then Bantang counted out $5,000 and gave it to the Middle-Eastern man.

"You know the cut," Bantang told him. "Four thousand for the Mandarin, one thousand to your boss."

Without so much as a thank you, the Middle-Eastern man stuffed the money under his shirt and went out the back door.

"Jihadist vulture," Bantang grumbled. "If only the Boss trusted a more reasonable bank, like one in Switzerland."

Bantang took a bottle of whiskey from the kitchen cupboard and opened it. He took a mighty swig, gargled with it and swallowed. Then he passed the bottle to the haki, who at this point was too intoxicated to speak, even if he wanted to.

"The ships we take are never reported as being stolen," Bantang told him, pocketing another $1,000 in cash and then closing up the vault after putting the rest of the money inside. "They're repainted, reflagged and sold for a percentage through the Shanghai Chinese. We split the cargo, and the Boss keeps the money, except what we pay the Muslim terrorists to stay out of our way and what we pay our informants. That, my friend, is how the world goes round."

THEY WERE SOON on the sekoci again, zipping along the water at what felt like supersonic speed.

The haki's head was drowning with colors and voices and faces. Sometimes when he glanced over at Bantang, he thought he saw a happy girl driving the boat instead. And even though the haki couldn't remember exactly where they'd been just a few minutes before, he couldn't shake the notion that a monkey was chasing them.

Bantang told him they had one more errand to run. They were soon at another island, this one long and thin, like a finger sticking out into the channel. There was no dock for them to tie up to. Bantang ran the motorboat right up onto the beach, which, from the haki's point of view, seemed to go on forever.

Just up from this beach was a dirt road that was home to a handful of waterfront establishments. Like the other islands visited this night, these businesses were mostly saloons and lounges.

The big building was trimmed with bright green neon lights. It was called *Kucing Jantan Rumah*—roughly translated, Home of the Tomcat.

It was a brothel, one of the largest in this part of Asia.

Bantang and the haki went around to the rear entrance and let themselves in. They met a woman who looked to the haki like a madam in the rear vestibule; she was coming out of a room that had a hidden door that went flush up against the wall as soon as it was closed. The haki got a brief glimpse inside this room and saw it was filled with communications equipment: telephones, radios and such. Odd for a brothel, he thought.

Bantang and the madam had a brief discussion, and then Bantang passed her a packet of money. She handed him two glasses of champagne and disappeared upstairs.

Bantang gave one glass to the haki and they toasted and drank.

"The girls who work out of here go all over Asia," Bantang told him. "They have regular customers among ship captains, military people and the police. But they are also our spies— and they are much better than the CIA or the Russian spy network. From these people we know which ships are heading our way, which ships to target and attack. The girls also have contacts in the newspaper business, and that assures us that such attacks never get into the media, so the population of the world does not know when a ship is taken here like they do every time a pin drops off Somalia.

"Not that it makes any difference; the insurance company just writes off the ship as being a loss anyway, as if it had sunk or caught fire or wound up in a boneyard. They don't have the time or resources to come after us. We are then able to commit the perfect crime."

But the haki wasn't really listening to him anymore. He'd caught a glimpse of several of the brothel's workers in the next room over and was now banging his head against the vestibule wall, trying not to have a drug-induced, involuntary orgasm.

THEIR ERRANDS DONE, they were soon speeding toward yet another destination. This one was not in the Phillip Channel, but was located back within the tangle of islands off Talua. They went under a wooden bridge that seemed a mile high and a mile long; It connected two islands that were homes to many lounges and bars. On a hill on an island nearby, a huge beer bottle was spilling out not magic air but a sea of beer on the trees below. On another island, they saw a wrecked, three-masted ship so old it seemed like something out of an old pirate movie. And while the haki had managed to shake the notion that a monkey was chasing him during all this, he believed now that the fish under their boat were mad at them because they were going too fast.

They soon arrived at yet another island just as the sekoci ran out of gas.

"Happens every time," Bantang said.

He managed to drift through the island's expansive lagoon and reach a long, crooked-finger dock sticking out from the beach. It was obvious this island was different from the others they visited this night. It was hidden among a gaggle of other islands probably twenty miles in from the Phillip Channel. It had only one approach, and the water surrounding it was very shallow, especially on the north side, which featured a stout sandbar. There was no way a large vessel, such as a major warship, could ever get anywhere near this place.

Still, it was within sight of the bright lights of Singapore just on the horizon.

"This is where we live," Bantang told the haki. "Blakam Padam, our little hideaway. The locals call it Pirate Island."

There were no neon brothels or rowdy saloons here. This place looked like a military camp. There was a barracks, an armory, a mess hall and shops to service the large number of small attack boats. Many men in red bandanas were in evidence here, too: at least eighty or so, maybe more. They were mostly clustered in small groups, sitting around campfires, drinking whiskey and talking loudly.

Most interesting, hidden on a rivulet nearby was a large boat, a seagoing yacht bigger than the one that had taken them to the hijacked tanker. This yacht had been fitted out with many weapons and had extra-large fuel tanks on its rear deck, a most unusual vessel.

Bantang walked the haki around the site, talking as they went.

"You will get your cut of anything we make," the white-haired pirate was saying. "You are poor, just like us, no? You want your piece of the world, too, right? You want to go to Singapore someday and live like a king? That's what we all want.

"If we make money, you make money. And not just robbing safes on passing tramp steamers or stealing oil from medium-size fuel ships. We are prepared to take down larger ships here. Super tankers. Container ships. The sky is the limit. And if you should get hurt or even die during an operation, we are good about that. We will send your share to your family, if you have one. Or to your friends. We will take care of you, even after death."

They walked deeper into the camp. There were many small shacks in a row next to the barracks. They had open walls, and the haki could see boxes containing handheld GPS units, night-vision goggles and old mobile phones. The armory was filled with weapons—M-16s, AK-47s and shotguns, plus many more boxes of ammunition.

Again, many of the pirates were drinking near the camp's little beach, next to the lagoon. Still tripping and drunk, Bantang and the haki headed back in that direction.

They took their place near a group of pirates and were each handed a bottle of Chinese beer. One pirate started admiring the haki's wristwatch. The haki pulled it away immediately and with one glance, Bantang told the man to desist, much to the haki's relief. The last thing he wanted was someone taking a close look at his watch.

Fifty feet up from the beach was a large structure more

elaborate than the others. It was built of concrete and steel, not rope and teakwood, and seemed to have a substantial foundation underneath it. It had a wraparound porch and two armed men loitering outside. They were wearing black bandanas, a sign, Bantang explained, that they were part of the Boss's elite personal bodyguards. The building they were guarding was obviously the camp's headquarters.

A man stepped out of the building's front door and onto the porch. That's when the haki saw Zeek Kurjan for the first time.

Tall, thin, with a cracked nose, dark skin, steely eyes and a long black beard that was tied in braids and held together at the ends by black ribbons, he was wearing a loud purple shirt and purple pants, not jeans, and high black boots over his pant legs. Two long, thick gold chains hung around his neck and reached almost to his belt. The belt itself contained two sheaths that held large combat knives. A black do-rag covered his head. Though Zeek was known to employ doubles for security purposes, stand-ins who dressed and wore their hair and beard like him, the haki was sure this man was the authentic item. He looked as cruel and ruthless as advertised.

Another sekoci arrived shortly thereafter. It tied up to the finger dock and four people got out, two pirates and two men wearing Indonesian military uniforms. They walked past the clusters of pirates and up to the HQ building. They had a brief discussion with Zeek, at which the head pirate let out a great, sinister roar. Whatever news the military men delivered, Zeek was pleased by it.

The Pirate King started barking orders. Two of his bodyguards scrambled out of the HQ and ran to a building at the rear of the camp. They soon returned, dragging a middle-aged man between them.

This man was obviously a prisoner of the pirates. His clothes were in tatters, and judging by the cuts and bruises on his body, he'd been beaten and mistreated for some time. He was taken into the HQ, after which Zeek's booming voice could again be heard, along with that of the hapless prisoner pleading for his life.

After a few minutes of this, the man was dragged back out onto the porch of the HQ. A bell was rung three times, ordering the pirates to gather round.

Zeek soon reappeared and addressed his men.

"Our friend here is ready to end his vacation with us," he said, pointing to the beaten, broken man. "Who wants to help me bring him home?"

The pirates cheered lustily, raising their fists over their heads. All of them wanted to go.

Bantang grabbed the haki's hand and raised it for him.

"You do not want to miss this, my brother," Bantang said.

A SMALL FLEET of armed sekocis set out from the pirates' island. Zeek's speedboat was in the lead.

The trip to the island of Sumhai took about twenty minutes, winding in and out of the dizzying channels separating hundreds of islands in the Talua region. There were no happy girls with them this time. All of the pirates were drunk and high on drugs, including the haki. But he could see they all had something else in them, too—a look of bloodlust, like men going into a battle that they knew they would win, no matter what.

Sumhai was actually two islands separated by a narrow shallow canal. The larger of the two had a couple of dozen huts, a small sugarcane field and a pen containing a few pigs and goats. The smaller island contained a graveyard: a small hill with one tree and a collection of crude stone markers.

The sekocis' noisy approach woke up the village's residents. Soon people were flowing out of their huts, wearing rags for bedclothes. But on seeing the pirates, they went into a panic. Parents hustled children back into their shacks. The pigs and goats were set free, allowed to run into the jungle and hide. The men put on their clothes and grabbed broomsticks as weapons.

The fleet of sekocis landed on the island's beach. Pirates climbed up into the village, waving their weapons around and shouting orders. Like clockwork they rounded up the island's thirty or so residents, forcing them to the water's edge.

A cheap plastic chair was set up on the beach, and only then did Zeek get out of his speedboat. He sat in the chair and stretched his legs. He looked at the gang of frightened villagers staring back at him and smirked. He signaled his bodyguards, who then dragged the prisoner off his boat.

A gasp went through the villagers when the beaten man was thrown at their feet. A woman and two teenage girls ran to him and helped him to his knees.

They were crying: *"Bapak! Bapak!"*

Father, father.

Zeek once again signaled his bodyguards. They roughly broke up the reunion, pulling the wife and daughters away from the beaten man.

The wife tried to hit Zeek, but the bodyguards kept her at a safe distance.

"Why are you mad at me?" Zeek asked her, his voice dripping with sarcasm. "Even though he still owes me money, I have returned your husband to you. Your daughters now have their father back."

The woman suddenly looked hopeful.

"But there is a price," Zeek went on darkly. "In fact, he and I recently negotiated the terms of his release."

Zeek gave a third signal to his bodyguards. They grabbed the youngest of the daughters and threw her at his feet. The villagers gasped again. Zeek scanned his gang of pirates, selecting one who looked more intoxicated than the rest. He motioned him forward.

Zeek told this man simply: "A present for you."

The pirate proceeded to brutally rape the girl, while Zeek's bodyguards forced her mother, sister and father to watch.

It seemed to go on forever. The girl's father was on the ground weeping uncontrollably, her mother and sister hysterical.

When it was finally over, the mother screamed at Zeek: "God will punish you for this!"

But this only amused the pirate captain further. He grabbed the mother by her hair and brought her face up to his.

"You have it all wrong," he told her. "You see, *I am* the punishment of God. That's why I'll live forever. If you kill me, I just come alive again. I do not bleed; I can't be drowned. I am here to do His bidding. And if you had not committed great sins, like those fools on those three ships in Singapore for instance, then God would not have sent a punishment like me upon you."

With that, Zeek drew out one of his knives and slit the woman's throat.

"This is the bargain your husband made," Zeek told her, as the woman began choking on her own blood. "This is the ransom he agreed to pay."

At that point, the second daughter broke away from the bodyguards and managed to lunge at Zeek. She slapped him hard across the face.

"You are a woman!" she screamed at him. "Your beard is like pigtails on a little girl!"

Zeek froze. He looked at the daughter with an almost befuddled expression, as if even he couldn't believe what she'd just said. But it was obvious her words had cut him deep.

Still the Pirate King recovered quickly. His face didn't turn crimson. His cold, dark eyes didn't bug out, nor did he reach for his knife again. Instead, he turned the hysterical girl around so she was facing the crowd and then he embraced her from behind. He began whispering in her ear, rocking her and stroking her hair, as if he was comforting her.

And she did calm down. For a moment.

But then slowly, Zeek reached down and took the two ends of his gold chains and crossed them. Then he brought them up to the girl's throat, wrapped them around her neck and suddenly pulled them tight. The girl began choking. The pirates cheered. The girl fought and fought, but Zeek only howled with laughter as he slowly strangled the life out of her.

The villagers started screaming. Even though armed pirates surrounded them, some started throwing rocks at Zeek, others attacking the pirates themselves with broomsticks. Gunfire filled the air.

Zeek let the dead girl fall to the ground, then roared: "Give them all a bath! They need to be cleaned."

That's when the slaughter began.

Some villagers were shot at random. Others were forced to the ground, the pirates holding them down so Zeek's body-guards could shoot them in the head. Some villagers managed to break free and run, but armed pirates chased them into the woods or the water and hacked them to death with machetes. Others were simply stomped to death where they lay.

The haki was anxiously fingering his wristwatch during all this. Between the drugs and the alcohol, he couldn't believe his eyes. Everywhere he looked he saw unspeakable horror. Not ten feet away from him, an elderly woman was being raped. Over there, a man was being beaten with nailed sticks; behind him, three children put inside sacks and stomped to death. Over there, an old man killed by scalding hot water.

Some villagers were tied to trees and savagely kicked until dead. Others were impaled on their own farm tools. Children were thrown into barrels of boiling cooking oil. Others were held under water on the beach until drowned.

It lasted only about ten minutes. But by the time the pirates were through, all of the villagers were dead.

When it was over, Zeek, who had watched it all approvingly from his cheap plastic chair, screamed to his men: "No one can beat us because we have the courage of lions, the cunning of foxes, the long-sightedness of ravens, and the wildness of wolves!"

His men cheered and some tried to repeat his words. But exhausted by the rampage, many of the pirates simply collapsed to the ground. They were all covered with blood, like hyenas after a feeding. Those few still on their feet looted the meager belongings of the poor village residents, then burned down their huts. Bodies were left where they fell. Already, buzzards were circling the island, awoken and drawn here by the scent of blood.

Finally, the pirates prepared to leave—and that's when the strangest thing of all happened.

Returning to their boats on the beach, some pirates fired off a few rounds from their weapons, one last gesture of the defiance.

Bantang came up to the haki. The white-haired pirate was also covered in blood. He looked at the haki and sensed his shock. "Don't worry," he said. "You'll get used to it."

They stumbled down to the beach, intent on getting back to the sekoci they'd come in on. They were about to climb into the boat when a booming voice behind them yelled, "Stop!"

The haki froze. So did Bantang.

They both turned to see Zeek, standing twenty feet away, pointing at them. The pirate boss snapped his fingers and two of his bodyguards ran up to where the haki and Bantang were standing. They ripped the weapons from their hands and dragged them over to Zeek. In seconds the haki was facing the Pirate King himself. He'd yet to be this close to him and he realized now that his face was ravaged by scars and burns. And his eyes were indeed completely black.

"You—the new one," Zeek harshly said to him. "What's the matter with you?"

The haki tried to stay cool. He just shook his head.

Zeek laughed evilly. "But look at you," he said.

A small crowd of bodyguards and pirates had closed in now.

The haki looked himself up and down, but didn't know what Zeek was talking about. But the others nearby knew.

"He is too clean!" one cried.

Zeek gave this pirate a playful slap on the cheek.

"Yes—exactly," Zeek said. "He is too clean."

He raised his hands as if to indicate the rest of his gang. "Look at my sons," he said. "They are dirty. They are sweaty. They wear the blood of others on them."

Then brushed his hand against the haki's chest.

"But you, my friend," he said. "You are clean. Too clean."

The haki froze. Zeek was right.

"You did not participate," Zeek told him, his mock humor fading with every word. "You drank my whiskey. You took my Ecstasy. You handled my girls. Yet, now, when everyone else joined in, you hold back. You remain clean. Why?"

The haki opened his mouth and tried to say something,

anything. But nothing would come out. There was nothing to say. He had stood and watched the bloody rampage, but he had not taken part in the savagery.

Suddenly, Zeek was right in his face.

"That means you are either a woman or a spy," he said, so close his rancid breath was almost suffocating. "And I don't have the time right now to find out which one it is."

Zeek called over two of his biggest bodyguards.

"We don't need his kind in our family," he said. "Take him—and make it hurt. And leave him among the stones as an example."

The bodyguards immediately grabbed the haki and dragged him across the shallow, narrow channel that led to Sumhai's second island. The one with the graveyard.

Zeek then turned his attention to Bantang. "Where was your judgment—letting this person get so close to us?" he asked the white-haired pirate.

Bantang could not answer. He was too scared to even talk.

"We will bring up this matter back at the base," Zeek said.

Bantang was tied up and thrown into a boat. With that, the rest of the pirate band jumped into their sekocis, and together they all disappeared into the night, Zeek included.

Meanwhile, the haki was forced up to the second island's only tree, the bodyguards punching and kicking him the whole way. Once there, one bodyguard threw a rope over the tree's limb and fashioned a crude noose on one end. The other bodyguard took out his machete. It was clear that hanging wasn't the only thing they had planned for him.

One bodyguard took off the haki's wristwatch, looked at it, then tossed it away like a piece of trash. Then both bodyguards started dancing and performing martial arts moves around him, drunkenly flailing at him with the tips of their machetes.

They were cutting him with each turn—laughing anytime they hit him. But they tired of this quickly.

One bodyguard came right up to his face. "So—which is it?" he sneered at the haki. "Spy? Or woman?"

The haki didn't answer. The man put his machete up against his throat and started to draw it across.

That's when the haki pretended to lose his footing and fell to the ground. When his would-be executioner went to haul him back to his feet, he realized the man had taken off his prosthetic right leg, the end of which had a long, thin knife attached.

The haki plunged this knife deep into the pirate's stomach and tore upwards, twisting it to puncture his heart.

The pirate fell over, dead before he hit the ground.

Then, picking up the dead man's machete, the haki slashed the other pirate in the groin, pulled the machete out, then slashed him again across the neck as he fell toward him, killing him.

Both bodyguards were dead in five seconds.

Then the one-legged man retrieved his wristwatch and his prosthetic leg, dove into the water and started swimming madly out to sea.

9

THEY RESCUED TWITCH about a half-mile off the coast of Sumhai Island.

Batman and Crash swooped down out of the night in the team's tiny work copter and plucked him from the waves just as he was sinking for the last time, struggling badly and signaling with a fading laser pen.

They pulled him onboard and laid him on the bench in the passenger compartment. He was in bad shape—cold and wet, his bronze makeup running down his face. His fake teeth had fallen out, and he had blood on his shirt and hands. He was trembling uncontrollably due to the drugs in his system. A small river of heroin, cocaine, methamphetamines and LSD was still coursing through his veins.

He was shaking with anger, too, at what he'd just seen on Sumhai Island. Twitch was a veteran of Delta Force; he'd fought in some of America's bloodiest if most secret battles.

He'd endured the horror of the messy ending at Tora Bora, leaving his leg behind in the bargain. He'd lived through the awfulness and degradation of Walter Reed's infamous Building 18. The combination of these had affected him so much, he'd almost taken his own life.

But he'd never seen anything like what he'd witnessed on Sumhai.

"Are you OK?" Crash yelled at him over the noise of the helicopter's spinning rotor. "Talk to me. . . ."

But Twitch didn't reply; he couldn't. Instead he handed his wristwatch to Crash. Within was a tiny camera and a locator-transponder that was activated at the wearer's discretion. It was Twitch hitting this panic button that led to them picking him up just in time. In fact, the transponder was still beeping faintly.

"I got pictures," he finally gasped, just barely able to speak. "I got pictures . . ."

"And I'm asking you if you're OK," Crash barked back at him.

But Twitch just fell off the passenger bench.

Crash picked him back up, checked his pulse and flashed a penlight into his eyes. His pupils were dilated and rolling back into his head. His pulse was 200 beats a minute. He was grasping an old empty plastic Coke bottle like it was the most precious thing in the world. When Crash tried to take it from him, Twitch pushed him away.

Crash leaned forward and yelled in Batman's ear: "We gotta get to where we're going chop-chop, before he goes into shock."

Then Crash wrapped a blanket around Twitch, pulled him tight, and tried to get him to stop shaking.

"Those bastards," Twitch kept mumbling. "Those bastards . . ."

THE ISLAND WAS known as *Mengutuk Hantu Pulau*.

Literally, Cursed Ghost Island.

The name was no joke; this place had earned its spooky reputation. It was a narrow, tree-covered piece of rock located at the convergence of where cold water coming down the Malacca Strait collided with warm water flowing out of the Phillip Channel, creating a fog that permanently enshrouded the island.

This made it a virtual graveyard for ships. Vessels losing their way in these strange waters over the centuries, with one wrong turn, were sent crashing against the mountains of jagged rocks that surrounded the atoll, sinking them and washing the victims' bodies ashore.

Cursed Ghost Island and its fog and its skeleton beaches. The highly superstitious locals avoided coming anywhere near this place or the waters around it, believing them to be haunted. Only the dead lived here.

But anyone looking hard enough this night might have seen the bare outline of a ship anchored in the island's biggest cove, hiding in the mist. It was Team Whiskey's boat. Rusty, oily, with a single stack and four cargo masts, technically it was a DUS-7 coastal freighter, a type of vessel used for short trips between islands or up and down coastlines, and not for transocean odysseys. Just a hundred and twenty feet long with a width of twenty-four feet, it looked every bit of its fifty-plus years afloat. It was so battered and unassuming, anyone seeing it washed up on a beach somewhere wouldn't have given it a second glance.

In the eyes of Team Whiskey, these were all assets. When Kilos offered to provide them a ship from which they could run this, their second paid operation, the vessel the company had in mind was one of its so-called "workboats." These barely disguised, intentionally misnamed vessels were actually long-range mega-yachts, high on the comfort scale, full of communications equipment and sometimes weapons, and looking like something from a James Bond film. It would have been world class, but for what Whiskey knew they had to do, it would've stuck out mightily in a sea full of container ships, super tankers, steamers and fishing boats.

No, the DUS-7 was what they needed, and in the end, it's what Kilos gave them. Along with the ship, Kilos had also provided a crew of five Senegalese nationals. Widely regarded as excellent sailors, these five longtime employees of Kilos Shipping knew their new jobs were not the same as those of typical seafarers. They were loyal, they could drive the ship in all circumstances, and if needed, they knew their way around combat weaponry as well. But because their names were just about impossible to pronounce, the team just referred to them as the Senegals.

The team had nicknamed their new ship, too. They called it the *Dustboat,* which again was apropos. But it did have another important attribute: While it might not have been as sexy as a Kilos workboat, it was much faster than it looked. This was because it had not one, but two propulsion systems.

Its primary means of motion was a dual diesel-based system that turned twin screws and moved the ship at about eighteen knots in a calm sea. But because the DUS-7 was specially adapted by Kilos for cargos that absolutely had to get there—"sensitive shipments," in the company's parlance—the company's engineers had added a small gas turbine as a second propulsion unit. Hundreds of gallons of seawater sucked into huge tanks in the hold of the ship were condensed and, using power from the spinning turbine, shot out the back of the ship at high velocity in the form of jet sprays. When the ship needed some extra speed and the crew turned on these jets, it was like switching on an afterburner in an F-16. With this added power, the little freighter could top forty knots, faster than some of the U.S. Navy's speediest warships.

And there was another asset: Because in the freighter's former life it had transported those highly sensitive cargos to some of Kilos's shadier customers, the ship also had a so-called Rubber Room hidden deep within its lower decks. It was a compartment where up to ten tons of cargo—usually arms and ammunition—could be carried and sealed off behind false panels that even the most ardent NATO search party would miss.

In this hidden storage cabin now sat Team Whiskey's small arsenal of weapons, communications equipment and various gadgets of the special operations trade. It was also where they kept the $50,000 that Kilos had paid them for their first job. Or what was left of it.

So this was their ride—this was how they got to the Malacca Strait and its environs.

It was also the same punctual boat Twitch had robbed three times to quickly make his bones.

ONCE THEY'D ACCEPTED Kilos's offer for this second gig, they'd sailed at double power to get here from Aden. But even though they'd reached speeds in excess of forty-two knots, they'd arrived a day too late. Twenty-four hours before getting here, Zeek's men had murdered the three Kilos crews in Singapore Harbor, his revenge for the killing of his brother Turk off Somalia. The first blood in what would become a nasty little war had been spilled even before Whiskey made it past Sri Lanka.

So, it was not a good start. In fact, the team had learned through Conley, the security guy, that old man Kilos had taken the news of the Singapore murders so hard he had to be hospitalized. But the shipping czar had sent them a message that said, now more than ever, the world had to be rid of Zeek. And this made Whiskey even more determined to do their job well.

But even before the Singapore murders, the team knew that just killing Zeek himself would not be enough. They knew they had to take down his entire organization, too. If they didn't, then some underling would just take over for the Pirate King and move his operations to East Africa, where they would cause more problems for international commerce and especially Kilos Shipping. As it was, Kilos had stopped all its ships from going anywhere near Singapore.

So, just lopping off the head of the snake was not Whiskey's goal this time. They had to start cutting at the tail of the vile serpent and work their way up, making sure that when they were done, no part of the creature was left squirming.

The problem was, intelligence on Zeek and his inner circle was virtually nonexistent in these parts, which is what led to

Twitch's undercover mission, the type of assignment he'd done many times in his tenure with Delta Force. Mixing in and keeping his eyes and ears open had been one of his specialties back in his special ops days, and he was the best of all the team members in doing it.

But now, as the tiny work copter descended through the mist of Cursed Ghost Island, lining up for a landing on the DUS-7, Batman and Crash wondered if they'd asked too much of their colleague this time.

BATMAN SET THE copter down on the makeshift landing pad near the stern of the ship. Nolan and Gunner were already there, waiting.

It took all four of them to get Twitch out of the copter. His body was limp and, judging by his nonstop mumbling, he seemed to be slipping in and out of reality. The plan was to immediately bring him down to the ship's tiny sick bay and treat him before he briefed them on his last hundred hours.

But though he was still severely under the influence, once below and out of the elements, Twitch insisted he give them his report now: that Zeek and his crew were so evil, time was of the essence. So they led him down to the ship's galley and pumped him full of aspirin and coffee. Still wrapped in a blanket and clutching his empty Coke bottle, Twitch told them everything.

Taking the Ecstasy, darting back and forth between islands, his trip to the Red Skull Bar, to Brothel Beach, to the hijacked ship, to the Great Fortune Lounge, to the pirates' hidden base—he admitted he couldn't remember exactly what happened when and in what order. He'd skipped around to so many islands at such high speed, under the influence of such potent drugs, it was hard for him to keep it all straight, especially the locations of those various islands. His last real lucid thought, he said, was when he robbed the *Dustboat* for the third time on his way to proving he had the beans to be a pirate. After the twins waking him the next night, most everything was a blur.

Except one thing. What was crystal clear was the massacre he'd just witnessed on Sumhai Island. As proof, he'd taken many pictures of the atrocity, and with a USB hookup and the push of a button, these pictures were soon being displayed on Batman's laptop.

The first few photos showed some of the locations Twitch had visited earlier in the night. Undercover photos of the Great Fortune Lounge, the Red Skull Bar and Brothel Beach. A few shots from the hijacked tanker. Even a couple from the drug-fueled party on the yacht.

But it was the photos of Sumhai Island that sickened the other members of the hard-bitten team. The pictures were disturbing and graphic. Kids, mothers, fathers, the elderly, all sadistically murdered, their bodies treated like trash. There was some disappointment that the team hadn't been able to pick up Twitch sooner; that they might have prevented the slaughter on the island. Once again, they'd arrived too late to prevent a mass killing.

But the plan had been that Twitch would hit his panic button only as a last ditch effort, and that's exactly what he did. And looking at the gruesome pictures just made the team even more determined to find Zeek and give him the same medicine they'd doled out to his brother.

AFTER THEY VIEWED the photographs, Twitch ended by telling them how he was able to get the drop on his two would-be executioners and finally make his escape. Then, with his debriefing complete, he put his head in his hands and fell silent again.

Crash brought him down to the ship's tiny sick bay, checked his vitals, gave him a sedative, and waited for him to drift off to sleep. Meanwhile, the other team members remained in the galley, gathered around a map of their operations area.

It was time to plan their next move.

"Did he ever say anything about the twelve grand?" Batman asked Crash when he returned.

Crash shook his head no. "Not unless he's talking about it in his sleep," he said.

The money the team used to help Twitch make his bones had come from the stash Kilos had given them as payment for their first job. They'd looked on it as a reasonable investment or an acceptable loss, depending on the eventual outcome of the mission. But it was still their money, and they had to assume most of it was blown to the four winds by now. But as Batman kept reminding them, it would be nice to somehow recoup the loss. No matter what the situation, he was always the team's "money man."

They knew some of what Twitch told them sounded more like Alice in Wonderland than solid intelligence. The drugs he'd ingested in order to maintain his cover had been some kick-ass stuff and the team was amazed he'd held it together long enough to get away.

The problem now was finding the pirates again. The team knew some of the locations of Twitch's recon mission, because every time he took a picture with his wristwatch, the time stamp also contained his transponder location. But just about the only place he *didn't* take a picture was the most important place of all: the pirates' hidden camp. So the team would have to look for it.

Problem number two was the size of Zeek's gang. From what Twitch told them, and what they'd seen in the photographs, the ruthless pirate controlled what amounted to a small army of at least eighty men, many more than the couple dozen the team had been expecting. Even worse, as the recruitment of Twitch had shown, Zeek was looking for even more thugs to join his murderous crew. The numbers were definitely in Zeek's favor.

"But we got the air asset, and that's a plus," Nolan said, addressing the issue. "And we got some firepower at the bottom of this ship. Plus, up until a few hours ago, Zeek had no idea that someone was in the area looking to fry his ass. When he finds his two boyfriends out on that island full of pinholes, he'll know something is up. His MO is to create fear—and then milk it. But still, he might freak out a little, which will be good for us."

"And there's something else we can key in on," Batman said. He pulled a small stapled booklet from his pocket, titled *Superstitions of Indonesia*.

"I downloaded this earlier," he said. "And there's some interesting reading here. I quote: While it might be called culture, tradition, religion or superstition, a lot of Indonesian customs add up to the same thing: an attempt by Indonesians to influence future events by small, seemingly unrelated actions."

He passed the book around for the others to peruse.

"Translation: They're superstitious as hell," Batman went on. "We already know they believe in magic. And we know Zeek thinks of himself as lucky, or blessed by God, the fucking egomaniac. But if we can get him thinking that things *aren't* so overall rosy for him and his gang, that might have a detrimental effect on him, too."

"Well, we have to find him first," Crash said.

THEY SPENT THE next hour trying to plot Twitch's stops on their map. It took some doing, but eventually they were able to match most of the photos with most of the locations their colleague had visited during those last few hellish hours.

From there, they developed their war plan. In the old days, they would have had all the resources of the CIA, NSA, the FBI, spy planes, spy satellites, listening stations—you name it—at their disposal. But now it was just them and their wits. Which meant they had to go with their intuition and gut instincts, just the sort of thing that got them in trouble back at Tora Bora. But they didn't know any other way.

At the end of it, Nolan said: "I know we figured the way to beat these guys was either quickly or quietly. I think this time, we do it quickly rather than quietly."

Batman was nodding. "You read my mind. One, two, three. A kick in the nuts. A punch in the face."

He slammed his fist on the table.

"Then . . . a knife in the heart."

The others grunted their approval.

"And that way," Batman added, "maybe we can still get some of our money back."

10

Skull Island

THE MONKEY AT the Red Skull had been sick all day.

The night before, while lapping up spilled beer from the bar as he always did, he'd ingested a substantial amount of methamphetamine, which had been spilled by an intoxicated patron, along with a half of Rohypnol pill, also known as the date-rape drug.

The monkey spent the rest of the night and most of the next day hanging by his tail above the rickety piano, urinating on himself.

The owner of the bar, Miss Aloo, took this as a very bad sign. The monkey never got sick. But business had been slow the whole day as word of the macaque's malady spread. Neighboring businesses up and down the street even burned incense to keep the monkey's bad spirits away. The whole island felt uneasy.

But as soon as the sun went down and the small navy of boats belonging to the smugglers and the drug dealers and the pirates and happy girls began tying up at the Skull's docks, the bar filled up as usual, reassuring Miss Aloo that the danger had passed and it would be just another typical Friday night. The monkey, though, stayed in his perch, angrily gnawing on the paper napkin that served as an ill-fitting diaper.

By 11 P.M., the bar was as smoky and crowded and rowdy and dangerous as always. Besides the pissing monkey, the talk was about the murder of two of Zeek's bodyguards the night before on the small island off Sumhai. That thirty villagers had also been killed wasn't as much on the patrons' minds as Zeek's men getting cut up. Everyone *knew* who slaughtered the villagers and why—no one crossed the most powerful pirate in Indonesia and got away with it. But who had the balls to kill two of his right-hand men?

The words on everyone's lips were: *Ku-sang do-tang*.

Roughly translated: "Wait for the next shoe to drop."

THAT CAME AT precisely eleven-thirty.

Every Friday night, Zeek had three Chinese money-counters go to the Red Skull and tally his week's take. They had an electric-powered bill counter, carried a set of books, and prepared payments for people in Zeek's employ, including his army of pirates.

But Zeek's money-counters were having an off night as well. They had all of the pirate's operating cash out of the hidden vault and laid out on one of the kitchen's cutting tables as always. But their bill-counting machine had been breaking down ever since they'd arrived. The island's notoriously unreliable electricity had been working intermittently, stopping the machine cold and losing the totals, meaning the counters had to start all over again.

Zeek's bagmen were also late getting to the Skull. These were the people who actually distributed money to Zeek's gang members and other people who worked for him. Heavy showers sweeping through the area were slowing travel by water in some parts. Where usually the paymasters would do their secret knock on the Skull's back door sometime just after sundown, tonight they were actually arriving past 10 P.M. and later.

So when the money-counters heard a secret knock on the back door around eleven-thirty, they routinely hit the open buzzer to let the visitor in. But instead of the typical pair of scruffy pirates walking in to pick up their packs of money, three huge men in ski masks and carrying assault rifles burst in instead.

The money-counters thought it was a joke until the first

gunman through the door hit the nearest counter with the butt of his rifle, sending him flying over the table of money and knocking him unconscious.

This was enough to wake up the two armed men who were supposed to be serving as guards for the money-counters, but who were usually the most inebriated patrons in the Skull. Both received the same treatment, the butt of an M4 assault rifle right on the temple, collapsing each to the floor. Oddly, the three masked gunmen were whistling throughout most of this, terrifying the bar's innocent kitchen workers, as Indonesians consider it highly unlucky to whistle around food. When the gunmen intentionally started spilling boxes of salt on the floor, the kitchen staff fled to the walk-in freezer, locking the door behind them and leaving the two remaining money-counters to deal with the invaders alone.

One of the masked gunmen checked the door leading into the bar itself. But there was so much noise coming from the front of the Red Skull that none of the patrons realized anything unusual was going on in back.

"What do you want?" one of the money-counters finally asked in horror, reaching for a piece of hollowed-out wood he always kept nearby.

"What the fuck do you think we want?" one of the gunmen snarled back, knocking the lucky piece of wood out of his hand and crushing it with his boot. "We want the money. All of it."

The gunman threw a box of garbage bags at them, but the two money-counters hesitated, even though they were looking down the barrels of three assault rifles.

"We can't," one blurted out. "Zeek will kill us . . ."

"Don't worry about Zeek," another masked man told them. "Zeek's broke. He's out of money. We're only here because he can't pay us what he owes us. Now start stuffing those fucking bags!"

That was it—that was all it took.

The money-counters quickly filled the bags with packets of cash and handed them over to the gunmen. Then they hit the floor and covered their heads with their hands.

"Now stay down there and count to five hundred slowly," one gunman warned them. "Or we'll blow your fucking heads off."

The robbery complete, the gunmen turned to leave when they heard an ungodly screech behind them. They spun around to see the bar's brass-colored monkey flying through the air, fangs bared, diaper in place, coming right at them.

There was no time to shoot it; instead, one of the gunmen swung his rifle like a baseball bat, hitting the creature dead on and sending it spinning into the kitchen wall.

Then the robbers went out the door.

THEY MADE A clean getaway.

Or at least it seemed that way at first. The three masked gunmen—Batman, Gunner and Crash—had left the work copter, engine running, in the weeds behind the Red Skull while they robbed Zeek's bank. It took them not ten seconds to get back to the aircraft after the theft—but that's when the problems began.

Batman jumped in behind the controls; he was the most accomplished flier of the team, having joined Delta right out of the Air Force. But Gunner and Crash had trouble stuffing the bags of money into the copter's tiny open cockpit. There were six bags in all, containing nearly $60,000. But they were mostly filled with packets of small bills, and some of the bags were packed so tight the sides were ripping. They also had no way to tie off the tops of the bags once they had twisted them closed. The result was a comedy of errors trying to get all the loot on board.

In the mad rush, Gunner tried sitting on the moneybags to keep them from blowing out of the cabin during takeoff. But as soon as Batman lifted off, some packets burst and streams of stray bills found their way out of the bags and out of the helicopter altogether, raining down on lucky drunks stumbling the muddy roads of Skull Island below.

Batman was pissed. He'd planned this operation down to the last detail—or so he thought. He knew, like every enterprise, Zeek's business ran not so much on his total worth but

on cash flow. Take away the operating funds, people stop getting paid, and trouble usually results. Thus the idea to rob
Zeek's depository. But Batman was also intent on replacing
the $12,000 the team had invested in Twitch's undercover
operation; Anything beyond that would be a happy profit. But
now that profit was going out the window—literally—all because Batman didn't bring any twist ties.

The trail of falling bills continued as they climbed out over
the water and headed east. Finally, Gunner and Crash managed
to hand-tie the bags and stow most of them under the seats. But
by that time, more than half the loot had blown away.

"Maybe we shouldn't have smacked that fucking monkey!"
Crash yelled above the racket of the rotor, still trying to catch
some stray bills swirling around them. "What's it say in the
book about that?"

"Screw the monkey!" Batman yelled back to him. "Just try
to keep at least twelve grand of that for us!"

Then Batman forced himself to stop thinking about the
money and concentrate on their next destination. He checked
his watch.

Somehow, they were still on schedule.

FINDING SKULL ISLAND hadn't been a problem. Twitch had
remembered its name from his night of involuntary debauchery, and it was on most of the maps they'd downloaded of the
area.

Determining that Mirang Island was their next destination
had been a little more difficult. Twitch had recalled lots of
color, lots of activity, and a long white beach that "seemed to go
on forever." He'd estimated that it had taken a speedboat ride
of about twenty minutes to get there from Skull Island—that
is, if he had his sequence right.

The team was able to cop some color satellite maps from
the Internet and found a long, thin, finger-shaped atoll off the
northwest edge of Batam. From space it looked like a miniature version of downtown Las Vegas: one of those places that
needed no streetlights because the honky-tonk provided all
the illumination anyone would ever need. When some quick

calculations told them it was conceivable that a sekoci fast boat could get from Skull Island to Mirang in twenty minutes or so, they felt they had their place.

The flight over from Skull to Mirang took just five minutes in the work copter. Batman was rated in fighters, big planes and helos; for him, flying the copter was like driving a small, slow economy car. He had to constantly remind himself not to exceed the chopper's maximum speed, as this was rough on the hardware and hell on fuel consumption. Still, they made it to Mirang in record time.

They flew over the downtown first, confirmed it was an orgy of neon lights and waterfront saloons, then headed for the southern end of the island. Here was another well-known feature of Mirang: the vast, isolated, Piniti-Hatan graveyard.

The place was enormous. Nearly five square miles in area, it was an immense field of craggy trees, overgrown grass, weeds, boulders, and of course, graves and gravestones—hundreds of thousands of them.

Batman studied the cemetery from the air. "Maybe this is where *we* start to get lucky," he yelled to his teammates.

He landed the copter in the darkest part of the sprawling graveyard and the three men climbed out.

"Fucking hey . . . look at this place," Gunner said. "Is this where every person who drops dead in Indonesia gets planted? There's like a million graves here."

"It's already giving me the creeps," Crash said. "Are we sure this is the right thing to do?"

Batman looked around, making certain no one was nearby. "It's part of the plan because of what it says in the superstitions book," he told them. "You want to reread the book now? After we're already here?"

They began walking among the graves. They were here not to steal a body, but to steal funeral flowers. Trouble was, they'd landed in an area of older graves, and they could see only patches of covered-over ground and grave markers.

"Damn—no flowers anywhere?" Batman asked.

"I think the book said some Indonesians bury the funeral flowers with the body," Crash said.

"Well, we don't want to roam too far away from the copter," Batman said. "So, I guess we start digging here."

Retrieving some entrenching tools from the aircraft, they selected what looked to be a relatively fresh grave and commenced digging. But after five minutes of hard work, they still hadn't found any flowers or plants. They kept at it, until they heard a bone-chilling *clunk!* Crash's entrenching tool had hit the top of a coffin.

"Oh God," he cried. "Is that what I think it was?"

Before anyone could answer, Gunner's boot went through the top of the flimsy casket and he found himself implanted in a corpse.

"Jesuszz fuck!" he screamed. "Jesuszz!"

Crash pulled him out and they quickly threw dirt back onto the broken coffin and grave.

"I'm telling you," Gunner said, trying to calm down, "we shouldn't have smacked that monkey or spilled the salt or whistled during all that. This bad-luck shit must work *both* ways here."

"Let's just try somewhere else," Batman told them.

They found a second relatively new grave and started digging again. But no sooner had their shovels hit this ground than they heard a dog start howling in the distance. It unnerved Gunner so much, he dropped his digging tool and unslung his M4.

"Goddamn," Batman scolded him in an urgent whisper. "Can you calm down, please?"

"Do you remember what the book said about hearing a dog howl in a graveyard after midnight?" Gunner asked him, looking around nervously. "It says, 'if a dog howls past midnight, it signifies a wandering earthbound spirit on the premises.' Like in a ghost?"

"You memorized *that*?" Batman asked him.

"Hey, it was your book—you said to read it," Gunner shot back at him.

And now Crash was getting caught up in it. "Well, what the fuck time is it?" he asked as the dog began wailing again.

"It's five minutes to midnight," Batman said. "Not that it

makes a piss hole of difference. The Indonesians are the super-stitious ones, guys, remember? Not us. *Them*."

The dog howled again. It seemed closer this time.

"What did it say about howling *before* midnight?" Crash asked Gunner seriously.

Gunner tapped his forehead in an effort to remember. "I think if a dog howls at the stroke of midnight, it signifies death in the family," he said. "What happens before, I don't know."

The two men began digging furiously. Batman didn't know whether to laugh or chew them out. "You guys are unbeliev-able," he said.

They finally found some dead flowers beneath the dirt and quickly did what they came here to do: rub them all over their hands and faces and battle suits.

"These are lilies, right?" Gunner kept asking. "And or-chids? They're the kind to use."

"Two minutes to midnight," Crash said, hearing the dog howl again.

They both turned to Batman. "Enough?" Gunner asked him.

Batman just shook his head. He grabbed some loose flow-ers. "Yeah—let's go."

With that, both men sprinted to the copter. Batman climbed in after them.

"One minute to go," Crash said.

Batman again just shook his head. He hit the throttles and pulled up on the collective.

"I really made the right choice hooking up with you two."

THE FLIGHT TO the other end of the island took just two minutes.

They easily relocated the white beach that "went on for-ever." Batman put the copter down behind a jetty that was partially hidden by jungle. Gazing over the jetty with their night-vision goggles, the three men spotted a building washed in green neon among the many bars and dance clubs along the waterfront. But this place was not some wooden box on stilts. It was a huge, ornate old building of mixed Asian and Western design, with many floors and windows. It looked more like some groovy apartment building than a whorehouse. The sign above the front door read KUCING JANTAN RUMAH—Home of the Tomcat.

"Gentlemen," Batman said. "Behold the brothel at Brothel Beach."

THE HOOKERS SMELLED them coming.

Even before Gunner kicked in the back door, some of the prostitutes inside the brothel had detected the scent of dead lilies and overripe orchids blowing in the hot night air. That's why the six women taking a tea break in the back room were already freaking out when Team Whiskey burst in.

The sight of their M4s, their black camos or their other-worldly night-vision-equipped helmets didn't faze the hookers one bit. It was scent of the dead flowers on them, and even worse, the mud on their boots.

"Is that dirt from a graveyard?" one girl asked frantically after the trio exploded through the door.

Batman was stumped for a moment; they all were.

He finally replied: "Yes, it is."

The hookers lost it at that point. "God help us!" one screamed. They started to push past them, trying to get to the back door.

"Wait—how many people are here?" Batman shouted at them. "Where's the madam? Where are all the radios?"

But the six prostitutes, all scantily clad, gorgeous and Asian, weren't listening to him. They were manhandling him out of the way now. "I don't know and I don't care," one told him, rushing by.

With that, the hookers fled out the back door.

Batman slammed the already-splintered door behind them in frustration. Then he signaled Crash and Gunner to check out the hallway leading into the main part of the cathouse.

What an odd beginning, he thought.

According to Twitch's debriefing, the brothel doubled as Zeek's intelligence-gathering center, so Whiskey was here to destroy it. Their *moyens d'entrée* was the smell of funeral flowers because, according to the superstitions book, any house in Indonesia that smelled of flowers placed on a grave would be considered unlucky forever and would have to be abandoned by those who lived there. Having dirt from a cemetery on one's shoes apparently brought even more bad luck.

But as it turned out, the team had arrived bearing *too much* misfortune. As word quickly spread throughout the brothel about the sudden appearance of the flower-scented, muddy-booted visitors, the result was a virtual stampede of call girls going out the front door of the cathouse, with an equally frantic mad dash of clients going out the back. The problem was, Twitch hadn't been able to remember exactly where the spy center was located within the huge whorehouse, and that's something Whiskey had to know if they were going to grease it. But weapons cocked or not, no one would stop long enough to talk to them.

It was total chaos by the time the team members found their way to the front parlor, the center of the whorehouse's universe. It was as if someone had planted a bomb in the place. Call girls were practically knocking the team members to the floor in their rush to escape.

Batman caught an elderly, extremely made-up woman rushing by. He correctly identified her as the house madam.

He held her by the arm. "Zeek is running out of money," he told her, hurriedly reciting his prepared lines. "And we're here to collect what he owes us."

"He owes us money, too!" she barked back at him. "But I'm not staying around to collect. Not in this place."

"So, where's all his radio equipment?" he asked her. "His spy gear?"

But she had already broken away from him and was halfway out the door. She called over her shoulder: "I don't know who you are, but I wouldn't stay around too long. When more people find out about the bad luck in this place, it won't be pretty."

With that, she and the remaining call girls were out the door. Just like that, the place was empty.

Batman, Crash and Gunner just stood there and looked at each other.

"Jesuszz, now what?" Gunner asked.

Batman shrugged. "We gotta toss the joint, I guess."

Crash and Gunner shrank back. The whorehouse was enormous; just judging by the number of call girls taking flight, there had to be more than a hundred rooms in the place.

"Can I go on record as saying: 'Eewww?'" Crash asked.

They climbed the stairs and began their search. They found just empty bedrooms on the first and second floors, but the higher they got in the building, the stranger things became. On the third floor, many of the rooms had chains and restraining equipment attached to the walls. Whips—and whipped cream—seemed to be the most prominent features on the fourth floor. On the fifth floor, they found rooms filled with large rolls of plastic and bubble wrap. On the sixth floor, many rooms had adult-size diapers scattered about, some used, some not.

"There's not enough booze in the world to get that image out of my head," Crash had said on this discovery.

But still, they could find no communications equipment or anything connected to what they'd envisioned Zeek's spy center to look like.

And yet Twitch had said he'd momentarily glimpsed the inside of the place. "What did we miss?" Gunner wondered.

Batman thought a moment, then asked: "Where's the last place you'd want to go in a place like this?"

Crash and Gunner answered almost simultaneously: "The kitchen."

They raced back downstairs, made their way to the rear of the building and went through a door next to the lounge where they'd first come in. Here they found a stove, a refrigerator and a dining table—but nothing to indicate a spy station.

"It's here though," Crash said, adding with unintended irony, "I can *smell* it."

He took out his combat knife and started jabbing the walls. The first three thrusts hit solid wood. On the fourth try, the blade went through a thin piece of plastic veneer. One well-placed kick knocked half the wall down. On the other side, they found a room full of shortwave radios and computers, bracketed by two hidden doors that ran flush to the wall. This was Zeek's version of an intelligence-gathering center, right down to the secret entrances.

They searched the place, but nothing surprised them very much at first. The shortwave radios were made on Taiwan; the knock-off computers in South Africa.

"Not exactly MI-6 headquarters, is it?" Crash observed.

But in the bottom drawer of the computer table, Gunner found a notebook containing dozens of e-mail addresses. One of the entries was clearly marked *Indonesian Naval Intelligence Center*. Another *The Malaysian Secret Service*.

"Interesting cybersex partners these chicks had," Gunner said, reading through the notebook.

He turned it over to Batman, who flipped randomly through it until he came to a page of names and e-mail addresses printed entirely in red ink. He started reading the names, written in a sort of pigeon English, when he realized some of them were familiar. Jiang Zemin. Wang Zhen. Hu Jintao. Zeng Qinghong.

"Do those guys own restaurants or laundries?" Crash asked, reading over his shoulder.

Batman laughed darkly. "They own half the fucking world," he replied. "These are top guys in the Communist Chinese government."

Beside each name was an indication—things such as *Likes 5th Flr* or *Owes $$$ for 6th Flr*—plus a calendar date, some recent, some from years past.

"If this means what I think it does," Batman said, "I predict Pampers will be opening a factory in China soon."

They heard a noise outside. Crash looked out a nearby window and cried, "Holy crap!"

Gunner and Batman joined him and saw a crowd of people coming up the street, carrying torches and, yes, some of them, pitchforks.

"Christ, is this because of us?" Batman asked.

His answer arrived a moment later when a Molotov cocktail came crashing through the kitchen window behind them.

Before they could react, another firebomb came through the front door. Then another through the battered rear door.

"These people don't fuck around!" Gunner said. "A few dead flowers and they want to burn the place down . . ."

Within seconds, three large fires were spreading on the bottom floor of the building.

"What should we do?" Crash asked Batman anxiously.

Batman started firing his M4, tearing up the banks of radios and computers inside the spy room. "Just in case!" he yelled over the gunfire.

The other two did the same thing—for about five seconds.

Then Batman stuffed the phone book in his back pocket, along with some DVDs he'd found along the way, and said: "Ladies? After you."

They left the way they came—punching through the flames and out the rear door. A minute later, they were back out on the beach and running toward their copter, avoiding the huge crowd that by now had surrounded the building. By the time they were airborne again, this crowd had grown to several hundred people, including a police car and a fire truck.

As the team watched silently above, the mob continued throwing firebombs into the brothel, this while the firefighters hosed down nearby buildings to keep the blaze from spreading.

The brothel was soon totally engulfed in flames, lighting up the night for miles around.

"There's some ammunition we could have saved," Gunner observed. "That entire place is going to melt."

While the huge fire was attracting a lot of attention on the beachfront, many of the clubs along the shoreline, some just a few doors away, remained packed with people partying and dancing.

Batman finally turned the copter away from the island and headed for home.

"Just another Friday night on Mirang," he said.

11

SNAKE NOLAN WAS woken by the sound of the team's helicopter returning to the DUS-7.

He was lying on his bunk in his cabin, just one deck below the makeshift landing pad near the stern of the old ship. The compartment was pitch black and, until this moment, completely silent.

His body shook when he heard the thump of the copter setting down. This set his heart racing. His throat began to constrict. He really didn't want to do what came next, but he had no choice.

He'd managed to hold himself together up to this point. Though it took a lot of work, he'd been able to throw himself into the mission, busying himself with the planning, the logistics, the overall command of the team, reviewing maps, reviewing intelligence, doing the same things over and over, until he would literally pass out from exhaustion, only to wake anywhere from one to five hours later and start all over again. Some might call it burnout, but he'd passed the burnout stage long ago.

It was no way to be. No way to live. But it was what it was, because if he did it any other way, he'd be forced to think about what his life was *really* like, and he just couldn't take that. Not now.

He'd been operating on this self-imposed autopilot for almost a year, trying his best to avoid the demons that had plagued him since that shard of rock took out his eye in Tora Bora. His sham trial. His incarcerations. His frequent escape attempts. His mad marches across the desert to get back to that place where his old life ended and this awful new life began, as if by retracing his steps he would make it all right the second time, get his vision back and catch up to and kill the monster who had murdered 3,000 of his countrymen and crushed his own heart at the same time.

Einstein said madness was doing the same thing over and over and expecting a different result. Nolan was a walking, talking, living, breathing example of that particular bit of lu-nacy. He'd been able to dig an escape tunnel a quarter-mile long with nothing but his fingernails, but as hard as he tried, he couldn't escape this loss of soul, couldn't figure out how to get it back, to reverse time to when they were still chasing bin Laden, the Marines were still on their way to the blocking point, and his superiors, his country, and his commander in chief hadn't let him down.

But it was impossible, because he wasn't Superman, or Ein-stein, or even the old Snake Nolan, though he was killing himself on the inside trying to prove to everyone on the out-side that he was all three of those people and more.

The long beard, the matted, uncut hair, the dirty clothes, the cracked fingernails. *That* was the uniform he felt more comfortable in, because that's who he really was. Someone from another world, not this one.

The proof was in the writing on the wall. Literally. Because just as the mud walls of his jail cell in Kuwait had displayed an orgy of scribbling and nonsense, so, too, his cabin wall here on the *Dustboat*. Numbers, dates, names, locations. Arrows pointing here, arrows pointing there. Arrows pointing every-where and nowhere.

He didn't know what any of it meant; it just came out of him and he had to write it all down until he dropped. So it was no wonder he felt like he was no better, but actually getting worse—and that no matter what he did, sane or not, he would never be able to shake the feeling that he was falling. Never hitting anything. Just endlessly falling.

A second metallic thump over his head made him jump again; the copter was down for good. The sound knocked his equilibrium so off kilter he had to hang onto the bunk just to stop his cabin from spinning.

No, he *really* didn't want to do what came next. But again, he had no choice. There was no magic formula to change the way things were.

He got off his bunk and steadied himself. He checked the time: 0240 hours. Batman had completed his part of tonight's assignment. Now it was his turn.

* * *

HE MET BATMAN, Crash and Gunner coming down the access ladder.

Beside their flight equipment and weapons, they were carrying six ripped garbage bags full of money. Batman was also carrying a stack of DVDs.

"How'd it go?" Nolan asked them.

"Only fucking crazy," Crash wearily replied.

Gunner nodded rapidly in agreement; they both looked like they'd seen a ghost.

"It all went well," Batman told him, calmly. "We did what we set out to do. Zeek now has his cash-flow problem and he lost his version of Langley, Virginia."

He pointed to the bags of money. "And we might have gotten our twelve grand back and a few dollars more. So, it's all good."

"What's that smell?" Nolan asked them. "Is that you guys?"

"Yes, it is," Crash replied. "The flower thing came off slightly askew."

Crash and Gunner continued on below. Batman stayed with Nolan until they were out of earshot.

"You sure you want to do part two?" Batman asked him. "Because I don't mind going back out there tonight. I can take a quick squirt, drink a cup of coffee, and be good to go in no time."

Nolan shook his head. "Don't tempt me," he said. "But, I have to do this myself."

Of them all, Batman best understood what Nolan was going through. Because they had been officers back in the SOF days, they were closest kindred spirits. Though they had never talked deeply about anything since Whiskey reunited, Batman was pretty sharp. He could see the torment in Nolan's eyes.

"OK," he finally told Nolan. "The Senegals are refueling the copter and it's working like a charm. You still got about three hours of darkness left; should be plenty of time. Just keep your wits about you. It's like flying around another planet out there."

Nolan let out a long slow breath. "OK—I'll go wake Twitch and get the show on the road."

They shook hands, and Nolan eyed some of the titles of the DVDs Batman was carrying.

"*'Tokyo Cheerleaders Part 6*?' '*Bangkok Booty Part 23*?' What's with this stuff?"

Batman shrugged.

"Research," he said.

NOLAN WALKED FORWARD to Twitch's cabin, finding him already awake and sitting on the edge of his bunk.

A small plastic bag containing several red onions hung from his doorway.

"What's this?" Nolan asked him.

Twitch just shook his head. "Crash hung it there about thirty seconds ago," he replied, his voice raspy and barely above a whisper. "Keeps the bad spirits away. I guess he thought he was doing me a favor."

Nolan came in and sat in a chair across from Twitch. It had been twenty-four hours since they'd rescued him from his long, strange intelligence-gathering mission. While he looked slightly better, it appeared he needed a couple of weeks to recuperate. Or maybe a couple months.

"How about you?" Nolan asked him. "Are you sure about this?"

Twitch shrugged. "It has to be done," he said, softly. "And I'm the only one who can do it. The memories are slowly coming back in bits and pieces. . . ."

He let his voice trail off, and at that moment, Nolan realized he and Twitch weren't that different, at least when it came to having issues with toys in the attic. Both suffered from what might be called acute separation anxiety—separation from their life before their Delta careers came to such a tragic end.

Twitch spoke again. "Look at it this way," he said, once more barely whispering. "If I was still in Delta and this mission had to be run, I'd run the mission."

Nolan shifted nervously in the chair. "Me, too," he said.

Twitch got to his feet, still a little unsteady. "Then let's go," he said.

They made their way up to the ship's makeshift ready room. Here they climbed into their combat suits—black camos, jump boots, and a belt and holster for their Glock 9s, all courtesy of the hidden Rubber Room.

Their flight helmets were as elaborate as any fighter pilot's. They had universal communications capability, meaning the wearer could make calls on the radio, on a sat phone, or even on a plain old cell phone without having to take his hands off the aircraft controls. They also had built-in night-vision goggles, and in Nolan's case, an elongated scope that fit over his good eye. Both took M4 assault rifles from the weapons locker as well. Nolan also had a good luck charm with him: his old keychain, which had a device that would beep in response to a wolf whistle as an easy way to find it. He'd carried it with him every day since joining Delta.

They climbed up to the copter platform. Two of the Senegals had refueled the tiny aircraft and had attached a 50-caliber machine-gun pod and a spool of ammunition to a hard point on the left-side undercarriage. They'd also hooked an extra fuel tank on the right side for balance and backup, and had reattached the doors in case the copter had to fly at high altitude. With all this done, the little aircraft was ready to go.

Nolan climbed in behind the controls, started the engine and felt a wave of anxiety wash over him. This was the moment of truth, the moment he'd been dreading. His father had owned a Cessna 210 and had taught him the basics of flying when he was just in his teens. Later on, the Army had trained him in rotary aircraft as a prelude to joining Delta Force. So Nolan knew how to fly. But he'd yet to do it in combat with only one eye. And while he'd taken a couple of test flights in the work copter during their mad dash to Indonesia, this would be his first night flight as a cyclops. Overall, a scary situation.

He was forcing this test of will on himself, dangerously facing his fear, just to prove that he wasn't *that* over the hill— or around the bend. If he was going to lead the rejuvenated

Team Whiskey with any kind of effectiveness, he had to successfully complete this mission. But his hands were shaking so much, he was sitting on them just so Twitch and the Senegals wouldn't see.

It was now 0300 hours. The wind started kicking up, and the ever-present mist began swirling around the DUS-7. Nolan did a check of his instrument panel; everything looked green. The two Senegals walked around the copter one last time and then gave him the thumbs up.

He adjusted his special night-vision attachment, a gift from Kilos before they'd left Aden. It was a detachable spyglass that worked just like a standard pair of night-vision goggles, except just for one eye. It fit into his helmet's visor, and just by tapping it, he could zoom in, zoom out, or go wide angle. Like all night-vision apparatus, it gave the world an eerie emerald glow.

He did one last check of the controls; everything was still looking good. He glanced over at his passenger, and that's when he noticed Twitch was holding his empty Coke bottle. Nolan started to ask him about it, but then changed his mind.

"Strap in tight," he told Twitch instead. "This might get bumpy."

They lifted off, shaky at first, but somehow Nolan got them airborne.

But no sooner had they cleared the ship when suddenly a swirl of crumpled dollar bills began flying around the cockpit, blinding them. Nolan quickly lost the horizon and the copter began to fall. He pulled up on the collective, increased power and swatted the bills out of his way, clearing his vision again. The next thing he knew, they'd broken through the mist and were up and over the island's tree line, heading east.

But Nolan was instantly soaked in sweat, heart pounding, hands shaking, his equilibrium again thrown out of whack. He found himself praying that some warning light would pop up on the control panel, just to give him an excuse to return to the ship. But the entire panel remained green.

This was such a foolish thing to do, he thought. He wasn't

in any shape to fly a helicopter, day or night. Not in his condition.

Then he felt Twitch's hand touch his right arm. He had the cap off his Coke bottle and was spilling the air from it onto Nolan.

"You're doing just fine, sir," Twitch said to him, his voice low, despite the sound of the copter's spinning rotor blades. "It's a great night for flying."

And just like that, Nolan's fears drained away.

NOLAN HAD SERVED in dozens of locations around the world since joining the military. He'd seen some fairly exotic places, especially with Delta Force, but he'd never seen anything like the nightscape spread before them now. In this part of Indonesia, nicknamed the Talua Tangs, hundreds of islands stretched out as far as his nightscope allowed him to see, glistening as if floating atop an emerald sea and illuminated by a bright half moon.

Batman had been right; it was otherworldly. If the entire Earth were made up of only islands and water, it would look like this.

The largest island within his field of view was no bigger than half a mile around. Some were smaller than a football field. Yet more than two-thirds of these islands had lights visible, indicating *someone* was living on them. Off in the distance, as always, was the green-yellow glow of Singapore.

The whole scene was surreal—and seeing it through the eerie emerald of the night-vision gear only added to the dreamlike effect.

Their mission tonight was to find the pirates' hideout. It would not be easy. Batman knew how to get to Skull Island and, by extension, Brothel Beach, because Twitch had taken pictures with his watch cam of those places, and the images came with transponder stamps. With that information, they had found them with the help of an Internet satellite map.

But after the drugs really kicked in, Twitch started taking the photographs less frequently, stopping altogether just before he reached the pirates' hideout, and not starting again until he'd moved on to Sumhai Island. So on this flight, they would attempt to retrace the steps he'd taken before he'd gotten so high.

To do this, Nolan had worked out a plan using techniques learned in his Delta Force days. Twitch had seen many things while in the company of the pirates the night before, but he couldn't remember seeing any of the bandits refueling their speedboats. Yet the pirates had no problem flying around in their swift sekocis, engines at full throttle. This told Nolan the pirates must have had access to a fuel facility somewhere close to their hideout, and that their hideout must be somewhere close to the islands Twitch had visited with them.

So if they could find some of the landmarks Twitch was sure he saw after leaving Brothel Beach, they could establish a search radius by guessing the distance a boat with an almost-empty fuel tank could go from there. Within that radius, must lie both the pirates' fuel depot and their hideout.

Or Nolan hoped that was the case.

"I remember seeing a large billboard on one of the islands we went past," Twitch told him now, his voice still low. "It had a big beer bottle on it. And after that we'd gone by a wrecked, three-masted ship washed up on a beach. But before all that, we went under a bridge that connected some islands where a lot of nightclubs were.

"At the time, the beer bottle sign seemed as big as a mountain. The wrecked ship looked like it was left over from the real old pirates days, and that bridge looked like the Brooklyn Bridge. It was sort of like being in Disneyland. If Disneyland was a place for druggies."

It took them a half hour of flying over island after island, but finally Nolan spotted what he thought might be Twitch's "Brooklyn Bridge." It was ten miles south of Brothel Beach, at the edge of an island inlet surrounded by a halo of pink light. And it *did* seem like it was big enough to connect Brooklyn to Manhattan. Made of basic bamboo-and-rope construction, it was surprisingly high and at least a quarter-mile long. It was strung with blinking party lights and gas-fueled candles.

"That's definitely it," Twitch said softly, as they flew over the structure at about 5,000 feet, out of earshot from anyone below. "Now, I think the beer sign was after this . . ."

They began scanning every island near the big bridge, gradually working their way outward. They saw a lot of boats moving among the many islands: freighters, small tankers, fishing trawlers. But it was odd: While things were bustling below them on this Saturday night, they didn't see any of the fast sekocis the pirates used. Nolan had the distinct impression Zeek's men were lying low.

This time it was Twitch who spotted it first. Off to the west, probably five miles from the bridge, an old Carlsberg Ale billboard, complete with a huge bottle, stood atop a hill of palm trees. It looked like something from the '50s.

"Yeah, that's it," he told Nolan.

Beyond the beer sign, Nolan spotted a large uninhabited island with a particularly rugged coastline. A place where a ship might wash up. It took them five more minutes of burning precious fuel, but finally they located the wreck of an old three-masted schooner.

"OK, the trifecta," Nolan said, fist-bumping Twitch in triumph.

But now came the hard part.

If they assumed that night the white-haired pirate, Bantang, had left the hijacked tanker in Phillip Channel with a near-full tank of gas, then visited Skull Island and Brothel Beach before heading back for Pirate Island, how far would his remaining gas take him? Nolan figured the answer had to be twenty miles or less, because according to Twitch, Bantang had pushed the sekoci's powerful engines hard, and the boat did not seem to have a large fuel tank.

No sailor, in a big boat or small, ever wanted to get caught out in the water with no gas. Indeed Twitch recalled Bantang's motorboat running out of fuel just as they'd reached the pirates' hideout.

So Nolan commenced a long slow orbit, starting at the island where the wreck was and working his way out. They scoured every island below, paying attention to those few that did not have any lights burning on them, as they figured it would probably be a darkened island that held Zeek's headquarters. But it was frustrating, because there were *so* many islands and many of them, dark or not, looked the same.

At first the search seemed useless. There were even more islands in this part of the Talua Tangs, all shapes, all sizes. Worse, they were all thick with jungle, their canopies being almost impossible to penetrate even with the night-vision goggles.

"They could have bonfires burning down there and we wouldn't see them," Twitch said. "I don't think smoke could even get up through those trees. It's the perfect camouflage."

But then they got lucky.

Nolan had a good feeling just before he spotted it; then Twitch saw it, too. Not on an island, but on the water. A long thin oil slick.

It didn't seem that unusual at first. The water among the hundreds of islands was heavily traveled by boats of all sizes, they used gasoline or diesel, and most leaked some fuel. But this was different. This slick was leeching out of a small, dark, triangular island about fifteen miles north of Beer Bottle Island and almost a straight shot from where the three-masted schooner was beached. The slick was several shades of blue, green and red. When enhanced by the night-vision goggles, it almost looked psychedelic floating on the calm water.

Nolan eased the copter down to twenty feet, both he and Twitch looking in all directions to make sure no one else was in the vicinity. Hovering above the oil slick, they turned their night-vision goggles on high and looked into the jungle on the triangular island. Both immediately saw a steel pipe, maybe six inches in diameter, running out of the forest and along a small, rocky beach before ending in the water, just where the slick began.

Nolan thought it conceivable that an island-hopping tanker could pull up to the end of this pipe, hook on and pump fuel into a storage tank hidden in the jungle. Had they found what they were looking for?

"I'd like to think we hit the jackpot," he told Twitch. "But . . ."

Then they got lucky again.

"Here comes company," Twitch announced softly.

Nolan looked over his right shoulder and saw three fast boats approaching the island. He immediately pulled up on the copter's collective and they went straight up, fast, climbing back to 5,000 feet and out of sight. He began circling the island.

The three boats arrived just off the end of the pipe. One stayed in place while the two others landed on the rocky beach. Sure enough, they could see four men get out of the two boats and walk into the jungle, each carrying what looked to be a gas tank.

"They're filling up," Twitch said. "But they're also being careful, leaving a guard boat offshore."

"After what happened last night and now earlier tonight, I can see why they'd be nervous," Nolan agreed.

They continued orbiting, and in a few minutes the four men emerged from the jungle, obviously carrying full gas tanks. The tanks were loaded onto the two boats, which soon departed. Nolan followed them.

It was not a minute later that they spotted a small island with a lagoon on its western side and a sandbar on its north. About half the island's forest had been hacked down, and in the clearing they saw a low two-story concrete building along with many small huts, a barracks and a mess hall. A crooked-finger-type dock stretched into the lagoon, with berths for a few dozen fast boats. Most important, there was a large yacht docked in a stream located away from the rest of the boats.

"That's the place," Twitch confirmed. "I'll never forget it as long as I live."

Sure enough, the two boats they were following pulled up to the dock and those aboard climbed off, carrying their recently filled fuel tanks with them.

Nolan fist-bumped Twitch again.

"Good work, my brother," he said.

* * *

THEIR RECON MISSION was a success. But on a hunch, Nolan flew the copter back to the island where the pirates' fuel depot lay hidden. The third fast boat, the one that had been keeping guard, had taken off in another direction, heading toward another dark island nearby.

"Let's see where those other guys went," he said to Twitch.

They found the pirates' boat beached on the next island over from the fuel depot. The tree cover wasn't quite as thick here, and there was a tall cliff on the island, somewhat unusual. Nolan focused his nightscope on the cliff and spotted two pirates walking toward it. Twitch saw them, too. Nolan moved the copter around the island, and that's when they got lucky again.

On the other side of the cliff was a large satellite dish.

"Jesus, what are these guys doing—talking to Venus?" Nolan asked. "Those things went out of style in the '80s."

Twitch's memory started flooding back again. "They showed me one of these old portable telephones they use," he said. "They really were stuff from the '80s, pull-out antennas and all that. But the reason they used them was they knew these days, people eavesdrop on cell phones, but don't bother with the old shit. They told me whenever Zeek was in trouble he'd put out a call on this old phone system and all his friends would come running."

Nolan patted Twitch on the back. This was an important find. Not only had they discovered Zeek's hideout and where he kept his fuel—they'd also uncovered the heart of his communications network.

But more important, they had both proved to themselves that they could still handle a hazardous mission without freaking out. The question now was: What should they do about all this?

"We don't have the firepower to deal with the hideout," Twitch said. "But the fuel tank and the sat dish? I think we got to take them out now. These guys are slippery and they're unpredictable. We could come back out here tomorrow night or even in a few hours, and it could all be gone."

Even though it would be tipping their hand to the pirates,

Nolan had to agree. "If we deprive them of fuel and a way to call their friends, it will make our ultimate goal easier. It will also let them know that someone is out to get them for real this time. That could go either way for us. But we've got to take the chance."

NOLAN KNEW TAKING out the satellite dish would be easy. At least twenty feet across, it was a fat target.

They waited for the two pirates to depart, and once they were out of sight, Nolan eased the copter down to a point just above the top of the cliff. Moving the aircraft sideways a bit allowed Twitch to lean out the right side door and aim his M4 down at the large umbrella-shaped dish.

"Anything in that superstitions book about shooting up one of these things?" Twitch asked Nolan. "Ten years of bad phone service or something?"

"Let's hope not," Nolan told him.

That's all the prompting Twitch needed. He opened up on the dish, his rounds shredding it as if it was made of paper. And suddenly he was screaming like a madman.

"Can you hear me now?" he was yelling wildly as he fired away. *"You fuckers! Can you hear me now?"*

HE DESTROYED THE antenna in less than thirty seconds. Taking out the pirates' fuel tank would be harder.

First they had to find it. It took nearly a dozen passes over the heavily forested island before Twitch finally spied a silver-colored fuel tank through not only a canopy of jungle but a blanket of camouflage netting as well. Now they had to figure out the best way to destroy it.

Putting the copter into a hover close to the tank and firing the gun pod wouldn't do. The tank looked capable of holding about 2,000 gallons. The resulting explosion would probably vaporize them and their copter. Standing off at a safe distance and shooting at it would probably not work, either—there was a good chance they'd run out of ammunition before one of their rounds penetrated the forest, the camouflage netting and the tank itself.

The third option was for Nolan to strafe the tank, making passes like a fighter pilot, hoping a close-in fusillade would puncture it, but not so quickly that they couldn't get out of the way first.

But there was a hitch. Nolan was barely a copter pilot—and hardly a fighter pilot. And he knew there was a difference between flying and flying well. Just as someone who drove a Chevy pickup truck could conceivably drive a ten-speed Kenworth double trailer rig, it took years of accumulated experience to keep it on the road. Even though his anxieties had eased since he'd left the ship, he had concentrated most of his energy on just staying in the air. Any extracurricular activities would be a challenge.

He checked the time. It was already getting light and they had only about five minutes left before they would have to head back to the ship. So they had to do something fast.

He told Twitch to strap in as tightly as possible. He then rose to about 2,000 feet, turned the copter around, pushed the nose down and began his dive. Right away the aircraft started vibrating madly. The controls became heavy and the engine began screaming. Even Twitch seemed concerned.

But Nolan knew there was no turning back. About five hundred feet above the fuel tank, he hit the gun-pod trigger and kept it depressed until he finally peeled away just about fifty feet out. He'd been able to follow the gun pod's tracer rounds as they streaked through the jungle toward the bare silhouette of the tank—and this initial barrage looked impressive. But there was no explosion. They would have to go around again.

Soaked in sweat again, Nolan once more climbed, turned the copter over and began a second dive. He started firing farther out this time, trying to concentrate on the line of red tracers as it tore through the trees. His dive was steeper and it lasted longer, but again, no explosion—just some flaming branches.

"We only have ninety-three shells left," Twitch reported, checking the pod's readout screen.

Nolan climbed for a third time. He was not diving steep enough, which meant not enough of his rounds were hitting the target in a concentrated area.

This time, he climbed to 2,500 feet, turned and pushed the nose of the copter into an extremely sharp dive.

Twitch let out a yelp as they started going nearly straight down. Nolan hit the trigger, and somehow Twitch recovered enough to stick his M4 out of the copter's open door, adding its bullets to the gun pod's rounds.

Nolan was using all his strength to keep the copter steady in the suicidal plunge—but the big Kenworth was starting to run off the road. Just as he thought he was going to lose it, there was a sudden bright flash followed by a plume of deep red fire. Only then did the force of the explosion hit them. Nolan turned the copter immediately, but it was the shock wave that actually saved them, throwing them sideways about a hundred feet, away from the fireball.

The explosion was gigantic. Though the noise was a bit muted—more of a *whomp!*—it was all Nolan could do to regain control of the copter. He pushed the throttle forward, getting them away just as the flames were licking at the tail rotor. Looking behind him, Nolan saw a huge hole in the jungle and the remains of not one, but actually three fuel tanks burning furiously.

Mission accomplished. . . .

He returned to the controls and the job of escaping, and only then did he realize that Twitch had been hit. A piece of shrapnel had come through his open doorway, ripped through his safety harness and tore into his upper right arm.

"Jesuszz, Twitch—talk to me!" Nolan yelled to him over the noise of the copter's engine going full out.

"I'm still feeling no pain, sir," Twitch yelled back. "And it's just a nick. I'm OK."

But he was bleeding, and at that moment, Nolan realized they didn't have any bandages on the copter.

They looked around the cockpit for something, anything that could serve as a dressing. But the aircraft was small and spare to begin with, and they found nothing.

That's when Nolan reached inside his flight suit and pulled out something else he'd been carrying with him: a small, slightly torn U.S. flag. He handed it to Twitch. "Use this," he said.

Twitch looked at the flag and quickly realized he'd seen it before.

"This is the team flag," he said, astonished. "Our flag from Tora Bora."

Nolan didn't say anything. He just concentrated on getting the copter on course and back to the ship.

Twitch applied the flag to his shoulder and soon the bleeding was down to a trickle.

Then he said to Nolan: "Our flag—you kept it after all these years?"

Nolan nodded slowly and just said: "Yeah—after all these years."

12

Pirate Island
The next night

ZEEK'S GANG MEMBERS were creatures of the night.

They did their robbing, hijacking, whoring, drug-taking and killing after dark. Then, like vampires, they were home before dawn, sleeping during the day, only to rise again when the sun went down.

That's why, this night, none of the pirates were aware their fuel dump had been blown up less than twenty-four hours before. Most had been passed out in their bunks at the time of the explosion a few miles away; some were so intoxicated, a small atomic bomb wouldn't have roused them. The noise, the smoke, the flames—Zeek's army noticed none of it. Even those pirates charged with standing watch had been asleep when the dump went up.

The chow hall bell began ringing madly around 2100 hours, waking the pirates. Usually this was the signal for the first meal of their upside-down day. But those stumbling out of the

barracks felt a different vibe around the camp. Nights like
this always started with a communal meal of boar and noodles, followed by more drinking. But those pirates approaching the mess hall couldn't smell any boar cooking, nor could
they see the steam that always filled the compound from the
boiling of the noodles. And there was no alcohol anywhere to
be found. All this was odd.

There was another strange thing: As the gang had taken a
large ship not forty-eight hours before, many expected to get
their share of the booty tonight, and to be paid by the gang's
paymasters. Saturday was payday for Zeek's band. But none
of the bagmen were in sight.

Zeek himself hadn't been seen since the night before, but
this was not unusual. The Boss slept during the day as well,
and sometimes well into the night and even the next morning.
But now, the pirates saw that Zeek's concrete HQ was surrounded by his *Badan Menjaga,* his personal bodyguards, the
dozen trusted inner-circle types who wore the coveted black
bandana. They had set up 50-caliber machine guns behind
sandbag barriers on all four sides of the building and were
warning away any pirate who came close. Some of the older
brigands on hand had been part of Zeek's gang for more than
ten years. They'd never seen anything like this.

One of Zeek's lieutenants appeared in the mess hall and
began ringing the communal bell again, a long series of three
rings each. This was the signal that all the pirates should muster up and pay attention.

The lieutenant waited for the last of the group to assemble
inside. When the mess hall was full, he began speaking.

"The Boss wants you to know trouble might be coming," he
told them starkly. "We've had a couple problems lately."

A nervous murmur went through the crowd; the news was
totally unexpected. The officer revealed that two of the gang's
members had been murdered two nights before, just after the
rampage on Sumhai Island. Then, less than twenty-four hours
ago, the pirates' fuel dump had been blown up.

"The Boss is sure that we're dealing with a rival gang," the officer went on. "Or maybe something connected to his brother Turk getting iced a little while ago. But either way, he says, don't worry. We all know it's hard to find us here."

He spread his arms to indicate the hideout's natural defenses. The pirate camp was on the edge of a lagoon that was so shallow it was hard for deep-water boats to get anywhere close to it. The lagoon itself was protected on three sides by heavy jungle, and the curve of the camp's beach was such that, even on the fourth side, looking in from the north over the sandbar, it was extremely difficult to see the pirates' encampment with the naked eye. In their many years of pirating, no one had ever come looking for them here.

The officer went on. "The Boss is sure our location is still a secret, because there are so many islands out here, it would take weeks for someone to search each and every one. But if this rival gang *does* find us here, we will take care of them quickly, because we are still the biggest gang in the area, and the Boss says when we get rid of these guys, it will make us that much stronger."

The hungover pirates let out a groggy cheer. Then the officer signaled the chow hall crew to proceed. But instead of laying out the meal, they began distributing the gang's drug of choice—Indonesian Ecstasy. This batch was filled with extra methamphetamine, to keep the fighters wide awake for whatever might be coming.

But what would that be, exactly?

The answer came a few moments later.

IT BEGAN WHEN someone spotted two lights out on the water just beyond the entrance to the lagoon.

One was bright white, with a small red light beside it. Running lights for a good-sized vessel, the pirates figured. As word went around camp about the mysterious lights, two more popped on. The same white and red combination, about five hundred feet from the first two. Then two more blinked on about two hundred feet from them. Then four more—and four more after that.

Within a minute, it appeared that more than a dozen large boats had suddenly materialized off the pirates' shoreline. Was this a fleet of lost fishing boats that wandered over from the nearby Pautang Channel? Or were these mother ships, launching a rival gang's fleet of fast boats? If so, this meant Zeek's gang was about to be overwhelmed by a horde of enemy pirates.

Zeek's men had to find out what was going on. With their officers' blessing, a handful of them climbed into one of their own fast boats and headed out of the lagoon. Not thirty seconds later, those back on the island heard five distinct *pops!* Then the fast boat floated back in again.

The five pirates were still in it. They were all dead—each with a massive gunshot wound to the head.

The pirates began to panic. Many ran to get their weapons, which they usually kept in their fast boats. But suddenly a long stream of tracer fire came out of the night, tearing into the gang's boats along the crooked finger dock and systematically exploding them like car tires. As the pirates reacted to this, another stream of tracer fire riddled the island's generator hut. In an instant, the power plant blew up and all the lights went out.

Pirate Island was suddenly in the dark.

Aboard the DUS-7

NOLAN CLIMBED INTO the passenger seat of the work copter and strapped in.

"Now comes the hard part," he thought aloud.

He laid his M4 across his knees and put his helmet on. He was dressed in his usual battle suit with several belts of ammunition slung over his shoulder. He was anxious about the upcoming action.

Batman climbed in behind the copter's controls. Nolan was happy to let him do the flying; just getting inside the copter still gave him the shakes. Batman did a quick check of the flight systems and saw everything was green, including the

50-caliber gun pod attached to the copter's left-side hard point and the APO—the asymmetrical piece of ordnance—they were carrying on the right.

Close by on the mid-deck, the Senegals were putting the finishing touches on an unusual weapon, a throwback to the Vietnam era: five M2 50-caliber machine guns attached to a steel frame about ten feet long. A single belt of ammunition fed each weapon, ninety rounds per belt. A rudimentary camshaft had been slotted through the M2s' firing mechanisms and attached to a pulley on one end of the steel frame and a large rotating bolt on the other. Depending on the amount of cranking done on the pulley, from one to all five of the weapons could be fired at once.

The steel frame sat on a wooden pallet supported by four hydraulic jack stands. The pallet could be hand-moved up and down, and left and right, but not very far. Gunner, the contraption's designer, had assured them that if all went well, a whole lot of aiming and moving wouldn't be needed for this cannonade machine to work. One of the guns had just taken out the pirates' rubber boat fleet and their generator. But would all five work in concert when they needed them? That remained to be seen.

At the far end of the DUS-7, Gunner and Crash were reeling out a long rope, on the end of which were fourteen wooden rafts, built in the *Dustboat*'s tiny workshop. Each raft held a battery-powered searchlight and a smaller blinking red light. Called a Bailey String, it was an old British trick from World War II designed to make an enemy think there was a squadron of unknown warships offshore when no such ships existed at all.

Like the cannonade machine, the rafts were about deception, which was just about the only advantage Team Whiskey had in its mission against Zeek. Though they had wounded their adversary by robbing his bank and busting up his spy ring, his fuel supply and his communications system, there was no getting around the fact that they were outnumbered at least eight to one. They were also somewhat limited in their ammunition, had no real heavy munitions, and had a diminishing supply of aviation fuel. If they were going to get Zeek, it had to be tonight, on their terms. And it all had to happen in less than five minutes, because after that, the element of surprise would be gone.

"Cutting through all the bullshit," Batman said to Nolan now, "what do you think the chances are that all this hocus-pocus is going to work?"

Nolan didn't answer right away. It was an odd question. When they were in the military, they never talked about how good a plan was, or their chances of making it. They just went and did it because it was their duty. Even their first job for Kilos, saving the *Global Warrior* from Turk's gang, had been undertaken with that mind-set.

But this—this was different. They were directly taking on a superior force, in their enemy's territory, against overwhelming odds, for—well, for a paycheck. Though there was an ancillary reason to rid the world of Zeek and his scum, basically it came down to the fact that they were now mercenaries doing a job that they would get paid for if all went well. And if things didn't go well, there would be no one left to get paid.

Their plan was simple then—or as simple as they could make it. Now that they'd gotten the pirates' attention with the Bailey String, and by popping their rubber boats and killing their electricity, they would use the copter to attack the pirates from the south side of the lagoon. This way, they hoped the confused brigands would flee to the north side of the camp, to the small sandbar located on the only side of the small island that was in any way exposed. Waiting for them there, just 300 feet offshore, would be the DUS-7 and the Senegals and their cannonade machine.

"Our chances?" Nolan finally replied. "Ten of us against eighty or so of them? I'd say fifty-fifty."

Twitch had just climbed into the back of the helicopter. He'd heard what they were talking about.

"Fifty-fifty?" he said to Nolan. "Once again, always the optimist."

With that, Batman hit the throttles and eased the overloaded copter into the air.

* * *

BACK ON THE stern, Crash and Gunner watched the copter go overhead. That was their cue to start the next part of the plan.

They tied the rope holding the Bailey String to the stern railing and climbed down to a rubber boat cinched to the back of the unmoving ship. Gunner was carrying a backpack filled with explosives.

Once in the rubber boat, Gunner carefully laid down the backpack. Then Crash handed him his M107 sniper rifle. The huge weapon was still warm from the five shots Crash had just fired, taking out the five pirates who had come out to investigate the mystery lights off the island's shoreline.

"You're sure you know how to use it, right?" the ex-SEAL asked him.

Gunner studied the big M107. "Hey—I'm the weapons guy here, remember?" he said. "I can fire anything."

With that, Crash went over the side of the rubber boat and into the water.

"Jesuszz, I thought it would be like bathtub warm down here," he gasped. "It's freaking freezing."

"Global warming," Gunner told him. "Or cooling? I don't know, ask Al Gore."

Gunner handed Crash the backpack full of explosives. Crash strapped it on—and immediately began to sink.

Gunner reached down and grabbed him, pulling him back to the surface.

"Damn, are you going to be able to do this?" he asked his colleague. "That pack is too heavy for you to swim with."

Crash readjusted the pack and tried it again. He didn't sink this time, but it was obvious that the loaded backpack was weighing him down.

"Are you sure you can make it?" Gunner asked him again.

"I have to," Crash told him. "Just take good care of my gun."

With that, he swam away into the dark.

Gunner watched him go, then looked the sniper rifle up and down again. Yes, he was the team's weapons master, but he'd never dealt with this type of gun before. It was a third longer than a typical combat weapon and felt twice as heavy. Its scope was almost as long as its barrel, and it had an elaborate foldout brace on its tip to steady it when it was fired. It took an enormous 12.7mm round. If it hit right, a bullet that size could cut a person in two.

Gunner climbed back up to the stern of the ship. His job now: If any of the pirates directed anything, from a flashlight to a searchlight at one of the Bailey String rafts or the *Dustboat* itself, he was to shoot them immediately with Crash's M107. This way they would eventually stop trying to find out what was going on out beyond their shoreline.

But as Gunner tried to set himself on the stern, he studied the weapon a third time and just shook his head.

"How the hell does he shoot this thing?" he said.

THE WORK COPTER circled the island once, and its occupants took stock of the situation below. Crash was on his way. Gunner was in place. The blacked-out DUS-7 was anchored where it needed to be, the cannonade machine armed and ready to go. It was time for the copter to make its presence known.

Flying with no running lights, Batman pushed the aircraft down to just twenty feet and flew right over the pirates' HQ, gun pod blazing, making an ungodly noise. The barrage tore into the concrete structure, causing an explosion of fire and rock. The attack was on—and the clock was ticking.

The flash from the explosion lit up the entire pirate camp. In its glow, the pirates could be seen scattering or hitting the dirt. Batman turned the copter over and pointed it toward the finger dock. He squeezed the gun pod trigger and took out many of the pirates' boats that hadn't been sunk in the initial barrage from the ship.

Another twist, and now Batman had lined up in back of the main group of pirates, coming at them from the south. He opened up again with the gun pod while Nolan and Twitch added rounds from their M4s. From ground level, it was hard to figure out just what was going on. There was a lot of smoke, dust and spray in the air—and a lot of noise. Many of the pirates couldn't even see the helicopter; many thought the gunfire was coming from the ships offshore. At this point, Zeek's black bandana bodyguards started firing their 50-caliber machine guns, but not at any real targets. A lot of their return fire was falling harmlessly into the lagoon.

Batman turned the copter around and strafed the HQ again. They were so close to the ground that Nolan could see chips of concrete flying off Zeek's lair. Again, he and Twitch added their M4s to the fusillade, blasting any pirates who came within their enhanced field of vision.

Once Zeek's elite bodyguards realized they were being attacked from both air *and* sea, most of them scattered. But a few regular pirates stood their ground and finally seeing the copter, raised their weapons to get a shot at it.

This didn't deter Batman. He dove even lower on the camp, the gun pod spitting out massive streams of tracer fire. A lot of this was now hitting its mark and the copter crew could see pirates falling to the ground, wounded or killed, some of them in pieces.

The team's plan seemed to be working. Those pirates who could were fleeing toward the north end of the lagoon. The unlit, darkened DUS-7 was lying in wait for them; the Senegals had the cannonade machine ready to fire. Their fusillade would come from nowhere, and the pirates would have nowhere else to go. At least that was the plan.

Nolan just hoped it worked—this time.

The last of Zeek's bodyguards were close to all-out panic by now. They began waving their 50-caliber machine guns around madly, but again, they couldn't find anything real to shoot at.

Amid the chaos, one bodyguard turned on his ancient portable phone, only to find there was no service. Other bodyguards tried their phones, also to no avail. They'd never been told that, just as their fuel dump had been destroyed, their secure, if antiquated, phone system had lost its transmitting dish.

Now it seemed tracers were washing all over the island, like a wave crashing to shore. The remaining bodyguards freaked out and started firing wildly in all directions, but wound up cutting down some of their own men. They were still convinced a small offshore navy was bombarding the pirates' camp, while a ghostly aircraft of some kind was shooting at them from above.

One of the bodyguards finally took out a personal cell phone—a strict violation of Zeek's rules, but a necessary act of desperation. Under the intense fire, he called the only people who could help the pirates in a situation like this: their partners in crime, the Indonesian military. Dialing the local naval headquarters, the bodyguard, saying he was under direct orders from Zeek, hastily explained that the Boss needed assistance on Pirate Island quickly, and that he was willing to pay any amount of money to get it.

But the Indonesian naval officer on the other end of the phone turned him down flat. Not because of the danger—but because he'd heard Zeek wouldn't be able to pay.

"Word is your boss got no money to operate," the officer said. "And that he has much bad luck on him."

The bodyguard was stunned. He'd heard nothing of this—but he had to think quickly.

"We will pay you in girls," he told the navy officer.

But the man said no again. "All your girls are gone, too. Your brothel is empty. Your whores are on their way to Bangkok."

Again, the bodyguard was shocked.

But he had one more form of currency to offer the officer.

"Ecstasy," he said. "One thousand hits, free to you."

The officer just laughed at him and started to hang up.

"OK—make it two thousand," the bodyguard said, pleading.

There was a long silence. Then the officer said, "Make it three thousand and you've got a deal."

THE WORK COPTER made more passes over the camp; the gun pod was lit and smoking, and Nolan and Twitch were spraying gunfire everywhere. His anxiety gone, Nolan felt the adrenalin pumping through his body. He was high from it.

Soon, the next part of the plan would kick in: finding Zeek himself. Nolan was getting psyched for that.

He had plans for Zeek. They all did. The photos Twitch had taken of the massacre on Sumhai were impossible to erase from his mind. As hideous as it sounded, he wanted to do to Zeek what Zeek had done to those innocent villagers. Scald him to death. Drown him in boiling oil. Tear open his guts and leave him to try to stuff them back in.

People going into combat have fantasies, too—and these were Nolan's. But he knew they were stupid, unworkable, and that dead is dead and their plan to quickly ice Zeek and his gang was the only way to go.

The trouble was, Twitch was harboring the same kind of fantasies. And he planned to act on them.

THE COPTER HAD turned and was making another low-level run, firing at the pirates to keep them moving toward the north end of the beach when Twitch suddenly unbuckled his seat harness and jumped out.

Neither Nolan nor Batman knew he was gone until they swung around from the last strafing pass and saw their colleague on the ground, in the middle of the chaos of pirates running toward the sandbar.

"Jesus—I don't believe this guy," Batman said. "Is he *trying* to get killed?"

"That's a distinct possibility," Nolan replied.

TWITCH WAS WELL prepared.

He was wearing his black camouflage battle suit. His flak vest. His oversized Fritz helmet with blast visor and multi-wire connections. Armored knee pads and black high-top paratrooper boots. He was carrying his huge MX automatic carbine with a belt already fed into it and two more crisscrossing his chest. He also had an extra-long, razor-sharp serrated Gryphon-Terzuola combat knife.

Best of all, he had his empty Coke bottle. As soon as he hit he ground, he poured some of the air on himself. Then he went to work.

The sudden appearance of a futuristically dressed soldier in their midst panicked the pirates further. No one tried to shoot him or stab him or challenge him at all. They were just trying to get away from him . . . and for good reason. Twitch was firing madly at them, cutting down pirates all around him. He put the carbine on his right hip, and while firing with one hand, used his combat knife in the other to slash and cut pirates running past him.

Nolan and Batman could see flashes of the whole thing through their night-vision equipment. It looked like something from a real-life *Rambo* movie, right down to the bloody bandage Twitch was wearing on his arm, covering his wound from the night before.

"We've got to get him back!" Nolan yelled to Batman. "Before those guys get wise and cut him to pieces."

Batman pushed the copter up and around again as Nolan got ready to grab Twitch and haul him back into the chopper. But by the time they'd returned to the spot where Twitch had jumped out, amid the fury and the smoke and the dark and flames, they discovered their colleague had vanished.

THIS WAS WHAT Twitch wanted to do: kill as many pirates as possible with his own hands. No bombs. No strafing attacks. No sniper rounds fired from a quarter mile away. He wanted his face to be the last thing many of the pirates would see. He wanted them to feel the horror the people of Sumhai had felt. Twitch thought he owed that to them.

He moved quickly through the dust and smoke, firing nonstop at anyone he saw, slashing anyone close to him. He was running on the loose sand—and that alone was remarkable. Usually he had a hard time running on such a surface with his prosthetic leg. But now he was moving with the grace of an Olympic sprinter. Make that an *invisible* Olympic sprinter.

He broke into the chow hall and shot it to pieces with his carbine. Some pirates seeking refuge here had hidden under the tables. Twitch hunted down every last one and shot them without mercy. Then he fired into one of the propane tanks near a cooking table until it blew up and started a massive fire.

When several more pirates tried to flee the burning building, Twitch cut them down like animals. He finally ambled outside, barely aware of the burning timbers falling all around him.

He walked into the next building, a workshop where the gang repaired their boat engines. Again, some pirates had tried to hide here, squeezing themselves in amongst the tools and old engine parts. Again, Twitch calmly hunted them down, stabbing those he could reach with his knife, shooting those he couldn't. Before leaving, he fired into a full gas can, causing an explosion that quickly engulfed the wood and rope structure. He moved on, the screams of more pirates burning to death ringing in his ears.

He coolly shot several more pirates who were running past him, and then stumbled into the next building over—the gang's tiny sick bay.

There were six pirates in here, all in beds, some in bandages, others suffering from drug overdoses. All were unable to move. Twitch walked from bed to bed, shooting each ailing pirate in the head.

Then he reached the sixth bed. Here, he found a man lying on his back, his head and face covered with bandages, a blanket pulled to his chin. Twitch ripped the bandages from the pirate's face—and was stunned.

He recognized the man.

It was Bantang, the white-haired pirate.

He'd been viciously beaten all over his body and his left arm had been cut off. This was Zeek's punishment for allowing the "haki" into their midst. Twitch just stood there, looking at the broken man, even as Bantang was looking up at him, a monster in black armor holding a gun that looked like a small cannon.

Twitch slowly raised his visor and let Bantang see who he was. The pirate's eyes grew large.

"You?" was all the pirate could say.

"Me," Twitch replied.

Bantang started crying. "Shoot me," he said. "Please—just shoot me."

Twitch put the barrel of his carbine next to Bantang's ear.

The pirate was trembling mightily.

"Please—do it," he pleaded.

But Twitch never moved the gun. He squeezed the trigger, firing a round into the pillow, blowing out Bantang's eardrums in the process.

Then, he turned on his heel and walked out.

THE SWIM IN from the DUS-7 had been brutal.

Crash became exhausted halfway across the lagoon; at one point he even thought about turning back. Swimming with the backpack was harder than anything he'd faced during Hell Week back in his SEAL training days. And with that memory, he realized that brutal training had been more than a dozen years ago, and he was that much older now. His mind began racing. Maybe he had to stop fooling himself. He wasn't a SEAL anymore—he was an ex-SEAL. And there was a big difference.

But turning back would mean he'd failed the rest of the team, and he'd rather die than let that happen. So on sheer determination, he pushed himself across the lagoon, past all the gunfire, and finally reached his target: sitting alone, at its own berth in the stream, far from the finger dock, Zeek's armored yacht. It was the vessel they were sure the Pirate King would use if he did eventually move to the east coast of Africa. No matter what happened then, the team thought it was crucial they destroy this vessel. By doing so, at the very least, they would know that any move west by Zeek would be delayed if not thwarted.

The question had been, how to do it? The copter and the rest of the team would have their hands full with the heavily armed pirate army. Shooting up the yacht with assault weapons would damage but probably not destroy it. Plus, they needed that ammunition to deal with the pirates.

So they decided to place a large explosive charge under the yacht's hull and detonate it. That's what the explosives in Crash's backpack were for.

Once he'd reached the yacht and regained his strength, Crash went to work.

He took out the heavy explosive charge and, diving underneath the vessel, attached it under the hull at the all-important center point. But getting the charge to stick took longer than he'd anticipated. The only available adhesive was marine duct tape, which didn't work very well under water.

With his lungs about to burst, Crash finally got the charge to hold, and desperately swam to the surface. It took him almost a minute to catch his breath, as gunfire and tracer rounds streaked all around him. He had two more dives to make: one, to attach the underwater detonation cord, and another to arm the fuse. He planned to set the fuse to 120 seconds, enough time for him to swim a safe distance away.

He went below again and attached the detonation cord fairly easily. But when he returned to the surface, he found three pirates wearing black bandanas standing on the yacht's midship railing, looking down at him.

This was disastrous. Crash had no weapon with him, not even a knife. And these three were pointing AK-47s at him.

He instantly dove again and set the fuse. AK-47 bullets were zipping through the water all around him, the noise they made when breaking the surface nearly splitting his eardrums. He stayed down as long as possible, but he was trapped. The yacht's dock prevented him from swimming in that direction, and the gunmen were firing into the water on the remaining three sides. Once again, his lungs threatened to burst.

He went back to the surface again to find two of the pirates had jumped into the water. They grabbed him and began pummeling him. Crash tried his best to break away, but he couldn't. They all went underwater, the pirates trying to slash at him with their knives, and he had nothing to fight back with. He was certain he was going to die here, either drowned, gutted, or blown up.

A strange calmness came over him, though. He thought: If this is the end, at least he'd accomplished what he wanted. He'd put Team Whiskey back together, and they had done *some* good, right?

He somehow broke away from his attackers, but was cut in many places—and by this time he barely had the strength to reach the surface and take in a breath. He was sure it would be his last, but he needed it anyway.

So he surfaced, drew it in—and awaited his fate.

The two assailants surfaced right beside him and came at him with knives glistening.

Then he heard three of the most beautiful sounds ever: *Pop! Pop! Pop!*

A bullet for each of his two attackers in the water and for the one who had stayed on the railing, firing at him. All three pirates cried out—then died instantly.

The next thing Crash knew, he was alone, surrounded only by the bloody water.

"Gunner," he thought.

He'd figured out how to fire the large sniper weapon, and like a guardian angel, he'd been watching over him.

An instant later, Crash began swimming like hell.

Twenty seconds after that, the yacht blew up. The explosion was so powerful it lifted the huge vessel right off the water and sent it crashing back down again.

It broke in two and immediately sank to the bottom.

THE WORK COPTER was going over the armed yacht just about the time it blew up. Batman had to turn on the jets to escape being caught up in the explosion.

"Fucking Crash!" Batman yelled. "SEALs come through again!"

Nolan scanned the lagoon and saw the team's sniper calmly swimming back out to the channel, free of the heavy backpack. He and Batman did a fist-bump. A major part of their plan had just been accomplished. The armed yacht was gone. So no matter what happened, Zeek and his gang weren't going west to Africa anytime soon.

But Whiskey wasn't done yet.

Again, Nolan was glad he was not flying the work copter. Batman was throwing them all over the sky, shooting here, dodging stray enemy fire there, always wary that something as small as a ricocheting AK-47 round could bring them down as quickly as a SAM missile.

Finally, Batman got the copter pointing north again, and that's when they realized most of the pirates were just where they wanted them to be—at least fifty of them were crowded on the tiny sandbar on the northern side of the beach, the last place they could go. Batman pulled the copter into a hover about 100 yards away from where the pirates were congregated.

Nolan felt a twinge in his stomach. He could see through his night-vision scope that most of the pirates were milling around, completely exposed, hoping the attack was over. They had no idea what was about to happen to them.

"Man, this is fish in a barrel," he said to Batman, knowing their plan worked *too* well. "These mooks don't have a chance."

Batman could only shrug. "What else can we do, Snake?" he asked, adjusting his own night-vision goggles. "Capture them and rehabilitate them? Give them a slap on the wrist and tell them not to be bad boys anymore? You saw what they did to those villagers—and God knows how many other people. These guys are garbage."

Nolan couldn't disagree. Zeek's gang was a brutal bunch. But again the feeling came over him. Doing dirty ops for his country had been one thing. But doing it for a paycheck? Quite another. . . .

He pushed the sat phone to ON and called the DUS-7. When one of the Senegals answered, Nolan said just one word: "Now. . . ."

Hidden in the murk, behind some high reeds, the gallery of machine guns on the old freighter opened up. Their streams of fire filled the night with tracer rounds. With a minimum of moving back and forth, the fusillade hit just where the team wanted it to go, directly into the crowd of pirates caught out in the open on the constricted sandbar. The barrage lasted less than thirty seconds; some of the pirates looked like they were fast dancing as they were getting hit. When it was over, most of Zeek's gang were dead or dying.

Batman took the copter out of its hover and slowly flew above the killing field. Already the sands were running thick with blood. He fired single shots from the gun pod at any body he thought was still moving. Nolan also added a few rounds from his M4.

It took about a minute, but finally they could see no more signs of life below.

All the pirates were dead.

NOW CAME THE hard part.

Batman once again put the copter in a bone-crunching turn and was soon back hovering over the compound.

"Am I still green on this thing?" he yelled to Nolan.

Nolan looked out the open doorway and checked the object the copter was carrying on the right-side hard point. Again, for this flight, instead of hauling around an extra fuel tank to balance the gun pod, the copter was carrying the APO, the powerful "asymmetrical piece of ordnance"—Delta-speak for homemade bomb.

It was Twitch's concoction, a mixture of gasoline, diesel fuel and Jell-O, all soaked up into rags and old newspapers. The canister, made of an empty fuel tank, was also filled with nails, screws and bolts—instant shrapnel. Sandpaper and a nine-volt battery served as the contact fuse. In all, it weighed close to 200 pounds.

The target: Zeek's concrete headquarters.

"It looks good," Nolan yelled back to him. "Or as good as it can look."

Batman replied: "Then hang on."

He put the copter into a sharp left turn, swooped past the concrete building, turned again, and was now heading right back for it. Nolan could see people shooting at them from several of the building's windows. He slung his M4 out the open doorway and fired back. Then, flying as fast as the work copter could go, Batman yanked the release lever, and the homemade bomb fell off the bottom of the copter, just twenty feet above the building.

The explosion was tremendous. Batman put the copter into a fierce left turn, but still the shock wave almost knocked the aircraft out of the sky. Batman quickly recovered safe flight and, climbing to two hundred and fifty feet, overflew the concrete building—or what was left of it—once more. The bomb had been delivered right on target and had worked perfectly. The building was now a pile of burning rubble falling into a newly formed hole.

"Nice shooting," Nolan told him with another fist bump.

But then they saw something strange: a river of water was gushing from the lagoon to the blast site. It took them a few moments to realize what was going on. The bomb had worked so well, it had blown a hole down below the island's water table, creating a huge crater and collapsing the beach all around it. Water from the lagoon was now quickly filling this crater. The lower parts of the island, including what was left of Zeek's headquarters, would soon be under water.

"Shit! This is not good!" Batman yelled.

"Get me down, quick!" Nolan yelled to him.

A burst from the gun pod made sure the bodies of several scattered bodyguards nearby were really dead. Then Batman put the copter down, landing about twenty feet from the burning, sinking building.

Nolan immediately jumped out. He had his M4 in one hand and a small disposable camera in the other. This was the most important part of the mission. He had to get proof their job was finished, that Zeek was dead.

He ran up to the demolished building, finding it even more obliterated than they had previously thought. It was little more than a heap of smoking rubble, and the water from the lagoon was quickly filling a large area all around it.

As Batman watched nearby, Nolan started moving among chunks of concrete, trying to get to the bottom of the pile before the sizzling water submerged them. Zeek was known to dress in purple, so Nolan was looking for anything that bore that color. It was a race against time, as the lagoon water was coming in fast.

Nolan moved one piece of concrete to the side and saw a leg and an arm sticking out of the rubble. Both were wearing purple. He snapped two pictures—but suddenly sensed someone was behind him.

He swung around and almost shot the person—until he saw it was Twitch, standing there. He looked dazed and was white as a ghost.

"What the hell did I just do?" he was mumbling. "Was that real?"

Nolan wanted to throttle him for his dangerous behavior, but there was no time for that. Instead, Nolan just told him to help move the rubble near the body before the water covered it all.

Then he yelled back to Batman in the work copter: "All we have to do is move a couple more rocks, snap a few more pics, and we're home free!"

That's when Batman received a call from the DUS-7. It was Gunner. All he said was: "We got company . . ."

THE DUS-7'S LOW-TECH, rudimentary surface radar set had picked up a blip moving up the Pautang Channel toward Pirate Island.

Within thirty seconds, using his night-vision goggles, Gunner could see a small warship heading in their direction. It was an Indonesian Navy patrol boat.

The team had found evidence at Brothel Beach that Zeek had ties to the Indonesian military. Plus, Twitch had seen a boat similar to this one standing by the night that Zeek's gang seized the oil tanker.

Had the pirates or the bodyguards gotten through to their allies-in-crime somehow? Was this ship investigating reports of the battle? Or was its presence here simply a coincidence?

There was no way to tell. But while fighting a bunch of bloodthirsty pirates was one thing, going up against the Indonesian Navy was quite another. Their patrol boats were heavily armed and known to carry antiaircraft missiles.

"Time to go, guys," Batman called to Nolan.

"But we only have one more piece to move," Nolan yelled back.

"Nope—let's go now!"

Nolan didn't want to argue. He pulled Twitch off the rubble, took a few more pictures, then ran back to the copter. He threw Twitch onboard, then scrambled on himself.

They rose above the smoldering compound and headed into the night. Meanwhile the DUS-7 had hauled anchor, picked up Crash, and was quickly leaving the scene as the Indonesian gunship approached.

Nolan checked his watch. The attack had lasted just four minutes and thirty-five seconds.

He was not happy, though. "We did everything but the most important thing," he said.

"Don't worry it," Batman told him, slapping him five. "He's dead. You got pictures. Let's go get paid."

13

Aboard the DUS-7
Two days later

ON THE MENU tonight was steak *au poivre*.

There were also orange *patates*, Maltese vegetables scorched in *vin de pêche*, and bourbon profiteroles for dessert. Never had the DUS-7's galley smelled so good.

The rusty old freighter was passing off the southern tip of Sri Lanka, heading west through heavy fog. Already halfway across the Indian Ocean, its destination was the Port of Aden.

Team Whiskey's job was complete, and now they were heading home. What would happen to them when they reached Yemen was anyone's guess. They'd have some money to spend, soon at least $20,000 each. But after that was gone, who knew? A return to their jobs at the secret Saudi super-mall was a gloomy possibility.

But this was a time for celebration. Sitting around the mess table now were the five team members plus Mark Conley, the representative from Kilos Shipping. Conley had flown aboard the DUS-7 in one of the company's luxurious helicopters just before sundown. He'd arrived with the makings of the feast, along with Mikos Kilos's personal chef. Conley also carried a briefcase full of money, the team's second $50,000 payment in less than a month.

The operation against Zeek had been a success, even if no one on the outside could agree what happened to him. Malaysian newspapers were reporting Zeek had been killed in a gunfight with his own bodyguards. A Jakarta radio station claimed the Pirate King had committed suicide. Some Internet postings and even some tweets said Zeek had died while working on a bomb and that his body had been obliterated. Indonesian law enforcement was calling his death the result of a turf war, noting the robbery at the Red Skull Bar and the burning of the brothel on Mirang as proof, because Zeek was connected to both.

One thing was for certain: By the next day, the battleground on Pirate Island had been cleaned up. All the bodies had been taken away and the remaining camp structures burned and bulldozed. The Indonesian military had decided to raze the camp for its own protection.

"You guys did your jobs well," Conley told them now as he opened a bottle of champagne and poured each man a glass. "Everyone at Kilos Shipping is pleased, especially the top man. He's still broken up over what happened to our crews in Singapore—the fact that the cops never bothered to look into their murders shows you the grip Zeek had on this area."

Conley raised his glass in a toast. "But just as Zeek kept his word to get back at Kilos Shipping for killing his brother, you guys kept your word in getting Zeek before he could do any more damage. For that, we thank you."

They drank their champagne and then Nolan presented Conley with a large manila envelope. Inside was a written account of the action against Zeek's compound plus the photos Nolan had taken of the pirate's demolished headquarters.

"This is what Mister Kilos paid us for," Nolan told Conley. "We hope he's happy with the results."

Finally the meal was laid on. The team members were worn out and beat-up, but also in good spirits—even Twitch.

So the conversation flowed. More champagne was opened and more toasts were made, to one another, to Kilos Shipping, to Senegal. When the celebration reached its height, Conley put a briefcase on the table and opened it. Just like the first time, it was filled with fresh, crisp packets of cash. Fifty thousand dollars in all.

"With this, Mister Kilos sends you his undying gratitude," Conley told them. They toasted the shipping magnate yet again and drained their glasses. Then they opened the first bottle of scotch.

But no sooner had the sixty-year-old Macallan been poured when one of the Senegals came into the mess and whispered something in Nolan's ear. The team leader was needed up on the deck immediately.

With Batman in tow, Nolan went up to the main deck to find a huge U.S. Navy warship had pulled up alongside the DUS-7.

Batman moaned. "This can't be good."

It was past dusk, and the ship—the guided missile cruiser USS *Robert J. Messia*—had come out of the fog behind them, barely registering on the DUS-7's rinky-dink surface radar.

A radio message from the Navy ship told the freighter to kill its engines and prepare to be boarded. The reason? Antiterrorism patrol.

But Nolan sensed there was more to it than that.

A launch left the Navy ship and motored over to the DUS-7's access ladder. Five people came aboard: three armed sailors and two men in civilian clothes.

Nolan and Batman met them at the railing. The civilians flashed their ID cards. They were from the ONI, the Office of Naval Intelligence. Basically CIA agents of the high seas, the agents looked like spies out of central casting. Cheap haircuts. Off-the-rack clothes. Aviator sunglasses even though it was nighttime.

One was older and shorter. He was Agent Harry, and he did all the talking.

"Mind if we ask you folks a few questions?" he asked.

"Do we have a choice?" Nolan replied.

Both agents shook their heads no.

They led the pair down to the mess hall. The agents groaned when they spotted Conley.

"Why am I not surprised to see you here?" Agent Harry asked the Kilos rep.

"I'm a globetrotter," Conley replied, not thrilled to see the agents, either. "You guys got nothing better to do than harass private ship owners?"

The agents took out notebooks. "And you got a problem helping out your country?" Harry asked.

Nolan indicated the bottle of expensive scotch on the table. "We're a little busy here, guys," he said. "What's on your mind?"

"Like we said—just a few questions. . . ."

"Such as?"

"Such as, what was this ship's location two nights ago?"

Nolan started to answer, but Conley cut him off. "Two nights ago, I believe my crew was in, let's see, was it Hong Kong?"

The agents didn't bother to write this down. They noticed the briefcase of money, the expensive food and the newspaper clippings about Zeek's demise scattered on the mess table.

"Old man Kilos is sure feeding you guys good," Harry said. "Keeping you up-to-date as well."

He pointed up toward the main deck.

"And that copter up on the stern? Not the Ferrari with rotor blades, the other one. The work copter? Just a little bit beyond civilian specs, don't you think? Gun pod? Bomb mounts? In fact, it nearly matches the description of an aircraft that was . . . ah, 'borrowed' from a location in Saudi Arabia recently."

Conley just laughed. "Get to the point, will you?"

Agent Harry asked, "I suppose you guys were nowhere near the Pautang Channel two nights ago?"

Everyone shook their heads on cue, even the Senegals, watching all this from afar.

"No—why?" Conley asked. "Something happen we should know about?"

"Just a little dust-up with a local bad guy," Harry dead-panned. "A pirate type. Someone bombed and strafed his hideout—in a helicopter. This after fucking up a couple of his businesses the night before. If you take a closer look at those newspapers, you can read all about it."

Conley got up, indicating it was time for the agents to go.

"Well, thanks for the news flash, guys," he said. "But you're impeding commerce here."

The agents closed their notebooks; they knew this was fruitless. Nolan and Batman escorted them back up to the deck.

"You could do worse than be hooked up with Conley," Agent Harry told Nolan on the sly. "But that doesn't mean we're not aware of who you guys are."

The ONI agent looked him in the eye and said: "Message received, Major Nolan?"

Again, Nolan started to respond, but this time he stopped himself.

"Have a good ride back," he told the agents instead. "Don't fall in."

As the agents started down the access ladder, Harry turned and said one last thing.

"Just remember," he told them. "Out here—word travels fast. Good or bad. Accurate or not. It might look like a big ocean, but everyone knows everyone else's business. So, be aware—someone's always watching."

With that, the agents departed.

RETURNING TO THE mess hall, Nolan poured them all another drink, and Conley turned his attention back to the briefcase full of money.

"You guys earned this in spades," he said, pushing the briefcase toward Batman, the team's moneyman. "And it was a pleasure working with you again."

Conley shook hands with each member of the team. Then he asked one of the Senegals to inform his copter pilot that he was leaving. The chef had already packed his travel bag.

But then Conley's cell phone rang. He had a quick, hushed conversation. The team members could hear only bits and pieces of it, but Conley kept saying, "I don't believe it. Who knows about this?" He paused and said, "OK—hold on. I'll ask them."

He turned back to the team. "Well, the squid cops were right: Word *does* travel fast out here."

"Why? What's going on?" Batman asked.

"This is one of our contacts in Mumbai," Conley told them. "An Indian Navy warship has been hijacked by Somalis somewhere near the Maldives. It's a brand new high-tech vessel, highly automated and worth about a hundred million bucks. The pirates are threatening to kill the crew and blow it up if their demands aren't met."

"Tough situation," Batman said, pouring the team another scotch.

"It sure is," Conley said. "That's why the Indian government wants to know if you guys can get it back for them."

PART FOUR

The Taking of the *Vidynut*

14

AT FIRST, THE Indian Navy thought its new fast-attack boat had been lost at sea.

The futuristic warship, christened the INS *Vidynut,* had been on a shakedown cruise near the Maldives Islands as part of its final sea trials before commissioning. It was designed and wholly built by the Indian Navy itself, which had made extensive use of lightweight composite materials in its construction. That's why Navy officials feared the *Vidynut*'s hull had given way, and the 180-foot-long, 1,000-ton ship had gone down with all hands during stormy weather in the Kardiva Channel, northwest of Male, the capital of the Maldives.

But the *Vidynut* had not sunk, at least not yet. A different fate had befallen it.

The ship had made a scheduled port call to Male, where it took on fuel and stores for the 800-mile voyage back to its home port of Mumbai. Most of the twenty-man crew had been given shore leave in the pricey, internationally known vacation spot, with its officers invited to dine at the president's mansion. Just four sailors were left on the ship during its last night in port.

Sometime after midnight, two small boats came up alongside the *Vidynut,* and a dozen armed men climbed aboard. They brutally murdered the four sailors on watch, and as other crewmen returned from shore leave, they were seized and viciously beaten. Most were tied up below.

The invaders had collected all the weapons on board and forced those sailors assigned to bridge duty to prepare the ship to sail. Once the captain and his officers returned, they, too, were overpowered, beaten, and put below. Just like that, the highly advanced warship was in the hands of armed intruders.

Those intruders turned out to be Somali pirates.

AT LAST REPORT, the *Vidynut* was heading west. The pirates had met cohorts on other ships along the way, and it was now estimated there were at least thirty gunmen on board, almost twice the number as the hostages. The story of the hijacking had not yet reached the media; at the moment, the Indian government preferred the public to think their showpiece, one-of-a-kind fast-attack vessel—versions of which they hoped to sell to other countries—had sunk rather than been taken over by Somali gunmen. The assumption was that the pirates were intent on getting back to Africa and ransoming the vessel, the first warship taken by seaborne bandits in the modern era.

It was by far the most audacious act yet by the Somali pirates, carrying out a bold hijacking an entire ocean away from their home waters. The Indian government was deeply embarrassed and wanted nothing more than to get their warship back quickly, but quietly.

Those few who knew about the situation were guessing the Somalis' asking price for return of the *Vidynut* would be at least $100 million.

"BUT WHY US?" Nolan asked, taking a deep gulp of coffee. "I mean, other than the fact that we happen to be in the same time zone? We're just five guys. India has one of the largest navies in the world. Can't they do anything?"

In just a few minutes, everything had changed aboard the DUS-7. The booze and food had been taken away and the team was drinking cups of strong Senegalese coffee. Conley had remained on board. He was keeping a line open to his contact in Mumbai, and this person was trying to answer as many questions as possible about the hijacking. The mess table was now covered with maps of the Indian Ocean.

"Yes, India has a huge navy," Conley said in response to Nolan's question. "But this thing has turned into a political monster. Above all, the Indian Navy doesn't want to be in the position of having one of its warships fire on another. It's bad for business."

"How about their other armed forces, then?" Nolan asked him. "They must have their own version of Delta Force. Can't they attempt a rescue?"

"Their top special operations unit is called MARCOs," Conley replied. "Basically Indian Marine commandos. But most of them were deployed to the Kashmir a few weeks ago, and it would take at least two days for them to get their shit together to even attempt a rescue. By that time, the pirates will be almost halfway to Somalia and out of range of their helicopters. The MARCOs are not exactly a rapid-reaction force, I guess."

"Makes you wonder if the pirates knew that before they started this operation," Batman opined. "Maybe they've been doing their homework—the scary little bastards."

Nolan drained his coffee and poured another.

"OK, but don't the Indians have an aircraft carrier?" he asked Conley. "Get the commandos to the carrier, launch them from the carrier to the hijacked ship. Simple."

"Again, a good idea," Conley said. "Trouble is, their carrier, the *Viraat,* is currently in Japan on a goodwill cruise, which is what it does about ninety percent of the time."

"Not exactly taming the Mighty Main, are they?" Gunner said.

Conley held up his finger and listened for a moment to his contact on the other end of the phone. Then he said: "Well, I guess it wasn't like some of them weren't trying. We just heard a force of Indian Army soldiers training on the Maldives when all this happened jumped on their helicopter and took off after the ship, thinking they could get it back. Trouble was, they weren't trained for these things. They were just regular troops, with no experience in seaborne ops. They took off, got lost, ran out of gas and crashed into the ocean probably fifty miles short of their goal. All thirty-five of them drowned. They would have been national heroes if they had managed to pull it off. But . . . listen, rescue missions and such? We're actually beyond all that now."

"What do you mean?" Nolan asked.

Before Conley could answer, his laptop started beeping.

"Good, finally," he said. "I'll let my friend tell you directly."

He opened the laptop and went to the Skype Web page. He pushed a few keys, then set the laptop on the mess hall table in front of the team. They were soon looking at a live video image of Conley's contact in Mumbai.

His name was Nigel Scott. He was a middle-aged Englishman, balding but dapper. He was sitting in an office overlooking Mumbai Harbor, smoking a cigarette and drinking what they assumed was coffee. He seemed a bit ruffled, as if he hadn't slept in a while.

"Give them the 411, will you, Scotty?' Conley asked him, opening up the audio connection. "Explain the difference between a rescue mission and a recovery operation."

Scott lit one cigarette off another.

"I'll put it to you bluntly, gents," he began, his face filling the laptop's screen. "The way the Indians are looking at this thing now, that ship's crew is as good as dead. There are several reasons for this. First, the four guys the pirates killed in Male weren't just shot, they were butchered, horribly, with machetes. When the Indian government contacted some ex-FBI profilers about this, the profilers told the Indians these pirates are so vicious, there's no way they'll let the hostages survive. The pirates want to ransom the boat and are prepared to wait as long as it takes—days, weeks, months. But they don't want to deal with the hostages, caring for them, feeding them and so on. They're just an unwanted complication. The ship itself is the real prize.

"As proof of this, the Indians discovered that someone on the ship managed to surreptitiously open a communications link on the main control panel—so Mumbai can hear a lot of what the pirates are saying on the bridge. And what they've heard confirms that the profilers were right: The pirates were talking about how they're going to kill the crew whether a deal is made or not."

"Sounds like these guys have taken a page from Turk's

book," Batman observed. "Why bother with the human baggage?"

"Now, the pirates contacted the Indians early on by sat phone," Scott went on. "And the Indians, of course, told them they don't deal with terrorists, which is what everyone says at the beginning of these things. The pirates pretended to be pissed off, threatened to kill the hostages, but again, it makes no difference because the people eavesdropping on them know they're going to execute the crew no matter what—probably sooner rather than later—and there's really nothing the Indians can do about it."

"So what does all this mean?" Nolan asked him.

Scott let out a long stream of smoke. "Well, to put it bluntly, it means the Indians want to concentrate on just getting their ship back."

"Man, that's fucking cold," Batman said.

"Well, welcome to the real world," Scott said. "But they're just being practical. And they want to protect their investment."

"OK, so the crew is gone," Nolan said. "So what? All the Indians have to do is pay a ransom to get the ship back. I'm sure they've got an extra hundred million sitting around—it's not like they're spending it on slum dog urban renewal."

"Yes, but there's a point everyone is missing," Scott said. "You see, NATO and others who are trying to stop the Somali pirates are scared to death of setting a precedent of pirates hijacking military ships and then getting paid huge ransoms to give them back. That would be an escalation of this whole Somali pirate thing that no one even wants to contemplate."

"So?" Nolan asked.

"So, with the Indian crew dead," Scott said, "as soon as that ship reaches Somali waters, NATO is going to sink it. And they've already told the Indians this. Simple as that. When it happens, I'm not sure what kind of spin the Indians will put on it. Maybe they'll just stay with the 'hull broke and it sank' story. But once that ship reaches the pirates' home waters, it's as good as gone."

"So, again, what do they want us for?" Nolan asked him.

Scott almost seemed amused by the question. "Well, they want their ship back—*before* NATO sinks it. And that's where you guys come in. They know the handful of you just greased almost a hundred monkeys in Indonesia. More importantly, they also know you rescued the *Global Warrior* without firing more than a dozen shots. Word gets around about these things, and so they look at you as experts in both beating overwhelming odds and keeping the gunplay to a minimum when necessary. Bottom line: they'd like the ship back, intact, without using excessive force."

Nolan needed a few moments to let all that sink in. They all did.

"That must be some ship," Batman said, breaking the silence.

"It's a bit of a national treasure," Scott said, again somewhat amused. "Home-designed, home-built, and all that. Computers run everything. It practically sails itself. Can engage multiple threats. Packed to the gills with firepower. And eventually they want to sell them around the world. So it's very valuable to them. And they'd rather not see it sink. Or get too mussed up, if you chaps are able to get it back."

"Easy for them to say," Nolan told him.

Scott wearily lit another cigarette and blew out a cloud of smoke. "Well, again, they're being realists. They know it's much easier to recover a ship if there are no hostages on board to worry about. . . ."

He let his voice trail off.

Nolan said, "But still, it doesn't answer the question: Why are we their first option? How do they know we didn't just get lucky in Indonesia, or aboard the *Global Warrior*?"

Again, Scott was brutally frank. "Well, you're not *exactly* the first option. Blackwater—or whatever they are calling themselves these days—already turned the Indians down on this one."

"Blackwater turned them down?" Nolan said to Batman. "That tells you something."

Batman asked, "What? That they're getting fat and lazy?"

"No," Nolan replied. "It tells you they don't take on jobs they know they can't do."

He looked around the mess table. With the scotch and steaks gone, the team had returned to looking beat up and worn out. Crash was like a mummy, wrapped in a mile of bandages as a result of his fight in the water at Pirate Island, Twitch still had that 1,000-yard stare in his eyes. Gunner looked like he hadn't slept in a week. Even the usually animated Batman was dragging ass.

"Can we really do this?" Nolan asked them gravely. "So soon after the Zeek thing? I mean, personally, I can hardly think straight."

"That's probably the scotch," Batman told him. "But it might be a moot point anyway."

He turned back to Scott on the screen. "I hope they realize it will be a major effort just for us to catch up to this ship. We could chase them across the entire Indian Ocean and still not make it."

"The Indians are aware of that," Scott said. "But if you do, and you figure out a way to get the job done, it could be a big payday for you."

Nolan thought for a few more moments. He asked Gunner, "What's our supply situation—I know it's not good."

Gunner read from a list. "We're very low on 50-caliber ammo; we're very low on M4 ammo. The copter's gun pod is completely empty, and its gas tanks are almost dry. We're OK on ship fuel at the moment, both diesel and turbine. But we'll burn most of it out if we decide to really put the pedal to the metal and start chasing this ship."

Nolan turned to Conley. "Can Kilos help us out?"

Conley nodded. "You guys were there when we needed you," he said.

"I mean, do you have one of your 'special ships' nearby?" Nolan asked him. "The ones that carry your 'special cargoes?' "

Conley checked his BlackBerry. After a few moments he replied, "It so happens that answer is yes. And we also have a heavy-lift copter available for delivery. But remember, it will be potluck. We just never know what's available."

"So are you interested or not?" Scott asked them. "The Indians are going nuts waiting for an answer."

Again, Nolan looked at the team gathered around the table. The unknown was if they were in any shape to take on another mission so soon.

Finally Nolan asked Scott the big question. "If we do this, and do it right, how much are we talking about?"

Scott didn't hesitate. "If you get the ship back—and, of course, recover the bodies of the crew, if possible—the Indians will give you two million dollars cash. No questions asked."

Batman whistled. "That's some serious fucking coin."

Even Twitch was paying attention now. They all were.

Crash mumbled through his bandages. "Beats going back to the mall."

Nolan massaged his tired temples. The whole thing was so weird and unexpected, a big decision that had come at him right out of the blue.

"Let's take a vote," Batman suggested.

Nolan knew it was the only thing to do. He couldn't deny the team a chance to make such a huge sum of money, even if they didn't have any idea how they were going to pull it off.

Finally he said to them, "You've heard it all. You got the facts. So, for a two-million-dollar split, raise your hand if you want to try to save this boat."

Everyone around the table immediately raised his hand. Even the Senegals standing nearby voted yes.

Nolan rubbed his weary head again, but finally raised his own hand.

"It's unanimous, I guess," he said to Scott. "Tell them we'll take the gig."

There was some high-fiving and grunts of approval around the table, except from Twitch, who shifted uncomfortably in his seat.

"Now I know how an undertaker feels," he said.

15

THE KILOS HELICOPTER arrived just before midnight.

It was an S-64 heavy lifter, a civilian version of the U.S. Army's CH-54 Skycrane. Pimped for night flying and sea duty, it had been built especially for the shadowy shipping company to move large pieces of contraband between vessels at sea under cover of darkness. A huge crate shrink-wrapped in black plastic hung from its cargo sling.

On the bow of the DUS-7, flashlights in hand, Nolan and Batman guided it in. The ship was 100 miles west of the Maldives and just ninety miles behind the hijacked Indian warship. A combination of the small freighter's great speed and the captured warship's low cruising rate of fifteen knots had closed the gap between them significantly.

Conley had flown on to Mumbai, taking the Kilos chef with him, but not before talking to his contacts inside the U.S. intelligence community. His sources told him the U.S. was watching the commandeered ship via spy planes and drones. He also learned that, while the U.S. could understand India's desire to have a private company to retake the ship before it reached Somali waters, the Pentagon was less than happy to learn that private enterprise was a group of ex-Delta Force guys who had a major beef with Uncle Sam. When Conley told that to the team, they knew it was official: They were now foreign mercenaries.

The big copter approached the ship gingerly. It took some maneuvering, but finally the S-64 was able to rest its load on top of the freighter's hold hatch. Nolan and Batman hastily unhooked the wires and, with a wave to the pilot, sent the aircraft on its way.

They contemplated the delivered object for a moment. It was much bigger than they had expected; they only really needed two kinds of ammunition. But they had no idea what the shipping company had sent, except that the captain of the container ship had said he hoped they'd find it "helpful."

Batman patted the side of the tightly wrapped crate.

"I wonder what's underneath all that," he said. "A couple *tons* of ammo, maybe?"

"Let's find out," Nolan replied.

It took them five minutes just to cut the plastic wrap off the cargo. Then they had to pull apart the crate itself, which took another ten minutes. When it was open, both men were stunned at what they found inside.

"You've got to be *fucking* kidding me," was Batman's response.

It wasn't a crateful of ammunition or even more machine guns. It was an M102 field gun, an artillery piece that at one time was the mainstay of the U.S. Army's infantry forces. It was a powerful weapon, big and bold on two wheels, weighing almost two tons, and capable of firing high-explosive shells up to seven miles. But what the hell were they going to do with it?

"Jesus Christ," Nolan said. "We needed ammo for our pop guns, and they send us an atomic cannon."

AN HOUR LATER, the team was gathered back in the mess hall.

Outside, the sea was beginning to swell and the wind was growing stronger. The coffee cups were starting to rattle in the ship's galley.

Several things had happened in the past hour. They'd managed to tie down the artillery piece with chains, ropes and electrical wire to a spot near the front of the ship. The delivery also included forty-eight rounds of high-explosive artillery shells. The team stored them in an empty lifeboat locker nearby.

The Indian government had given them access to a classified Indian Navy Web site where they were able to get a GPS reading on the *Vidynut*. With their dual propulsion systems working overtime, they were now within seventy-five miles of the hijacked warship and still closing fast.

Most important, Team Whiskey had been able to download blueprints of the *Vidynut,* which they were studying now, even as the Indian Ocean outside was sounding a little more agitated.

The *Vidynut* was, indeed, futuristic in almost every respect. Aside from its virtually complete automation, the ship itself looked like it was going 100 knots even when it was standing still. It was all curves and smoothed-out right angles; anything that could be flared on the drawing board had been. It was also stuffed with a lot of sophisticated electronics as well as extensive communications and radar arrays. Though the only weapon visible above deck was a four-inch naval gun on the bow, belowdecks there were six automated missile launchers: four for short-range attacks and two for long-range engagements. The *Vidynut* could sink a ship four times its size from more than fifty miles away.

Its superstructure was three levels high, beginning about one-third of the way down from the bow, and took up the middle of the ship. The bridge was located at the top of the superstructure in a swept-back, all-glass bubble, its roof festooned with antennas and spinning radar dishes. The ship's stern was devoted to holding the long-range missiles themselves, plus an elaborate, almost stylish-looking exhaust stack that would have seemed at home on a Klingon warship. The deck was so cluttered there was no way the team could ever land their work copter on the hijacked missile boat.

Not that they would have to. After tossing around many ideas for an hour or so, the team had come up with a simple— make that *very* simple—plan to recover the ship and collect their two million dollars. And it was the blueprints that gave them the idea.

Assuming they were able to catch up to the *Vidynut*, their first objective would be to get as close to the warship as possible without arousing the pirates' suspicion. Because the DUS-7 was such an old ship, they were hoping the hijackers would not suspect them of being anything other than a rust-bucket freighter moving through the Indian Ocean.

Once they were within range of the *Vidynut*, though, they would fire one shell from the M102 artillery piece, hoping for a hit on the ship's propellers, which—due to the craft's ultra-modern, shallow-hull design—were just a couple of feet below the water line. With its props disabled, the ship would be dead in the water.

And that was it. If the ship had no means of propulsion, it couldn't get to Africa. If it couldn't get to Africa, NATO couldn't sink it.

The *Dustboat* would just sit a safe distance away, snipe at the pirates if they showed their faces, but basically wait them out. Conley had told them the Indian ship had only about a three-day supply of food and water. Soon the pirates would get hungry, thirsty and hot. Eventually, they'd crack.

The plan fit perfectly with the team's own supply situation. While they were extremely low on M4 and 50-caliber ammunition, they had plenty of supplies and now the artillery piece. It was an incredibly simple way to make a cool two million.

But it was not to be. Because just moments after putting the finishing touches on the idea, just as they heard the wind outside getting louder and felt the ship's rocking get a little rougher, one of the Senegals came down from the bridge holding the latest weather report. A huge complication had just appeared on the horizon.

A storm was blowing up from the Cape of Good Hope, aiming right for the middle of the Indian Ocean. With heavy rains, high winds and particularly high seas, the gale was already going full force, and the *Vidynut* and the DUS-7 were heading right for it.

But that was not the problem. The problem was, the DUS-7 was still some seventy-five miles behind the *Vidynut*, meaning they would be hit by the full force of the typhoon's 100-knot winds, which would probably blow it farther from the hijacked ship than they were now. By the time they recovered, the *Vidynut* would be that much closer to Somali territorial waters—and they'd be so far behind, it would be almost impossible for them to make up the lost time and distance.

Batman did the calculations. When he realized their gloomy conclusion, he threw the weather report across the mess hall.

"The way this thing is blowing in," he said angrily, "there's no way we're going to catch that freaking ship."

16

IT WAS DARK. It was hot. It smelled of oil, blood and urine. It was crowded and grown men were crying. The ones who were still alive, that is.

Vasu Vandar was in hell. He just hadn't died yet.

Vandar was captain of the INS *Vidynut*. What had started out as a night of high honor, dining at the home of the president of the Maldives, had turned into a nightmare when Vandar returned to his ship to find it had been taken over by the Somali pirates and the intruders had brutally killed four of his men. Then he had to endure the humiliation of getting under way at the point of an AK-47.

Now he and most of his crew were stuffed inside the stern bilge station, a tiny compartment located at the bottom of the warship, just waiting to die. The compartment, filled with heating pipes, fuel lines and pumps for the ship's toilets, measured just ten feet by six feet. This is where the pirates had put them—fourteen men in all, plus the bodies of those they'd killed.

There was no light in here, no food or water. The sailors were barely able to breathe. Vandar had told his men not to talk, but he could hear many of them weeping. Others were hallucinating, going mad, crying out. Vandar couldn't blame them for that. He was going mad as well.

He knew by now that there was no way out of this. He also knew ransoming the crew was not part of the pirates' agenda. They wanted the ship. He and his men were just complications.

Vandar also realized no help was coming. The Indian Navy's only aircraft carrier was way up in Tokyo Bay, throwing flowers at the Japanese. The *Vidynut* was far beyond the reach of any of India's helicopters. He also knew it was not likely the Indian government would accept another country's direct help in saving them.

"We have had a navy for 5,000 years," he thought glumly. "And now, when we need them, they are nowhere to be found."

He tried to will himself to accept the cold fact that the end was near for him and his men; it was a hard thing to do. But whether they were to be shot or stabbed or just simply left in here to suffocate, Vandar couldn't imagine them lasting much longer. The only question was why the pirates were waiting so long?

He could now hear some of the men praying, their way of spending their last moments alive. Vandar was dealing with his last breaths in a different way. When he was captured, though the pirates had searched him, they'd missed a pen he always kept his pocket. It had a tiny light attached to it to help him write in the dark when the ship was training under black-out conditions.

He was using this bare light now, and this pen, to write aimlessly on the compartment walls.

THE STORM HIT just after 2 A.M.

The sound of the water crashing against the hull rose in volume, and soon they could feel the *Vidynut* being tossed around like a toy. This only added to the misery of the sailors jammed into the small, hot space. Some began wailing again. Vandar ordered them to quiet down, to save air. In his heart, though, he was praying the hull's composites *would* fail, and that the ship would break up in the tempest. A death by drowning would be preferable to suffocation in an airless space, inches away from a dead man.

He was startled, then, when he heard furious pounding at the door of the compartment. It opened, and he could see three of the pirates standing in the dull light of the passageway.

They began shouting: "Captain! Captain! Who is the captain?"

Vandar froze for a moment. Why did they want him? Did this mean the killing was going to begin?

The pirates cocked their guns and appeared ready to fire into the crowded compartment.

"Who is the captain!" one yelled, aiming his weapon at those men clustered near the door. Finally Vandar called out: "I am."

Two of the armed men crawled into the space and dragged him out. Then they shut the door and locked it once again, sealing the rest of the crewmembers inside.

The pirates dragged Vandar up to the main deck; the boat was swaying so much by now that they kept losing their grip on him. Vandar had gone through some big storms in his twenty-year career with the Indian Navy. Without even seeing it, he could tell this was one of the worst.

They reached the main deck and the gunmen forced him up onto the bridge. Here, he found two of his sailors who hadn't been taken below. One was at the helm—a young seaman who looked like he was about to die from fright. He had a bleeding, untended wound on his arm. The other, without much more experience, was watching over the ship's vital systems. He, too, looked extremely frightened. He was bruised and bleeding, as if he'd been pistol-whipped.

Outside, the storm was raging as if the vengeance of Vishnu had fallen upon them. The rain and wind were horrific and the waves looked as high as mountains. There were more than a dozen pirates on the bridge and they were all holding onto something, trying to stay upright as the ship was thrown all over the sea. One pirate, though, was away from the others; he was huddled in the far corner of the bridge, watching over something he'd apparently plugged into an electrical outlet.

One of the pirates walked up to Vandar, coming nose to nose with him, even though the bridge was rocking mightily. This pirate was obviously the gang's leader. He had an enormous scar running across his neck, as if he'd had his throat slit at one point. He had few teeth and a lazy eye, and he smelled awful.

He also had a huge machete in one hand, and Vandar was terrified that this man was going to hack him to death right here.

Instead, he addressed Vandar in rough, broken English.

"Are we sinking?" he asked, his voice betraying a bit of urgency.

Vandar was so thrown by the question, he asked him to repeat it.

"Are we sinking!" the man roared at him, raising the machete.

Vandar did a quick scan of the ship's critical systems. He saw no red blinking lights, and no alarms were ringing. This meant, in theory at least, they weren't in danger of going down. Not yet, anyway.

But Vandar wasn't going to tell the pirate that. "You must release my crew so we can sail this ship properly. If not, we *will* sink."

For this, he received the butt of the machete across his face. The blow sent him sprawling across the bridge.

"We know this is robot boat!" the gang leader screamed at him. "It goes by itself. But in this? Can it go by itself *in this*?"

"I don't know," Vandar told him truthfully, from the floor. The *Vidynut* had a small crew precisely because of its extensive automation, but it hadn't yet passed its sea trials and had never gone through anything like the storm blowing outside.

"You are the captain!" the pirate screamed at him, picking him up off the deck. "Either you tell me truth or we kill the lot of you right now."

Vandar collected himself and tried to appear calm, but it was impossible.

"What do you want to know exactly?" he asked the gunman.

"Are we sinking?" the pirate leader asked him again.

Vandar replied, "No—not yet."

"Will we sink?"

"I don't know," he answered.

"How will we know if we are sinking?"

Vandar indicated the main panel of status monitors.

"If this lights up and starts making noise," he told the pirate leader, "then it will mean we are sinking."

The gang leader hit him again with the machete handle—this time in the stomach. Then two other pirates picked him up and prepared to drag him back to the bottom of the boat.

As this was happening, the pirate who had been sitting in the far corner of the bridge popped out of his seat.

"It is charged!" he exclaimed.

He walked over to the pirate leader and, in full view of Vandar, revealed what he'd been watching over. It was a battery for a video camera and it had been recharging, slowly as it turned out.

But now the battery was full—and this was making the pirates very happy. One handed the pirate leader a video camera.

The pirate leader turned back to Vandar and inserted the battery into the video camera like someone would put an ammo clip into a gun.

"Soon," he hissed at Vandar, "our show will begin."

Vandar was dragged back to the bottom deck and thrown back into the bilge station. He squeezed himself in, trying his best to stay away from where the dead bodies lay. Many of his men were wailing openly now, and he just didn't have the heart to tell them to stop.

Instead, he just returned to his corner and resumed writing his nonsense on the wall.

He'd been out of Hell for less than five minutes.

THE *VIDYNUT* SLOWLY sailed its way out of the storm by morning, riding out the last of the wind and surviving the final gigantic waves.

The sky cleared, and the last stars of the night came into view. Off on the eastern horizon, the first rays of dawn were poking through the remaining wisps of the storm clouds.

The pirates on the bridge all breathed a sigh of relief. The worst had passed. They could now proceed with their plan.

The pirates had planned the taking of the *Vidynut* for months. They'd monitored the Indian Navy's public Web site, where the admirals bragged about their new warship and its sea trials and how the revolutionary vessel would be available for foreign sales someday.

This particular gang of pirates—the Swoomi Clan—had hijacked cargo ships off Africa before and had extracted million-dollar ransoms in return of vessels and crews. It sounded like a lot of money, but after dividing it up among the pirate hierarchy, their clan leaders, the Muslim radicals who provided them with the weapons and fuel, and the Eastern European cartels that handled the negotiations, there wasn't a lot left to go around.

That's when they'd hit on the idea of taking the *Vidynut,* knowing that for the same amount of work, and just a little more travel, they could hold the warship for tens of millions of dollars—with no middlemen looking for a cut.

They had prepared very carefully for the takeover, attending to every detail, right down to how they would get rid of the crew. As a way of making their reputation, part of their plan was to videotape the crew's execution and then release the tape to the jihadist media, where they knew it would get widespread airplay and garner their gang a lot of respect.

What they hadn't anticipated was their video camera's battery pack running out of power. Originally, they were going to execute the crew the night they took over the ship. But with no power for the video, the crew's death sentence had to be postponed.

But now, with the storm subsiding and the camera's battery pack charged again, it was time to move to this next step.

"Start bringing them up," the gang leader told his men as soon as he detected those first rays of sunlight peeking over the horizon. "We'll do them five at a time."

His men responded by pulling back the safeties on their AK-47s.

But the top pirate held up his hand.

"But we won't waste bullets," he said. He pulled his razor-sharp machete from his belt. "We'll cut them to death instead."

THE SLOWLY RISING sun continued to burn its way through what remained of the storm clouds, making the new day hot and humid. A thick haze enveloped the surface of the water.

The pirates went to the bottom of the boat and opened the bilge compartment. They dragged out five of the Indian crewmen and tied their hands behind their backs with duct tape. Forced up to the main deck, the terrified sailors found more pirates waiting for them. All were chewing qat and brandishing machetes.

The Indian sailors were pushed to the mid deck next to the superstructure and made to kneel. Their heads were put on the deck railing and held down by the pirates' feet. There was much chatter among the hijackers as the qat began to take effect. Some of the pirates were sharpening their knives; others were pushing and squabbling with each other as to who would take the first bloody swing.

Finally, the pirates decided that the executioners would be selected based on seniority. The first victim, the sailor who was unlucky enough to be at the end of the group of five, was the ship's cook. He was wailing uncontrollably; he knew what was coming.

Two pirates readjusted his head on the railing, ripping his shirt back so his executioner would have a better view of his neck. The executioner laid his machete on the man's nape and cut it slightly, giving him a mark to aim for.

The executioner then let out a growl, raised the razor-sharp knife over his head, and started to bring it down—when the pirate commander screamed from the bridge.

He stopped in mid-swing.

"The camera is in the wrong position!" the leader yelled down to them. "The sunlight is going directly into the lens. We won't be able to see a thing."

The pirates moved the small 8mm camera around to a handful of locations, arguing about the best place to film the beheadings. Meanwhile, the five Indian sailors were still being held in place, terrified by what was going on around them.

Finally, all was ready again. The first victim was once again held down. The video camera began rolling. The victim began wailing again. The executioner raised his machete once again—and once again began to swing. But at that moment, the boat was hit by a rogue wave, a leftover from the storm. It was enough to knock the executioner off-balance. The machete came down—but it missed the man's neck, slicing into his shoulder instead.

The victim let out a horrifying scream as his blood started dripping onto the deck. The other pirates laughed and started taunting the executioner for his bad aim. The assassin spit out

his wad of used qat; it disappeared into the low haze still surrounding the ship. He looked up at his commander, watching
it all from the bridge of the ship, and grunted once more in
determination.

He raised the machete a third time and now swung it with
anger. But again, halfway down, the ship was suddenly
slammed by something much stronger than a rogue wave. This
time the entire vessel shook from stem to stern, so much that it
knocked all the pirates off their feet, the executioner included.

The ship had hit something.

Or more accurately, something had hit the ship.

There was a monstrous screeching noise at the same time
as the blow; the unmistakable sound of metal hitting metal.

All this occurred simultaneously, and it took a few moments for the pirates to realize what had happened: An old,
rusty freighter had come out of nowhere and rammed the Indian warship so violently it had opened up a gaping hole on
the aft starboard side.

Before the pirates could react, this ship hit the *Vidynut*
again, this time much harder, further opening the gash it had
made. This collision was so severe, the *Vidynut* went over at
least thirty degrees, almost capsizing.

Several pirates were thrown into the water. Automated
warning signals started going off all over the warship as it
painfully righted itself. In the confusion, the five Indian sailors marked for execution were able to scramble away.

All in a matter of seconds.

The dumbfounded pirates thought this old freighter had
simply struck the warship by accident. But when the freighter
plowed into the *Vidynut* a third time, this collision more
violent than the first two, they knew it was no accident. This
third blow hit them with such force, the snout of the freighter
was now stuck in the gash it had created on the side of the
warship.

The pirates panicked. None of this was making sense.
That's when they saw four people—an enormous white man
and three Africans—aiming a large gun from the mid deck of

the freighter back toward the rear of the *Vidynut*. These men fired this gun as if they were trying to hit the *Vidynut*'s propellers, but the angle was all wrong and the still-choppy seas caused the big gun to widely miss its mark. Its shell instead struck the ship's stylish exhaust housing, blowing it to pieces.

Those few pirates who weren't in complete shock tried firing at the men on the freighter. They had anticipated some kind of a rescue attempt might be made on the Indian ship, but had been expecting helicopters or mighty naval ships from the United States or somewhere. It just did not compute that an old rusty ship like this would carry such a powerful gun.

The men on the freighter ignored the pirates' gunfire and loaded the gun again. They aimed it crudely, once more using nothing but raw muscle-power to move it farther down the deck, and fired again. But as before, the rolling seas and the bad angle prevented an accurate shot on the propellers. Their second shell took off the *Vidynut*'s entire main deck stern section with a massive explosion.

And seconds later, a fire broke out on the next deck below.

NOLAN WAS WATCHING all this while dangling from the top of the DUS-7's forward starboard cargo mast.

"I knew aiming that damn thing would be a problem," he thought, swinging around to get a better view of Gunner and three of the Senegals as they struggled to move the two-ton artillery piece even farther down the deck. "It will be impossible to hit the propellers now."

He looked over at Crash, who was hanging from the next cargo mast over.

"Stay cool!" he yelled over to him. "Wait for my signal."

"You got it!" Crash yelled back.

Just how they made it here, and how they found the *Vidynut* in the middle of the vast ocean, in the middle of the massive storm, with not even the basic search coordinates, was almost inexplicable. Nolan was hardly a religious man, or a superstitious one. But after what had happened in the past few hours, he was considering becoming a little bit of both.

They had spent a good part of the night caught in the middle of the typhoon. Not just high seas, not just waves crashing against the freighter's battered hull: The decks were lit up by so many lightning flashes, the interior of the ship was bright as daytime. The winds had howled like a chorus of banshees. More times than anyone could count, the ship almost went over. They lost their GPS system and the radio. When both of the ship's water pumps burnt out from overuse, the crew thought they'd met their end. Even the Senegals, with thousands of years of seafaring excellence in their DNA, grew nervous.

At the height of the gale, Crash and Gunner, remembering their experience on the ground in Indonesia, fled to the ship's galley and hastily made good-luck onion bags for every member of the crew. They insisted everyone wear them around their necks, and no one turned them down. They also tacked onion bags all over the engine room, and spread sugar all over the bridge.

At first, none of the mumbo jumbo appeared to do any good. The ship was lifted out of the water several times by waves that seemed impossibly high. The lightning grew even fiercer and more frequent. The wind took off their communications mast and even lifted their anchor chain, blowing it right off the deck.

Then, at one point, all four of the cargo masts began glowing with the most fantastic light—as if the lightning that had hit them had also inhabited them. It was frightening and fascinating.

St. Elmo's Fire . . .

That's what the Senegals began shouting. Nolan had never seen anything like it. None of them had. At one point, it was so bright it seemed as if the entire ship was about to burst into flames.

But then a gigantic wave hit the *Dustboat* head on and washed right over them. And when they emerged from the other side of the deluge, the mysterious light was gone. They soldiered on from that point, holding on tight, their onion bags swinging around their necks, and gradually the storm went away.

And when the sun came up, not knowing where they were, or even what direction they were going, what did they see through the haze, not a mile away?

The *Vidynut*. Still heading west.

Nolan had never experienced anything like it.

But miracle, good luck, or whatever, it meant their "simple" plan to recover the Indian warship had also gone up in smoke. Because by using their long-range night-vision scopes, they could see the executions of the Indian sailors were about to take place on the deck of the warship. They could actually see the machetes glistening in the early-morning sun.

To the team's credit, there was no discussion about it. No thoughts of payment versus humanity. On Nolan's orders, the Senegals went to full double power, and in the only way they could think of disrupting what was sure to be a bloody slaughter, they T-boned the *Vidynut* going a full forty-two knots, knocking it back nearly twenty feet.

This collision, and the second, even more violent one, probably would have been enough. It was not part of any plan to get stuck in the side of the warship. But that's what happened when they hit the *Vidynut* the third time, melding them together like a pair of unlikely Siamese twins. Try as they might, the Senegals on the bridge just could not get the two ships to separate.

This forced Gunner to move the big gun quickly to the stern, to try to get a shot at the *Vidynut*'s propellers, the one remaining component from their original plan that might work. But again, the firing angle was all wrong—and as a result, they'd taken out the ship's exhaust stack and a large portion of the stern main deck. And they'd also started a fire. This on a ship they were supposed to be recovering intact.

But they couldn't think about that now. The real question was, what to do next?

The rules had changed. The warship's crew was still alive, or at least some of them were. Whiskey had to save them. But *how* could they get over to the warship to do this? There was no way they could use ladders or gangplanks. And it was too long of a jump from where the *Dustboat* had lodged itself in the *Vidynut*. Plus, trying to use the unarmed helicopter, either to drop them on the ship or to actually land on it somewhere, would be too dangerous. This left only one way to board it: swinging over by a rope.

That's why Nolan was up on the cargo mast.

One way the team had tried to stay in shape during their dash from Yemen to Indonesia was shimmying up and down the DUS-7's cargo masts, a throwback to their old Delta obstacle-course days. So hanging from the top of the forty-foot-tall mast was not foreign to them. But swinging from one ship to another? That would be different.

Nolan was dressed in his black camouflage suit and had his M4 slung over his shoulder. He was carrying a bag of hand grenades: some flash, some frags. He also had a large knife given to him by the Senegals.

Crash was similarly dressed and equipped, though he still had a bandage around his head. Nolan yelled over to him: "Are you ready?"

Crash yelled back: "Absolutely!"

Their ropes were attached to the tops of portside cargo masts. They had knots on the ends for them to hold on to. They would have to jump off the starboard mast, swing over the deck of DUS-7, past the portside mast, back up into the air, then let go and land on the Indian warship. Even during the most extensive Delta Force training, Nolan had never done anything like this.

He signaled the Senegals below. On his call, they raked the *Vidynut*'s decks with fire from the cannonade machine. It used the last of their valuable ammunition, but caused lots of noise and smoke, and the ricocheting rounds kept the already-panicking pirates off balance.

The fusillade lasted just six seconds. When it ended, that was Nolan's cue.

He squeezed his onion bag, put the knife between his teeth and thought: "Here goes nothing."

Then he jumped off the mast.

He was airborne for only a few seconds and then he was down again. He'd swung over to the Indian warship perfectly, landing on the deserted stern, barely scraping his knees in the process. He couldn't have done it better.

Crash was a different story. He, too, had swung over, but he'd done so with too much force, too much velocity, too much enthusiasm. And he held onto his rope for too long. As soon as Nolan landed, he looked up to see Crash sailing through the air—and right over the ship, landing with a splash on the other side.

"Damn," Nolan cursed. "We should have worked on that a little more."

BATMAN AND TWITCH were more successful getting aboard the hijacked ship.

They'd both scrambled up to masts as soon as Nolan and Crash had vacated them, grabbing their ropes as they came back. With no hesitation, they swung over to the *Vidynut*, too. Batman, in particular, lived up to his nickname, flying through the air like an acrobat, landing on two feet like a pro. Twitch was right behind him, also arriving gracefully despite his artificial leg. Like two superheroes, they had their weapons up and ready—which was good, because a half dozen pirates were huddled under the superstructure's overhang not fifty feet away from their landing spot near the bow. They all had their heads down or were looking the other way, but they were armed to the teeth.

It was up to Batman and Twitch to disable the *Vidynut*'s deck gun; that was their role in the new plan. While they had no idea whether the pirates knew how to operate the highly automated bow-mounted gun, the team couldn't take the chance that it would be used against the DUS-7. Luckily they landed within an arm's length of the weapon and were quickly all over it, looking for ways to render it inoperative without destroying it.

But suddenly the air around them was full of bullets. Batman and Twitch hit the deck to discover the clutch of pirates huddled below the superstructure had finally spotted them and were now firing at them.

"How many of these guys are on this fucking boat again?"

Twitch cried as he and Batman competed for the little cover the deck gun afforded them.

"I think we're going to find out," Batman yelled back.

He looked over his shoulder and all he could see was the bow of the ship and the foggy water beyond. Unless they wanted to get wet and leave the deck gun to the pirates, they were trapped.

They tried to attract the attention of Gunner and the Senegals on the DUS-7, which was riding only a few feet away, still stuck into the side of the warship. But their colleagues were down around the freighter's stern, providing cover for the five Indian sailors who'd just escaped execution. The same men who, just seconds before, were lined up to be beheaded were now huddled at the rear of the warship, hiding from the pirates.

This was distracting them, so Batman and Twitch had no choice but to use what little ammunition they had to fire back at the group of pirates, causing the pirates to intensify their return fire.

"What are we going to do?" Twitch yelled to Batman. "I had more ammo back in Tora Bora than I have now."

"Keep firing," Batman replied. "I'll think of something."

But no sooner were the words out of his mouth when Twitch ran out of ammunition.

"OK, this is serious now," he yelled over to Batman, who was running very low on ammo himself. Meanwhile, the pirates firing at them seemed to have an endless supply of bullets.

Again, Batman knew if they jumped overboard, there was no guarantee they'd be able to get back up again. Plus, there would be nothing stopping the pirates from shooting at them while they were floundering in the water.

So they had to disable the gun somehow and then seek cover. Batman took out a pair of wire cutters and began desperately looking around for a power cable or a hatchway that led to a power cable, something he could cut to immobilize the deck gun with minimum fuss.

But the weapon was self-contained. There were no wires or cables or anything running in or out of it. The gun and its covering were flush with each other and to the deck itself. Even the gun's swivel mechanisms were flush with the deck. Batman couldn't find a space where he could fit a credit card, never mind a pair of wire cutters.

"This isn't going to work," he yelled over the gunfire to Twitch. "Can you check your end?"

Twitch knew what he meant. As Batman laid down a barrage of gunfire, Twitch popped up and looked into the weapon's forward-pointing barrel. It was clear for as far down as he could see.

"It's not capped, if that's what you mean," he reported back to Batman.

Batman contemplated the deck gun for a moment. Like everything else on the ship, it was swept back, as if it was being permanently buffeted by a stiff breeze. And it also looked expensive. But he couldn't worry about that now.

He slid his M4 over to Twitch, then took out a frag grenade and pulled the pin. While Twitch fired another barrage toward the pirates, Batman popped the grenade's safety, jumped up, and dropped the grenade down the gun's barrel. He and Twitch hit the deck.

The grenade blew up a moment later. The sound was more muffled than Batman would have thought, and for a moment, as he lay there with his hands over his head, he thought that maybe he'd disabled the weapon without causing too much damage.

But then there was a secondary explosion—something inside the gun had lit off, possibly a shell. This time the explosion rocked the entire ship, covering him, Twitch, and even the pirates with a rain of burning shrapnel. When Batman dared to look up again, all that was left of the gun was a smoking hole in the ship's deck.

"Damn," Batman said. "Another million down the drain."

The explosion finally got Gunner's attention. He'd just reloaded the M102 gun when he saw Batman and Twitch frantically waving at him. They pointed to the band of pirates that was slowly advancing toward them from under the superstructure.

Gunner held up his hands, as if to ask, *What should I do?*

"Shoot them!" Batman screamed over the noise of the waves and the gunfire.

Gunner didn't hesitate. With his tremendous strength, he turned the small artillery piece around, did a rough aim at the unsuspecting gang of pirates, and fired. The shell exploded just thirty feet in front of Batman and Twitch, again bringing a shower of hot metal cinders down on them.

But when the smoke cleared, the pirates were gone, vaporized by the powerful blast. Unfortunately, a large portion of the ship's lower superstructure was gone as well.

"Put that on our tab too," Twitch said dryly.

They were safe for the moment and their immediate task was complete. The naval gun wouldn't be a threat to the DUS-7. But the ship was still full of armed pirates, and Batman and Twitch were out of ammunition.

They scrambled over to the forward anchor housing and hid behind its tall, flared enclosure. From here they could see the results of the team's actions so far: a gaping hole in the side of the warship's hull, another gaping hole on its main deck with a small fire burning within, and a third smoking hole where the naval gun used to be. A quarter of the superstructure was gone, another part of it smoldering. The rear exhaust housing was gone and the back of the ship was in flames.

All this in a span of about two minutes.

"God damn," Batman said. "By the time this is over, we'll owe *them* money."

THERE WAS JUST no way Nolan could go look for Crash.

Though he had landed cleanly, the team CO's arrival had not gone unnoticed. There were pirates all over the deck, confused and in small groups hiding from the chaos of the past two minutes. But they weren't so bewildered that they'd held back shooting at Nolan, who looked like he'd just fallen from the stars and into their midst. No sooner had he reached the ship and gotten to his feet when he was dodging a blizzard of bullets. He immediately went back to hugging the deck.

In the new, hastily conceived plan, he and Crash would

have set about finding the rest of the Indian crew—if they were still alive, that is. But the main deck was now a free-fire zone, and Nolan could hardly move without inviting a hail of gunfire. It would have been suicide for him to crawl to the port side and look over the edge for Crash. A ladderway about ten feet away from him led belowdecks, where the rest of the Indian crew might be. If he could make it there, he might be able to press on with his mission. But at the moment, even that seemed impossible.

But then a shell from the DUS-7's field gun went over his head and smashed into the rear starboard side of the superstructure wall. Nolan thought it might have been another errant shot by Gunner, but at least it killed several of the pirates who'd been firing at him, at the same time knocking a trio of lifeboats sky high and into the water.

Nolan was up and running even before the dust had settled, moving like a madman. He dove into the ladderway and went down headfirst, a stream of gunfire following him so closely one bullet took off the heel of his boot. He landed on the second deck in a heap, bruised and battered but in one piece.

"Sorry, Crash," he whispered.

He got to his feet and started running down the second-deck passageway, his M4 up and ready even though he had fewer than a dozen rounds in his magazine. The smoke from the many fires they'd started had mixed with steam from broken pipes down here, and the combination made navigating the passageway difficult. Even worse, water was pouring out of the bulkheads and down ladderways, and he could hear electric wires shorting out. Some kind of red hydraulic fluid was also leaking out of the ceilings. It looked like blood mixing with the water beneath his feet.

He came upon two pirates who'd been wounded by shrapnel and had managed to crawl into a stairwell before dying. Nolan made certain they were dead, then took their AK-47s and moved on.

He checked every cabin, every compartment, every passageway he came to, looking for more crewmembers, but finding none. His gut was telling him they were all probably in one small place, and according to the blueprints, the smallest compartments on the *Vidynut* were at the bottom of the ship.

He headed deeper into the ship, going down two more ladderways. The lower he went, the more breathing became a problem. He was sure a lot of plastic was used to build the futuristic warship, and now it was burning unabated, filling the ship with toxic smoke. Soon he couldn't see his hands in front of him.

He somehow found a ladder that led to the very bottom of the ship and climbed down into this passageway. Moving as fast as he could, he felt as if he was seeing everything through a fish-eye lens. Breathing heavily, coughing in the smoke, the lights blinking on and off. The noise coming from above was deafening as the artillery piece roared away—once, twice, a third time. Gunner, shooting at God knew what.

"There'll be nothing left," Nolan said to himself.

Then, amid this symphony of sounds, he heard something different: people crying. He moved toward the noise and found himself at the end of the passageway. He stopped for a moment to wonder what would happen now if one of Gunner's shells hit below the waterline and this expensive piece of shit just collapsed in on itself. Would he even have a chance to get out?

The wailing was coming from the last hatch in the ship. Nolan gave its wheel lock a spin and the door opened with a whoosh. He stepped back and a mass of bodies fell out.

At first Nolan was sure they were corpses—and some of them were. But some started gasping for breath as soon as they hit the deck, each gulp bringing little more than a lung full of smoke. Nolan had found his sailors. He was amazed so many were still alive.

He helped up those who could get to their feet, leaning them against the bulkhead and shaking some back to reality. There were ten in all, but some were babbling incoherently. Others were crying. Still others were throwing up. Nolan tried calming them down, telling them they were OK, that he was going to get them out. But most seemed oblivious to what he was saying.

The ship's commander finally found his way out of the putrid compartment. His face was streaked with dirt and tears. He wrapped Nolan in a massive bear hug, weeping uncontrollably and overjoyed that help had come.

But then he looked around and asked: "Where is the rest of your rescue force?"

Nolan just looked him in the eyes and said: "I'm it . . ."

Captain Vandar was stumped. "You are U.S. Special Forces? Army? Navy SEALs?"

"I'm a private contractor," Nolan replied quickly.

Vandar's enthusiasm waned for a moment when he realized his rescue party was just one man, in a dirty combat suit, carrying three battered rifles and sporting an eye patch.

"Let's get your guys up to the deck," Nolan told him, handing him one of the AK-47s. "If we're lucky, they can get over to my ship."

Vandar hugged Nolan again. "We owe you a huge debt of gratitude," he said. "We will not forget this act of kindness and bravery in saving us and our ship."

"We'll see about that," Nolan said under his breath.

Nolan lined up the sailors. The ones in better shape he put at the front, the others were at the back. He urged each man to take hold of the shirt of the man in front of him, this way they would stay together. He was hoping all of them had the strength to reach the top deck, but at the moment, he wasn't sure any of them would make it.

Still, they had to get moving. The ship was rocking back and forth mightily now.

"Are you ready?" Nolan asked Vandar.

The ship's captain also took stock of his men—wounded, sick and disoriented. He turned back to Nolan and said, "OK, you lead. We'll follow."

BACK UP ON the deck of the DUS-7, Gunner was moving around like a madman.

The M102 field gun was normally assigned a five-man crew. While that was mostly for set up and break down, just loading the gun was an intensive five-step process: open the breech, let the spent shell fall out, load in the new shell, close the breech, pull the activation cord and fire the round. This didn't take into account aiming the two-ton weapon and re-aiming it after the recoil from the previous shot inevitably knocked it off its mark.

Gunner's first two shots back when all this began were pure misses. Impossible angles, rolling seas, bad aiming. He never even came close to hitting the *Vidynut*'s propellers, which was why both ships were still tooling along, still making fifteen knots, still awkwardly joined at the hip. His next few shots were attempts to save the lives of the five freed Indian sailors, and Batman and Twitch, caught alone on the bow of the warship. Another shot unintentionally allowed Nolan to get belowdecks to do his thing.

From there it had just devolved into battle between the pirates firing at him with AK-47s and him firing back with un-guided, high-explosive shells better suited for taking out tanks and pillboxes. He screamed "Damn!" every time he saw another piece of the expensive *Vidynut* disappear in a fiery flash. The gun was so powerful, whenever a shell hit the ship, it nearly pushed it over on its side. And every time he actually hit any pirates, the destruction was so complete he would blow up their weapons, too.

He imagined he could see a ghostly calculator, floating in space next to him, adding up the toll for the damage he was causing. A hundred thousand dollars for this, two hundred thousand for that, a million for that other thing.

Still, after five minutes of this, the situation remained chaotic. Batman and Twitch were still trapped up on the front of the *Vidynut,* with no ammunition for their M4s. Those Indian sailors who'd almost been executed were still stuck at the back of the warship with no weapons at all; joining them were their two colleagues who'd somehow managed to escape from the bridge. The pirates were still firing at both groups and at the DUS-7 from positions up near the bridge and behind the clutter that made up most of the ship's deck behind the super-structure. With no more small arms ammo left on the *Dust-*

boat, the Senegals had been reduced to firing flare guns, which, while forcing some of the pirates to keep their heads down, had started several more fires on the *Vidynut*. So Gunner had no choice but to keep firing the big artillery piece to protect his colleagues and the Indian crew.

But the ultramodern warship was taking a hell of a beating in the process.

NOLAN RETRACED HIS steps, leading the line of freed sailors up the lower passageway, up the ladder, to the third deck, and then to the second. The higher they climbed, the louder the noise and thicker the smoke became.

When the line of sailors finally made it to the hatch leading out to the main deck, Nolan called them to a halt.

"This will make you a very big hero back in India," Vandar told him. "We will not forget what you have done for us here today."

Nolan indicated they should all be quiet. Then he opened the hatch leading to the main deck.

Nolan went out first; Vandar was right behind him. They looked around the main deck—and were stunned. The top of the warship was a mess of twisted metal, rivers of spraying oil and multiple fires, devastated by the DUS-7's artillery weapon in its battles with the enemy gunmen. The damage had at least tripled since Nolan had gone below just two minutes ago.

Vandar surveyed the scene—and nearly collapsed. His demeanor changed immediately.

"This is bad," he started moaning. "Very, *very* bad . . ."

Nolan and Vandar, telling the rescued sailors to stay in place, fought their way through the smoke and flames, stopping at the aft part of the smoldering superstructure. Nolan, judging by the number of pirates' bodies among the wreckage on the deck, estimated at least half the hijackers had been killed. But by the amount of fire still coming from the top of the superstructure, he guessed most of the remaining hijackers were up on the bridge, and there were still at least a dozen of them. It was just about the only place on the ship that wasn't on fire, or smoking heavily.

"That bridge alone cost almost thirty million!" Vandar groaned.

As if on cue, another shell from the DUS-7 streaked over the heads, causing them to hit the deck. It smashed into the main mast just behind the bridge, sending it crashing down on the top of the control center's glass bubble.

Vandar groaned again. "You are destroying us in order to save us."

Nolan spotted Batman and Twitch still holding on at the bow. He signaled them to come aft, which they did under cover of Gunner sending yet another shell smashing into the superstructure.

They made it to the front edge of the superstructure; Nolan and Vandar were at the back end. Nolan slid his M4 across the deck where Batman could retrieve it. He immediately took out six of the twelve rounds Nolan had left and gave them to Twitch. Nolan now had an AK-47 as his primary weapon, as did Vandar. They took up positions near the two aft stairways leading up to the bridge: Nolan on the portside, Vandar going over to starboard. Batman and Twitch had similarly positioned themselves near the bridge's forward stairways. Now, they had the four bridge entrances covered. And thanks to Gunner and the field gun, just about the entire deck under the bridge was either thick with billowing smoke or crackling flames.

The pirates were trapped.

The four began firing up at the bridge, but it was impossible to tell if they were hitting anything or not. Their barrage didn't last long in any case, as they all ran out of ammunition at just about the same time.

"Now what?" Batman yelled to Nolan.

Nolan had to think. "I'd like to get those mooks out of there somehow without totally wrecking the place," he yelled back to him. "I mean, it would be good to keep at least one thing intact!"

"I think that ship has sailed!" Batman yelled in reply.

Nolan reached into his satchel and produced what he

thought was a flash grenade. He told Vandar, "Shield your eyes—these things can burn your retinas."

With that, Nolan threw the grenade right through the broken rear windshield of the bridge. He was prepared for a blinding flash—but got a tremendous explosion instead. It was so powerful that it blew out every remaining window on the bridge and in the cabin below it.

Only then did Nolan realize that he'd thrown a frag grenade into the bridge instead of a harmless, if blinding, flash grenade. More damage . . .

That was enough for him. He had to end this.

The warship was smoking and on fire in a dozen places already, and it was a miracle they all hadn't been killed. But too many innocent people *had* died in this incident: the Indian sailors murdered during the takeover and those who'd crashed in their helicopter trying in vain to reach the ship.

Nolan strongly suggested Vandar look away. Then he put his fingers to his mouth and whistled loudly. Gunner heard him. Nolan just pointed to the bridge and gave the knife-across-the-throat sign. Gunner understood.

He and the Senegals repositioned the field gun and loaded it. One more signal from Nolan confirmed what he wanted them to do. Gunner pulled the firing cord and, for the first time, the field gun opened up directly on the *Vidynut*'s bridge.

It took five high-explosive shells crashing into the ship's control center before all fire from the pirates ceased. Nolan signaled Gunner to stop. Then, from the four stairways, the team members and Vandar climbed up to the bridge deck, already knowing what they would see. The bridge was no more than a heap of jagged metal and broken glass. The pirates who'd hidden there were now just small piles of smoldering bones.

This little war was over and the *Vidynut* was back in friendly hands.

But at what a cost. Once again, Nolan looked around at the fires, the many holes in the ship's deck, the part of the superstructure where the bridge used to be. It had all happened in less than ten minutes.

But amid the sound of crackling flames, they heard a voice calling out to them. They rushed to the port side of the ship to see Crash down below. He was holding onto one of the lifeboats that had been blown overboard earlier in the fighting and had become entangled on other wreckage hanging over the side.

Batman looked down at him and said, "How's he going to explain this one to his grandkids?"

Retrieving a heavy rope, they were soon lifting their wayward colleague up to the deck.

"You know how long I've been yelling down there?" he barked at them, climbing up over the railing.

But then he stopped and looked around the Indian ship. It was burning and smoldering in so many places, he couldn't count them all.

"Wow," Crash said. "What the hell happened up here?"

Nolan wiped his dirty, sweaty brow.

"Just another job well done," he said.

IT TOOK A while to search the *Vidynut* to make sure every pirate had been killed. They found thirty-three bodies, but figured at least another dozen had been blown to pieces or burned to dust. It worked out to about one artillery shell per dead pirate. And it was many more hijackers than the team had expected to face.

Extracting the DUS-7's nose from the gash in the side of the *Vidynut* took a long time and a lot of muscle power. Only with the entire complement of freed Indian sailors lined up on the DUS-7's deck pushing against their ship, plus the Senegals reversing the freighter's nearly burned-out engines did the two vessels finally come unstuck.

But just as soon as the ships were separated, the *Vidynut* began listing violently to starboard and taking on water through the hole made by the DUS-7. This set off a mad rush through the smoking ship to seal off a slew of watertight compartments and prevent it from sinking. Even tightened up, though, the ship was still left listing almost thirty degrees.

Finally, the *Dustboat* took the warship under tow and

turned back east, calling in their position and heading toward Mumbai.

In the next few hours, they were buzzed by several U.S. Navy P-3 patrol planes, and more than once they thought they could see way, way up the thin contrails of a TR-1 spy plane looking down on them.

Around noon they were met by two Indian destroyers heading west at full speed. It was touch and go getting the *Vidynut*'s towline attached to one of the ships. When that was done, the freed Indian sailors were transferred to the second destroyer.

Each sailor shook hands and hugged the Team Whiskey members and the Senegals before departing. Commander Vandar gave Nolan his captain's hat and sword—a huge gesture of respect. The team CO accepted the gift graciously and bid Vandar good-bye.

As Vandar walked the shaky gangplank to the destroyer, Crash said only loud enough for Nolan to hear: "And don't forget to put that check in the mail."

THE TEAM CONTACTED Conley, who was in Mumbai, and made plans to hook up with him. While this was happening, another U.S. Navy aircraft came into view and buzzed the *Dustboat*. It wasn't a P-3, though. It was an SH-60 Seahawk helicopter.

It circled the DUS-7 at such a low altitude, the team members finally got the message. It wanted to land.

Crash guided the gray camo copter onto the ship's forward cargo hatch, the same place the Kilos copter had delivered the field gun just the night before. That was now hidden away, as were all their weapons.

Once the copter touched down, two men climbed out. Dressed in civilian clothes and sunglasses, they were the ONI agents, Agent Harry and his sidekick.

Nolan and Batman groaned when they saw them. They met the agents at midships.

"Really—don't you guys have anything better to do?" Nolan asked them.

"Plus, your fan Conley jumped ship," Batman added. "So there's really no one here for you to harass."

Agent Harry looked them up and down and shook his head. "Black camos for sea ops?" he said. "You either got a lot to learn or you just like dressing up to play soldier."

Nolan bit his tongue again. "What can we do for you?"

Both men took out their notebooks. "Just routine stuff again," Harry said. "Like where have you been since we last spoke? How did you get that gash on your bow? And how much did the Indians pay you for their recovery operation?"

Nolan just laughed at them. "You guys want a cup of coffee or something? Or a drink?"

"OK, message received," Harry said. "But please understand, we have to do these things. It's our job to go through the motions. I mean, we find out everything eventually anyway."

"Well, thanks for stopping by," Nolan told them.

They closed their notebooks and started to walk away, when Harry stopped and took an envelope out of his shirt pocket.

He handed it not to Nolan, but to Batman.

"I almost forgot," he said. "Mister Graves—this is for you."

Batman looked it over. "What is it? My draft notice?"

Harry shook his head. "No—actually it's from the U.S. Treasury Department. They've successfully gone through the Ninth Circuit Federal Court to get a recovery order against all held materials at your former residences on Park Avenue, on Martha's Vineyard and, through a British court, in the Bahamas."

"What the hell does that mean?" Batman asked.

Harry's smirk became a dark smile.

"I'm not an accountant," he said. "But what I think it means, Mr. Graves, is that you're now dead broke."

PART FIVE

Protecting *Chastitsa Zvyozd*

17

Mauritius
Four days later

NOLAN WAS DOWN $5,000.

It had happened so quickly. One round of baccarat, a couple of spins of the roulette wheel, a disastrous turn at the blackjack table. Five grand, gone in less than a half hour.

Nolan's reaction was typical. He walked down to the beach, ordered his next drink to be a double, and asked the cabana girl if she could bring him some more suntan lotion.

It had been like this for four days now. The team was staying at the ultraluxurious *Nadee'd* resort on the island nation of Mauritius. Nolan had never seen a place like this, never realized such a place could even exist. If heaven has a beach, it will look like this.

Mauritius was located about 650 miles east of Madagascar; 1,500 miles from the east coast of Africa. It was a playground for the ultra-rich and ultra-beautiful, in the middle of nowhere, surrounded by the warm waters of the southern Indian Ocean. This was where the team had come to heal their wounds, to chill out, and spend some of the money they'd earned . . . and stolen.

They were here at Conley's suggestion. The food, equal measures French, African, Chinese and Indian, was out of this world and the booze was never-ending. And the women—even with only one good eye, Nolan knew he'd never seen women so beautiful, so sensuous, and so available as the ones he'd met here.

The team had spent their days hanging out on Union Beach, a pristine, white-sand shoreline that looked like something created by a film studio's special-effects department. Palm trees were perfectly placed every few dozen feet, many with small shade huts and hammocks attached. Each of these stations had two gorgeous waitresses at their beck and call, massages and applications of suntan lotion included. And when it got particularly hot in the midafternoon, the waitresses just couldn't resist going topless and dragging their customers into the water.

So losing a bit at the tables didn't bother Nolan much. These memories were worth the scratch.

The DUS-7 was docked at a marina belonging to the Mauritius Coast Guard. Located on the south side of the island, it was far from the armada of mega-yachts that frequented the mid-ocean paradise. Resting in a double-locked vault at that marina's office, under constant guard by the Senegals, was the team's growing bundle of money: the $50,000 payment from Kilos Shipping for their mission against Zeek, their original payment from Kilos for saving the *Global Warrior,* and the proceeds from the Red Skull robbery less the money that went out the helicopter's windows, and most surprisingly, the entire two million fee from the Indian government, which Conley managed to shame Delhi into paying since their crew had been saved even though the futuristic *Vidynut* was nearly a total loss.

It all added up to more than $2.1 million, mostly in hundreds, with some thousands, and literally kept in a bundle to avoid the taxman. They had tied the bundle together with rope and duct tape and stuffed it in a sea sack that was now resting in the Coast Guard's vault.

Their plans at the moment? Nothing more complicated than getting more drinks, playing more games of chance, and meeting more women. They were booked at the resort for an open-ended stay.

IT WAS JUST after noontime on their fourth day that their order of drinks was delivered not by a topless waitress, but by a man in a thick wool suit.

"Am I hallucinating again?" Nolan asked, raising the brim

of Vandar's captain's hat to get a better glimpse at the man. He was middle-aged and looked like a former boxer. His face was big and beefy, scarred under both eyes, and featured an oft-broken nose. Pasty and white, it appeared like he hadn't spent more than two minutes in the sun in his entire life.

"Can we help you?" Batman asked him.

The man pleasantly passed around the drinks and took a seat near the team.

"Was nice work in Malacca," he said in a thick Eastern European accent. "And getting warship back for Indians? You guys getting famous."

No one on the team knew what to say. They were supposed to be keeping a low profile.

"How do you know about us?" Nolan finally asked the man.

"We hear about you on the Twitter," the man replied. "Everyone know about you now. Word is around. They say: 'These *parni* can do anything. Protect you. Save life. Get ship back.'"

"What's Twitter?" Crash asked.

"So, you made us," Nolan said to the stranger. "Is this just a hello?"

The guy shook his head. They could all see that he was packing a huge handgun under his thick blue suit coat.

"Is hello and is also to ask question," he replied. "Are you guys interested in some more work?"

Twenty-four hours later

"MAN, THAT PLACE on Mauritius was a real dump," Crash said.

The rest of Team Whiskey did not disagree.

The five of them were standing on a helipad near the entrance to a place called Kinkokos. It was a Greek island fifty miles southeast of Athens, one of hundreds of islands of the Aegean Sea. Kinkkokos was one big privately owned resort. Featuring rolling hills, lush fields, waterfalls, bubbling streams, with exotic plants growing everywhere, it boasted mansions, a marina and landing pads for a fleet of helicopters. It was all surrounded by miles of pearl-white beaches and incredibly clear, blue water. In many ways, it *did* put anything on Mauritius to shame.

The team had just been deposited here by a Boeing 234UT helicopter, a long-range dual-rotor aircraft that was as luxurious as anything any of them had ever flown in. It had carried them over from Athens airport after a private jet flew them up from Mauritius. They'd been hired for another job, one not so clear-cut as their previous gigs. The man they'd met on the beach in Mauritius—they knew him only as "Bebe"—represented a "family business" based in Moscow. Exactly what this family business did was still a mystery. But the team certainly had some theories about that business . . . and the nature of the "family."

The family was hosting a weekend party for its myriad associates. This fête was to take place on a cruise liner the family had leased for the occasion to sail the Aegean Sea. There would be some business to attend to, but mostly it would be a bash above the waves. Each guest was bringing his own body-guards, a limit of two, but Bebe was under orders from the family's patriarch to hire some extra security to supplement the paid guns looking out for their guests. That's where Team Whiskey came in.

They were here now to meet the head of the family business—indeed, he was the owner of Kinkkokos Island. An oversized golf cart driven by two enormous goons carried them up the long driveway to a huge traditional Greek-style mansion that sat atop the highest hill on the island. They were met by two more enormous goons at the front door. The team members were carrying rucksacks and their personal weapons; this made the goons nervous. While Batman insisted on keeping the sea bag holding their money, the goons told them to leave their guns at the door. They were then escorted through the mansion to a piazza in the back.

They found a man sitting by a crystalline pool, reading

a newspaper. He was short and stout, with a ruddy face and a shaved head. He was at least seventy years old and he, too, looked right out of a movie—if the movie was about fabulously wealthy Russian gangsters.

The goons made their presence known. The elderly man, clad in a gaudy silk bathrobe, looked up at the team members and frowned.

"Who the hell are you?" he asked in a thick accent.

The team was stumped. This was the right address, wasn't it?

"We're the marine protection service," Nolan answered. "We'll be helping out on the cruise liner—for your party?"

The man looked them up and down. Then he said: "You look like you're here to cut grass, to rake leaves. You don't have uniforms. Emblem patches, nothing. And you, you're half blind. And this guy's a gimp. He's got a peg leg."

Twitch took a swing at the old man. His haymaker missed, and the two goons were soon on him, lifting him up between them. The rest of the team stayed in place; they knew Twitch didn't need any help. He was a fierce Delta-trained warrior, as the two goons were about to find out. Using a combination of karate, jujitsu and judo, he proceeded to beat both men unconscious, ending with an excruciating kick to the groin to each, courtesy of his metal foot.

In seconds the pool area was flooded with armed men, running to defend the Russian godfather. But he just waved them off.

"OK, you guys are hired," he said as the unconscious goons were carried way. "But if you're going to work for me, we must get you clothes that are new."

THE CRUISE SHIP was named the *Althea Dawn*.

It was 900 feet long, had sixteen decks, six pools, twenty-four bars, ten dining rooms, and accommodations for nearly 1,000 high-paying passengers.

But this was not a typical cruise liner. Rather, it was leased from an Italian company that dealt only with well-heeled clients. There were no closet-sized rooms on this ship. The smallest stateroom was as big as a luxury suite in a five-star hotel; most of the staterooms were penthouse-size or bigger. Each was on the outer part of the ship, complete with balcony and water views. There was a lavish casino, two giant, well-appointed function rooms, and many private rooms for dining, partying or other activities.

The galley and kitchen rivaled the best restaurants in Paris. The kitchen staff numbered nearly 100; the boat's crew outnumbered the guests three to one.

The cruise ship was leaving out of the port city of Kronos, located just two islands over from Kinkkokos. Though the plan was to sail around the Aegean, for security reasons, there was no set course. The ship would travel 1,200 miles in the two and a half days of sailing, at times doubling back on its route to confuse anyone who might be planning to do it harm.

The ship had arrived at Kronos earlier that morning, docking at a private berth at the far edge of the tourist city. A large tent had been erected on the dock. A parking lot nearby was filled with limos and SUVs, all with dark-tinted windows.

Passenger loading began precisely at noon. Looking stiff in their new dark blue combat suits, Nolan and Gunner stood at the gangway and checked out every person who came aboard. Each guest had to have an invitation signed personally by Bebe. That invitation was watermarked and had a red stripe embedded in it to thwart counterfeiters. Plus, Bebe was close by, still in his thick woolen suit, eyeballing everyone who walked up the gangway. If the team members had any question about a guest, they just looked over to him for a thumbs-up.

As it turned out, no one tried to crash the party. The passenger list was unusual, though. Fifty middle-aged and elderly men were the first to climb aboard, each with his two bodyguards, each unmistakably Russian or Eastern European. There was little doubt what these people did for a living, these "family associates."

Once they were aboard, a small army of young women was allowed up the gangway. There were exactly two hundred of them, and they made the girls back on Mauritius look like also-rans in a 4-H beauty contest. Most were blond—

Scandinavians, Germans, Czechs—with a few Asian and African beauties as well.

But most odd, the last guests to come aboard were a half-dozen professorial types, all wearing tweed jackets with elbow patches despite the heat, and all smoking pipes. Each had the required invitation, but still Nolan and Gunner looked to Bebe to personally vet them. Each got a thumbs-up.

There were dozens of Greek police in the area, watching all this activity. But underscoring the power of Bebe and his friends, they stayed a respectful distance away from the boarding process.

Everyone was finally loaded aboard—fifty business associates, 100 bodyguards, 200 party girls and six college professors. Everyone's luggage had been X-rayed, but by Bebe's orders, the only verboten items were explosives. Handguns, Uzis, ammunition and drugs were allowed onboard. One particular elderly guest brought a briefcase that was stuffed with cocaine, and a large bottle of Viagra.

Meanwhile, Batman was in the work copter, flown up from Mauritius on a family-leased cargo plane. He was circling endlessly over the cruise liner while Crash and Twitch were in scuba gear checking the hull of the ship for mines or explosives. They found none.

One hour after the loading process had begun, Nolan reported to Bebe that, by his criteria, all of the guests had passed muster. Again, Batman—circling above—reported nothing irregular. No smaller vessels were spotted near the cruise ship, no suspicious types were watching them from the docks.

The *Althea Dawn* left the dock at Kronos just after 1330 hours. In beautiful weather, it headed for the open sea.

THE CRUISE SHIP had everything for everybody—except one thing: locations for the team to set up their 50-caliber machine guns.

Bebe had supplied them with four Russian-made Dushka powerhouses and several miles of ammunition. It wasn't that their employer didn't want the hardware to be seen. Just the opposite. He'd encouraged the team to be as visible as possible, to make their high-powered guests feel more secure. The cruise liner just didn't have any ideal crossfire points to set up four giant machine guns.

The team finally settled on a four-corners approach: two weapons on the main deck bow, two on the stern. The weapons were attached to the railing with huge vise grips, supplemented with bike chains and electrical wire. The plan was for the team members to patrol the decks during the day carrying their personal weapons. If trouble struck, they would rush to these four gun posts and defend the ship. At night, three of the guns would be manned at all times, on a rotating basis, with each gun commander equipped with night-vision goggles.

Meanwhile, the work copter would be either airborne or ready to fly at a moment's notice. Bebe not only had encouraged the team to be armed at all times; he wanted the work copter parked on the stern of the boat, in full view of the largest pool. The copter was scarier-looking than ever, fitted with a second gun pod, two wing-mounted rocket launchers, and permanent M4 mounts. The former mall-cop copter was now loaded down with weapons.

Between the team's firepower and the small army of bodyguards aboard, Nolan was confident they could ward off any attack by . . . well, by whom? That had yet to be made clear.

So, once they were under way, Nolan sought out Bebe to explain the overall situation to him. He found him at the bar on the top deck.

"Comrade One Eye," was how Bebe greeted him. "Will have drinks, you and me."

Nolan got a soda water. He was on the clock.

"Just who are we protecting you guys from?" he asked Bebe directly. "Pirates? Rivals? Someone's navy?"

Bebe smiled, displaying a mouthful of gold teeth.

"Your specialty is pirates, right?" he asked.

Nolan shrugged. "I guess."

"So you are protecting us from pirates then," he said, and added: "But maybe more."

"Really?"

Bebe downed his shot of vodka. "See it this way," he said. "Every man aboard ship has enemies—dozens at least. Rivals. Wannabes. People wanting to settle score. If someone sink ship, they get rid of many, many top adversaries in one swoop."

Bebe never stopped smiling as he said all this; Nolan knew this was not a good sign. The Russian was holding something back.

"You're paying us a lot of money," he told him. "And whether you tell me everything or not, it's still the same fee. So, if you want us to just keep a lookout for pirates, then so be it—though I'm not sure how many pirates there are in the Aegean Sea. But, if you want to level with me, then maybe we can really protect you from *everything* that's out there."

Bebe mulled this over, then motioned Nolan to come closer. "OK, here is scoop," he said. "We get gossip that someone will definitely attack ship during cruise. Rival business. Jealous of us. And somehow, someway—they want to try to get us all. I get information from sources that are very firm. Never wrong. And I'm getting updates by hour. Chatter says attack will come. No matter what."

"Why don't you just cancel the trip, then?" Nolan asked him. "Turn around and everyone can go home safe."

Bebe laughed. "You don't know my world. Is simple rule. You never show fear. Is better that whole ship sinks than to cancel big party. That's how everyone feel. The trip must go on—we must be prepared to fight off whatever is coming—or we look like schoolchildren."

NOLAN LEFT THE bar and went to the suite that had been supplied to the team. It was an expansive space with a dining room, a game room, a sitting room, a full bar, big-screen TV, two balconies, and a half-dozen bedrooms spinning off it. It was *nothing* like the *Dustboat*.

Crash, Twitch and Gunner were on hand, getting ready to go on duty. Each was wearing his new deep-blue combat suit, courtesy of their client. In reality, their new uniforms looked like something designed by NASA. They were thick, hot, uncomfortable—and ugly.

"What's the 411?" Gunner asked him. "Are these guys for real or paranoid? Or both?"

Nolan pulled out a soda water from the bar.

"They're for real," he told them. "No doubt about that. But let's make sure we know where the life preservers are kept. This might get a little funky somewhere down the road."

"That's great," Gunner said gloomily. "Just when we thought we'd had our share of funky with the Indians."

In their own way, these three rarely seemed anything but motivated despite all they'd gone through. But at the moment, Nolan thought they looked troubled. He'd sensed it right away.

"What's the problem?" he asked them. "You guys don't like the accommodations?

Crash spoke first. "It's the money," he said bluntly.

"The money? For this job? Two hundred fifty grand not enough for you to sail around on this tub for two and a half days?"

"No, it's a lot," Crash said. "*That's* the problem. Add it to what we made squashing Turk, squashing Zeek, and what the Indians just gave us, we're almost up to two and a half million bucks."

"Two million, three hundred eighty-five thousand, to be exact," Nolan told them. "You guys want to count it or something?"

Gunner spoke up. "We're just concerned about the security," he said.

"Security?" Nolan asked. "We got it here with us. Batman prays over it every half hour. You can't get better security. Plus, we agreed not to put it in a bank, just in case someone comes looking for taxes or something."

"You just hit the nail on the head," Gunner said. "Not the banking thing—but who's watching over it for us."

Nolan was stunned. "The Batman, you mean? He's the money guy of the group. He's the best guy to look out for it."

The usually reticent Twitch spoke up. "Sure, he's the money guy—but he's also another Bernie Madoff. He was on the run when we hooked back up with him. He has more guys chasing him than you do. Plus we just found out the government seized all his assets. He's beyond broke at this point."

Nolan put his drink down. This was getting serious.

"Are you saying you don't trust him with our money?" he asked them directly.

"Do you?" Crash asked.

Nolan was pissed. "Let's remember who we are talking about here," he said. "This is a guy who's saved the lives of each one of us more than once. Me, in Kosovo. Gunner, in Sakrit, Twitch and Crash, that gunfight outside Beirut. He'd take a bullet for any one of you."

The three men nodded uncomfortably. Crash said, "But money changes people."

Nolan was starting to burn. "Yes, I guess it does," he said. "It's changing you three right before my eyes."

A tense silence descended on the suite.

Nolan finally broke it. "OK, so what do you want me to do? Split it up so you'll all have your own piece? Do we really want to be all walking around with a half million dollars in our pockets?"

"What we want is for you to talk to him," Gunner said. "Just make sure that he's copasetic with the money, that's all."

"I mean," Crash said, "now that we know he's seriously broke, have you actually *seen* the money since we came aboard? How do we know he isn't making a side deal with these Russian meatballs? Or that he won't disappear with it when we're not looking? Take off in the copter and just fly away? You got to admit, that's just about what he did to those suckers he had for clients back in the States. And what's stealing a couple million bucks mean to a guy like that anyway? He's used to stealing *hundreds* of millions. To him, we've made chicken feed compared to that. It would be nothing for him to disappear with it."

Nolan started to say something, but stopped. They were right, of course. He trusted Batman, but he was the only other officer in the team, and maybe that was affecting his judgment. And he couldn't let that happen, no matter what he thought of the guy.

He drained his water, then said, "OK—you guys get out on deck patrol. I'll go talk to him."

NOLAN FOUND BATMAN out on the stern, sitting by the work copter.

"What's the good word?" he asked Nolan cheerfully.

"I believe it's pronounced: *Bratva krasnayai,*" Nolan replied. "Or maybe *Krasnaya mafiy.*"

Batman laughed. "Yeah, Red Mafia? Is that who you think these guys are?"

Nolan shrugged. "Who knows? Who cares? They paid up, right?"

"They did," Batman replied. "I counted it and tested every bill—and it's all legit. No counterfeits. No bogus script. A quarter of a million dollars in the ship's vault, along with the rest of our stash. We'll need to get a new sea bag soon, by the way."

Nolan had known Batman for almost fifteen years. They'd gone through Delta training together. There was a bond there. Even though they'd been out of touch after the Tora Bora mess, when the group got back together, it was like they'd missed no time at all.

On the other hand, Nolan had no idea what had gone on with Batman after he returned to civilian life, other than he'd been caught up in the Wall Street scandals. There was a big hole in the time line there.

Batman lit a cigarette—which was funny, because Nolan never knew him to smoke.

"You never did tell me what the hell happened to you back in the States," Nolan said to him. "We've been back riding together for more than a year now, but I still haven't heard the story."

Batman took a long drag on his smoke. "What's to tell? I went into high finance after leaving Delta and got caught up in it. We all did. Making money. Making *more* money. Even when we went to the higher-ups and told them maybe we should cool it on all these exotic trades and stuff—they just said: 'Shut up and make more money.' That's the short version of a long story."

He took another drag, held his breath, and let it out slowly.

"Not as exciting as almost punching out a judge and going off to find bin Laden on your own," he added.

"There's no statute of limitations on either of those things," Nolan said gravely.

Batman laughed and nudged him. "Man, you're still uptight," he said. "Here, take a drag of this and relax. We're on a roll here."

Nolan didn't smoke but Batman nearly forced the cigarette into his mouth. Nolan took a drag—and spit it out immediately.

"Jesus—what is that? *Pot?*"

Batman just smiled. "Hey, I don't know. Bebe gave it to me. Takes the stress away. Take another hit."

Nolan held up his hand and refused.

Batman said, "What's the matter? Afraid you'll get the one eye red?"

Nolan ignored the comment. He said instead, "You know, at one time maybe you were able to swim in a pool filled with money. But the guys, they've never come close to the amount we've earned in just this past month."

"It will be good for them to see how the other half lives," Batman said.

"Well, let's make sure of that, OK?" Nolan said.

Batman looked at him strangely. Then a light went on behind his eyes. "Hey—is that what this is about? Those guys are worried because I'm the one holding the money?"

Nolan shrugged, feeling the slight effects of the inadvertent drag of reefer. "I told them they had no reason to be."

Batman was upset. "That cash is safe with me. I'm not a crook. I wouldn't rip off those guys. What are they thinking? That I'd just suddenly take off? Leave them high and dry?"

Nolan just shrugged again, but didn't say anyhthing.

Batman was getting agitated now. "I'm embarrassed by what I did, Snake. And I'm sorry. And that's why I rejoined this merry band. I had a bit of trouble living with myself. Sure, I made some serious coin—and now it's gone. But I lost a lot more than that. My wife—my kids. Back in the States. I haven't seen them for months. That's *my* prison sentence. Because of what I did, I'm a man without a country."

Nolan looked him straight in the eye and said, "So am I."

BEBE'S BUSINESS MEETING started with the sound of a ringing bell.

On this signal, all of the male guests and their bodyguards were summoned to the ship's central function room, located on the fifth deck. Nolan had three of the 50-calibers manned, on display as the family associates walked by, each man flanked by his hired heat, except the half-dozen professor-looking types, who looked even more out of place than before. Per Nolan's plan, the work copter was in the air, Batman noisily circling the ship. But like the big guns, it was for show more than anything else.

Once everyone was inside the function room, Nolan and Crash stood guard at the only door that led in and out of the place. Nolan didn't want to know what was going on inside. That was not part of the job.

But Crash's curiosity was stronger, and eventually it got the best of him. The door leading into the function hall was made of frosted glass with intricate designs cut into it. The designs were made of clear glass, providing hundreds of peepholes.

Crash couldn't resist taking a peek.

"What the fuck?" he gasped, pushing his eye against the window. "This is weird . . ."

Nolan was embarrassed by Crash's behavior, but the curiosity was getting to him, too.

"What is it?" he asked Crash in a hushed tone.

"You gotta see it for yourself," was his reply.

Against all his instincts, Nolan put his good eye up against the glass and looked inside. What he saw was baffling.

The men were sitting around a huge table covered with rocks. All shapes. All sizes. Nothing but rocks.

It didn't make sense.

Had he seen them dividing up drugs, or gold, or diamonds, or even weapons, he would have understood.

But rocks?

"What the hell is up with that?" Crash asked him.

Nolan had no idea—and it wasn't like he was going to ask anyone, especially Bebe.

"If they want to pay us a quarter million for protecting rocks," he told Crash, "that's fine with me."

THE BUSINESS MEETING lasted just thirty minutes.

The attendees streamed out of the hall when it was over, laughing and joking in several languages. Some of their goons were carrying suitcases they could barely get off the floor.

The guests walked past Nolan and Crash like they weren't there. The last person out of the room was Bebe.

"Business over for a while," he told them. "Now party begins."

"How long will it last?" Nolan asked him, checking his watch.

Bebe laughed. "Maybe forever," he replied.

WHEN NOLAN WALKED the main deck and found Gunner at his machine-gun station having his picture taken with two gorgeous women, he knew the celebration had begun. A third was wielding the camera. They were all wearing micro-bikinis, and all were drop-dead gorgeous.

"How could I resist?" Gunner said to Nolan as he walked by. "They said they're crazy about my uniform."

Nolan gave him a mock salute and kept on walking.

He next came upon the so-called Big Pond. It was an Olympic-size swimming pool, also located on the main deck, which featured a semisubmerged wraparound bar. The pool area was already crowded with party girls, again all of them out-of-this-world beautiful. The business associates were just starting to wade into this area, followed by their bodyguards. Soon the champagne was flowing like water.

About 200 feet above the pool, the work copter was hovering; it was Batman's way of telling a joke, as in: "I got *this* place covered."

Two beauties walked up to Nolan and tried to get him to drink a glass of champagne. They said his eye patch was sexy.

He politely declined their offer.

"Maybe when I'm off duty," he told them—and kept on walking.

Just as he was passing the far end of the pool, he saw a group of women remove their bikini tops. There was a great cheer from those sitting at the submerged bar, and soon more of the women took off their tops. Waiters with trays arrived, filled not just with drinks, but also with bowls of cocaine. A slight yelp from the deep end caught Nolan's attention; one of the guests was having sex with one of the party girls in full view. Music was playing, people were cheering. It was like a live-action porn flick. The party had been on for exactly five minutes.

Nolan kept on walking, leaving the peals of delight behind.

It was like being a mall cop again.

IT ONLY GOT worse—or better, depending on the point of view—as the afternoon went on.

Nolan walked the decks continuously, sweating in his new uniform, looking in on various staterooms and halls, the game rooms and the casinos. He saw the same thing in each one: men, women, drugs, debauchery. Liquor flowed; waiters rushed through the passageways pushing carts full of so much food, there seemed to be no way it could all be eaten by the people on the ship. The sweet scent of marijuana was everywhere, and everyone he saw seemed to be sniffing their way through a nonexistent head cold.

All of this would have bothered him in his previous life, before everything changed at Tora Bora. But now? The only thing bothering him was *how little* all this was bothering him. It sounded like a cliché, but he'd joined the U.S. military to fight for truth, justice and the American way, only to find that the American way had little to do with truth or justice, at least as far as his case was concerned.

He was smarter now. This sort of thing—what Bebe was up to—was what made the world go round. People with their little miserable lives could either ignore it or carve off a piece for themselves. But whatever they decided to do, Nolan knew it wasn't up to him to stand in their way. He had no pension. He had no retirement fund. All that had gone away the moment he decided to pursue bin Laden on his own. And though he felt deep down that he was pursuing him still, he was in no position to turn down any job that would bring some money his way. They'd been fabulously lucky in the past month with their maritime security thing, and he would have been crazy to give it up just because he didn't approve of the people who were paying the bills. For him, now, looking out for number one had to be a full-time job—because no one else would do it for him. Not anymore.

Or at least that's what he was trying to tell himself.

THE AFTERNOON SLOWLY turned into twilight.

The *Althea Dawn* meandered its way through the sea, passing islands, escorted by dolphins, heading into the last of the sunset, and all the while the work copter flew cover overhead and the team members walked the decks, heavily armed, sweating in the late-day heat, making sure everyone was safe to party.

The first sign of trouble came just after the sun went down. Batman had just landed to refuel when a passenger yelled that small boats were approaching the ship. Nolan had just sat down in their suite for a cup of iced coffee when he heard the person calling out on the starboard side. He rushed to the deck, alerting the other team members on walkie-talkies Bebe had supplied. But by the time he got outside, the boats had disappeared.

Nolan searched the water with his night-vision scope, looking for anything out of the ordinary, but finding nothing. The boats, if they existed, could have been from any of the nearby islands—fishing boats, yachts and ferries all sailed these waters, and he tried to explain this to the crowd that had gathered near the scene. But still, word went around the ship quickly that someone was stalking them.

Things eventually calmed down and the party resumed. Nolan returned to walking the decks, checking on the team members now manning the highly visible 50-caliber machine guns. Scantily clad girls and thug-like men roamed from room to room, doing drugs, having sex, and on many occasions, videotaping the activities.

At one point, Nolan thought, "Who can keep this up for two more days?"

Then he remembered the guest who'd come aboard with the briefcase stuffed with cocaine and Viagra.

And he had his answer.

NIGHT FELL.

At about 2100 hours, Nolan's radio beeped. Bebe wanted to see him in the top-deck bar.

He made his way to the top of the ship, where he found the Russian sitting with four shots of vodka and a half-dozen sat phones spread out before him.

He was ending a phone call when Nolan approached. Bebe held up his hand, freezing Nolan for a moment. The Russian downed the four shots without stopping to take a breath, then indicated the bartender should pour four more. Then he signaled Nolan to sit down.

"Bad news getting worse," Bebe told Nolan, who was finally able to get a glass of iced coffee. "Friends on land telling me chatter say attack on us is coming imminent. No ideas how, just that it hits soon."

Nolan could sense Bebe was concerned, and that was not a good thing. He wracked his brain thinking of what form this attack might take.

Some things he could dismiss out of hand; this wasn't a bad action movie they were living in. He was sure the attack would not come in the form of a rogue cruise missile or a torpedo fired from a submarine owned by some secret organization that wanted to rule the world. A suicide attack like on the USS *Cole* was the more likely possibility—but between the team members on deck and Batman constantly circling overhead, and everyone being equipped with night vision, they would see something like that coming from far away and in plenty of time to stop it.

"Are you sure every bodyguard on board has been cleared?"

Nolan asked Bebe as he dove into his second quartet of vodka shots.

"Done a dozen times," was Bebe's rough reply. "Plus, it would take *every* bodyguard on board to be dirty to turn on us all."

"How about those eggheads that came onboard—the guys who look like college professors?"

Bebe laughed. "They *are* college professors and they were needed on this voyage. But we have their wives and families at secret locations to be released only when we all come home safe. It is not them. Threat is coming from someone else."

Bebe downed four more shots, but they seemed to be having zero effect on him.

"Most important is that vast majority of peoples on ship don't worry about what we know," he told Nolan. "Everyone must have good time or whole thing has been failure."

NOLAN LEFT BEBE as he was ordering four more shots, and resumed his rounds.

He checked with Gunner, Crash and Twitch. All was well with them. They were constantly scanning all sides of the ship, bow to stern, with their night-vision goggles. No vessel had come within a mile of the *Althea Dawn* all night.

He found Batman on the back end, fueling up again. Like the others, he'd seen nothing suspicious, and his aerial field of view was up to twenty miles in all directions. Their prior conversation on money matters forgotten, Batman took off again in the work copter to once more circle the ship.

Not thirty seconds later, gunfire broke out.

It came from the port side, near the bow. Nolan rushed down the deck, picking up Crash along the way, pushing through a caravan of waiters delivering a ton of food somewhere. Up on the bow they found two bodyguards firing into the dark waters with huge handguns. Nolan quickly got them to stop shooting and asked what they were firing at.

Through slurred, broken English, one said he'd seen two boats full of men dressed in black approach the side of the ship. But the other man claimed he saw just one boat, and the men on board were all wearing white, not black. The bodyguards argued about this, waving their guns around wildly.

As Crash disarmed the two goons, Nolan scanned the waters below. He saw nothing. He called up to Batman, who also reported seeing nothing. Both bodyguards were highly intoxicated; so much so, Nolan was surprised they hadn't killed each other instead of just throwing bullets into the water.

But the gunfire had attracted the attention of just about everyone on the boat. In less than a minute, a large crowd had gathered on the bow. A ripple of uneasiness went through the passengers.

This got Nolan thinking: "How can *I* take another two days of this?"

HE WALKED BACK to the stern, hoping to catch a cool breeze.

The moon was up, and it seemed an idyllic scene if it were not for the imminent threat of an attack on the ship. He stared at the moon and his mind wandered. He was engaged once, long ago, to a beautiful girl. She'd wanted to sail the Med for their honeymoon.

"I guess this is as close as I'm going to get," he thought aloud.

But then a feeling came over him. It was the same feeling he'd experienced just before they'd found Zeek's fuel supply that night. The same feeling he had when he was about to win a hand of poker.

The ship had been threatened, and Bebe had hinted that the people behind the threat were gangsters and criminals, just like Bebe and his friends. The top of the food chain when it came to criminal activity in Eastern Europe.

In other words, they were smart.

And smart people would not openly attack a boat full of heavily armed bodyguards and a security team, with an armed helicopter flying over it.

They would do it a different way.

But how?

Had he forgotten anything? Every passenger was checked coming aboard. Every piece of luggage, every hired goon.

Bebe had had the ship swept for bombs prior to bringing the team into the mix, and they had swept it again, inside and out.

What was left?

Nolan looked out on the ship's wake. Microscopic animals and algae churned up by the ship's propulsion gear left a trail of eerie phosphorous as the vessel moved through the calm, tranquil seas.

The ventilation system? he thought. No—the ship was not a closed system, so sending poison gas through it might affect a handful of people at the most. Plus, it was too James Bond-ish.

The water system? Nolan looked around him. Who the hell was drinking water here? No one. Or not enough people to score a major kill like Bebe's contacts were telling him was coming.

Air, water and . . .

At that moment, Nolan heard a small commotion below him. Two men were out on the service balcony at the very bottom of the ship. They were kitchen workers. One dumped a bucket of garbage overboard; the other had a large white bowl full of a black substance, moist and oily. He also had a spoon with him. They were talking in hushed tones, speaking Greek. They had no idea Nolan was watching them.

Throwing the garbage overboard had attracted a gang of seagulls that now were trailing the boat. The two men seemed very interested in the seagulls and began throwing more food to them. One seagull was braver than the rest and kept coming closer and closer to the service balcony as the men continued to throw out scraps. Once this gull got very close, the worker with the bowl took a spoonful of the black substance and flung it into the wind.

The seagull caught a mouthful of it in midair. In an instant, it turned over and nose-dived into the sea, scattering bloody feathers everywhere.

Nolan couldn't believe it.

"Son of a bitch," he whispered. "How could I be so dumb?"

BEBE WAS JUST ushering his guests into the main dining hall when Nolan found him.

"You and I have to go down to the kitchen immediately," he told Bebe as inconspicuously as possible.

But Bebe was not happy to hear this.

"This most important meeting of trip," he told Nolan. "This is the big meal where money changes hands. Do you know of missile heading for us? Or explosive boat coming alongside?"

Nolan was firm. "No—but money changing hands might not be an option if you don't come with me right now."

THEY WALKED INTO the ship's kitchen two minutes later.

A small army of cooks and waiters were madly preparing meals for the guests three decks above. It was a snapshot of controlled chaos, like a restaurant reality show. Nolan quickly spotted the two men he wanted to question.

Still not happy, Bebe followed him across the kitchen to where the dinner's first course was being prepared. The two men Nolan had spied out on the balcony were surprised to see the heavily armed Nolan and the woolen-suited Bebe standing behind them.

Nolan zoomed in on an enormous bowl of caviar, aka Russian Ice Cream. The two men were hovering over it. He turned to the man he'd seen throwing the black stuff to the seagulls. He seemed to be a Greek national, but it was hard to tell.

"Speak English?" he asked the man.

The man nodded nervously.

Nolan took a spoonful of the caviar and handed it to him.

"Eat this," he ordered the man.

The man's face turned white.

"I cannot," he said in a thick accent. "Too expensive for a worker like me."

"If it's good enough for the seagulls, it's good enough for you," Nolan told him. "Eat it . . ."

The man started furiously shaking his head no. Now the rest of the kitchen crew was paying attention.

Bebe nudged Nolan aside. He towered over the kitchen worker.

"Eat," he told the man.

The man was so frightened, he wet himself. The caviar had

been spiked, it turned out, with the venom of the Sydney Funnel Spider, one of the deadliest toxins in the world. One drop the size of a pinhead was enough to kill several hundred people. And that's how it had been smuggled aboard: a drop encased in wax and affixed to the end of a common pin hidden in the kitchen worker's sewing kit. Sherlock Holmes wouldn't have found it.

"Eat!" Bebe roared at him again, taking out his massive handgun to make his point.

When the kitchen worker finally put the spoon to his lips, Bebe forced it between his teeth and made him swallow. The man's eyes went wide—and blood instantly gushed from his nose and mouth.

He dropped to the deck, dead before he hit the floor.

THE CRUISE SHIP returned to Kronos two nights later.

The guests were ushered off, each picked up by a limo or armored SUV. Once again, the Greek police were nearby, but did their best to ignore what was going on at the berth.

Up on the top deck, Bebe and Nolan sat at the bar again, a bottle of vodka and two glasses in front of them. Nolan was finally drinking, finally feeling relaxed. The team had done their job well here—and it was good to know they could again save a ship without destroying it.

Bebe was in the best mood Nolan had seen him. From the Russian's point of view, the trip couldn't have gone better. The guests were safe, and there were no more incidents after the first night. Those who knew about the grisly episode in the kitchen had nothing but admiration for Bebe's skills.

As for the worker who had poisoned the caviar—well, he was now sleeping with the fishes along with his busboy accomplice.

"You men are good," Bebe said to Nolan. He passed him a briefcase. Nolan opened it—it was full of U.S. greenbacks.

"What's this? You already paid us."

"Is your tip—your bonus," Bebe boomed.

Nolan scanned the money. He was getting good at estimating just how much money a briefcase could hold. This one looked to contain $50,000.

"This is too generous," Nolan heard himself saying.

"Stop with the shit of a bull," Bebe said. "Just count it!"

Nolan downed his shot of vodka. "I'm not going to count it," he said. "I trust you."

"Count!" Bebe insisted. "If you guys want to make it in this business you must learn this: Never to trust anybody. Never to trust especially those peoples who owe you money."

Nolan counted the money. He was right: It was an extra $50,000.

"Put money down on new copter," Bebe said. "You ride around in dinky car that barely flies. You need SUV with rotor blades."

"I'll look into that," Nolan told him.

"You can go far in this business," Bebe said again. "But secret is, be careful who you do business with. Some criminals more trustworthy than others. Never trust Syrians. Never trust Iranians. Never trust French. And never, ever trust Chinese. No good to even be considering business with them, because they will stab you in back when you're not looking and then sell someone the knife. Everyone else, though, just count money. *Always* count money."

They did another shot.

"Thanks for the advice," Nolan told him. "I—we appreciate it."

Nolan hesitated a moment, then said: "I must ask you something. And please don't take it as a sign of disrespect."

Bebe laughed. "Be careful, Cyclops," he said, patting his wool suitcoat. "I still have gun."

Nolan went on. "I looked in on you and your friends during your first business meeting, when you were making your deals. I thought I would see gold, or jewels, or raw diamonds. But all I saw was rocks."

Bebe roared bearishly. "You peeked?" he said. "You are good spy, because peeking gets you shot and you did not get shot."

He poured out two more vodkas.

"You see us not with rocks," he said. "You see us with this."

He reached into his pocket and produced a plastic bag containing . . . a rock.

"Is rock, true," Bebe told him. "But not rock from here."

He pointed up at the stars. "Is rock from up there."

Nolan had to think a moment before this made sense. Then it came to him. "Meteorites?" he asked.

"Is meteorites, yes," Bebe said. "Per pound, most valuable commodity in world these days. More precious than gold. Jewels. Plutonium. Anything. We steal them. We deal them. We trade them. Is why six professors were here, to verify what we have is real. Do you understand, my friend? Our big new business is selling *chastitsa zvyozd.* 'Pieces of the stars.'"

Another two shots of vodka. "Never stop looking for something more valuable than what you already have," Bebe told him. "That's the secret. And here's a few more . . ."

Over the next thirty minutes, Bebe imparted a boatload of knowledge and intelligence to Nolan. He told him about the various people he'd dealt with over the years. A surprising number of his contacts were intelligence operatives from European countries, and not just those of the former Soviet bloc. Weapons always were at the center of these dealings. Weapons for cash. Weapons for gold. Weapons for pieces of the stars.

"Many guns out there," Bebe said. "Problem is, many people don't know how to use. They just feel bigger and better if they have them. Countries or criminals. Having weapons makes dicks grow longer. It's very dangerous situation."

Nolan just shrugged. "We are not naïve enough to take sides," he told Bebe. "We know what this world is like. We are just trying to make as much money as quickly as possible and then give it all up before someone who doesn't like us locks us up."

Bebe laughed and took a huge gulp of vodka. "Is story of my life," he said. "But if it is just money—quick money that you want—you should always be looking for the ship, *Dutch Cloud.* But you must know this already."

But Nolan shook his head no. He'd never heard of the *Dutch Cloud.*

"Is container ship that goes missing right after 9/11," Bebe told him. "Top secret. Big secret around the world. Is ghost ship. People see it, then they don't. What is in its containers? No one knows. Lots of guesses, rumors, speculation. But of this is sure: big bounty on that ship. Find it and you get fifty million, cash."

Nolan was fairly drunk by now. Still, he was fascinated by the story—and the prospect of making fifty million.

"Fifty million?" he asked Bebe. "To be paid by who?"

The mobster laughed again.

"By your own CIA," he said. "Who else?"

At that moment, their attention was diverted by something in the sky. They both looked up as a shooting star passed over their heads.

Bebe laughed out loud again.

He shook Nolan's hand vigorously, then said: "Is God telling me—I must get back to work."

PART SIX

South to Zanzibar

18

Port of Aden
Yemen

MARK CONLEY UNLOCKED his office door and stumbled inside.

It was midnight. He was hot, sweaty and exhausted. He snapped on the air conditioner and collapsed onto the couch. He'd left here a week ago, but it seemed more like a year. He'd spent a piece of that time on the DUS-7, helping Team Whiskey get what they needed to recapture the *Vidynut*. Then he went on to Mumbai to await the outcome and, at the end, finally collect the team's fee. He'd met them on Mauritius, paid them and left them on the beach with the topless waitresses.

He hadn't talked to them since, which was fine with him. They needed a rest and he needed a break. The onetime gig to kill Zeek and stop him from being a problem to Kilos Shipping had, with the *Vidynut* incident, unexpectedly turned into something much larger and much more visible. Despite asking the Indian military for confidentiality in the matter, Conley had been dodging calls about Team Whiskey since leaving Mumbai—inquiries from rival shipping companies that needed the team's brand of security were pouring in. Conley was familiar with MySpace, Facebook, Twitter, texting and plain old e-mail. But never did he think that word about Nolan and company would make the rounds so quickly.

But now that he was back at his home base, he hoped it was over, that the wave had crested. Though he'd turned into something akin to Team Whiskey's booking agent, it was also important that he get back to doing his real job, running security for Kilos's Middle Eastern operations.

No such luck. A glance at his blinking answering machine revealed fifty-four waiting messages, three times the normal after a week away.

Maybe I should get voice mail, he thought.

He wearily hit the PLAY button and listened to each one. Many were from the same people he'd avoided earlier, representatives from rival shipping companies looking to hire Team Whiskey.

Of the fifty-four messages, one stood out. It was from a friend of a friend, a British doctor who lived on the Channel Island of Jersey, off the west coast of France. As his was the only call that didn't involve maritime security, Conley called him back.

Dr. Stevenson lived in a small village on the western edge of the island and frequented a pub that sat on a cliff looking out on the Atlantic. The pub also served as a boardinghouse, one of whose recent guests had prompted Stevenson's call. The middle-aged man had shown up at the small hotel about a month before. He didn't have much money and, when he was sober, which wasn't very often, was wary of the other guests. He especially feared anyone connected with the sea—shipping, pleasure boating, the Royal Navy—and in his more inebriated moments, expressed particular concern about a man with one leg. Oddly, the guest was a naval officer himself of some sort, or at least he signed in with the unusual name of Lt. Commander Q. Zee.

The strange man spent his days on the cliff near the pub, looking out to sea in good weather and bad, trying to separate the container ships from the yachts, waiting for something he seemed to hope would never come.

At night, after partaking of a few drinks and other intoxicants, he would hold court in the pub's bar, telling horrible stories of murder and mayhem on the high seas. He would also hint that he held a secret of immense proportions, something that would wreak havoc on the entire planet if the wrong men learned of it. All this he would tell the pub patrons and the tourists, as they bought him anisette until he passed out and the pub owner's son carried him to his room.

Though at first the owner feared the man's presence would eventually drive business away, this was not the case. The tourists loved him, and even the locals liked to listen to him. He was that much of an oddity.

One night, the man collapsed and died. Dr. Stevenson performed the postmortem and attributed the death to alcohol poisoning and an overdose of cocaine. The stranger's body was laid out in the village's small clinic. His few possessions, including a change of clothes and a BlackBerry, were stored in the pub's attic.

The following night, people came looking for the dead man—but they weren't interested in claiming his body. Wearing dark clothes and ski masks, five men invaded the pub just before closing time, terrifying the owner, his wife and a handful of drunken patrons. They were looking for the man's possessions, tossing his room with the precision of people who'd done this sort of thing before. But on finding nothing, and fearing the police would soon be on their way, the raiders departed, leaving in a helicopter that had landed on the far side of the cliff.

The pub owner's son had stolen the man's BlackBerry just minutes before the invaders arrived, justifying it as payment for back rent the stranger owed when he died. Confessing the theft to his father, the young man gave the BlackBerry to Dr. Stevenson, who at one time had served as a medical officer with the British SAS. After examining the device, the doctor began to believe the stranger's claims that he knew a dangerous secret that had worldwide implications. His clue? The seemingly ordinary BlackBerry turned out to be a sophisticated communications and data storage device of the sort used by intelligence services.

On the device, the doctor discovered entries that indicated something extremely valuable was buried on a pinprick of land off eastern Africa, close to the island of Zanzibar. The device contained information on this small island—a place that showed up on very few maps—and directions on how to get there. It also held personal data on the dead man—much of it encrypted—that further indicated he was not some kook.

Judging by some of the security codes he found, Stevenson determined that the dead man had been a highly trusted courier for some country's intelligence service.

Possibly Great Britain's MI-6.

Or even the CIA.

"I DON'T UNDERSTAND why this character buried this thing in the first place," Crash said, draining his glass of Egyptian beer. "If it was so freaking valuable, why is it hidden on an island no one has ever heard about?"

Conley had anticipated the question. The team was sitting in a dockside bar near the Kilos building in the Port of Aden.

The team had just returned from their side-job with Bebe and the mobsters, picking up the DUS-7 in Mauritius and finally making the twice-delayed sail back to Yemen. Conley was astonished to hear the story about their gig on the cruise liner, shocked that the team had worked for the Russian Mob.

"Dangerous people who do dangerous things," Conley told them. "I don't know many people crazy enough to get in bed with the Krasnaya mafiy. No Americans, anyway."

At this, Nolan told him point-blank. "We're not Americans. Not anymore."

They'd retired to the bar on the water and ate and drank, and Conley told them about his conversation with Dr. Stevenson and the saga of the mysterious courier.

"The doctor was able to break into the guy's personal information on the fake BlackBerry even though it was encrypted up the wazoo," Conley said. "Whoever this guy was, he was an expert in handling extremely sensitive items, many of them stolen. Intelligence documents, industrial espionage, weapons designs, things like that. He'd been doing it for years, always worked alone, and he wrote everything down. He'd been using this little-known island to bury the especially hot items until things cooled off. Because this place doesn't even show up on a lot of maps, he thought it was better hiding valuable stuff there than using safes or security boxes. He would hire seaplanes or private boats to drop him off, telling them he was doing scuba diving or survival training or some such bullshit. He would bury the item and then come back for it the same way.

"This last time, though, the plane he'd hired to go pick up the item crashed on the island. He was the only survivor and now he was stranded. He eventually ran into some drug-dealing pirate types who were also using the place to hide their stash. He paid them to take him off the island, but he didn't want to carry the item with him while he was traveling with them. So it stayed behind, still buried.

"When he got back to civilization, he came to believe that certain people were chasing him, thinking he had the treasure with him. Instead of going back for it, he went into hiding. This drove him a little nuts, I guess, because he also developed a powerful drug habit and a drinking problem, which added to his paranoia. By the time he made it to that boardinghouse on Jersey, he was a mess. The thing was, he was right—people *were* after him. And if he had waited just one more day to die, those people would have gotten the most important thing Dr. Stevenson now has in his possession."

"And what is that exactly?" Nolan asked.

"A treasure map," Conley said with a straight face.

"You've got to be kidding," Batman said.

Conley shook his head. "It was hidden on the faux Black-Berry along with all the other secret stuff. It's a map of that island, and it shows where he buried this ultravaluable something-or-other."

"And what does this have to do with us?" Nolan asked him.

"Well, how else will you know where to dig when you get there?" Conley replied.

The team members laughed, even Twitch.

"Why are you so convinced we'd want to do that?" Batman asked him.

Conley refilled his beer mug. "One reason is, Stevenson says he thinks he knows what the treasure is, and that he can get it back into the hands of the right people."

"So?" Nolan asked.

Conley smiled. "So, in addition to giving me a finder's fee, he's agreed to pay you five million to get him there and back safely."

The team was stunned.

"Five million?" Crash said. "The doctor knew how to save his pennies."

"Ever meet one who didn't?" Conley asked.

"Plus, there must be something in it for him at the end of the road, too," Batman said. "Something gy-normous."

"I'm sure there is," Conley replied. "But in this case, you guys are little more than taxi drivers. Get him there, help him dig for the buried treasure, and get him back. Maybe a week's work—and you got another five million to lug around with you."

The team was almost overwhelmed; it seemed like the big money just kept rolling in.

"But why us?" Gunner asked this time.

Conley shrugged. "The island is located in pirate-infested waters off Africa," he said. "Stevenson needs someone he can trust, and he wants to do it quickly and quietly. You might have to work on that quiet part, but as far as getting him there and back, I think it's doable."

Conley replenished his beer once again.

"Besides," he said, "what else you guys got to do?"

DR. STEVENSON FLEW in the next morning.

He looked the part of a man of intelligence and leisure; middle-age, in good shape, with a shock of graying hair. He was dressed plainly, thank God. The team had fretted he might show up wearing a safari suit, a pith helmet, jodhpurs or worse.

They met him at the dockside bar. He was accompanied by a younger man named Squire who appeared to be hired security. His tattoos ID'd him as ex-SAS, as in Special Air Service, the elite British special ops group. A good guy to have along.

Stevenson had the map, taken from the encrypted fake Black-Berry. But he had some unsettling news for Team Whiskey.

"Once I was able to fully decrypt this, I discovered I wasn't the first one to get into its pants," he told them.

"Translation, please?" Crash asked.

"Someone else logged onto the device shortly before I got ahold of it," Stevenson said. "Possibly right before the owner moved into the boarding house on Jersey. They might not have gotten in as deep as I did, but they were able to extract some information."

"And that means?" Nolan asked.

"It means someone else knows about this island," Stevenson said. "And they probably know that something extremely valuable is buried there."

"Which means someone else might be trying to get to the treasure?" Batman asked.

Stevenson nodded solemnly. "Precisely."

Nolan looked at the others and shrugged.

"Nothing like adding a little excitement," he said.

THEY'D BARELY BEEN able to resupply the DUS-7 when they set sail again.

The Senegals were still onboard. So, too, was the field gun Kilos had provided them for the *Vidynut* recovery. They put the artillery piece on a one-foot-high elevated platform with heavy-duty springs underneath and side railings usually employed as loading assists. The odd arrangement was designed to reduce the big gun's recoil, keep its aim true, and avoid tearing up the deck—as they discovered it did during the retaking of the *Vidynut*.

The cannonade machine was disassembled, with two of the 50-calibers put onto swivel mounts, one on either side of the work copter's open bay, and the three others put on the DUS-7's bridge. The ship's helipad was reinforced and enlarged to handle helicopters even bigger than the work copter.

More ammunition was loaded aboard—finally—along with more fuel. The gas turbine was recalibrated, and the entire communication suite was updated with better GPS and worldwide sat-phone coverage.

All this was done in just one day by Kilos engineers working at the Port of Aden facility.

THEY SET SAIL at midnight.

Slipping out among the fleets of container ships moving about the watery crossroads of the Middle East with their weapons hidden, they looked like just another coastal freighter, battered, dented and badly in need of a paint job.

Once they were under way, Nolan made the mistake of climbing up to the bridge and joining the Senegals for a drink. He was off the clock, and after what had happened in the past two weeks, he needed a break any time he could get one.

But drinking with the Senegals wasn't like taking a shot of vodka or downing a few beers. It meant tossing back a concoction known as *mooch,* a brew of fermented apples, hops, grain alcohol and pulverized qat, the slightly hallucinogenic stimulant plant many people in North Africa chewed on a daily basis.

The first few gulps of mooch were like nirvana. The sea was calm, the sky was brilliant with stars, and the DUS-7 was moving along at almost forty knots—which was exhilarating in itself. As one of the Senegals steered the ship and stayed sober—the designated driver—Nolan and the other African sailors toasted each other and exchanged war stories. Gradually, Nolan started to relax.

Things began to go wrong about an hour into the drunk-fest. The Senegals were funny guys, with many stories about their exploits fighting as mercenaries in Africa. Nolan thought he might have laughed *too* hard, something that had never happened to him before. He got dizzy, found himself gulping for air, his face became flushed and his stomach was suddenly aching. Just about this time, the sea started rolling. The wind came up and the waves began to build. Within fifteen minutes, they found themselves in the middle of a storm not unlike the one that had preceded the battle for the *Vidynut.*

And very quickly, Nolan found himself seasick. Another first.

He managed to stagger down to his cabin and collapse on

his bunk. He rocked and rolled with the ship, tossing and turning, the nonsense he'd written on his walls seeming to revolve around him, suspended in air. He prayed for the ability to hurl, yet was unable to.

This was not like him. He was embarrassed enough that the Senegals saw him turn white; he would be horrified if the other Whiskey members witnessed him in this condition.

Though it was his stomach that was twisted, it was really his head that didn't feel screwed on right. Not a year ago, he was going mad in the hellhole in Kuwait, digging his way out not just to escape, but to walk across Iraq, Iran and Afghanistan into Pakistan to continue his pursuit for Target Number 1. Yes—less than a year ago. But it seemed more like just a few weeks.

Now he was almost a millionaire, out on the open sea, far from that windowless rat hole of a prison cell. He was eating well, living well, fighting well, and developing a reputation that could bring him millions of dollars more.

Yet it just didn't seem right.

There were things missing. Things he'd left behind, back in his old life. People and things.

He sat up straight in his bunk, desperate to shake these thoughts. He'd worked on conquering his demons after getting out of Kuwait, and at the moment vastly appreciated the mall-cop job for easing the transition. He'd won a major internal victory by flying the work copter that night over the Talua Tangs—with a little help from Twitch's magic air. They had stomped Zeek. They had stomped the Somali pirates. They had prevented a bunch of very rich gangsters from being poisoned to death. And more millions would soon be theirs.

But still, he was feeling empty. Why?

Showing physical weakness was one thing—displaying any further mental issues would be hard to come back from.

He had to get back up on deck.

Climbing the ladder was rough. The ship seemed to be going one way every time he started going the other. At one point, it felt as if the *Dustboat* was turning completely over, that the sea would come rushing in and that would be the end of him.

But he blinked his eyes, and everything became more or less level again.

Somehow he made it to the main deck and was able to look out on the raging waters of the Indian Ocean. The waves were so high, their spray looked like tsunamis. There was so much water going back and forth, it was like the lights around him were melting and flowing into one. It was almost psychedelic. He was immediately soaked to the skin.

But then something caught his eye. Not on the deck, but on the water, beyond the hellish waves. First, it was just a yellow light. Then he saw a green one, than a red one. They were all dull, barely visible, maybe 1,000 feet off the port side.

It was another vessel—a container ship, heading north, painted mostly black with a white bridge. It looked weirdly empty for some reason, like no one was steering it. Like it was devoid of any human life or control.

Could it be?

Suddenly, Nolan felt 100-percent sober. He ran up to the bridge, bursting in and surprising the still-jovial Senegals. He retrieved the bridge's pair of powerful nightscope binoculars and ran back out to the railing.

He pointed the spyglasses at the ship and studied it up and down, bow to stern, with his good eye.

Could it be?

He ran to the back of the DUS-7 and focused on the container ship's stern as it disappeared into the night. He *had* to see its name.

It seemed like it took forever, trying to focus the scope for his one eye, looking through the water and spray and the waves. He finally got the binoculars to focus, though, and he was stunned by what he saw. The ship's name was the *Dutch Cloud*.

The ghost ship Bebe had told him about.

He ran back up to the bridge, his heart on fire. He asked the Senegals if they'd also seen the name of the ship.

As one, all of them replied: "What ship?"

19

NOLAN SPENT THE rest of the night up on the bridge, scanning the sea-surface radar, hoping the phantom ship would reappear. Five hours of searching produced nothing, though. He monitored the radio all night, too, trying to pick up any stray transmissions. Again, he came up empty.

He finally fell asleep on a cot on the bridge and was awakened by the rays of the morning sun streaming in the window. The bad weather had passed, and Gunner was standing over him with a pot of coffee.

"Breakfast of champions," Gunner said, pouring him a cup.

Nolan got to his feet. His head was pounding, but at least it wasn't spinning anymore. The Senegals offered their apologies for causing his condition, but he waved them away.

"Ma faute," he told them in their native French. "My fault."

His thoughts went back to the craziness on the deck just a few hours before. It didn't seem real to him now; it was more like a dream. Had the storm been that big—or had it just been a squall? Had the fermented apples gotten to him—or was it the qat? Had he just fallen asleep here on the bridge and imagined the whole thing?

He rubbed the fog from his eye and checked their position on the control panel. Despite having passed through the storm, they were still making good time. They were already 500 miles out from Aden and just a little more than a day's sail from the spot where the mystery island was supposed to be.

Their course was taking them right through waters most frequented by Somali pirates, but Gunner and the Senegals were already joking about it.

"Let them try to attack us," Gunner was saying, just itching to use the artillery piece again. "They'll wish they stuck to chasing zebras."

THEY SAILED ALL that day and into the night with no problems. The seas stayed calm and the steady wind helped push them closer and closer to their destination.

The team spent most of their time in the galley, playing endless rounds of poker and drinking coffee, sleeping only in two- or three-hour shifts.

About ten-thirty the next morning, Nolan had just won a big hand when one of the Senegals came down to interrupt the never-ending card game. He'd spotted something up ahead.

It was not a phanton container ship. Rather it was a much smaller boat, a half-mile off their port bow. It was about the size of the DUS-7, but of much more modern design. It looked like a research vessel, all white with lots of antennas and satellite dishes poking out of the top. The problem was, it was obviously drifting.

Within five minutes, they had pulled up close to the vessel and the Senegals had caught it with a grappling hook. Nolan and Crash went over and climbed up to the bridge, where they discovered two crewmembers slumped over the controls—both shot in the head.

They went below and made their way through several cabins packed with digging utensils. Shovels. Picks. Buckets. Tarps.

"Maybe an archeology team," Nolan said, scanning the stuff.

They moved into the galley, and here they found the ship's passengers. Five white men, steroid-pumped muscles, dressed in black, with empty shoulder holsters—and powdery noses. Each had two bullets in his head.

The galley had been ransacked of food and water. A liquor cabinet in the kitchen was empty. There were no guns on board, but plenty of empty ammunition boxes. Bloody prints on the galley deck showed the murderers had been barefoot. It all led to one conclusion.

"Somali pirates," Crash said.

Nolan nodded. "No doubt about it. They must have caught these guys with their pants down, snorting their lunch."

They both tasted a bit of the powder left on the table. It was cocaine.

"I'm guessing these morons were drug runners," Crash observed. "Drug runners who thought they'd go digging for something maybe?"

"Bingo again," Nolan replied. "They just picked the wrong time to play Indiana Jones."

The team had no choice but to move on—recovering the bodies of drug mules wasn't in their plan. They made a sat-phone call to the International Maritime Hotline in London and reported what they had found and where. Then they hung up before giving any of their own information.

TWENTY MINUTES LATER, they came upon another boat drifting in the water.

There was no doubt who this vessel belonged to. It was a long, thin motorboat with dual engines and a small control house. There were ten black gunmen aboard it, all dead. All were barefoot; all had been shot multiple times by a large caliber weapon. The boat itself was riddled with bullet holes and barely afloat.

"And here are our perps," Nolan said, studying the boat full of bodies from the nose of the DUS-7 and seeing it was filled with food, bags of cocaine, and liquor bottles. "Ten less Somali pirates to worry about."

But what had happened to them?

Gunner was the weapons expert. He looked at the carnage from stern to bow. It appeared that, just as the pirates had probably surprised the drug runners, someone had probably surprised the pirates. But who?

"From the angle of the bullet holes?" Gunner said, shaking his head. "Hard to say."

Just then, they heard a low, droning sound. An airplane was coming at them out of the south. It was an updated Grumman Goose, a two-engine, high-wing seaplane usually seen island-hopping in the Caribbean or the Pacific.

It flew right by them, close to their port side, going very fast and disappearing into the darkening clouds to the north.

"Someone out here running pirate-watching trips?" Crash asked dryly.

The droning noise gradually faded away, but then grew loud again. The plane passed them again, this time on their starboard side, flying south, very low.

"Someone on board must have forgotten something," Gunner said.

"Either that or they're trying to get a good look at us," Batman replied.

Now the seaplane turned yet again and came back a third time. This time, Nolan sensed something was wrong.

It was slowing down and passing them on the port side again. It seemed almost like it was going to attempt a landing.

"Maybe they're in trouble?" Crash wondered. "Maybe they need us to rescue them."

That idea was shattered by what happened next. As the innocuous plane went by, they could see two of the windows in the fuselage were open. Suddenly bullets were flying all around the bridge. It took the team a few moments to realize the gunfire was coming from the passing airplane.

"What the fuck?" Crash roared. "Whose fucking air force is that?"

Gunner yelled, "Now we know who killed those pirates."

The team sprung into action. They lowered the blast visor on the bridge and everyone grabbed their M4s. Gunner ran outside to one of the bridge-mounted 50-calibers, newly installed in its movable seat. But there was a problem. The machine guns elevated only 45 degrees—when the Kilos engineers installed them, it had never dawned on them they might be needed to shoot at airborne targets. They were meant strictly for battling pirates and seaborne adversaries. The same was true for the 50-calibers installed near the stern railing.

Now the plane was turning and coming back. And unless it flew really, *really* low, the team's best weapons would be useless against it.

Dr. Stevenson and Squire had appeared on the deck by now, attracted by the commotion. They were carrying two high-powered hunting rifles.

The plane went by again, strafing the upper deck, hitting the cargo masts, and perforating the work copter sitting unshielded on its landing platform. Everyone in Team Whiskey fired back at the attacker with their M4s, but the effort was stymied by lack of range and the airplane's speed.

The plane turned and strafed them again on the port side, heavily damaging their life boats and snapping their main communications antenna.

This was getting serious. Nolan knew a well-placed barrage from the airplane hitting the bridge or the fuel supply could cripple them at least, and at worst, sink them. Yet there was no way they could fight back against the attacking aircraft.

"Blow smoke and come to all stop!" Nolan told the Senegals suddenly. The others were puzzled by the order, but it soon made sense. The *Dustboat* quickly slowed to a crawl and smoke began billowing out of its stack, creating a temporary smoke screen. Meanwhile, Nolan borrowed the doctor's hunting rifles, handing one to Gunner. Together they climbed the two starboard cargo masts.

The plane turned and approached them again on the starboard side. The ship had emerged from the smoke cloud by now, meaning Nolan and Gunner had to act fast. They drew a bead on the airplane with the high-powered rifles. As it went by strafing the deck below, Nolan and Gunner opened up from atop the masts.

They missed the plane's pilot but shot the two men who were firing at them from the passenger compartment. The plane staggered for a moment. Their bullets had caught one of its engines, too. It started smoking and dipped a little before regaining its lost altitude. Now the low drone was replaced by the sound of an engine backfiring.

The plane did not turn back toward the DUS-7 this time. It continued flying south, a cloud of oily smoke trailing behind it. It finally disappeared over the horizon.

The doctor quickly checked everyone for injuries. Incredibly, no one had been hit in the strafing attack. But again, the ship's new communications tower had been shot to pieces, and one of the portside cargo masts had been cut in two. Worst of all, the work copter had taken a dozen rounds to its rotor and tail section. The damage was irreparable; their air asset was out of commission.

Looking at the trail of smoke still visible in the southern sky, Twitch said, "So much for our welcoming committee."

THEY SPOTTED THE island about a half hour later.

Though the skies were clear and the ocean still calm, their destination, sitting out on the southern horizon, was mostly engulfed in fog.

"No wonder no one can ever find this place," Crash said, standing on the bridge, scanning the murky place through high-powered binoculars. "It reminds me of our old digs back in Malacca."

Gunner was right beside him, also studying the mist-enshrouded island. "Isn't this where King Kong lives?" he asked.

Nolan was looking at the place through his special one-eye scope. He couldn't disagree with his colleagues. Lots of thick jungle, waves crashing on shore. Even what appeared to be an extinct volcano. It was right out of a '30s Hollywood movie.

Then he spotted something else. Anchored a few hundred feet off the north end of the island was the seaplane that had shot at them. This was not a big surprise.

"I know the first thing we have to do," he said.

THEY WERE SOON within a half-mile of the island. Their communications were out, but they still had sea surface radar, and this allowed them to sweep the waters around them in case any other vessels were nearby. They spotted nothing.

They made for the seaplane. Nolan, studying it through his spyglass as it bobbed in the shallow waves off the rocky shore, could see the two open windows he and Gunner had shot at; streams of blood dripped down the fuselage beneath them. The cowling on the plane's left engine was also up, as if someone had tried to fix the damage the team's high-powered gunfire had done. Nolan was familiar enough with this kind of plane to know it could still fly on one engine. Which meant it could still be dangerous to them.

They moved the DUS-7 to within a hundred feet of the moored seaplane. One more check of the surface radar told them they were still alone on this side of the island. A scan of the nearby shoreline also turned up nothing.

Gunner had been manning the M102 field gun since the seaplane was spotted. He took it very personally when someone shot at him. This would be his measure of revenge.

When Nolan gave him the signal from the bridge, Gunner loaded the weapon, closed the breech, eyeballed the aiming guide and fired the gun. The crashing waves masked most of the sound as the shell hit the seaplane below the wing root, blowing it to pieces and collapsing the fuselage in on itself. The plane sank in mere seconds, going down with one big glub. A cheer went up from the DUS-7. It had been a perfect shot.

"He's getting pretty good with that shooter," Batman observed.

Watching it all from the railing with the rest of them, Twitch said: "I hope we didn't need that thing to get out of here."

THE DUS-7 CONTINUED its way around the island. Reaching a large outcrop of rock in the southwest side, they picked up a small blip on the sea surface radar. Peering through the fog, they could see some type of vessel anchored on the far end of the island.

It was important that they keep their presence here secret, so Nolan ordered the DUS-7 to back away out of sight. Then he and Batman went out in a small boat and paddled up to the rocky outcrop. Using it as cover, they were able to see the vessel, anchored about 1,000 yards away.

It was a catamaran—a large one. Easily 200 feet long, it was two hulls connected by a bridging section and a large bow structure.

"Seaplanes? Catamarans?" Batman said. "Is there a casino out here?"

Nolan studied the catamaran and concluded it was probably built as a car ferry. But at the moment, it wasn't cars but digging equipment being offloaded from it. They could see a work barge transporting a front-end loader and a small army of men with shovels to the shore.

"Whoever these guys are, they're not screwing around," Nolan said. "They got enough stuff to dig up every inch of this place."

"Which gotta mean they're looking for the same thing we are," Batman replied.

They returned to the DUS-7 and had the Senegals bring it back around to the northeast side of the island. Here they found a small cove surrounded by high coral reefs. Large waves were crashing onto these reefs, however, making the inlet's entrance an extremely hazardous passage.

Nolan asked the Senegals if they thought they could maneuver the DUS-7 past the reefs and into the cove, in order to hide it close to shore. They assured him they could. But from that commenced ten minutes of high drama as the West African sailors inched the freighter through a channel barely thirty feet across. The DUS-7 itself was twenty-five feet wide; the clearance was so small, both sides of the ship scraped against the cement-like coral going in. It was brutal to watch, but in the end, an amazing feat of seamanship.

Once inside the calmer waters of the inlet, the ship nestled itself near some overhanging flora, practically unseen from the waters beyond the reefs.

They had their hiding place.

THEY WENT ASHORE in two boats.

Nolan, the doctor, Squire and Crash went in one; Batman, Gunner, Twitch and one of the Senegals in the other. The rest of the Senegals remained on the DUS-7, their weapons ready, with the engines muted on idle.

The two boat parties hooked up and immediately plunged into the jungle. The island was about a half-mile around and, besides the rocky beaches, it appeared to be all jungle and one volcanic mountain. Some streams ran through it, but their water was curiously the color of blood.

Not two minutes into the jungle, they came upon the wreckage of a small two-engine De Havilland seaplane. It had crashed into a thick tree bank and had made it to the ground remarkably intact.

The passenger compartment was empty, but the two pilots were still in their seats, still wearing their company uniforms and even their hats and headphones. Their skeletal hands still clutched the controls, condemned forever to fly a doomed plane.

"This must be the crash the mystery man survived," the doctor said. "That means it all started right here."

They continued through the jungle, heading south, walking carefully with their weapons up, ever aware that they weren't the only ones on the island. Twitch was in the lead, scanning everything around him with each step.

He suddenly held up his hand, bringing the team to a stop. He said not a word, just pointed to the ground about two feet in front of him. Nolan looked over his shoulder.

Barely visible in the heavy foliage was a large square pit dug into the hard sand. It was about ten feet deep. At the bottom were a dozen bamboo sticks, sharpened ends pointing up.

"Punji sticks," Twitch said. "Looks like monkey shit on the tips. If the fall doesn't kill you, the infection will."

Nolan looked deeper into the pit and saw bones at the bottom. Animal? Human? It was hard to tell. But his guess was the booby trap had been here for a while, probably set up by pirates or drug dealers. Because of its location right off the beach, it was meant as a cruel warning to anyone who would come here looking for buried treasure—of any kind.

Once the rest of the team saw the trap, Nolan told them, "We all got to watch our step. These things are guaranteed to ruin your day."

TEN MINUTES LATER, they reached a clearing, only to make another gruesome discovery: three bodies stuffed under some rubber trees, barely hidden in the brush. Each had been bound and gagged; each had two bullets in the back of the neck. The bodies were still warm.

"Are you thinking what I'm thinking?" Batman asked Nolan.

Nolan nodded grimly. "I'm guessing these guys are what's left of our seaplane crew," he said. "They were hired guns who were paid to sink or at least turn away anyone who came close to this island. But it's like what usually happens with rookie hit men: their employers get rid of them to keep them quiet, whether they've succeeded or not."

"But who whacked them?" Crash asked.

Nolan checked the ammo clip in his M4.

"Let's find out," he said.

THEY STOLE UP onto the beach near where the huge catamaran had anchored. Dr. Stevenson carefully studied the men on shore nearby. All were dressed in black battle suits and stocking caps. He immediately recognized them as fitting the description of the armed men who'd invaded the Jersey Island pub that night.

"My guess is they're South Africans," the doctor said. "The witnesses in the pub that night were mostly tourists. They said the raiders spoke with British accents, but strange ones."

The team watched as the catamaran crew tour off another front-end loader and more stacks of digging tools. Team Whiskey, by contrast, had brought only hand shovels and entrenchment tools.

"Frigging guys *are* serious," Batman said. "And if they spot our tub and know that we're on the island, they'll hunt us down like . . ."

His last few words were drowned out by a loud whistling sound. A moment later, a flash of metallic light passed over their heads and landed squarely on the work barge bringing the front-end loader to shore. The explosion was so large it knocked everyone in Team Whiskey's group to the ground. They wisely remained there and waited. When the smoke cleared, they looked back to the beach and found nothing left of the barge, the front-end loader or the men accompanying it.

Suddenly, more shells came screaming through the air. This was not their M102 firing; these were large-caliber naval gun shells going over their heads. The barrage hit the beach, causing another minor earthquake.

Nolan jumped up, climbed the nearest tree, and—using his special spyglass—spotted a military ship coming toward the island from the east, moving very fast. He reported this to the team below.

"Who the fuck could it be?" Crash asked.

"Can you ID it?" Batman called up to him.

Nolan was able to read the numbers on the side of the ship. "P331," he said. "It's a destroyer."

Batman pulled out his BlackBerry, called up a special foreign navies app and started typing in Nolan's information.

"God damn," he said after a few moments. "Who ordered the *khoresht*?"

Nolan couldn't believe it. "That's an Iranian ship?"

Batman confirmed it: "It's the *Jamaran*. Fifty-eight hundred tons. Guided missile destroyer. It was deployed to the Gulf of Aden a few months ago to help control the pirates. Looks like it's gotten involved in some extracurricular activities instead."

As he was speaking, the Iranian vessel unleashed a ferocious barrage of ship-to-ship missiles. They all hit the catamaran, blowing it to pieces. It was a frightening demonstration of enormous naval firepower.

"Christ—we'll be part of tomorrow's shish kabob if they find us out here," Crash said. "And we got no way to call for help."

"So what else is new?" Twitch said.

THE IRANIAN DESTROYER anchored close by the wreckage of the catamaran.

It lowered four boats and began ferrying people to the shore, about two hundred and fifty feet away. The personnel in the boats were all dressed in civilian clothes; none was wearing a military uniform. Each had a shovel or a pick, and in that way they looked like an army of archeologists. But each was also carrying an assault rifle or a machine gun. Some were also lugging military-style metal detectors and even portable ground-imaging radar sets. Looking like a large jackhammer, each instrument required three men to drag it across the ground while a fourth took readings of what it saw beneath the surface. Like a very elaborate mine detector, it could spot things buried almost ten feet underground.

The sun was starting to go down. The men who were ferried ashore worked on setting up a base camp and building two huge bonfires, using wood already gathered by the people their naval guns had just obliterated.

Watching all this from the jungle nearby were Nolan and Batman; the rest of the team had returned to the *Dustboat*.

This was a disturbing development. There had always been a chance that they could dig up the treasure and avoid the people in the catamaran. But trying to get away from the island—treasure in hand or not—would be almost impossible with the Iranian warship on the scene.

"There's got to be about a hundred and fifty of those assholes already on shore," Batman said, eyeing the Iranian base camp. "And what? Another three or four hundred still on the ship?"

"At least," Nolan replied, studying the situation with his special spyglass. "I'm guessing these guys on the beach are Pazdaran. The top Iranian special ops group? Remember them from the Battle of Herat?"

"Just barely," Batman replied. "And, you know, for this being a secret treasure, a lot of people seem to know about it."

"Well, maybe these guys don't know *exactly* where to dig for it," Nolan theorized. "I mean, why else would they have so many people with so much equipment?"

"They do seem to be settling in for the night," Batman said, noting the Iranians were building several more bonfires and setting up tents. "If you're right, they might not start searching for the treasure until tomorrow morning."

Nolan checked his watch and said, "Which means we only have a few hours to find it—in the dark."

"But finding it will only be half the battle," Batman said. "We still have to get away."

Nolan thought a moment, then packed up his spyglass.

"Let's find the damn thing first," he said. "Then we'll figure out how to get out of here."

THEY RETURNED TO the DUS-7 and helped cover it completely with tree branches and vines. Then, leaving the Senegals on board, the rest of the team went back into the jungle, following the map found on the faux BlackBerry.

Again, the fact that the Iranians had come ashore with metal detectors and portable ground radar imaging units suggested they weren't really sure where to start digging. Whiskey barely had a shovel and some entrenching tools. However, they did have the original map. They were hoping this gave them an important advantage.

The map, crudely drawn, had been scanned and downloaded to the mystery man's device. Though not elaborate, the version Dr. Stevenson had been able to recover did list some GPS coordinates as longitude and latitude. So in a way, looking for the treasure would be an exercise in "geocaching"— hiding an object at specific GPS coordinates to be found by someone else.

But the map actually showed *three* sites where the treasure could be buried—just why the dead man had chosen to give more than one location was a mystery. Most likely he wanted to make it harder for anyone who eventually found the map. The only real clue was a note that said the real treasure was buried in a "black spotted bag."

After a tough slog through the heavy jungle, the team reached the first GPS point indicated, praying they would hit paydirt right away. The site was on a small hill on the north end of the island, not far from where they'd sunk the seaplane. The hill was covered with heavy vines, and the sandy ground was almost solid with roots. In fact, it was hard to tell where the vines ended and the ground began.

Using their night-vision capability, they were able to locate a spot near the GPS coordinates that appeared to have been dug up relatively recently. Still, the re-digging was arduous— much worse than what they had to do back in the Mirang Island graveyard, Crash reported. Their shovels were practically useless here; at least the entrenching tools were sharp on the business end, allowing them to cut through the vines that had grown over the recently disturbed ground.

They took turns on the entrenching tools while Gunner kept watch. It was during a turn by the doctor and Batman that they hit not another tangle of vines but a piece of solid wood.

"Bingo," Batman whispered, quickly adding: "I hope . . ."

They'd hit the top of a long, narrow wooden box—a coffin, they thought at first. But further digging revealed it to be a wooden shipping crate bearing U.S. military markings.

They pried off the cover and found within a pair of Stingers, the small portable surface-to-air missile that allowed a single person to shoot down an aircraft as big as an airliner. There were four more boxes under the one they'd uncovered, equaling ten Stingers in all.

"Jackpot!" Crash cried. "Right?"

At first, they all thought they'd guessed right by digging here. But then reality set in.

"This isn't it," Stevenson said. "Stingers are available all over world—and can be had on the black market fairly easily. Our dead courier friend didn't deal in things so pedestrian— and let's face it, this is hardly a pot of gold worth sending a Iranian warship to uncover."

Plus, on closer examination, they determined the missiles were old, rusty and probably unworkable. At the very least they'd have to be recalibrated and expertly cleaned before anyone even thought of using them.

"He's right," Nolan said. "No way everyone got so hot and bothered about ten old missiles."

THEY MOVED ON to the second dig site.

Their GPS device told them it was on a beach on the western edge of the island, about a quarter mile from where the catamaran was sunk. The digging here was just as tough. The beach was rocky on top and muddy beneath, so with every two swipes of the entrenching tool, the mud flooded back in, filling half the hole again.

But after some heavy work, they finally hit something that was not mud. It was a large metal box this time, almost the size as the crate the Stingers were in. It took all their muscle power to pull it out of the ground, after which they discovered it had not one, but two combination locks on it. This presented a problem: Shooting the locks off would make too much noise; the Iranians were not that far away. Plus, if this box contained Stingers as well, a bullet in the wrong place would blow them to Kingdom Come. But they were running out of time.

Gunner stepped forward, indicating the others should move back. He studied the two locks, but then put his fingers under the box's lid and began to pry it open. It seemed impossible at first; the box appeared to be solid metal. But Gunner was incredibly strong and eventually, he was able to bend the lid away from the combination locks and off the box completely.

The others were amazed.

"Fucking guy eats his Wheaties," Batman said to Stevenson.

Beneath the lid was an old woolen blanket. Nolan pulled it away to reveal a large stash of brilliant, shimmering coins.

"Jesus Christ!" Crash exclaimed. "Are those gold?"

As it turned out, the answer was no.

Batman studied the coins—and then started laughing grimly.

"These are Soviet-era rubles," he declared. "The Russians used to make them in both coin and script. They look like gold, but . . ."

"But?" Nolan asked.

"But," Batman went on, "they are possibly the most useless currency on the planet at the moment."

There was a collective groan from everyone on hand.

"Strike fucking two," Crash said, throwing a handful of the coins into the water.

"This dead guy is dicking with us," Gunner declared ominously. "The shitty Stingers, and now this worthless Russian crap? Has anyone considered that this whole thing might be a gag?"

A gloomy silence fell over them. No one wanted to think that.

Finally Twitch said: "Well, if it is, it's a long way to go for a fucking joke."

THEY GRIMLY MOVED on to the third site, highly suspicious that they were on a wild goose chase. Finding and digging up the first two sites had taken much longer than they'd expected. The night had slipped away, and it was now only ninety minutes to dawn. The team was sure the island would soon be crawling with Iranian Special Forces.

Making a bad situation worse, the third site, according to the map, was located on a cliff just below the cone of the extinct volcano. They'd have to climb up to it.

This took almost an hour itself, and they were exhausted by the time they reached their goal. At first the ground here looked like concrete, but it was actually volcanic ash. Once the top layer was broken, it was like digging in hard sand. They went to work with the entrenching tools again, trying their best to stay on the spot the GPS was indicating.

More backbreaking work ensued, but finally they came upon yet another box. This one was plastic and about the size of a small TV. They opened it fairly easily and inside found a large, black spotted sack.

"Motherfucker . . ." Crash groaned. "I *knew* we should have started up here."

"If there's a jack-in-the-box in there," Gunner announced. "I'm going on a shooting spree."

They all recognized the sack as a "burn bag," used by spies and other special ops people to burn sensitive items safely should adversaries be closing in.

They opened the sack and found it was stuffed with rags and a small blanket. Stevenson searched through them until he found a wooden box not much bigger than a pack of cigarettes. Inside this box, he found a smaller metal box and opened it, only to find yet *another* smaller box inside. It was the type of container that held fuses for airplanes. Inside it was a wad of plastic wrapped in electrical wire. Unraveling this, they were left with a small jewelry box, something a ring would come in.

With much drama, the doctor opened this box—and took a look inside. Nolan was devastated. All the Whiskey guys were. The box held nothing but a tiny computer chip, something that might be found in a computer game. Sealed inside a little plastic case, it looked ordinary in every way.

"I knew it!" Gunner roared. "That prick was just yanking our chains!"

"This really *is* a bad joke . . ." Batman said angrily.

That's when the guy named Squire stepped forward. He had said very little, until now.

"No, gentlemen," he spoke coolly, inspecting the chip. "This *is* it. We've found the treasure—and it's just what I suspected."

Batman turned to Nolan and asked: "Is he nuts—or am I?"

Squire huddled them together.

"Let me explain," he said. He picked up the chip and held it for all to see.

"This little device can rule the world," he said. "Just watch."

He'd been lugging his laptop around with him all night; now the others knew why. With some precision, he slit open the computer chip's little plastic case, removed the chip, took the access panel off his laptop and then put the chip into a slot in the back. Then he turned the computer on and the screen lit up with an astonishing display of almost 3-D graphics.

Squire began punching the keyboard and, within seconds, those gathered were seeing some amazing things: classified documents from the Pentagon, the Queen of England's personal finances, the porn collection of the exalted leader of North Korea.

"This chip can go anywhere and do anything," Squire said. "No Wi Fi or wire connection needed. It's the ultimate hacking device—and the ultimate *spying* device. It can go through any firewall, through any security system instantaneously, and leave no trail behind. Military secrets. Industrial secrets. Personal secrets. It was stolen from the Chinese, who stole it from the U.S. And maybe the Chinese asked the Iranians to get it back for them, who knows? But our friend who left us these clues knew how valuable it was, and he also knew lots of other people would be looking for it. So he took himself out of the equation and left us to sort it out."

Batman looked Stevenson and Squire up and down—then said: "You know, something tells me you guys aren't exactly the real fish and chips."

Stevenson held up his hand. "No—I'm really a doctor," he said. "But my friend here is a private investigator—and ex-SAS. And if we ever get out of here, we will get this to its rightful owner—and we'll cut you guys in on the reward, above and beyond your fee, of course."

At that moment, they heard a commotion in the bushes nearby. Suddenly they were looking up at two Iranians holding assault rifles.

The pair smiled at them in a very disturbing way and raised their weapons.

One said: "We kill you all."

The team froze. Their weapons were on the ground, out of reach. Nolan could see the gunmen begin to squeeze their triggers.

But then both of them suddenly stiffened up, shocked looks washing over their faces. A bubble of blood showed up on both of their chests. They fell forward and hit the ground, dead.

Behind them stood two of the Senegals, bloody assault knives in hand.

"God damn," Batman exclaimed. *"God damn!"*

Nolan actually punched himself in the chest to get his heart back beating normally. Everyone in the team was checking his shorts.

"Comment savez-vous su pour nous sauver?" Nolan asked the Senegals. "How did you know to save us?"

"Nous avions senti un odeur de leur veni," was the unusual reply. "We smelled them coming."

Nolan took a deep breath and came back to reality. They had their Holy Grail—but they also had two dead Iranians who would have killed them all in seconds had they been able to. And this was a problem.

"These guys are going to be missed," Nolan told the others. "And when their comrades find them stabbed, they'll know someone else is on the island besides them."

"What the fuck are we going to do?" Batman asked.

Once again, it was Twitch who came up with an idea. "The Punji pit," he said.

Everyone understood right away. Gunner and Crash immediately began dragging the bodies into the jungle and down toward the booby trap.

But not far away, they could hear more people crashing through the overgrowth.

"We still got to get out of here," Batman said. "These assholes will stay here until they dig up every part of this island—and that means they'll discover the ship and we'll get the same treatment the catamaran got."

Then Nolan got an idea. He turned to Squire.

"The Iranians probably know they're looking for a chip, right?" he asked him. "I mean, maybe they don't know *where* it is, but they probably know *what* it is?"

The ex-SAS man nodded. "Probably."

Nolan smiled darkly. "OK—maybe we can get out of here yet."

He told the rest of the team to get going—all except Stevenson. "I'll need your expertise," he told the doctor.

As the others departed—including Squire carrying the ultra-valuable chip—Nolan took out his old keychain, the one that beeped in response to a wolf whistle, letting him know where he'd put his car keys. He always carried it with him as a reminder of better times past. He took off the back and removed its computer chip.

Then he gave the doctor his razor-blade knife and instructed him to insert his keychain computer chip into the tiny case that had held the mother of all chips and then reseal it by heating the knife with his lighter and touching its tip to the edge of the plastic. The doctor did so, being surgically precise—but Nolan knew they were running out of time. He could see a dozen pith helmets in the jungle below them, the heavily armed Iranian soldiers, getting closer all the time.

The operation and closing done, they hastily put the chip case back in the jewelry box, wrapped it in the electrical wire, put it back in the metal fuse box and then in the small wooden box. Putting this box back inside the burn bag, they wrapped it in the rags and the blanket, and then finally placed it inside the large plastic box.

Then they put the plastic box back in the ground and dumped dirt back in the hole. Covering it over, they spread the dirt around to hide the fact that anything had been dug up here recently, and then crawled away, just as the first half dozen Iranians reached the top of the cliff.

Had they taken just a few seconds longer, they would have been caught.

Now they were back in the jungle, but still surrounded by hostile soldiers.

"Now what?" Stevenson asked Nolan.

Nolan thought a moment and said, "Wish I knew."

THE REST OF the team reached the beach fifteen minutes after getting off the cliff.

It wound up taking all seven of them—Crash, Twitch, Gunner, Batman, Squire and the two Senegals—taking turns to drag the two dead Iranians down to the Punji pit. Once they were in sight of the booby trap, Batman suggested he go ahead and uncover the life rafts they'd hidden on the beach, making them ready for the others once they'd disposed of the two gunmen.

They all agreed, and with Batman plunging back into the jungle, the others hurled the two Iranians into the pit, then quickly moved toward the beach themselves.

They reached the cove about a minute later—only to find Batman nowhere in sight. And neither were their life rafts.

The Team Whiskey guys were immediately pissed.

"You've got to be kidding me," Gunner cried. "Where the hell is he?"

Crash said, "You mean, *this* is the time he picked to leave us high and dry?"

"Money talks," Twitch said grimly.

But at that moment, they heard some rustling nearby. They hit the ground, weapons up, only to discover Batman coming out of the bushes dragging two of their three rubber boats.

"Jesuszz, what's all the chatter about?" he asked them sternly. "You guys know better than that."

The Team Whiskey guys didn't say a word. They just loaded onto the life rafts with Squire and the Senegals and started paddling madly toward the DUS-7.

NOLAN AND STEVENSON crawled down the side of the cliff, doing their best to stay as quiet as possible. They were still in a fix, though. They had no idea if the rest of the crew had been able to get back to the *Dustboat*, and now there were even more Iranians around them than before.

They reached the lower jungle, somehow getting off the cliff without being spotted. But it was fully light, and without the darkness to shield them, and almost a half mile to go before they could even reach the cove, it seemed the doctor and Nolan were hopelessly trapped.

They avoided one group of Iranians, only to be cut off by another group that was operating a ground-imaging radar device. These Iranians were searching in large concentric circles, which meant that if Nolan and the doctor stayed where they were, they'd be discovered in minutes. Yet they couldn't go back the way they came; the cliff was swarming with even more Iranians.

It was strange because, almost unconsciously, Nolan yanked on his lucky onion bag, and just as two Iranian soldiers were about to walk right on top of them, they heard someone cry out in Farsi. The men working the radar dropped it and ran back into the jungle. Nolan and the doctor took the opportunity to scramble closer to the beach.

They soon found themselves at a point near the water but also close to the Punji pit. Some Iranians had come upon the booby trap and had found their two colleagues impaled on the bamboo sticks below. They were in the grisly process of taking them out of the pit, their post-mortem injuries disguising the stab wounds that had actually killed them.

Nolan and the doctor fist-bumped, and then continued making their way to the beach, and the ship beyond.

ABOUT TWO HOURS later the Team Whiskey group, hiding on the ship, heard a great cry go up near the interior of the island. They saw Iranian soldiers excitedly running to and fro and heard them singing and letting out yelps of joy.

The ruckus finally died down, and the Iranians made their way back to the south beach where their warship lay offshore. It was clear they were packing up and preparing to leave.

"I guess they found their treasure," Nolan said as they all looked on from beneath the camouflage. "Maybe now they'll be able to find their car keys."

AN HOUR LATER, Nolan was at the top of the DUS-7's forward port cargo mast, his special telescope up to his good eye, watching as the Iranian cruiser pulled anchor and slowly sailed away. He waited until the mast of the warship disappeared over the eastern horizon before climbing back down again.

Then he joined the rest of the crew in hastily removing the ship's camouflage. They wanted to get out of the area as quickly as possible.

Nolan and Batman were working on this alongside Squire and the doctor. Nolan asked Squire: "So—tell us, who have we *really* been working for all this time?"

Squire smiled. "My boss? His name is Bill Gates. Perhaps you've heard of him?"

"The name sounds familiar," Nolan deadpanned.

"Well, he's the owner of that ultimate, one-of-a-kind chip," Squire said. "And he's the one who'll actually be paying you—both your original fee, plus a piece of the reward."

Hearing this, Batman pulled Nolan aside and whispered to him: "That guy Gates took a bath in the last Wall Street crash—believe me, I know."

Nolan thought a moment, then turned back to Squire and said: "Ask him to make that cash, OK?"

PART SEVEN

The Last Battle

20

COGNAC.

Nolan had never tasted it, had never been able to afford it, or even wanted it if he had. But he was drinking it now.

A lot of it.

He'd never danced to disco music, either. Never liked the sound of it, or the beat. But he was dancing to it now.

And everything was spinning again, but now in a good way. The waitresses at the Aden dockside bar grew more attractive with each drink. The music was pulsating and erotic. In one corner, he could see Batman smoking hashish through a hookah. In another, Gunner had his head down in a bowl of beer. Close by, Crash was at a table making out with two, no . . . three women at once. Even Twitch was getting into it, pouring drinks and doubling as the gathering's DJ.

They were here again, in the same grungy dockside bar, celebrating their return from their successful adventure to Microchip Island. Though the bar was crowded, mostly with people from the Gulf States here to drink freely, the team had taken over the place, buying drinks and hits of hashish for all.

Dr. Stevenson and Squire had joined them earlier, but for only one drink. They had places to go—namely Seattle, Washington. With help from the Kilos finance department, they'd paid the team their fee for getting them to the island and back and made arrangements to wire their share of the reward once the Mother of All Chips was safely back home.

So the team was in high spirits, literally. Their coffers had increased again, practically overnight, and there was little sign of the uneasiness that Gunner, Crash and Twitch had felt recently about the money doings. Batman had totaled up their earnings: In just one month of operation, Team Whiskey had collected almost $7.5 million. When the reward arrived from Squire and Stevenson, that amount would grow to almost $8 million. Tax-free.

It was more money than any of them had ever had at one time—all except Batman.

Conley was also on hand for the celebration. He'd told them, "I'd suggest you guys go on vacation, but we know what happened the last time you tried that."

That got a big laugh, and then they drank more cognac, and some smoked more hashish, and Nolan took to the disco floor once more, gyrating in slow motion as two Middle Eastern beauties danced circles around him.

And everything was spinning. But in a good way.

BEEPING . . .

At first, Nolan thought it was part of the music—or maybe a side effect of breathing in too much secondhand smoke in the roomful of burning hashish.

Beeping . . .

Echoing in such a way, it felt like it was going in one ear and coming out the other.

Beeping . . .

Where was it coming from?

"It's your phone," one of the dancing girls yelled to him over the music. "You'd better answer it."

Nolan hesitated. He was always uncomfortable answering his cell phone. He never knew who might be calling him, especially if it was someone from the United States.

But he couldn't ignore it; that was not like him. Besides, it was killing his buzz.

So he flipped the phone open and was surprised to hear a voice that was familiar and instantly recognizable. But he couldn't imagine why this person would be calling him.

It was Bebe, the Russian gangster.

"I have news for you," Bebe began the conversation. "Are sitting at present?"

"I am," Nolan lied, shouting over the music. What was this about? he thought.

They'd received payment from Bebe with no problem, and even a big tip. Did the Russian Mob want the money back?

"Is good you are sitting," Bebe said. "Because news will make you faint."

"Please just tell me," Nolan said.

"Your friend, Pirate Zeek?" Bebe said gravely. "Is alive. He lives and is back at old tricks."

Nolan collapsed into the nearest chair. He thought for a moment that Bebe was drunk and this was his idea of a practical joke. But he knew that a guy like Bebe was always drunk and probably didn't play practical jokes.

"How do you know this?" he asked the gangster.

"A friend of friend of friend just sold him guns for new boat," Bebe replied. "Boat is modified Type 352 German minesweeper. Boat will bring Zeek and his posse across Indian Ocean to Somalia. Somalia warlords are waiting to give him open-arms greeting. They to give Zeek political asylum. Zeek to organize their Somali crazy people into better pirates, cause big trouble there. This his plan."

Nolan knew Bebe was on the level, for one reason: During their conversations, Nolan never told the gangster that they suspected Zeek's plan all along was to move his operations to Somalia.

"Check out what I say," Bebe went on. "I thought you should know this."

Nolan thanked him, and at the same time, tried to think of what to do next. Bebe actually gave him his answer.

The gangster told him: "Zeek person is dangerous and crafty—and has much luck in him. You, your friends, are good at job. But you must learn one thing: Zeek the Pirate? He doesn't die easily. You gotta kill a guy like that more than once."

With that, Bebe said good-bye and hung up.

And at that point, everything started spinning for Nolan

once again. But definitely not in a good way. In the blink of an eye, *everything* had changed.

He took off his onion bag and threw it across the bar.

Then he yelled, "Party's over!"

WORK ON THE DUS-7 began immediately.

Most of the damage done by the seaplane to the boat itself—holes in the deck, holes on the bridge—was patched but not painted. Two new cargo masts were quickly installed. The communication antenna was replaced.

The work copter was repaired by changing out the engine and replacing two rotor blades, but some of the bullet holes in the cockpit windows could not be fixed in time, so they remained.

The biggest change was in the ship's armament—a surprise, courtesy of Conley. The original customer for the M102 artillery piece needed to take delivery of it, so the field gun had to be hoisted off the DUS-7. But Conley had an even more interesting weapon to take its place.

It was an M198 155mm howitzer. This weapon was a monster. At eight tons, it was nearly four times heavier than the M102, and at thirty-six feet, its barrel was three times longer than the old field gun. In this case, size did matter. Not only could the M198 use a wide range of shells, from armor-piercing to high-explosive to anti-personnel—it could fire them more than twenty miles, in some cases right over the horizon, meaning the intended victim might not know their demise was coming. And despite its bulk, the M198 was actually easier to operate than the M102 because it came with a computer-assisted targeting system.

As Conley told the crew when the huge cannon was being installed, "Way back when, the people who were tracking down real pirates would have given their right arm for a weapon like this."

All the refit work was done by the same Kilos engineers who'd patched them up before the Zanzibar run. These were the people, many of them veterans of military navies, who assembled or disassembled a lot of Kilos Shipping's black-market weapons. They were used to operating at night, doing their jobs quickly and keeping their mouths shut.

THE WORK ON the DUS-7 was done inside Kilos's immense enclosed maintenance bay located next to the Kilos office building in Aden. By the next morning, the battered freighter was floated out of the bay and back to the Kilos loading dock where ammunition, fuel and more supplies were loaded on.

Nolan was belowdecks, helping to store shells for their new gun. More than eight hours had passed since Bebe's call, but he still felt sick. His head was pounding, his stomach twisted in knots. He was hoping the hard labor would exorcise some of these post-hangover demons, but so far, no luck.

How could this have happened? The team's entire reputation was built on the belief that they had put Zeek out of business back in Malacca. Their name had gone around the maritime world at the speed of light based on that one fact, and their sudden superstar status in that world had led to the three subsequent, highly lucrative jobs.

But now this? The revelation that they didn't even complete their biggest job successfully? To Nolan's battered psyche, this skewed everything. Their credibility. Their tactics. Their fees. None of it seemed justified to him. He was furious with himself. He was the first to admit that deep down, with each success, he'd fallen into the biggest pitfall a celebrity can face. He'd begun believing his own headlines.

Only one thing could right this wrong. They had to go do it all over again. Find Zeek and kill him a second time. If they couldn't do that, they had no business working as pirate hunters. And he knew the rest of the team agreed with him.

IT WAS NOW midmorning. Nolan was still sweating and aching from lots of heavy lifting and absolutely no sleep when he heard a collective groan from the deck above.

"Now what?" he grunted.

He climbed the forward ladder and saw what the grief was about. Down on the dock was a man dressed in a bad suit, wearing a bad haircut and cheap sunglasses, even though it was a cloudy day. It was an ONI agent. Not Agent Harry, though. It was his young sidekick.

Batman had already started down the gangway to talk to him, but Nolan called him back.

"Let me do this," he said.

Nolan went down to the dock and confronted the under-cover naval officer before the man could get any nearer to the ship.

"Private property, pal," he told the agent. "And there's no soliciting."

The agent ignored his remarks. He pulled out his ID card instead and, for the first time, Nolan actually saw his name: Agent Curt Hush.

"Where's your Uncle Harry?" Nolan asked him.

"Put out to pasture," Hush replied. "Forced retirement."

"How come?"

"Too old," Hush replied coldly. "Too out of it. And *way* too easy on you guys."

Nolan gave him a mock salute. "OK, thanks for the news flash," he said, starting to walk away.

Hush called after him. "I insist on asking you some questions right now. Or else . . ."

Nolan spun around. He was just itching to punch someone in the face.

"You *insist*? Why is that?"

"Because I've been keeping track of your recent activities," Hush told him. "And my bosses at ONI believe you might soon be directly interfering with the interests of the United States."

"So?" Nolan said with a straight face.

"So, it's in *your* best interest to comply this time," Hush told him, adding ominously: ". . . for many reasons."

Nolan immediately went nose to nose with him. "I get it now—you were the bad cop of the act. Is that it?"

"From what you and your friends are up to," Hush replied, getting heated himself, "you're lucky a real cop isn't here."

He pointed to the DUS-7. Even though the new 155mm gun had been covered with cargo nets and the mounted M2

50-calibers draped with packing blankets, it was obvious the ship had military weapons on board. In fact, the Senegals were in the process of lifting yet another pallet of artillery shells up to the deck at that moment. Kilos engineers were also completing some final repairs of the work copter.

"For instance," Hush said. "What's going on here?"

"We're repainting the ship," Nolan said plainly. "It's getting rusty on the gunwales."

"And where are the gunwales on this vessel, Major Nolan?"

"Beats me," Nolan replied. "But I know they're getting a fresh coat."

"Look," Hush said. "We know you're going after Zeek Kurjan."

"And you got a problem with that?"

Hush nodded emphatically. "Higher authority has a big problem with it. Higher authority thinks it's best we let the situation stand as it is."

"I don't speak 'Navy,'" Nolan said. "Just tell me what you're saying."

"Let Zeek go to Somalia to do his thing," Hush said directly. "Can I be any simpler than that?"

Nolan really laughed at him now—until he saw he was serious.

"What the hell are you talking about?" he growled at him. "This guy Zeek is a monster. He's a mass murderer. He's drug dealer. He kills kids, for Christ's sake. We thought we greased him already—you guys know that. But we missed him somehow, and now he's back and now he's got to be stopped again. So you telling me to hold back makes no sense to me. If we did that, it would be like letting him get away with it all."

The agent smiled disdainfully. "I don't expect someone like you to understand the intricacies of this," he said. "But there are logical geopolitical reasons for us to let this happen."

"Name one," Nolan challenged him.

"The Strait of Malacca is of much more strategic importance than the coast of Somalia or even the Gulf of Aden," Hush began. "These Somali mooks grab a cargo ship or some oil coming from Saudi Arabia? Who cares? It's all a scam anyway—the insurance companies just pay off the shipping company or they write it off as a loss.

"But if Zeek stays in the Strait of Malacca, he might get smart someday and decide to not hijack a ship there, but sink one or two or three ships. You block that waterway and you screw up commerce around the world. Even when they clear it, everything will cost more because the insurance rates will skyrocket. The military would have to pour in money and people to provide security."

Nolan laughed at him again—he couldn't help it. He'd dealt with pinheads like this for years in Delta. They got one little idea in their gray matter, and no matter how wrong it was, they stuck with it until their will was done, or another stupid little idea took its place.

"You're making my argument for me, genius," he told Hush. "We plan on icing this prick once and for all. It's our fault we didn't do it right the first time. So now we got to go back and do it again. But if we're successful this time, then *we've* done our jobs and *you* have one less problem to worry about. In fact, we'll send you a bill after we whack him."

It seemed to make too much sense. And, of course, the ONI agent wasn't buying it.

"No—there will be a problem if Zeek gets hit," he said.

Nolan was stumped. "But why? Who wants him to stay alive? Certainly not the Indonesians around the Talua Tangs. If he's out of the equation, they won't be under his smelly little thumb anymore."

"It's not the little Indonesians we're worried about," Hush said. "It's the Chinese."

Nolan just stared at him. "The Chinese? How do they have a dog in this fight?"

"They're Zeek's godfathers," Hush revealed. "They've been quietly providing his protection for years. They're the reason he's been able to get away with all this stuff. He's been sending them a percentage of everything he takes in—and they've been watching his back in return."

Nolan still didn't understand. He knew the Chinese government was run by a bunch of scumbags. Ripping off U.S. citizens with shitty products. Hacking into U.S. defense mainframes. Their involvement in the misery of Darfur. And a million other things. That sort of stuff didn't surprise him. But why would they get in bed with a common pirate?

"You're telling me those assholes in Beijing give a crap about a mook like Zeek?" he asked the agent.

Now it was Hush's turn to laugh. "And you call me a cub scout?" he said. "I'm not talking about the people in Beijing. They don't run that country. I'm talking about the crime syndicates in Shanghai. *They're* the grease that makes that whole enterprise go, and one of them—a guy named Sunny Hi—is very close to Zeek. *He's* the guy who provides him with cover."

"And he's in love with Zeek because? . . ."

"Because Zeek provides Shanghai with Happy-Happy girls," Hush replied. "Of all shapes and sizes."

"And ages?"

The ONI agent shrugged. "It's just another form of currency in that part of the world," he said. "You better learn that if you want to play with the big boys. And know this too: If you piss off Sunny Hi, he can make things very difficult for us. He can slow down seaborne shipments to the U.S. He can prevent our cargo ships from docking in China. He can convince his buddies in Beijing to stop buying U.S. Treasury notes. It's a long list—all of it bad."

Nolan tried to let this all digest. Then it hit him.

"You bastards," he swore at Hush. "You *knew* we didn't grease Zeek when you came to see us that first time. You just wanted the dirt on how we did it so—so what? So you could tell him how to avoid us next time?"

Hush's face turned crimson.

"Who the fuck's side are you guys on?" Nolan spit at him.

"Look, Nolan," Hush said, taking a step backward. "We know you've been able to make an incredible amount of money here in the last few weeks. Why don't you just relax and enjoy it. It's like making a killing at the poker table. You've got to know when to walk away. I mean, at the very heart of it, you're running an illegal enterprise here. Technically speaking, you're as much a criminal as the guys you've been paid to stop."

The whole Team Whiskey crew was crowded around them by now, listening to the exchange.

"And here's another thing," Hush said. "We know your situation at home. You play ball here and maybe we can help you with it. Get the military court to reverse its order. Get you back on home turf again. That's gotta be what you want, right?"

Nolan took a swing at him—but Batman caught his arm before he could deliver the blow. Nolan struggled, but only briefly. Punching the ONI agent wouldn't be good for anyone at this moment. He was furious, though, but not for the reason the others were probably thinking. Hush had hit him where it hurt and, for a split second, Nolan had actually considered telling him yes. For a split second he'd actually considered taking the payoff, just for a chance to go home.

But then he surprised himself again.

"Get fucked," he told the agent, as Batman and Crash held him back. "You didn't see what we saw after Zeek got through with those innocent people on Sumhai Island. You didn't see what he's done to people on these ships he's hijacked. Or the kinds of lives people were living under his little dictatorship. So you guys go get fucked and tell Sunny Hi he should fuck himself, too."

Nolan disentangled himself from the others and walked away.

"It's your choice, Nolan," Hush called after him, his voice a little shaky. "But just remember, orders go out, and the people who see them through don't necessarily know all the details. So, we can't be responsible for what happens next."

Nolan called over his shoulder: "Neither can we . . ."

21

Indonesia

ZEEK THE PIRATE died the night his headquarters was bombed.

He was shot, blown up and drowned during the surprise assault—but not before leading his men bravely against the mysterious, well-equipped and overwhelming enemy.

Zeek rose from the dead the next day, greeting the handful of his men who'd survived the sneak attack by fleeing into the jungle. Zeek was alive: They saw him, touched him. It was a miracle.

Or at least that's the story he'd ordered those surviving minions to spread throughout the Talua Tangs.

The reality was a lot less miraculous. Zeek had escaped the attack on his headquarters that night, not by divine intervention, but for two completely earthly reasons: One, he'd had the foresight, when he built his concrete HQ, to add a tiny bomb shelter beneath it. And two, a trio of his bodyguards, trapped in the shelter with him, had taken turns holding his head above water after the shelter flooded.

The real miracle was that Zeek's bomb shelter had held together at all. It had been built to withstand a blast from a hand grenade or an RPG, the biggest weapons a typical Indonesian pirate trafficked in. (It was actually intended as an anti-assassination safe room.) It was not designed to take a direct hit from a 200-pound bomb, homemade or not.

But it did.

Still, it wasn't exactly watertight. Even before the island's attackers had flown away, the shelter began filling up with water from the nearby lagoon. Trapped and unable to get out because of the tons of rubble over his head, Zeek ordered his men to take turns holding him up, allowing him to breathe from the small air space remaining at the top of the submerged shelter, while they held their breath until their lungs nearly burst. They followed his orders, terrified and in complete darkness, for more than twelve hours. In the end, all three died of exhaustion.

Lucky for Zeek, just minutes before the third one expired, the Indonesian military arrived to raze the camp. Hearing Zeek's screams, they dug him out of the watery grave, leaving behind the bodies of his three saviors and his similarly dressed body double in the rubble.

Zeek was lucky again that the local Indonesian military commander decided to remain his ally, but only because Zeek fulfilled the promise to give him 3,000 hits of Ecstasy, which could be sold for pure profit. So instead of putting him in jail, the military made arrangements for Zeek to recuperate at a private hospital outside Jakarta. He was released two weeks later, fit and trim, and determined to make good on his long-time desire to move his operations to East Africa, cash in on the easy pickings off the coast of Somalia, and renew his war of vengeance against his brother's murderers, Kilos Shipping.

But to do all that, he needed a boat.

Jacca Naval Base

ZEEK HAD NEVER owned a boat before.

He'd stolen many, hijacked many, killed for many. But in all cases, because he didn't want to leave any kind of paper trail for some overzealous law enforcement agency to pursue, he eventually sold them, flipped them or traded them for money or weapons.

He was a pirate of the high seas, yet he had no pirate ship of his own. Even the yacht blown up during the attack on his island headquarters and the one used two nights before had been on loan to him.

But things change.

He had a number of specific requirements in a pirate vessel. It needed room for at least one helicopter. It needed room for his new pirate army, made up mostly of ex-convicts and maritime riff-raff now in the employ of the Shanghai crime syndicates. It needed space for weapons and ammunition. It also needed a lifeboat, and that boat itself would have to carry a lifeboat of its own.

Plus, the ship had to have the many comforts Zeek felt entitled to while riding the seas: at least one hot tub, a big-screen TV, a bar and a pool. In other words, what Zeek needed was not so much a yacht that had some military faculties, but a military vessel that had some high-end amenities.

Enter Prince Seeudek. A third cousin of the Indonesian president's wife, he was extremely wealthy and very shady. Better known as the Playboy of Java, he'd bought a Type 352 German-built Ensdorf minesweeper several years before and had it converted to a pleasure craft while still keeping it listed as a ship of the Indonesian Navy. He'd handpicked his crew and gone off on his own military maneuvers, which usually involved sailing to and from the casinos at Monte Carlo. The 160-foot ship had room for weapons and helicopters, and also a hot tub, many large-screen TVs, a small interior pool, a game room and even a small dance club. It also had a lifeboat that, in turn, had its own lifeboat.

From the outside, the 352 looked exactly like a naval vessel. Inside, it looked like a boat even an oil-rich Saudi prince would envy.

The vessel wound up in the Zeek's hands shortly before his two-week recuperation was complete. Several Chinese businessmen visited Prince Seeudek in his Jakarta penthouse one afternoon and beat him to within an inch of his life. The next day, from his hospital bed, the Prince resigned as commander of the 352 and designated an obscure ethnic Chinese officer in the Indonesian Navy to be its new captain.

That officer's uncle was Sunny Hi, the Godfather of Shanghai.

ZEEK, HIS TWO remaining bodyguards and his new pirate band boarded their new vessel at the Indonesian Navy base at Jacca Bay—though not all at once.

It was midnight, and at Zeek's request, the lights on the southern end of the small naval base had been dimmed. Zeek and his bodyguards arrived at the dock in a black SUV with tinted windows, and they were quickly put aboard a motor launch usually reserved for high naval officers. It ferried them out to the 352, waiting at anchor a half mile offshore.

At the same time, Zeek's new army was belowdecks aboard a nearby Indonesian supply ship. They'd been waiting there since early afternoon, but were under orders to stay put until Zeek himself was aboard his new ship. Only then were they ferried over as well.

After that, a third vessel arrived next to the 352 and unloaded all of Zeek's new weapons and ammunition—bought on the Russian black market—plus his money and personal belongings. A brand-new helicopter gunship was also put aboard, along with a highly trained four-man Malaysian crew.

Zeek was just forty-eight hours out of the hospital at this point, but feeling fine. He'd spent the past two days at a luxury retreat on the nearby island of Kupang, looking into the backgrounds of those people who'd come so close to killing him. Thanks to a source inside the Chinese intelligence services, Zeek had learned his mystery attackers were American mercenaries, hired guns in the employ of Kilos Shipping. They were the same people who had killed his brother Turk— the same people against whom Zeek had sworn revenge. The same people who prompted him to order the murder of the three ship crews in Singapore.

The same people who, since the attack on his HQ, had been giving him nightmares.

Now Zeek knew who they were, knew their backgrounds, knew how to get to them. Eventually, he would deal with them as well.

But his biggest concern now was getting out of Indonesia— before someone tried to kill him again.

22

Port of Aden

THE DUS-7 WAS ready to sail by 1300 hours.

All the repairs were complete, all the weapons and ammunition loaded aboard. Its fuel tanks were filled, its gas turbine refitted and calibrated. The work copter was working again.

The only problem: Team Whiskey had no idea where Zeek was. Bebe's information said he'd purchased a quasi-military vessel and that he was sailing to Somalia and linking up with a band of Somali pirates similar to those his brother Turk had worked with before his death. So he was definitely heading west.

The shipping lanes between Asia and East Africa were like a superhighway, with hundreds of ships going back and forth between the continents every day. But it was an area encompassing hundreds of thousands of square miles, enough to make the biggest ship seem small. Blindly searching for and finding Zeek in such a huge area would be almost impossible.

Still, the team's plan was to rush the DUS-7 deep into the shipping lanes and simply start looking for this unusual ship that Zeek had acquired. They knew it was an inefficient way of searching for the notorious pirate. But they couldn't just sit in Aden, waiting for further news on him that might never come.

They had to go hunting for him.

NOT FIVE MINUTES before they were to cast off from the Kilos berth, though, Conley appeared on the dock. He knew what Whiskey planned to do, and was well aware of what havoc a resurrected Zeek could cause along the East African coastline.

And as it turned out, Conley was bearing two last-minute gifts for them: a small laptop and a plain wooden box. They had a quick huddle with him on the bridge.

"Good news," Conley told the team. "We've just been informed that Zeek's new ship has a maritime locator in it. A sort of miniature black box for ships. I don't think Zeek even knows about it."

"You're saying there's a 'chip in his ship?'" Nolan asked.

Conley nodded. "Exactly. Every Indonesian military ship has one built in, so they can be tracked by satellite."

"But we don't have a satellite," Crash said.

Conley passed the small laptop to them. "You do now."

Nolan turned the laptop on and was surprised to see a decrypted home page belonging to the Russian intelligence service pop up. A few keystrokes revealed that the page was connected to the Russian military's satellite system.

"With that, you can track the chip in Zeek's ship," Conley told them.

"But where did all this suddenly come from?" Batman asked Conley in amazement. "The news on the chip and this laptop? Is it something Stevenson and Squire left behind?"

"No—actually, it all just arrived here via special courier," Conley replied, showing them a large packing envelope with a no-name return address in Moscow. "I can't imagine who sent it," he added drolly.

Batman gave Nolan a hearty slap on the back.

"Wow, Snake," he said. "You have a godfather, too."

Conley gave them the second present: the wooden box. Inside was a very special artillery shell called a Copperhead.

"This one's from me," he told them. "You can actually guide this thing to a target, just like a smart weapon. The instructions are in the box. It might come in handy at some point. But use it wisely. They don't make them anymore. In fact, this might be the last one in existence."

THE *DUSTBOAT* SAILED all that day and into the night, heading southeast into the heart of the Indian Ocean sea-lanes.

The team spent the time making sure all the new equipment worked and that the ship's repairs were holding. They'd also wired the Russian laptop into their navigation system and begun monitoring satellite photos of the sea-lanes between

Indonesia and Africa. The whole chip-in-the-ship process was extremely simple. Once the vessel in question passed beneath the satellite, the satellite would acknowledge it and give it an electronic mark. This mark would then allow anyone with a slaved-in GPS device to keep tabs on the target ship even after the satellite had passed overhead.

The important thing was to get that mark.

But what would happen then? The team knew that, despite their new weaponry and their partial disguise as a rust-bucket freighter, they would be at a huge disadvantage going up against Zeek's new boat.

Nolan had Googled the type of ship Bebe said Zeek had bought and, while a Type 357 Ensdorf was officially considered a minesweeper, it actually carried a wide array of weapons. It had a five-inch gun on its forward deck, a fierce naval cannon that could tear into the DUS-7 with ease. It was also equipped with ship-to-ship missiles, another weapon that could fold the *Dustboat* like a tin can. Type 352s usually came equipped with an armed helicopter and many mounted machine guns. And according to Bebe's information, the ship was also carrying a small army of pirates Zeek had recruited for his move west.

Team Whiskey also knew they could expect no outside assistance in stopping Zeek. Agent Hush's visit had made it clear the U.S. Navy wasn't going to help. And contacting the NATO anti-piracy patrols would do them no good, because Zeek had yet to do anything wrong, piracy-wise, in their eyes. Plus, Zeek's connections to the Indonesian military establishment, and apparently to Chinese organized-crime lords, would most likely get him off even if NATO or any other anti-piracy forces actually did intervene.

So, it was up to Whiskey to stop Zeek on their own.

Again.

BY MIDNIGHT, THE team found themselves in the galley, once again drinking endless cups of coffee, anxious for something, *anything,* to happen.

Batman had arrived, dragging the moneybag with him.

This was not unusual as everyone felt better when the bag was in sight. It was stuffed with so many bills, though, it was getting hard to lift.

No one noticed anything different about him or the money-bag, but during a break in the conversation about Zeek, Batman suddenly picked up the bag and put it on the mess table.

"Anyone want to check the stash?" he asked them.

This was a first. The unwritten rule was, no one touched the money except the Batman.

"Why would we want to do that?" Gunner asked him, a bit nervously.

Batman looked right at Nolan. "Just so everyone can sleep peacefully, if we ever get to sleep on this mission."

Nolan was as surprised as the other three, but he knew where this was coming from: the talk he had with Gunner, Crash and Twitch that day on the *Althea Dawn*, and the discussion about the money he had with Batman a short while later. Trust issues were involved and had been simmering.

Batman pushed the bag toward Gunner, who just pushed it back. "I got no problems," Gunner said.

Batman pushed it toward Twitch, who barely seemed to notice. "Money can't buy me love," he mumbled.

Finally, Crash pulled the bag over to him. "You know, I think I'd like to feel it, smell it," he said. "I haven't seen it since old man Kilos first paid us."

He reached deep inside the bag and started pulling out tightly wrapped packets.

But it wasn't money. It was newspaper.

"What the fuck?" he yelled.

"I knew it!" Twitch said, suddenly coming to life.

They were all shocked—even Nolan. But Batman immediately calmed them down.

"I switched bags before we left," he confessed to them. "Our money's in a vault in a bank back in Aden that's secretly run by Kilos. It's safe, its insured, and it's even got two guards watching over it. And there's a special code to get in to see it."

He passed each man a Kilos business card with a number on it.

"Here's that code," Batman went on. "Any one of us can go there and get his share of the money at any time. No questions asked."

The three non-coms just glared back at him—like it was a practical joke. But it wasn't.

"And I told Conley, that if we don't come back, that money should be given to the families of those crewmen who were murdered in Singapore."

"But why?" Crash finally asked. "And why tell us now, like this?"

"Because this is not a job we're going on," Batman replied forcefully, even angrily. "It's a mission—just like the old days. No one's paying us for it. We're doing it because we have to. Just like back in Delta."

They knew he was right. They were going after Zeek only because they'd failed to complete the job the first time.

"We *have* to do it like this," Batman went on. "And we have to do it without the money being on our minds the whole time."

Crash, Gunner and Twitch were all still stunned and uneasy.

But Nolan reached across the table and fist-bumped Batman.

"I agree with him," he said. "We do this one not just for our reputation but for our honor. Like before, with Delta. That's got to be important to us. We can't forget that."

The others began to say something, but suddenly, the intercom squealed to life.

"Nous avons obtenu un success," they heard one of the Senegals cry. "We've got a hit . . ."

The entire team was up on the bridge in seconds. Studying the laptop screen, they saw a satellite photo display with a green blinking light at its farthest left edge. A line of script next to the blinking light read: *Indonesian medium warship.*

"That's got to be our boy," Crash said. "What other Indonesian ship would be way out there?"

"Looks like he's about 300 miles west of Sri Lanka," Batman said. That puts him about 200 miles east of us. If we pour it on, we can run into him sometime around mid-morning."

Twitch took it all in and asked: "Yeah—but then what?"

23

ZEEK'S SHIP, WHICH he'd christened the *Pasha*, had performed flawlessly since leaving the Java Sea.

It ran smooth and true through the Malacca Strait and out into the Indian Ocean. They'd sailed to Sri Lanka with no problems and stayed the night in the port of Ambalangoda to take on fuel. Anyone who saw them assumed they were an Indonesian naval ship and treated them accordingly. After fueling up, Zeek's well-connected Chinese captain told him they would be in Somali waters in less than three days.

Zeek had stayed awake for the entire trip so far—in fact, high on Ecstasy, he hadn't slept in a week. With the promise of trouble-free sailing ahead, though, he'd decided to retire to his spacious quarters to finally crash.

But no sooner had he unbraided his beard and taken a handful of barbiturates to help him sleep, the CO of his new pirate band, a man named Commander Fun Li, came to his quarters to tell him he was needed back up on the bridge.

Li was ex-Chinese special forces. He was a slight man, taut, muscular and fearless. He was a protégé of Sunny Hi, and thus was under orders to be devoted to Zeek. But even an egotist like Zeek recognized Li wasn't just some lackey. He was the real deal, brilliant when it came to strategy, tactics, intelligence and weaponry. The Pirate King had never had anyone as sharp and knowledgeable under his command before. It was Li's job to get Zeek, his ship and his new band of pirates to Somalia safe and in one piece. He was committed to doing it well.

Li escorted Zeek back up to the bridge. The agitated pirate entered the control center to find the ship's captain hunched over a large radar screen.

"Unwelcome company," the captain murmured to him.

Zeek looked at the seas around them. Nothing had changed since he'd left a few minutes before. It was a bright, sunny morning; the sea was extremely calm—sailing conditions couldn't have been better. There were four other ships within sight. One was about five miles ahead of them; it was a Panamanian-registered supertanker. They'd been following this ship since leaving Sri Lanka. Behind them, by about ten miles, was an old Filipino freighter heading for the Suez Canal. It had been following them since early morning.

Off to the portside, Zeek could see a rusty freighter heading in the opposite direction. Behind it by a mile or so was what appeared to be an even older freighter, also heading east.

So what was the problem?

It wasn't the other ships that were concerning the captain. Instead, he pointed to the sky right above the *Pasha*.

Zeek looked through the bridge window to see a small helicopter overhead, flying along, keeping pace with them.

He was immediately concerned.

"How long has that been up there?" he asked the captain.

"Five minutes," was the reply.

Zeek turned to Commander Li, who had the copter in his binoculars.

"What kind of helicopter is it?"

Li reported: "It's not a large aircraft. It could be from an oil platform or an oil exploration ship. Or . . ."

"Or what?"

"Or it could be a military craft," he replied.

This Zeek did not want to hear.

He pulled the binoculars from Li's hands and studied the copter himself. It was probably 1,000 feet above the *Pasha*, moving in perfect sync with the ship. It was hard to see what

color it was, or what type. It *was* small, though, which bothered him, because the copter that had led the attack on his
headquarters back in Indonesia had also been small.

Zeek had planned a carefree crossing of the Indian Ocean.
He had thought he'd covered everything. The ship, his political connections, his new army of bodyguards. The promise of
fertile new pirating ground.

But this helicopter . . . this worried him.

Zeek unhappily decided to forgo his sleep, took some meth,
and stayed on the bridge to watch the helicopter pacing them.

He asked Li about launching the ship's own helicopter—a
German-built Bo-105 gunship. But Li asked, to what end?

"Harassing that copter will just bring attention to us," he
said. "That's the last thing we want."

The 352 also had six 50-caliber machine guns onboard:
two on the bridge railing, two on the bow and two on the
stern.

Zeek pointed to the nearest 50-caliber and asked: "Could
we shoot it down if we wanted to?"

Li thought a moment. "Probably," he replied. "But again, it
would attract a lot of attention to us."

He spread his hands out to indicate the handful of ships going in both directions around the *Pasha*.

"So there's *nothing* we can do?" Zeek asked him angrily.
"Except watch the infernal thing?"

"Nothing else," Li replied.

And after twenty minutes, the copter flew away.

THE COPTER REAPPEARED two hours later, close to noon.

Once again, it was first spotted on the ship's air-defense
radar, a blip coming from the northwest.

It took up station right above the *Pasha* just as before, this
time moving as the sun moved, making it difficult for anyone
on the ship to look up at it very long with the naked eye.

Zeek had spent all the time between sightings on the bridge
in a highly restless state. He was fighting the contradicting
effects of the drugs he'd ingested—meth to stay awake, barbiturates to go to sleep—and losing on both ends. When the

copter reappeared, he ordered his two bodyguards onto the deck of the ship with their AK-47s close by, but following Li's advice, not in view. The same ships were in front of and in back of the *Pasha,* and as Li reminded him several times, the last thing they wanted was to call attention to themselves.

But Zeek was getting anxious. Who was in the helicopter? Who was watching him?

THIS TIME THE copter stayed above them for more than an hour. Tension ran through the ship the whole time. The bodyguards were forced to sit in the sweltering sun, looking extremely uncomfortable. The pirate army was told to stay below, out of sight. Meanwhile Zeek spent all this time on the bridge, looking into the sun, burning his retinas.

Once again he discussed with Li shooting down the copter—or at least trying to—and taking their chances with anyone who saw them. But again, Li talked him out of it. It would be impossible to keep other eyes from seeing such an action, and then reporting it. Zeek reluctantly heeded his advice.

At exactly 1330 hours, the copter disappeared again.

The tension eased, and for a moment, Zeek actually thought he could finally retire to his quarters and get some sleep.

But that idea was crushed when, at 1331 hours, the ship's radio screeched to life. The initial message was garbled and spoken in broken English, but the gist was clear. The *Pasha* was being told it should stand by and prepare for boarding by a NATO ship on anti-piracy patrol.

Zeek was instantly furious—this was the *last* thing he needed. This wasn't a typical vessel they were sailing here. Only a few members of European royalty had yachts that resembled military ships, and he was sure they didn't have compartments belowdecks filled with illegal weapons and newly recruited pirates. Political connections or not, Zeek was nervous at the thought of real military people tramping through his new ship.

The *Pasha* received three more messages via the radio, telling them to stand by, that the anti-piracy boarding party was on its way. During this time, Zeek made calls back to his friends at Indonesian naval headquarters and to Sunny Hi's personal phone, leaving frantic messages each time.

Waiting for the boarding party stretched on into the late afternoon. No NATO ship ever appeared. Replies to the radio frequency used by the mysterious caller went unanswered. The *Pasha* passed through a series of rainsqualls, but upon coming out of each one, they could still see no NATO ship, no changes at all, except that the Filipino ship that had been traveling behind them had been replaced by a rusty, broken-down coastal freighter.

Finally, Zeek and Li came to realize they'd been the victims of a hoax. There was no NATO boarding party on its way. The question was: Who would do this—and why?

By 1800 hours, Zeek was so wound up he could barely talk. It had been a bad day for him. He stormed back to his expansive cabin, determined to get some sleep, when he received yet another message from the bridge.

The helicopter was overhead again.

Zeek could not be contained this time. He signaled the crew to what amounted to battle stations, then climbed into his own battle gear and rushed back to the bridge, ready for war.

He told Li he had only one question: What was the best way to shoot down the helicopter—with the ship's machine guns or by sending their own copter aloft?

Li knew that, despite his deep connections, the wrong answer might get him a short trip over the side. But it was his job to stay cool and rational.

"If you want to shoot it down, I recommend shooting it down with the machine guns," he told Zeek. "Because launching our copter would give it a clue something was up. But . . ."

"But what?" Zeek asked.

"But we *mustn't* do it in front of witnesses," Li emphasized. "It would be too rash, and it would cause a lot of suspicions."

"What do you suggest then?" Zeek asked him.

"Let's move out of the shipping lanes," Li advised. "See if this pest follows. Once we are out of sight of prying eyes, you can do what you want with him."

Zeek saw the wisdom in this right away.

"Do it then," he said. "Move us—and hurry."

THE *PASHA* MADE a long, slow turn to the southwest at 1810 hours. They were now a few hundred miles west of the Maldives. Diverging here was not so unusual if the ship's destination was South Africa or even South America.

When the *Pasha* changed course, the trailing helicopter did as well. By the time the pirate ship passed over the horizon and beyond the sight of other vessels in the major shipping lanes, there was still an hour of sunlight left.

That's when Team Whiskey struck.

IT HAD BEEN a shoestring plan, badly stitched together with suggestions from all of them, yet somehow the team accomplished exactly what they wanted: They'd maneuvered Zeek out of the shipping lanes, away from any witnesses. They had him just where they wanted him, at least for the moment.

Sending the work copter to harass Zeek and radioing the phony NATO boarding message had been perfect ploys. The Pirate King was impulsive, paranoid, narcissistic and quick to anger. Making him aware that someone knew what he was up to, that someone was throwing a monkey wrench into his plans, had caused him to act irrationally, just as they had hoped.

And while his eyes, and those of everyone else aboard his ship, were looking skyward, focused on the strange little helicopter, they barely noticed that instead of the Filipino freighter following them, as it had all day, after going through the line of rainsqualls, the *Dustboat* had moved in behind them instead.

So, the trap had been set.

But right away, there was a problem. It had to do with the Copperhead shell Conley had given them. It was longer and narrower than a typical artillery shell and had two sets of steering fins, one near the middle and one on the end. These fins folded against the shell's body when it was being loaded into the gun and opened once the shell was fired. But this particular shell had been kicking around for so long, the fins would not stay flush when loaded into the M198 howitzer's breech. It wasn't a question of muscle power and jamming the shell in; it was more a surgical operation that Gunner, the weapons expert, just couldn't accomplish. Even with Nolan's help, he failed to squeeze the shell into the beastly M198.

This wasn't good, because the Copperhead was central to their plan against Zeek. Get him out in the middle of the ocean and sink his ass with the smart bomb/artillery shell from twenty miles away—that was the extent of it. As veterans of many asymmetrical engagements, the team knew few things went 100 percent right in combat. But all things considered, this was a good place to start.

But now it was getting dark, Zeek's ship was getting farther out of range, and Batman and Crash—in the work copter, still pacing the pirate ship—were watching the *Pasha*'s crew taking the tarps off their 50-caliber machine guns. But try as they might, those back on the DUS-7 just couldn't get the Copperhead shell to cooperate.

Finally, Twitch came up with an idea: Why not wrap rubber bands around the fins just long enough to get the shell inside the gun? Then they could snip the bands off once the shell was in place.

They took four rubber bands and put them in place as Twitch suggested—and the shell slid right in. Then, using the long, thin blade he always carried in his prosthetic leg, Twitch delicately snipped off the rubber bands and removed them from the breech.

It worked—but it had used up ten precious minutes. By the time the Copperhead was loaded, Zeek's ship was about twenty-two miles away, at the very limit of the smart shell's effective range.

Nolan called up to Batman in the work copter to tell him the gun was finally loaded.

"It's your show now," he told the copter pilot.

But no sooner had Batman received the message that a furious barrage of 50-caliber machine gun fire rose up from the *Pasha*. At the same moment, they saw the ship's helicopter gunship start its rotors, intent no doubt on coming up to challenge them. It was official: Zeek was trying to shoot him down.

"Are you ready to do your thing?" Batman yelled to Crash as he started dodging the storm of tracer fire.

"More than ready," Crash yelled back.

The ex-SEAL reached not for his sniper rifle, but for the team's laser designator. According to the manual, if Crash could hold a laser marker on the *Pasha*'s hull long enough, the Copperhead shell would lock onto the laser beam and follow it right down to the target.

But it was easier said than done, as the copter crew soon found out.

"We can barely hold steady over the boat," Batman yelled into his sat phone to Nolan. "And because these assholes are shooting at us, we can't stay in one place for very long."

"What do you recommend, then?" Nolan asked him.

"Just fire the goddamn thing!" Batman yelled in reply.

Nolan turned to Gunner. "Are you aimed?"

Gunner checked the M198's computer-assisted aiming calculators. "I'm in the ballpark," he said. "The readout says the ship is in the crosshairs."

"Then fire it," Nolan told him. "Before Batman has kittens."

Gunner didn't have to be told twice. He pulled the firing cord and the Copperhead shell exploded out of the gun with such sound and fury that, at first, they thought it had detonated inside the barrel itself. But that fear subsided as they watched the shell zoom toward the horizon, its steering fins extended.

Batman and Crash actually saw it coming, a flare of red fire arching across the sky. Now came the time to show some real fortitude. Batman stopped his aerial dancing act and put the work copter into a dive, ending up just 250 feet above the stern of the minesweeper. Holding on to his safety harness for dear life, Crash hung way out the copter's open door, pointed his laser marker at the *Pasha*'s rear deck, and did his best to keep it there.

Batman and Crash had both envisioned they'd have to stay like this for a substantial amount of time, but they were wrong. The Copperhead shell arrived just seconds after it was fired. It perfectly followed the beam of light shone on Zeek's vessel and struck with astonishing force. The shell sliced through the stern of the pirate ship, taking out the Bo-105 helicopter, its crew and its landing pad, then drove deeply into the hull and exploded in the engine room. The blast was so tremendous, it blew a hole out the back of the ship, utterly destroying one of its engines and disabling its main steering column.

Buffeted by the resulting shockwave, Batman and Gunner were astounded that the shell actually worked.

"Jesus freaking Christ," Batman cried. "Right on the freaking money!"

"We hit it," Crash kept saying. "We hit it!"

They hit it, yes—but they soon realized that they did not sink it. The pirate ship was going up the side of a wave when the missile struck. When it came off that same wave, propelled by the force of the blast, a great spray of seawater went through the blown-out hole, extinguishing the fire in the end of the ship with cosmic efficiency.

And incredibly, the *Pasha* motored on. It had lost half its power, smoke was billowing out of every orifice, and blown-apart electrical cables were sparking all over the deck. But the ship was still afloat and moving nevertheless.

Batman couldn't believe it; neither could Crash. When they relayed the news back to Nolan on DUS-7, the team leader couldn't believe it, either. If the Copperhead shell had hit just ten more feet toward the front of the ship, it would have sunk it like a brick.

"But we still got him by the nuts!" Nolan yelled back to them on the sat phone. "He's wounded. He's hurting. Now, we just got to finish the job."

"Roger that," Batman radioed back. "Let's hit 'em when they're down."

Crash put the laser designator aside and pulled his sniper rifle from the backseat. Batman put the work copter into another screaming dive. They passed through the smoke pouring

out of the back of the pirate ship and saw the deck was a scene
of mass confusion, the crew trying to fight what was left of
the fire and collect their dead and wounded. Batman turned the
copter sharply right, which put Crash and his weapon almost
even with the ship's wheelhouse.

Crash fired directly into the bridge. At the same time, Batman turned the copter so it faced the wheelhouse, and opened
up with the gun pod. The combined barrage lasted only a few
seconds, but caused extensive damage. Everyone in the control room—including the ship's Chinese captain and his two
executive officers—took bullets to the head and chest. Twelve
were killed outright. The bridge's main radio and communications suite exploded, and a main electrical buss blew out
every light on the ship.

Batman pulled the copter up and away and fired a barrage
at the smoking hole in the back of the ship, hoping to hit the
vessel's remaining good engine. He sprayed the deck itself,
killing some of those pirates who'd been firing the 50-caliber
machine guns at him. Finally, he and Crash ran out of ammunition. Batman pushed the copter's controls forward and they
quickly flew away.

On the DUS-7, Nolan had ordered the ship to full double
ahead, meaning their diesel engines were revved up to full
power and the small gas turbine was also running, increasing
their speed to in excess of forty knots. Within five minutes,
the *Dustboat* was just two miles away from Zeek's burning,
smoking wreck.

Nolan had Gunner load the big M198 again, this time with
a conventional shell. He fired and the first shell landed just a
few feet off the nose of the pirate ship. The explosion lifted
the front of the vessel out of the water and knocked it sideways.

Nolan helped Gunner reload, and the gun fired again. This
shell missed to port, but showered the pirate ship with shrapnel and a rush of superheated salt water.

A third shot—this one skimmed the bridge and nearly
took out the forward gun. The DUS-7 was now less than a mile
away, and the M198 was firing shells with incredible power

and violence. Nolan and Gunner reloaded the gun and fired it again. The pirate ship was turning wildly, and this shot went right through the main mast, blowing it to pieces.

"In the old days, 'de-masting' your enemy was the end of a battle," Gunner yelled to Nolan. "So we're getting close."

But no sooner were these words out of his mouth than they saw a flash from the pirate ship, and a five-inch shell streaked over their heads, landing in the water on their starboard side. The near-hit rocked the DUS-7 back and forth, causing a small tidal wave of seawater to wash over them.

Whether by fluke or defiance, the pirate ship was firing back.

"God damn!" Gunner yelled. "Too fucking close!"

Twitch yelled down from the bridge: "The Senegals want to know which way should we go?"

"Stay on his tail!" Nolan yelled back. "No matter what—stay right in back of him . . ."

This was the smart move. The pirate ship—though wounded—was still heavily armed. But no matter what condition it was in, it couldn't fire its heavy weapons backward.

Nolan and Gunner loaded the gun and fired again. This shot came even closer to hitting the pirate ship's forward gun, scraping it and taking out the entire bow railing before exploding in the sea on the other side.

The pirate ship went sharp to port. "Stay on him!" Nolan yelled, and the Senegals did just that.

The DUS-7 was now just a quarter-mile from the pirate ship and gaining fast. Nolan and Gunner could feel victory within their grasp. They loaded the gun and fired it again. The shell hit the pirate ship square on its main deck, blowing off half the port-side rail.

"Muthafucker!" Gunner screamed. "We got this asshole now!"

Nolan couldn't disagree. The burning ship was losing speed as the DUS-7 was gaining on it. The Senegals continued following Nolan's order to a T and stayed glued to the *Pasha*'s tail, not allowing the crippled vessel to fire any of its weapons.

Nolan and Gunner loaded another shell, and in aiming the gun, had the pirate ship's bridge in its sight. They knew it would be a direct hit. Nolan told Gunner to fire. But before he could pull the firing cord, there was a shout from the ship's bridge.

"We got company!" was all Twitch said.

Nolan and Gunner looked up into the gathering dusky sky and immediately saw what Twitch was talking about.

"I don't believe this . . ." Nolan gasped.

BATMAN AND CRASH were about halfway back to the DUS-7 when they saw what those on the ship saw.

They couldn't believe it, either.

Two U.S. Navy jet fighters were hurtling toward the DUS-7 at supersonic speed, flying in extremely low from the north.

They went by the ship so fast and so low, the *Dustboat* was rocked back and forth, buffeted violently by the combined shockwaves.

"What the fuck are these guys doing?" Batman exploded.

The planes were F-18 Super Hornets, the most powerful warplanes in the U.S. Navy and among the top fighters in the world.

Batman watched as the two jets pulled up and screamed off to the west.

He called Nolan on the sat phone. "What the fuck was *that* about?"

"I can only guess," Nolan shouted in reply. "The freaking ONI . . ."

It was the threat made good. The world would be better off if Zeek wasn't in Indonesian waters anymore—and killing him was not an option, because no one wanted to piss off the Chinese. So once again, Team Whiskey's intentions were being held hostage to the seamy machinations of international politics.

The question was, how far would the Navy jets go?

The two F-18s swung back around the DUS-7 and once again streaked over the freighter so low, the ship shook from one end to the other.

Then they turned yet again . . .

* * *

NAVY CAPTAIN RANDY Lynch was the flight leader of the F-18s. He and his wingman had left the aircraft carrier *USS Lincoln* in the Persian Gulf ninety minutes earlier after being assigned a classified anti-piracy mission in the Indian Ocean.

They'd been given a target described as a four-masted "tramp steamer." The boat was said to be "heavily armed and a danger to shipping." They were to intercept the ship, confirm its hostile intent, and "take all actions necessary to protect international shipping."

In other words, it was a pirate ship—and they were here to sink it.

Lynch had been a Navy flier for nearly fifteen years. He'd flown missions in Iraq and over Afghanistan. He'd shot at people and people had shot at him. This was the first time, though, that he'd been ordered to shoot at pirates.

On their next pass, Lynch and his wingman opened up with the F-18's nose-mounted cannons. They tore up the back of the rusty old ship and blew the top off the freighter's stack. They turned, and this time came in from the west. Opening up at 500 feet out, both planes walked a line of cannon fire right down the center of the vessel. There were a handful of secondary explosions this time, indications that there were weapons or explosives belowdecks of the old ship.

They turned again, knowing that fuel constraints and the coming darkness meant this had to be a killing pass.

But before they came in for this fateful strafing run, Lynch saw something odd happening on the ship. Someone had climbed up one of the freighter's masts, someone who didn't look like a Somali pirate. He looked more like a soldier, and he was madly waving a flag.

An American flag.

Lynch immediately broke off his strafing run; his wingman did, too.

"Pirate or not," Lynch radioed his partner, "there's no way I'm shooting at that. I just can't."

"Neither can I," the wingman radioed back. "Someone

might have got their wires crossed, because this didn't seem right from the beginning. I think I just suddenly ran out of ammunition."

"Roger that," Lynch said. "Me, too."

With that, the two fighters pulled up, turned as one and roared over the ship one more time. Then they disappeared into the approaching darkness to the northeast.

It took more than a minute for the roar of their engines to finally fade away.

DOWN ON THE DUS-7, the crew was laying flat out on the bridge deck amidships, the most structurally sound place on the boat. This is where Batman and Crash found them, hands over their heads, hot metal and smoke all around them. All except Nolan.

They'd landed the work copter just seconds after the F-18s departed and had immediately run forward.

"Jesus Christ!" Batman fumed, looking at the damage. "I probably know those Navy flyboys. And if I don't, I'm going to find out who they are and fuck them up."

The others were just getting to their feet. The Senegals were especially shaken up. They'd never had powerful jet fighters shoot at them before. Incredibly, no one was hurt.

Batman helped Gunner to his feet, then looked up at the mast and saw Nolan starting to climb down, stars and stripes in hand.

"Good thing he had a flag," Gunner said to Batman.

Batman just shrugged. "Yeah—go figure that."

It took a few minutes, but eventually everyone was back to breathing normally again. The damage report was not good, though. Some of their ammunition had gone off in the Rubber Room down below, and the deck was full of holes. The most extensive damage was in the engine room, though.

"They fucked up the feed system for the gas turbine," Crash reported. "And we have a major leak in one of diesels. We got about half our electrical power functioning. But we don't have any afterburner anymore."

Batman just wiped his hands over his sweaty head. "Could have been worse, I guess," he said to Nolan, who joined them on the bridge.

"Don't speak too soon," Nolan said.

He held up his arms and indicated the sea all around of them. Batman could see nothing but water.

In the confusion, Zeek's ship had slipped away.

24

Calzino Island
The Seychelles
Midnight

EIGHT PEOPLE WERE inside Lazy Joe's Bar: Four female college students from America, a bartender, a cook and two waiters.

Lazy Joe's was one of three businesses—the others were a hotel and a scuba diving shop—jammed into a trio of small, brightly colored waterfront buildings. They were the only buildings on the tiny island of Calzino, the farthest-out atoll of the Seychelles chain, northeast of Madagascar. Just a mile long and a half-mile wide, Calzino was all but devoid of trees and vegetation. Its harbor, small and shallow, took up most of its eastern side. The nearest land, another Seychelles island called Mahe, was more than 100 miles away.

Scuba diving brought the tourists here. Some of the most exotic reefs on Earth were close by, reefs that resembled monstrous, multicolored globs of light emanating from the ocean floor. The best time to dive these bizarre reefs was at night.

The four girls at the bar were restless. They'd been drinking since early evening while their male friends were out diving for the fourth night in a row. After many Cosmos, the girls decided they were leaving the island the following morning, with or without their boyfriends.

Calzino was just too boring.

But that was about to change.

THE FIRST GUNMAN burst through the door at the stroke of midnight, waving his assault rifle around wildly. At first, the patrons thought he was a policeman. He wore a black military suit and boots and a woolen cap. But there were no police on Calzino. The place was too small.

Without a word, the gunman shot the bartender between the eyes, dispelling any notion that he was law enforcement. The four girls screamed. A moment later, the plate glass window next to the bar exploded and two more gunmen burst in, firing their weapons indiscriminately. The girls screamed again, louder this time. The gunmen quickly knocked them to the floor and held them there with their boot heels. More gunmen appeared; two walked into the kitchen and shot the cook. When one of the waiters went to the aid of the girls, he was dragged out to the street and shot. Other gunmen broke into the hotel next door, roused the two employees and shot them in their beds. The three people who worked at the Night Dive marina were beaten, and one was shot trying to escape.

The gunmen then stole all their victims' wallets, emptied all the cash registers, collected all cell phones and seized the hotel's satellite phone. And that was it.

In less than three minutes, the little island of Calzino had been taken over by Zeek and his murderous crew.

NO ONE ON the island had seen the *Pasha* enter the harbor. Smoking and battered, the battle-scarred 352 had slipped in and dropped anchor just a hundred feet offshore.

Yet despite their brutal efficiency in seizing the tiny town, Zeek and his men had big problems. The *Pasha*'s captain was dead, as were all his first officers, the only people experienced in sailing the ship. All of the vessel's radios were destroyed, as was one of its two engines. The second engine was still working, but at only one-third power. Nearly all the electrical systems on board had short-circuited, all the navigation computers were down, and even simple things like the bilge pumps and the intercom were out of order.

Most critical, the pirates needed ammunition for their deck-mounted five-inch gun. Many of its shells had to be thrown overboard during the sea battle with their shadowy pursuers, when one of the fires threatened to blow up the ship's ammunition locker. This left the *Pasha* with exactly two shells, both of which were loaded inside the gun.

Zeek's new *capo,* Commander Fun Li, was extremely unhappy with this state of affairs. Yes, they had given their pursuers the slip. But the *Pasha* was barely afloat, and they'd lost more than three dozen men killed in the surprise attack. They'd made it here, to a safe harbor, but their most formidable weapon was practically useless. Li's military training had taught him to make the best of bad situations, to seize opportunity from chaos. This is why he'd strongly suggested to Zeek that the pirate band take refuge here on Calzino in the first place. It would allow them time to re-group.

And good news came just minutes after they'd arrived. The ship's engineers, all of whom had survived the sea attack, told Li that getting the ship's working engine back to 100 percent power required only one part: a power transfer knuckle. If one could be had, they could fix the ailing engine sufficiently to get the ship to Somalia with minimal delay.

But how could they get a power transfer knuckle?

Li made a phone call. Using the hotel's confiscated satellite phone, he spoke to a contact in South Africa who promised to airlift the critical part to Calzino immediately, along with a crate of five-inch naval gun shells. The engineers assured Li that installation of the engine part would not be a problem. With any luck, the *Pasha* would be rearmed and on its way the following morning.

When Li reported all this to Zeek, who had hidden himself away in his large, luxurious cabin, the Pirate King took the news as confirmation that God was still with him, that he had left all the bad spirits back in Indonesia—another reason he wanted to get away from his homeland—and that his run of luck, from surviving the sea attack to finding this tiny sanctuary, was still holding.

Only then did Zeek go ashore to see the hostages his men had taken.

THE GIRLS ON the bar's floor, still held at gunpoint, terrified and crying, gasped at the first sight of the fearsome Pirate king.

Striding in, dressed in brightly colored trousers, dress shirt and half coat, his beard in weird braids, his hair long and dirty, Zeek looked like something from a horror movie.

He scanned the shot-up bar, felt the veneer of the overly shellacked wooden tables, checked the overhanging aluminum lights for dust.

Then he casually pointed to the only brunette among the four girls and walked out. Two pirates yanked her to her feet and carried her, kicking and screaming, out the door.

The remaining girls could do nothing but cry as their friend was taken away.

THE TOP FLOOR of Calzino's three-story hotel held a penthouse of sorts. Slightly larger than the rest of the rooms, it had a massive waterbed, a hot tub and a small bar. The wall over the waterbed was adorned with the steering wheel of an old wooden ship; some very old spear guns and a diving helmet decorated the bathroom. When the room's curtains were opened, a large picture window provided an impressive view of the island's harbor and the ocean beyond.

This is where Zeek and the pirates brought the girl.

Zeek forced her to sit on the edge of the waterbed while his men ransacked the bar. They found only small bottles of white wine. Zeek drank one bottle in a single gulp, then had his men force the girl to drink six bottles, one right after another. She fought them mightily, but it made no difference. Her resistance only amused them.

On at a curt nod from Zeek, the other pirates left the room, closing the door tight and taking up stations in the hall outside. As soon as they left, the girl began to scream, then sounds of a great struggle could be heard. Eventually these sounds were replaced by the girl's pleas, begging Zeek to stop, and finally, by her sobs.

Then suddenly, the noise stopped completely.

The suite door opened and the young girl was flung out, landing hard on the hallway floor. She was naked, her face and chest covered with welts. She vomited, tried to get to her feet, and fell again.

One pirate slipped into the room. It looked as if a cyclone had gone through the place. Zeek lay on the bed, looking like someone who'd just finished a huge meal. The room smelled of blood and sex.

Zeek pointed to the curtains drawn across the room's picture window next to the bed.

"Open them," he ordered the pirate. "Then clean this place up."

His man complied, drawing back the curtains, revealing the view of the harbor and the ocean beyond.

The man took one look out at the water, though, and softly swore: "Damn . . ."

Lying just outside the harbor, silhouetted by the light of the full moon, was the DUS-7.

COMMANDER LI HAD spotted the rusty freighter seconds earlier.

He was standing on the wrecked bridge of the *Pasha*, hoping to get its computers working again, when the splintered masts of the DUS-7 appeared above the jetty leading into Calzino's harbor.

Li was both fascinated and highly troubled by the ship's sudden appearance.

"*They* made it, too?" he thought.

The last Li had seen of the rusty freighter, it was getting shot to pieces by two fighter jets. He knew the heavily armed freighter probably belonged to the merc unit Kilos Shipping had sent after Zeek, just as he knew the jets belonged to the U.S. Navy. So, he'd assumed it was a case of mistaken identity and that the pilots mistook their adversaries for pirates. So intense was this attack, though, the freighter seemed doomed to sink, just as the *Pasha* had seemed doomed just seconds before. Yet somehow, it also had survived.

Studying the freighter through his night-vision glasses now, Li could see that, like the *Pasha*, the freighter was extensively damaged. Two of its cargo masts were missing; its bridge was in shambles. Lockers, ropes, chains, housings, the typical things that cluttered a ship of this type, were all gone from the deck. It was obvious that whatever wasn't bolted down or working the freighter's crew had been thrown overboard. This told Li the ship's engines were also in bad shape, and that its crew had tried to lighten the vessel to keep it afloat and moving.

But *how* had their pursuers tracked them here?

Li again used the hotel's sat phone, this time to call a contact in the Indonesian Navy. He had a question for him: Did Indonesian Navy ships have AIS on them—as in an automatic identification system? The answer was yes, all Indonesian Navy ships had the chip-in-the-ship beacon. Question two: Had Prince Seeodek thought to remove his AIS beacon when he took delivery of the 352 minesweeper?

The answer was no.

Li was so furious he nearly threw the sat phone into the harbor. End of mystery—the freighter's crew had tracked them here via satellite.

Li called over two ship's engineers and ordered them to find the AIS beacon wherever it was on the *Pasha* and destroy it. Then he went back to studying the battered old freighter.

Thanks to his contacts in the Chinese intelligence services, Li knew a good deal about the people he believes were on the ship. Nolan, Graves, Kapula, Lapook and Stacks. He knew their lineage—from their glory days in Delta Force to their fall from grace within the U.S. black ops community, to their sudden emergence as the darlings of maritime security. He knew all about their battles, their gigs, where they'd been and what they'd been up to in the past month or so, even how much money they'd made. Li had done his homework on the

"Whiskey Team" before leaving Indonesia, knowing that Zeek might run into them again. And rusty ship or not, he recognized them as dangerous adversaries.

But he refused to believe the freighter's crew was double-lucky blessed, as some people back in Indonesia claimed. That they'd become ghosts on a ship called the *Global Warrior*, which allowed them to kill with ease a pirate crew run by Zeek's late brother. Or that they were able to spread so much bad luck on Zeek himself they'd caused him to go broke overnight. Nor did he believe the tale that, after fighting a typhoon while trying to catch up to the INS *Vidynut*, the freighter—which should have been a half an ocean away—wound up just a mile behind the hijacked Indian ship at the precise moment it needed to be there.

No—no one was *that* blessed.

True, they had come within a half-minute of sinking the *Pasha* and killing them all. But that bid had been foiled by their own countrymen shooting at them. How *un*lucky was that?

And finding them here at Calzino? Again, not some black magic. They'd simply had some earthly help called an AIS computer chip.

Yes, Li had studied them and tried to learn as much as he could about them. Just as he knew these people and knew what they had done, he also knew—as maybe the Whiskey Team didn't—that luck was like something you could pour out of a bottle. Each person had only so much of it, and at some point, it simply ran dry. And that's what was going to happen to these cowboys now. They were running out of luck. Li could just feel it.

The *Pasha*'s junior bridge officer now served as the battered ship's commander. Li ordered him to immediately reposition the ship so it was sitting in the center of the harbor, just twenty-five feet off the beach. This took several minutes, and when it was done, the *Pasha* was blocking most of the sightline from the harbor entrance to the small town itself.

In other words, it was in the way.

Now Li took a monstrous gamble. He ordered the *Pasha*'s weapons crew to man the forward-mounted five-inch gun and had another crew member turn on the ship's battery-powered searchlight and point it directly at the recently arrived freighter.

Then Li took the ship's bullhorn, positioned himself on the stern of his ship, and addressed the newcomers in perfect English.

He informed them that the pirates had taken over the town, had severed all communications, and were holding hostages, including four American females. They would kill them all if the Whiskey Team took any action against them. Zeek expected to leave the harbor at a time of his choosing with no interference from the team.

At that point, Li ordered his gun crew to fire a shell over the top of the freighter. Poorly aimed, the shell nevertheless sailed over the rusty ship, passing through the empty air where, had they not been destroyed, the cargo masts would have been.

Li watched now through his night-vision goggles as the people on the freighter scrambled to what for them must have been battle stations, one man each on bridge-mounted 50-caliber machine guns, one man back to the ship's tiny work copter. Two more manned the enormous howitzer these crazy people had somehow installed on the bow of their ship.

They also moved the freighter back from the harbor's entrance and behind the north side jetty, making it less of a target for the *Pasha*'s deck gun.

The pirate ship's gun crew stayed on station, but only fired that one shot. They had just a single shell left, and Li wasn't going to waste it.

Now it was time for Li to put himself into the mind of his enemy. The M198 was a powerful weapon—almost too powerful for this situation. If the freighter crew fired it at the *Pasha,* one shot might sink the 352 in seconds. But, because the freighter was rolling in moderate seas beyond the jetty, Li thought it almost impossible that its crew could get an accurate shot at him. And missing in this situation would mean taking out half the town—and that meant endangering the hostages.

And Li was sure the Whiskey Team had no more "smart

shells"; they would have used them during the sea battle. So the chances of a perfectly accurate shot at the *Pasha* were zero, and Li was sure the freighter's crew knew that as well as he did.

In other words, they were in a standoff.

Li zoomed in his night-vision goggles all the way so he could study the freighter up close.

The first thing he saw after focusing was a man with an eye patch, standing on the freighter's bow, also with a night-vision device, looking right back at him.

25

A FORTY-FOOT CLIFF on the north side of Calzino's harbor looked out over the jetty that formed one half the entrance to the small island's anchorage. This vantage point offered a close-up, unobstructed view of the DUS-7 freighter, anchored only a hundred feet away.

Commander Li ordered two of his best men to steal out of the town, climb up the cliff and set up a spy post. From their position, they could practically look right down onto the old freighter; they could even hear the people on board talking. An old pair of walkie-talkies taken from the dive shop kept these men in constant contact with Li.

No sooner were the two spies in place, though, when they reported a strange noise coming from farther out to sea. They could see everyone on the old freighter get their weapons up and ready. They even heard one of the crewmen yell: *"Who the fuck is this?"*

A boat was coming out of the north and heading toward Calzino's harbor at high speed. The spies worried it was law enforcement or even a Seychelles naval vessel. Then they heard raucous laughter and loud music playing, and they could see brightly colored lights draped around the boat's hull.

They reported back to Li: "This is not the police. It's the island's scuba diving boat returning to port."

Someone on the freighter fired a flare gun; the fiery shell went right across the bow of the dive boat. The boat slowed immediately, and the music and laughter abruptly stopped.

The freighter maneuvered slightly, blocking the dive boat's entrance to the harbor. In seconds, the small freighter was right up alongside the dive boat.

Watching it all through night-vision goggles, the spies reported the people on the dive boat looked confused and drunk. Sizing up the battered old freighter, with so many armed men on board, the people on the dive boat came to the only logical conclusion.

The spies heard someone on the dive boat yell: "Pirates!"

But then someone on the freighter fired another flare and yelled back: "We're not pirates. Send some people over. We'll explain everything."

The spies saw five people go from the dive boat to the freighter: the captain and his four diving customers, all wearing beachwear, baseball caps and sneakers. They had a quick conversation with the freighter's crew, distinct in their blue, very non-pirate uniforms, and then all went belowdecks.

The two parties emerged a few minutes later. The people in the beachwear climbed back onto dive boat and quickly disengaged from the freighter. They revved their engine and took off at high speed, away from the harbor and toward the southwest.

"They are certainly heading for the next island," the spies told Li. "They're probably going to get help."

Li checked his watch. It would take a boat like that eight hours or more to reach the next island, a hundred miles away.

He hoped his ship would be gone long before then.

As Li was following all this, he heard a commotion back on shore. He saw two pirates were dragging another girl out of the bar, tearing her sundress and forcing her up the stairs to the penthouse.

Another pirate came down, walked to the water's edge and yelled out to Li: "The Boss wants to know if we are going to be attacked anytime soon."

Li was perturbed that Zeek would be so cavalier about the situation, but he kept his cool.

"Tell him it's under control for the moment," he yelled back. "They will not attack—not just yet."

BUT LI KNEW the Whiskey Team *would* attack, somehow, some way. Their reputation depended on it, and it is what they'd done in the past. In fact, he could almost *hear* them plotting aboard the rusty freighter just beyond the jetty. They were cooking up something.

But what would it be this time?

Would they attack his larger force with a lightning-fast air strike as they did against Zeek's headquarters back in the Talua Tangs? Li thought the Whiskey Team might not because of the hostages involved.

So, would they wait until the *Pasha* put out to sea and fight another ocean battle, this one close-in and more reminiscent of the *Vidynut* incident? Li thought the Whiskey Team probably did not want this either, because this time they would not be fighting a ragtag bunch of Somalis in the ship-to-ship encounter, but rather a large, experienced armed force with a working naval gun *and* innocent lives aboard.

So, again, how would the attack come? Based on his knowledge of the Whiskey Team, Li thought he knew the answer. Other than the area around the harbor, the rest of Calzino's terrain was impassable. When he Googled the island earlier, the description read: "Made up of impenetrable fields of jagged rocks, an old granite quarry, and hundreds of pools of bubbling tar which present insurmountable obstacles to humans and animals alike."

This meant the Whiskey Team only had one option left—which was good, because Li would be ready for it.

He took a rubber raft from the ship and traveled the twenty-five or so feet to shore in a matter of seconds. Then he ordered his pirates to assemble in the street. Inside a minute, his small army was standing before him, except the people guarding the hostages, the two spies up on the cliff, and the crewmembers still on the *Pasha*.

Li told them he suspected the freighter crew would attempt a simultaneous attack-and-rescue mission. They would drive their ship into the harbor to get as close as possible to the *Pasha* for an accurate shot at it with their M198 howitzer. At the same time, they would use their helicopter to locate and rescue the hostages. If they were successful in both these things, the Whiskey Team could then back off and shell the town with impunity, dooming the pirate army.

"These people are worthy adversaries," Li told his men. "They not only found the *Pasha* moving in the shipping lanes, they successfully forced us into the open and they came close to sinking us and killing us all. So, to be clear, these people *will* attack us—it's just a matter of when."

It was a nightmare scenario that rattled many of the pirates. After all, they were brigands and outlaws, not elite soldiers. But Li told them not to worry, as he already had the perfect countermeasures in mind.

He told his men their biggest advantage was in their numbers. Roughly sixty fighters survived the attack at sea, along with twelve ship's crewmen who could use a weapon if need be. Nearly six dozen AK-47s firing at once would sent up a giant wall of lead, a gauntlet that even a ship the size of the freighter would have a hard time getting through. A ruptured fuel line or some kind of catastrophic explosion would spell immediate doom for the battered ship. Simply killing the ten-man crew in a long coordinated, fusillade also would work. Either way, the pirates would present a formidable field of fire—enough, Li told them, to turn the freighter's mad dash into a suicide mission.

He turned and pointed at the rusty freighter waiting on the other side of the jetty.

"We just need to keep our eyes on their helicopter," he told them. "When that copter moves, then they will move. They're reckless, and that means they're dangerous. We outnumber them almost eight to one. But we cannot allow them to surprise us. So—*watch that helicopter.* When it leaves, that's when they'll attack."

Li put the majority of his men along the harbor seawall, spacing them every five feet or so all along the brief shoreline. The rest of the pirates stood at the doorways of the three buildings. He ordered them to watch the skies around them at all times.

Li then checked with each man, making sure he knew his role, making sure his weapon was in working condition and that he had enough ammunition. He bolstered them with good thoughts and good morale, while forbidding them to take any kind of drugs until the battle was over. By the time he reached the end of the defensive line, his men were hyped up and just waiting for the freighter to attack.

But deep down, though he didn't want to admit it to himself, Li was anxious. He prayed for the supply copter to get there soon with the power transfer knuckle and especially the five-inch shells. When that happened, they could repair the ship and fire their five-inch gun at the rusty freighter at will, knowing the cowboys would probably not fire back for fear of hitting the hostages. They might even get lucky and sink the damn Whiskey boat before it even had a chance to attack.

But that all depended on when the supply copter arrived.

Only then would the equation change.

LESS THAN AN hour later, Li's prayers were answered.

It came at first as a low noise in the night. A drone, splitting the silence. Mechanical, powerful. Coming from the south.

It was a helicopter—a big one.

A moment later, it went over the town, an SA-321G Super Frelon heavy-lift copter. Unmarked, painted dark foreboding gray, it was flying low and fast.

It turned north over the harbor, making a lot of noise and gradually slowing down. The pirates on the seawall waved at it, and the people on the copter waved back. Everyone knew this was not law enforcement or a Seychelles military aircraft. This was what they'd been waiting for.

The copter continued its wide turn over the harbor. A man appeared in its open cargo door. There was a winch attached to it, and he was fastening a crate to the hook on the end of its rope. This box no doubt contained both the power knuckle needed to repair the ship's engine and the shells needed to load the *Pasha*'s deck gun.

The copter slowed further. Li yelled to crewmen on the *Pasha* to illuminate the ship's searchlight and guide the copter over to them so they could deliver the crate to the deck of the ship.

The crew complied, and the copter blinked its navigation lights in response. The men in the copter understood. The aircraft turned sharply out of its circle and headed for the pirate ship. For the first time since arriving on Calzino, Li actually relaxed. Because the helicopter had gotten here so quickly, he'd won his battle of time with the Whiskey Team. The advantage was now his.

Li lit a cigarette and waited. The copter passed over the cliff, going into its final turn—when suddenly there was a tremendous flash of light. It streaked through the darkness, over the harbor and hit not the helicopter, but the cliff just below it. The resultant explosion threw tons of rock into the air. This plume of debris shot straight up into the copter's rotors, disintegrating them. The copter came down fast, crashing on the cliff with a sharp, violent explosion.

It all happened so quickly, Li was stunned. They all were. It wasn't apparent at first what had occurred. Then Li realized the Whiskey Team guys had spotted the copter, deduced it was in league with the pirates and, knowing they probably couldn't hit it with a shot from the howitzer, did the next best thing: They fired a high-explosive shell at the cliff. The debris, in turn, downed the chopper.

Li was devastated.

"Now we're *all* stuck here," he groaned.

WATCHING THIS FROM the penthouse window, Zeek was instantly furious.

He made his way down to the street, pushing aside anyone who got in his way. He had a heated conversation with Li, and against his *capo*'s advice, ordered his men to retrieve the last two surviving dive shop workers and stand them up on the seawall. He then ordered the *Pasha*'s searchlight be beamed on them, and when he knew the people on the freighter were watching, he ordered two of his men stand up on the wall with the hostages, put their guns to their heads and blow their brains out.

Zeek laughed as the two men were executed, shaking his fist at the freighter. But just as quickly, the two pirates who'd performed the execution had their heads blown away in quick succession. They fell over just as promptly as the hostages, some of their blood splattering on Zeek's shirt.

They'd been shot by a sniper rifle, fired from the freighter.

Li screamed to his men to take cover behind the seawall. Zeek instantly disappeared into the night. Someone yelled that they should look at the helicopter on the freighter. Its blades were turning!

Another shout said look up on the cliff. Two black men could be seen there, brutally stabbing Li's spies. Their bodies were thrown off the cliff into the water below.

Shaken down to his boots that this had all happened so quickly, Li turned his night-vision goggles back toward the freighter, convinced the attack was coming at any second. And once again, he saw the one-eyed man in the blue combat suit standing on the bow, looking back at him.

But wait a minute, Li thought.

Something was different here.

Wasn't his patch over the other eye before?

THE FIVE REMAINING hostages were being held in the penthouse.

They were the four American girls and the last employee from the bar, a young African waiter. The girls had never entirely stopped crying, now several hours into this nightmare. The young man was in shock. Zeek had violated all of them.

They'd been left with Zeek's two remaining bodyguards, men who'd survived the attack on his island headquarters back in Indonesia by running into the jungle. Before going out to the street to preside over the ill-advised execution of the two dive shop employees, the Pirate King had given the bodyguards just one order: If the people on the freighter attacked, then one way or another, these hostages should not see the sun come up the next morning.

The bodyguards had smuggled a personal stash of Ecstasy aboard the *Pasha,* something forbidden by Commander Li. They had recently taken two hits apiece and, oblivious to what was happening on the street outside, were now staggeringly high. They'd been routinely molesting the girls, cutting pieces from their dresses with their razor-sharp knives just to hear them scream. But fueled by meth, coke and LSD, the pirates were soon raging with blood lust.

They had already gone through the hostages' personal belongings. But now, keying in on the young man's wallet, they found a picture of his mother.

The pirates punched each other in triumph. Their game could begin.

They took the picture of the man's mother and attached it to the far wall of the dimly lit penthouse. Then they forced the man to the other end of the room, put him on his hands and knees and told him to retrieve the picture. But as the man began crawling toward it, he was struck on the back with a gun butt by one of the pirates. He fell heavily to the floor, but was urged on by the pirates to try again. The man began crawling again, only to be kicked in the teeth by the second pirate. Crying now, the man tried a third time to get to the picture, only to be stomped on his neck by both pirates. The girls watched horrified as the man bled heavily from his nose and mouth.

Still, he tried again. But just as he was reaching for the photo, both pirates hit him with their gun butts, delivering a crushing blow to the man's spine. The man went into a violent convulsion, let out a bloody gasp and died, only inches from his mother's picture.

The pirates dissolved into fits of laughter.

"I just can't stop killing," one pirate roared to the other. "It's an addiction."

The pirates picked up the dead man and threw him aside.

Then they turned their attention to the girls.

One was wearing a locket around her neck. Ripping it off her, the pirates found a picture of her grandmother inside. She fought them violently to get it back, but to no avail. They tacked it up on the wall just under the big plate glass window.

Then they threw her on the floor at the other end of the room and said: "Go get it."

The girl started crawling, terrified and choking on her tears, knowing what was to come. She'd gone just a few feet when the first pirate raised his knife to slash her.

That's when the girl looked up and saw, reflected in the picture window's glass, a man incomprehensibly dressed in beachwear—Izod shirt, cargo shorts and designer sunglasses—but wearing a battle helmet and combat boots and holding an assault rifle with a bayonet attached to it. He was standing in the penthouse doorway.

Even more inexplicable, this man was smeared with tar—and feathers.

She looked right at him through the reflection and couldn't help but think: *Where did he come from?* He made a simple movement with his hand and mouthed two words to her: "Stay down."

She screamed and went flat on the floor. The pirate went to cut her—but then there were two shots. The pirate looked down at his chest and was astonished to see twin gushes of blood flowing out of him.

The whole room froze. No one said a word.

Then the pirate fell over, hitting the floor hard.

The other pirate was so shocked, he couldn't move. The man in the beachwear simply walked up to him and plunged his bayonet into his back. The pirate opened his mouth to scream, but was prevented from doing so by the bayonet slicing across his throat. He fell over a moment later.

The girl on the floor started to scream again, but Snake Nolan put his hand over her mouth and whispered urgently to her: "You're OK. We're here to save you."

TAR.

It was on Nolan's boots, on his hands, it was even in his hair.

The strange thing was—he also had feathers on him. Tarred and feathered.

Weird.

He'd done many forced marches during his days in Delta Force. He'd tramped across deserts, over mountain ranges, through jungles and swamps. Before that, he'd gone through some of the worst basic training imaginable. Crawling through pig guts with live ammunition flying over his head was just the beginning of those ordeals.

But he'd never been through what he'd experienced in the past half hour.

He, Crash and Twitch had just endured more than a mile forced run over the jagged rocks and tar pits that made up the impassable back end of Calzino Island. They'd been dropped off at a point on the far western side of the atoll by the dive boat, and while the pirates' attention was drawn to the DUS-7 and what Nolan hoped they believed was an impending frontal attack on the town, he and the others came in through the back door, so to speak. It was Team Whiskey's equivalent of Hannibal going over the Alps with elephants. They knew the only way to save the hostages was to come at the pirates from the direction they expected least.

And the people in the blue suits that the pirates had been watching? They were the American students who'd returned from scuba diving on the nearby exotic coral reefs. They were straw men. That's why Nolan, Crash and Twitch now sported the latest in J. Crew summer wear.

But they knew only half the mission was done. To successfully rescue the hostages, they had to get out of the little town fast. And their escape route had to be the way they came in— over some of the roughest terrain any of them had ever experienced. The question was, could their hostages take it as well?

Nolan pushed his helmet's visor up and tried to unstick his hand from his M4, but he couldn't. Both his hands and the weapon's stock were covered with tar.

Crash was with him; Twitch was watching the hotel's rear entrance, keeping an eye on their escape route. They'd been in the town for three minutes, taking the students' advice to look for the hostages in the penthouse first. But that was long enough. They had to get going.

Yet there was one more piece of business they wanted to attend to.

"Where's the head creep?" Nolan asked the girls.

They knew right away who he meant.

"He left when the shooting started out on the street," one girl said. "He never came back."

"Son of a bitch," Crash groaned. "I would have given anything to stick him."

"Me, too," said Nolan. "But that time's coming soon enough."

Nolan made his way to the picture window and, taking the laser designator from his pocket, blinked it three quick times toward the *Dustboat*. Almost instantly, a light near the M198 blinked three times in response.

"OK," Nolan said. "Now for phase two."

Just as the words were out of his mouth, they heard an enormous screech.

One of the M198 shells fired from the DUS-7's howitzer streaked over their heads and landed somewhere in the back of the resort, in the forest of granite stones and tar pits. When it hit, the whole building shook.

No sooner had the noise of the first shell exploding faded away when another shell went overhead—then another and another. It was Gunner, pouring it on.

"I'm glad he's on our side," Crash said, hearing another shell go over.

Nolan checked his watch and then said, "Time to go."

Crash went ahead to the hallway as Nolan started moving the girls out the penthouse door. But no sooner was he gone when Crash fell back into the room again.

"Freaking company," he announced. "Coming our way."

Everything just stopped and Nolan listened. In between the sounds of the howitzer shells going overhead, he could clearly hear footsteps rushing up the hotel's front stairs.

Voices were calling out: "Boss—where are you? *Boss*?"

Nolan just looked at Crash and grimaced. It seemed the pirates didn't know where Zeek was, either—and in light of the overhead bombardment, a lot of them rushed up here looking for him.

The pirates reached the top floor just as Crash locked the door to the penthouse. They were soon calling through the door for Zeek. Getting no response and knowing the hostages were in the penthouse, they tried opening the door, to no avail. Nolan put the four girls in the bathroom, telling them to get in the hot tub and to stay there no matter what.

As the pirates started to break down the door, another M198 shell went overhead and crashed in the rock forest behind the town. Nolan and Crash stood in the middle of the room and raised their weapons.

The door burst apart a moment later—splinters going everywhere. . . .

At least a dozen pirates were on the other side.

Nolan began to squeeze his trigger—Crash, too.

Then the lights went out.

Nolan fired first. With three rounds he shot the first three pirates through the door, killing them. One of them had a flare gun. It went off and sent a blinding, flaming missile streaking across the room, where it bounced off the plate glass window and right back into a fourth gunman's chest, blowing it apart and lighting the man on fire. Three more pirates lunged ahead, blinded by the burning flare. Nolan jammed his bayonet into one of them and shot the other two, using one bullet for each.

Crash used the butt of his M4 to knock another pirate off his feet; his boot to the gunman's throat crushed his larynx and killed him instantly. Nolan hit the floor, rolled to his left and fired his M4 point blank into a pirate's armpit, blowing out the man's rib cage. As this was going on, the pirates were firing wildly at them, but Nolan and Crash never stopped moving—that was the key. Bullets were flying everywhere, many of them tracer rounds. Nolan could hear them whizzing past his ears and feel their heat as they went by his face. None had hit him . . . at least not yet.

The pirate with the burning flare in his chest fell over, emitting ungodly screams and bathing the penthouse in a weird red glow. Another pirate lunged at Nolan, but Crash's fist came out of nowhere and punched the man hard on his temple. He fell into Nolan, knocking him to the floor again and finally separating him from his sticky M4, breaking off his bayonet in the process.

The next thing he knew, Nolan was crawling across the wet rug, trying to make his way through the crumple of bodies, bullets and blood, looking for something to shoot with. He found an AK-47 and started firing it at the door, but after just four rounds, it ran out of ammunition. Nolan tried to crawl back to the center of the room to find his own weapon, only to get punched hard in the jaw. He knew it was Crash who did it.

More tracer rounds bounced off the walls. Nolan lashed out with his field knife and, by pure luck, hit a pirate in his middle, toppling him. Nolan grabbed the pistol in the man's hand and, by the light of the flare, shot two more pirates—but then this gun, too, ran out of ammunition.

Nolan rolled over just as someone shot a stream of bullets into the floor. The penthouse's massive waterbed exploded, sending a deluge of hot water throughout the room and knocking everyone off their feet. The huge wooden wheel that had been tacked to the wall over the waterbed came crashing down on top of Nolan, almost knocking him out. He rolled out from under it and discovered that some of the spokes had come apart. They were fitted with sharp brass tips. He grabbed one and started swinging it at all the bodies he saw around him, hoping he'd hit anyone except Crash.

One of his swings connected. He heard a bone crack, and once more a pirate fell on top of him. Still without a weapon, he forced the piece of wood into the man's mouth and down his throat while pummeling with his other, very sticky hand. This stunned the pirate long enough for Nolan to grab his pistol and shoot him in the chest. Only then did the pirate's body go limp and Nolan was able to push him away.

The flare in the pirate's chest, splashed by the waterbed explosion, finally sizzled itself out, again plunging the penthouse into complete darkness. Just before the last of the illumination faded away Nolan caught a quick glimpse of Crash about five feet away, fighting desperately with two pirates, punching and flailing about wildly. Nolan shot one of the pirates in the buttocks, dropping him in an instant. Crash pushed the second one to the floor, where Nolan put a bullet in his head.

Suddenly a pirate was standing right over Nolan, looking down at him, reflected in the bare light of the moon outside. Nolan raised the pistol and squeezed the trigger, but nothing happened—*this* weapon was now out of ammunition. But an instant later, the pirate's chest was ripped open by three bullets. Crash had found Nolan's M4 and emptied it into the gunman. The man fell hard to the floor.

It seemed like a lifetime, but all this had taken place in no more than thirty seconds. And suddenly everything got quiet again. The penthouse was still except for the grunting and shallow breathing of the dying.

But then a beam of light shot through the room. Someone with a flashlight was walking over the dead and injured, inspecting the bodies. In the glare, Nolan could not see who it was. The light fell on him and Crash, who was now on the floor right beside him.

A moment of hope—the thought that the person with the flashlight might be Twitch—was dashed when the light lowered a little and revealed the face of another pirate, this one holding an AK-47 with, of all things, a bayonet attached.

Neither Nolan nor Crash had any weapons left. They were partially pinned under rubble and bodies. This pirate looked down on them, realized only they were alive among all his dead compatriots, and took two giant steps toward them.

Nolan looked into his eyes and realized the man was simply deciding which one of them to bayonet first.

The pirate's gaze fell on Nolan. He took one more step forward, raised his weapon, and started its downward motion—but suddenly stopped.

There was a strange noise, like someone opening a zipper, and the next thing Nolan knew, there was a long steel spear sticking out of the man's stomach.

A fishing spear, fired by someone from behind.

The pirate fell to the floor to reveal one of the girl students kneeling behind him, an old, expended spear gun still in her trembling hands.

TWITCH HAD BEEN so mesmerized and deafened by the M198 artillery shells going over his head and landing in the rock forest behind him, that he didn't hear the commotion going on up in the penthouse.

His job here was to secure their means of escape. But it was hard to ignore the ultra-bright balls of light that streaked across the sky, hitting about 2,000 feet away. It was like a fireworks show from a dream.

This was why he was so startled when the door he was guarding burst open and the four girl hostages stumbled out.

Nolan was right behind them. Twitch handed him a back-pack he'd been holding on to.

"OK, you know what to do," Nolan told him, as another shell went over their heads and crashed into the rock forest beyond.

"Roger that," Twitch told him.

With that, Twitch took out his empty Coke bottle and went about pouring some air from it on each mystified girl.

Meanwhile, Nolan hastily said to them: "Stay with my friend here. When he tells you to run, just start running and don't look back. We'll catch up with you."

But as Twitch began leading the female students away from the rear of the hotel, the one Nolan had saved from being slashed during the cruel game, grabbed the Whiskey CO by the arm.

"You *have* to come with us!" she told him, as if she would not take no for an answer.

"I can't," he said. "Not yet—now get going."

She started to protest, but she could tell Nolan was serious.

So, she grabbed him, hugged him, and kissed him full on the lips.

Then she disappeared into the dark with the others.

NOLAN RETURNED TO the penthouse, a little shaken, and flashed the laser pen six times out the window. Six blinks from a light on the DUS-7 was his reply. The M198 immediately stopped firing—and everything got quiet once more.

Crash took the backpack from him and reached inside. He produced one of the M198's artillery shells and carefully placed it on the floor.

It had a timer and fuse attached to it.

"This bit better work," Crash said.

"Well, it was your idea, wasn't it?" Nolan asked him.

Crash just shook his head. He, too, was covered with tar and feathers. "I can't remember back that far," he confessed. He looked the shell over. "It checks out," he declared. "As far as I can tell."

"Then let's do it," Nolan replied.

He peeked out the huge window and saw several dozen pirates below, still aligned along the seawall, hugging the concrete, eyes focused on the DUS-7, which had just stopped firing.

Now came the moment of truth. A problem that Team Whiskey knew they would face ever since they wound up at the entrance to Calzino's harbor: How would they deal with the pirates if they managed to get the hostages safely out of town? Just blowing up the *Pasha* and leaving it to NATO or the Seychelles government to sort out was never a consideration. With Zeek's connections, if they went that way, there was a good chance many of the pirates would either get off or get away, Zeek included.

No, the team was going to end it, here, with Zeek and his killers, one way or the other.

They faced two options, then. Once the hostages were out of danger, they could bombard the town with the dozen or so M198 shells they had left and then do what the brigands expected them to do: sail into the harbor and launch a brutal frontal assault, hoping that the big howitzer, the copter and their 50-caliber machine guns could sink the *Pasha* and kill all the pirates. But there were still dozens of enemy fighters on the island, all of them armed with AK-47s. Despite their big artillery piece and the air asset, there were still only ten warm bodies in Team Whiskey. It stood to reason some of them might not survive a battle like that.

So, Whiskey reached into its bag of tricks and came up with another way of dealing with the pirates.

Nolan and Crash set the fuse on the artillery shell, squeaked open the plate glass window, and gave the shell a mighty heave. It hit the pavement on the road outside—and bounced.

The clanging startled all the pirates nearby. They looked up to see Nolan and Crash looking down at them, giving them the finger.

Some pirates began pointing at them. Some began shooting at them. But some, out of pure curiosity, went over to investigate the shell.

And that's when it blew up.

COMMANDER LI WAS standing about 100 yards from the explosion. He saw bodies fly up in the air and he felt the concussion, the shock wave, and the heat. Shrapnel hit his arm, his forehead and his shoulder. They were all minor wounds, not that it would've made any difference.

He was momentarily confused because at first he thought this had been an artillery shell fired into their midst, and that the attack was on for real. But they had seen nothing shot off the freighter, nor had they heard the distinctive *whump!* of the M198 firing.

More confusing, he'd caught a glimpse of two men up in the penthouse looking down at the street just after the bomb went off. One of these men was wearing an eye patch, and it was over his left eye. But hadn't Li been watching this same man on the freighter for the past two hours? How could he be in two places at once?

All these thoughts went through his head in a split second— and suddenly it all fell into place. The hostages were gone. Rescued. The Delta Force guys had freed them. How? By coming over what had been advertised as Calzino's impassable terrain, and in the back door, right under Li's nose. And who were the people in the blue uniforms he'd been watching on the freighter? Stand-ins. Probably the American students who'd returned from diving.

So the Whiskey Team hadn't fallen back on their old tricks

after all. This was something new. Now, only the ship's mysterious shelling a short while ago didn't make sense.

Li was furious to the point of not being able to move or to
speak. But he recovered quickly and stood up amid the cloud
of debris. One thing he did know: No matter how skillful
their rescue of the hostages, the Whiskey Team members still
had to retreat the same way they came in, and this time they'd
have the hostages with them.

So had the shelling been an effort to create some kind of
path for them, to blast some part of the impassable terrain to
make it easier for them to get out?

Maybe . . .

In any case, blasted or not the Whiskey guys *had* to go
back over that hellish ground to escape.

And *that* meant Li would be able to pursue them.

He started running down the street, yelling that every one out
of two pirates lined up against the seawall should follow him.

This small army quickly came together. About thirty in
number, they ran through the dive shop and reached the far
edge of the town just in time to see the two armed men in
beachwear running into the forest of twisted rocks beyond.

Li had been right.

"If we get them now," he yelled to his men, "then we can
end this thing for good!"

The chase was on.

THE PIRATES RUSHED headlong into the chaotic, rocky land-
scape.

But right away, the terrain became far worse than Li had
imagined. When the Web site said this part of Calzino was
impenetrable and a danger to humans and animals alike, it
actually underestimated the conditions. *Thousands* of granite
slabs stuck out of the ground, looking like so many enormous,
twisted gravestones. Li's men soon discovered it was almost
impossible to run around the slabs or between them; most
were too close together. They were reduced to bouncing off
them, ping-pong style, with mixed results. In the meantime,
they'd lost sight of their prey in the dark.

"Spread out!" Li yelled to his men. "Call out if you pick them up again!"

Moving as fast as he could, Li was dizzy, trying to recall what else he'd read about the terrain on the southern part of Calzino. Just as he remembered the Web page had mentioned an old quarry on the far side of the island, he was introduced to Calzino's second impassable terrain drawback: He toppled into a tar pool.

The two pirates behind him were able to pull him out. Still, he found himself covered with the sticky stuff from the waist down. To add to the misery, just after coming out of the pool, he tripped and found himself covered in bird feathers. For some reason, there were hundreds of dead birds in the rock forest, and their rancid feathers were everywhere. It was disgusting.

Li resumed running. It was maddeningly hard work trying to quickly navigate around the stones in the dark, resulting in many bashed knees and elbows, as well as dealing with the tar pits, which came up at the most unexpected places. Just five minutes into the chase, Li and his men were bruised, battered, sticky and exhausted.

They reached a rare clearing. Several large pools of tar bubbled away. It would have been almost impossible for the pirates to cross—except the Whiskey Team guys had placed wooden planks across the pools, obviously when they were first sneaking up on the town. But they had made a mistake by leaving them in place during their retreat, because now Li and his men ran over them easily, avoiding the tar.

Once the small army was across, they were faced with a hill of granite blocks—some natural, some discarded when a quarry operated here. The hill was about fifty feet high, and there was no easy way around it.

Li and his men had no choice but to climb it, another grueling exercise. But it was worth it—because on the other side of the mound they found the large section of the rock field that had been blasted away by the howitzer's shells.

And perhaps the artillery shells *had* been shot here to clear away a particularly dense part of the rock field, and open up a path to the water, where Li was sure the dive boat was waiting for the Whiskey Team. But it appeared something had gone wrong. The shelling had destroyed a lot of slabs but had opened up a virtual ocean of bubbling tar in the process. The size of several large swimming pools, the pit was practically impossible to go around.

So where were the people they were pursuing? They certainly hadn't crossed this obstacle. Li used his night-vision goggles to scan the rock forest to the south and at last he spotted them again, the Delta guys and the hostages. They were in two groups. About five hundred yards away, with the light from the rising sun glaring off their brightly colored clothes, the four female hostages and one Whiskey Team guy in beachwear were moving with some difficulty through another field of slabs. About two hundred yards behind them were two more Whiskey Team guys, the ones who'd thrown the bomb out the window. They, too, were also moving as fast as they could over the difficult terrain.

But also from here, farther to the south, Li could see the remains of the old quarry—and at that moment, he realized that the fleeing hostages and their rescuers had been forced to take a wrong turn. Instead of heading for the sea, the escapees—unable to pass over the newly opened sea of tar—had turned inland and were now running toward the blind canyon that led into the old quarry itself.

"We have them," Li thought.

He hurried his men down the other side of the hill and toward the south, away from the water, following the tarry footprints that led them in that direction.

They soon reached edge of the quarry, and here the hellish terrain changed. No longer was it a field of giant, crooked monoliths. Rather, they were on the edge of a narrow, man-made road, cut out of deep, solid rock. This road led into the quarry.

Li called his men to a halt and took a quick head count. He'd started out with thirty men, and to their credit, despite many bashed knees and elbows, and many tumbles into the tar, all had been able to keep up with him. He had them check their weapons, making sure every AK-47 had a full ammo clip.

Then he contemplated the narrow man-made canyon. The road was tapered at the bottom of it, and the canyon's sheer walls were at least thirty feet high and impossible to climb. It was clear that this was a place of no escape; that there was only one way in and one way out. A scary proposition for any military commander.

Looking deeper into the twisting, turning canyon, Li could see the two Whiskey Team members who'd dropped the bomb onto the street running full tilt down the quarry road. Off in the distance, maybe a quarter mile away, were the main party of escapees, the four girls and the other Whiskey Team gunman.

"We've got them *for sure*," Li declared, but thinking to himself, "don't we?"

He ran everything through his mind. The Whiskey Team's stunning rescue attempt, their mysterious shelling of the rock forest, their throwing the time-delayed fused shell in among his men, then this crazy, bone-crunching pursuit.

Obviously, the first three things had been brilliantly planned. But just as his intuition had told him earlier, Li was certain the Whiskey Team had run out of its share of double-blessed luck. Maybe they'd become too clever, too intricate— but surely they had reached the end of the line when their artillery shells placed an insurmountable obstacle in their path instead of freeing them to make it to their boat and safety.

This was where the tide turned. The Whiskey Team was a bright star that had burned too quick. These three guys they were chasing were key players. Snuffing them out would enhance Li's street cred immeasurably. That was probably the most important reason of all to finish them off.

Li never really gave his men the go sign. He simply checked his weapon's ammo load and started running down the canyon alone. A second later, the rest of the pirates were right behind him.

The canyon twisted sharply right and fell off about twenty

feet before becoming straight again. When Li reached this sharp bend, he could see the shadows of two people moving along the canyon wall about a hundred yards ahead of them.

He leapt on the first high rock he came to and looked for the rest of the fleeing group farther down the canyon. He spotted them, now only about two hundred yards away. He rejoined his men and they ran on and on. It was a real foot chase now. As long as the fleeing group stayed in the canyon and thought someone was in pursuit, then they would eventually run right into a dead end.

The pirates ran a half-mile farther, slipping, gashing bones and skin, but never slowing down. The canyon began to twist and turn again, and more than once they got fleeting glimpses of some of the fleeing hostages and their rescuers going around the next corner, just up ahead.

Then they arrived at one particularly sharp turn, one too sharp to go around blindly. The team stopped and Li stuck his head around the corner. For the first time he could look down into the quarry itself, and there, out in the open, he spotted all of them: the three Whiskey Team guys and the four girls. They looked as dirty and banged up as Li and his pirates.

Standing in front of the far quarry wall, they were just realizing they had nowhere else to go.

They saw Li as soon as he saw them. A vicious gunfight ensued as the three Whiskey Team guys fired their weapons back at the small army of pirates. Li and his men took turns firing around the corner, expending lots of ammunition. It got to the point where pirates in the back were passing their fully loaded AK-47s to the men in front for them to use once their ammo had been expended.

This went one for almost five minutes, when the gunfire finally stopped.

Li looked around the corner again and saw the rescued and their rescuers were gone. He charged forward, and in seconds, he and his men reached the bottom of the quarry and found— nothing.

Except a rope ladder dangling from the farthest corner of the place.

At that moment, Li's walkie-talkie came alive. It was one of his lieutenants back at the town calling him.

The man said six words: "The helicopter is no longer there."

Li didn't know what he was talking about at first.

"Say again?" he shouted into the radio. "What do you mean?"

"You told us to keep an eye on the freighter's helicopter and tell you if it moved," the man explained. "Well, it's moved. It is no longer there."

Li's heart sank to his feet. A moment later, he heard the sound. He turned and realized the copter had swooped down behind them.

It sent a stream of bullets at the pirates as it went by, hitting a few. Some of the pirates fired their AK-47s at it, but the copter was moving too fast—and the pirates were practically out of ammunition anyway.

Besides, the copter was not here to kill them. It turned and fired six rockets at the wall up near the last bend in the quarry road, the place where the intense gunfight had played out. The resulting explosions effectively sealed the road shut.

And just like that, it was the pirates who were trapped.

Already they could hear the booming of the large gun on the rusty freighter sending a shell high into the air, heading their way.

Li fell to the seat of his pants.

The Whiskey Team guys had fooled him. Their plan wasn't like their assault on Zeek's HQ. Not really. Neither had they seen the need to turn into ghosts like when they retook the *Global Warrior*. Nor had they chosen to once more risk going toe-to-toe with the *Pasha* on the high seas.

"Damn," Li whispered as the M198 shell bore down on him. "It was Tora Bora. They were the pursuers that day. But today, they made *us* chase *them*."

26

BATMAN CAREFULLY PUT the copter down on the rocky beach, then helped each of the four girls climb out.

The dive boat was anchored nearby, bouncing in the high waves. Batman left the girls in the care of its captain, the unsung hero who had ferried the disguised Nolan, Crash and Twitch to the far side of the island in the first place.

What was sure to be a tearful reunion among the four rescued women and their scuba-diving boyfriends would take place soon, but after that, the dive boat captain would head full-speed to Mahe, the nearest island, hoping to find help.

The four girls, still in shock, thanked Batman profusely for what the team had done. Batman wished them safe passage then took to the skies again. Team Whiskey still had things to do.

He flew back to the quarry to pick up his three out-of-uniform colleagues. He found them still staring into the old excavation pit; some of the pirates' bodies continued to burn fiercely down below. It had taken just six M198 shells fired pinpoint into the quarry to annihilate the army of brigands. The team had been prepared to spray the thirty or so bodies with more gunfire, just to make sure they were all dead. But one look at the results of the bombardment told them that would not be necessary. No one could have survived that.

"Wow—I thought the party on that sandbar was bad," Batman said, looking into the pit and thinking back to the battle on Pirate Island. "But at least it was over in a few seconds for these guys."

Nolan felt his stomach do a flip. "Torn in half by machine guns or blown to pieces by artillery—dead is still dead. And we're not even at the end of it yet."

Without another word, they grimly reloaded their M4s, climbed into the copter and headed back to town.

In just thirty minutes, everything had changed. The hostages were safe, and combining the unexpected fight in the penthouse, the hand-carried M198 fused-bomb attack and the slaughter in the quarry, nearly two-thirds of the pirates were dead.

But now the team had to deal with those who remained.

As the copter approached the town, Nolan radioed Gunner and told him to initiate the next part of the plan. Gunner complied by loading and firing the M198, sending a single shell high over Calzino. This was not some high explosive he'd sent aloft, but a star shell—a bright retarded-flight flare that created an artificial sun over the tiny harbor even as the real sun was starting to break on the eastern horizon.

Those couple dozen pirates who remained in place against the seawall had no idea what was going on. Without their charismatic leader Commander Li, they weren't sure what to do. The purpose of the star shell then was to further distract the already distracted gunmen.

As they were looking up at the flare, wondering was it was about, the copter came in behind them. Flying parallel to the waterfront street, moving very fast and very low, it aimed its gun pod and opened up—and in one sweep, took out more than half the remaining pirates, some before they knew what hit them.

Those who avoided being cut down were faced with escaping into the rock forest or diving into the sea. Most chose the sea, only to be shot up by the Senegals firing the 50-caliber machine guns from the deck of the *Dustboat*. The few pirates who actually tried to disappear into the rock forest behind the town were hunted down and eliminated by the team members firing their M4s from the copter.

It was distasteful and bloody, but the team knew that just like back on Pirate Island, no mercy could be shown here. The pirates, if not murderers and sadists themselves, were working for one, so the world was better off without them. Plus, the team had to send a message to any other sea gangs in the area thinking about doing what Zeek's crew had tried to do. It was important that these pirate wannabes knew their life expectancy would drop dramatically if they ran into Team Whiskey.

The stiffest battle of the clearing operation turned out to be against the crewmen of the *Pasha*. They'd been almost an afterthought for most of the long, bloody night. But after dealing with the pirates on land, and dropping off Nolan, Crash and Twitch near the seawall, Batman dove on the ship and strafed it from one end to the other.

His actions were met with a hail of gunfire, but much of it was misdirected, underscoring the fact that the people on the ship were sailors and not seasoned fighters. The team's response, though, started a brief but furious clash in which the copter, the *Dustboat* and the team members on shore fired at the *Pasha* from three different directions. At one point, the tracer fire was so intense it blotted out the newly rising sun.

Finally, though, the people on the boat ran out of ammunition, and all firing ceased. The Senegals brought the *Dustboat* about a hundred feet into the harbor, and now with calm water below, Gunner fired off an M198 shell that hit the *Pasha* square on its tail, destroying its propulsion systems.

Everything quieted down after that. None of the team members were enthusiastic about going aboard the burning ship and searching it cabin by cabin to root out any dead-enders. So they just waited for them to show up on deck themselves, trying to escape the smoke and flames. When they did, Crash dispatched them with his sniper rifle.

It took about a half hour of this before the team felt certain most of their adversaries had been eliminated. Finally it was time for them to get down to the real order of business.

Finding and killing Zeek.

FROM WHAT THE team could determine, the Pirate King hadn't been seen since shortly after the executions on the seawall. That had been more than an hour ago, which meant he could be anywhere on the island by this point.

So, Gunner and the Senegals moved the DUS-7 even closer to the waterfront and directed the boat's powerful searchlight through the early-morning haze and smoke and onto Calzino's three buildings. And while Batman circled above, Nolan, Crash and Twitch began their grim search.

They started in the dive shop, an open-air building with few places to hide. Still, they tore the place apart, looked in every box, every storage cabinet and locker, even inside the anti-bends decompression chamber. But they found no sign of Zeek.

Next, they tossed the bar. The kitchen, the freezer, the cellar, the bar itself, under every table and couch, even in the rafters of the drop-down ceiling. Nothing.

The hotel was the most difficult to search. It was three floors, nine rooms, many closets and supply cabinets, a laundry and a kitchen—and there were dead bodies just about everywhere. Each corpse had to be checked, each air vent and bathroom searched. They even looked under the beds.

Nothing . . .

They returned to the street and had a short sat-phone conversation with Batman, still orbiting above. The sun was fully up now and in the early-morning light the little town looked surreal. With all the bodies lying about, it was like the set of a *Living Dead* movie.

Nolan took it all in and asked aloud: "What's that famous line? 'I've become Death, the destroyer of worlds.'"

"Bingo that," Crash agreed.

Their conversation with Batman was whether Gunner should bombard the town anyway, just in case Zeek was indeed still hiding in there, somewhere. They just couldn't bring themselves to do this, though. So instead, they decided that Batman should fly over the rock forest once again, to see if the Pirate King had somehow made it out of town and was lost among the stones.

Then the others searched all three buildings a second time.

But again, they found nothing.

AS THE SUN climbed steadily in the sky, the day grew hot. Nolan, Crash and Twitch, sweating madly, still sticky with tar and wearing the awful beachwear, went through the buildings a third time, again unsuccessfully.

Finally, they took a breather on the sea wall. Nolan didn't smoke, but he wished he could have a drag or two on a cigarette now—or even a joint would do.

They were all exhausted. They hadn't slept in almost three days, hadn't eaten in that time either, hadn't even downed a cup of coffee.

They'd eliminated Zeek's new gang, wrecked his new warship, wrecked his plans to move his bloodthirsty operations to Somalia. But none of them felt any sense of accomplishment, because they had not yet found the Pirate King himself.

They bitched and moaned for a few minutes, the only noise being the rumble of the *Dustboat*'s engines idling in the harbor and the faraway, high-pitched whine of the work copter flying over the rock forest again.

Their eyes naturally fell on the *Pasha,* just a couple of dozen feet off the beach. It was smoking heavily, flames shooting out of several openings, and it was listing badly to port. It was a wreck, but it was also the only place they hadn't searched.

They all came to the same conclusion simultaneously.

"Man, I don't want to do this," Crash said, speaking for all of them.

"It has to be done, though," Twitch replied gravely. "So, ship ahoy."

But it was as if someone had read their minds, because an instant later, a great crash came from the ship and a large part of the hull facing them fell open. At first they thought it was the result of the brief but vicious battle they'd just fought with the people remaining on the ship, a buckling of the lower decks or something. But then they saw this section of the hull was actually connected to a massive set of hydraulic hinges. It was supposed to open this way—courtesy of its previous owner, the Playboy of Java.

Out from the cavity behind it came a large, sleek motorboat, twenty feet long or more, its engine already running. It hit the water with a splash, turned a violent 180 degrees, and then headed out of the harbor at incredible speed.

"Son of a bitch!" Crash yelled. It had all happened so fast, none of them had been able to react. "There he goes!"

"Right under our noses!" Twitch cried.

It was true. In the instant he glimpsed it, Nolan saw Zeek,

long hair flowing, hunched over in the back of the motorboat with what looked to be about a half dozen of the *Pasha*'s sailors surrounding him. A seventh man was actually driving the boat. All of the sailors appeared to be armed not just with AK-47s, but with at least one rocket-propelled grenade launcher. They were creating a human shield around the Pirate King.

Nolan, Crash and Twitch finally got their weapons up and began shooting at the motorboat, but it was quickly out of range.

Then they heard gunfire coming from the DUS-7. The Senegals had spotted the escaping speedster and were firing at it, too. But it was swerving mightily and going too fast for them to get a good bead on it.

Then, just as suddenly, the work copter came out of nowhere, roared over the beach and began strafing the motorboat.

"Fucking Batman!" Crash yelled in triumph. "Right place, right time!"

But just as he was saying this, they saw a flash from the motorboat and a streak of light shoot up at the copter. There was another, brighter flash, and suddenly the copter began staggering in the air. The team knew what had happened: Someone on the motorboat had shot an RPG at the work copter. The missile had exploded—not inside the copter, but very close to it.

The copter wobbled to a complete stop in midair as the motorboat roared through a hail of bullets and out of the harbor completely. Somehow the tiny aircraft flew its way down to the end of the *Dustboat* and made what amounted to a controlled crash landing on the back of the ship.

"Damn!" Nolan yelled. "They got Batman."

The next thing Nolan knew, he was swimming. He had to get out to the *Dustboat* and this was the quickest way. He swam like crazy and before he could even think about it, he was being pulled up to the deck of the freighter by one of the Senegals. Crash and Twitch were right behind him.

Nolan immediately ran to the back of the ship where the

copter had come down, and saw a gruesome sight. Gunner and the other Senegals had pulled Batman from the copter, which was damaged but far from destroyed. But Batman was not in such good shape.

The RPG had taken his left hand completely off.

He was lying on the deck, bleeding and in shock. Gunner was trying to apply a tourniquet to the horrendous wound, but it was tough going.

Nolan knelt down to say something to Batman, but the pilot used his one good hand to grab him by the collar instead.

He said just one thing to Nolan: "Go kill that bastard."

THE WORK COPTER was leaking fuel.

A thin slice of shrapnel from the RPG blast had torn a slight hole in a fuel line under the passenger compartment, and aviation gas was spurting from it.

The copter's navigation system had also been blown out, as had its GPS antenna. And its radio battery was drained to nearly zero.

But it could still fly—and now Nolan, with Batman's blood still on him, was strapped into the pilot's seat. As he lifted off very unsteadily from the *Dustboat*, a great wash of anxiety and dread came over him.

His head was spinning; he was almost dizzy. He couldn't get the sight of Batman's mangled stump out of his mind. Of all the death and violence he'd seen just that morning, this is what sickened him the most.

He also hated flying the work copter. Hated the way it smelled; hated that he was now alone in it, unprepared, going off on what might be a one-way mission.

But his honor was at stake, and so was the team's. And, most of all, they needed revenge.

He headed out to sea, hoping the glare of the rising sun would help him find a tiny speck in a very large ocean. But it was still foggy in spots, making his search more difficult. He figured Zeek probably had at least a ten-minute head start on him. The pirate's escape boat was built for speed. In those ten minutes, he could have gone quite a ways, in any direction.

But Nolan guessed the Pirate King would head west, toward the African mainland. So he turned the copter in that direction, becoming almost overwhelmed with the smell of the leaking fuel as he did so.

He flew along like this for twenty minutes, but between the fog and his hands trembling on the controls, searching the water below was almost impossible. He kept losing the horizon and thinking he was turning upside down. The engine had already sputtered a couple times, and the smell of leaking fuel was growing worse.

Then he spotted something, about 1,000 feet below. It was a body, floating atop the waves, blood leaking out of it.

Nolan brought the copter down to a shaky hover directly over the body. It took him a few moments to realize it was actually one of the *Pasha*'s sailors. He'd been shot in the head.

Nolan continued on, flying low, now through dense fog and a minute later, found another dead sailor floating in the currents. A half-mile away, he came upon a third body, and then a fourth about a mile away from that. All had been shot in the head and left to bleed into the ocean.

Only then did Nolan realize what Zeek was doing. Just like Team Whiskey had done while nursing the *Dustboat* to Calzino, Zeek was gruesomely lightening his load so his getaway could be faster and his fuel could carry him farther.

NOLAN FOUND THE fifth and sixth sailors floating about five miles to the west of the last.

He was flying at just a hundred feet now, still furious, hands still shaking, the copter's engine popping every few seconds, and the smell of aviation gas almost choking him.

He finally broke out of the fog bank only to see a fusillade of tracer rounds coming at him. Before he knew it, he was looking straight up into the morning sky—strictly on instinct he'd pulled up on the copter's controls and avoided getting perforated by about a nanosecond.

He leveled out quickly and began shaking even worse than before. "Fuck me," he swore. "That was close. . . ."

When he looked below, he finally spotted Zeek's boat. In fact, he'd just flown over it. And indeed, it was moving very swiftly to the west.

Zeek was at the controls now; all but one of his loyal crew was dead and this last one was holding an AK-47. Nolan could see bloodstains and spent shell casings all over on the motorboat's rear deck.

Using up the remaining bit of the copter's radio power, Nolan called back to the DUS-7, now at least twenty-five miles to the south of him. He gave the Senegals his coordinates and told them he'd found the motorboat and was going to attack it.

That would be the last the DUS-7 heard from him.

Nolan had his M4 out. He checked the gun pod's readout and swore: It had exactly four shells left in its cannon.

He swooped down out of the sun and fired the four cannon shells at the motorboat. Only two hit, but fortunately they smashed into the boat's engine, setting it on fire. The last remaining sailor sent another barrage of bullets Nolan's way, but he was moving too quickly to get hit. The AK rounds passed by him harmlessly.

He swung the copter around and lined up on the motorboat's nose. With the gun pod empty, he stuck his M4 out the open door and squeezed the trigger. He didn't have to move the gun; the copter was doing all the moving for him. He went right over the motorboat, his rounds perforating its forward deck.

Nolan went around a third time and opened up again. This time his bullets pinged off the rear of the boat, close to where Zeek was sitting. He emptied his gun on this pass, and a few seconds later the motorboat's engine finally blew up.

Nolan shakily swerved the copter out of the way of the explosion. By the time he turned and made his way through the cloud of smoke and spray, he saw that the boat and the last sailor had been blown to pieces. But he could not see Zeek.

He began a frantic search for the Pirate King, endlessly circling the wreckage, but found nothing.

Then, out of the corner of his good eye, he saw a glint of light.

It was yet another escape boat. Smaller, and made of rubber, it had been ejected from the motorboat and instantly inflated just seconds after the engine blew up.

This escape boat had a remarkably large electric motor, and Zeek was at the controls. He was going west, heading for a shoreline that was now in view. Some part of terra firma was out there, the coast of Somalia perhaps, forty miles off in the haze.

Nolan knew if he allowed Zeek to get to shore, he'd never find him.

But what could he do?

His gun was out of ammo. His fuel was almost gone. The radio had lost all its power and the copter's engine sounded like it had blown a gasket or two.

Nolan didn't even think about it; he flew the copter about a hundred feet in front of Zeek's boat and jumped out, falling fifty feet to the ocean. The copter chased him down, as if it was angry at him for so suddenly ending its life.

He hit the water hard and wisely started swimming downward, not toward the surface. The copter hit a moment later, making an ungodly sound as the hot metal, the sparking electricity, and the still-spinning rotors smashed into the cold water.

The copter followed him down, seemingly unwilling to let him get away with its murder. Nolan abruptly changed direction and started swimming sideways. He felt one of the rotor blades hit the heel of his boot, one last blow of defiance as the machine kept sinking.

Nolan hastily kicked his way back up to the surface, breathing in a bit too soon and getting a mouthful of salt water for his effort.

He spit out the water and took another deep breath, mostly air this time. But the salt water had gotten up under his eye patch and was stinging his eye socket mercilessly.

Then he heard a noise behind him. He turned to see Zeek in his rubber escape boat bearing down on him.

The pirate was coming on fast—but this is exactly what Nolan wanted.

He drew out his combat knife, kept it below the surface. When Zeek sped by, he jabbed the knife into the boat and felt the satisfying sensation of the blade puncturing the rubber. He slashed it as deep as he could in the microsecond the opportunity allowed.

It nearly broke Nolan's wrist, but he was able to put a huge gash in the boat, losing the knife in the process.

The rubber boat started losing speed almost immediately. He saw Zeek look behind him, wondering what was wrong, then discovering that his getaway craft was losing air and was on the verge of collapsing.

Nolan actually felt a smile crack his bloody, salty face.

This ends right now, he whispered to himself.

He started swimming madly toward the sinking boat, and as he closed in on it, he could clearly see the terror in Zeek's eyes. At that moment he thought that maybe Zeek, the murderous Pirate King, was actually afraid of the water. He certainly stayed aboard the collapsing raft much longer than he should have. As it deflated and it started folding in on itself, a large chunk of it caught in the dying engine's propeller, quickly tearing the back half of the raft to pieces.

By the time Zeek finally bailed out, Nolan was on top of him.

Fueled by fear, Zeek became vicious. He pulled a knife and slashed wildly at Nolan, who came at him with only fists flying. Zeek wasn't sinking, but it was obvious he couldn't swim very well. Nolan just kept hitting him, trying to avoid his knife, then hitting him again.

This went on for what seemed like forever, Zeek swearing at him and screaming: "You? *You?*" as if he had known that it would come to this.

Finally Zeek lunged forward in an attempt to cut open Nolan's chest, but the blade of his knife got caught in his own long, stringy, wet hair.

When the entangled knife would not come out, Nolan saw his chance. He grabbed hold of Zeek's collar and began pummeling him about the neck, face and head. But the pirate was stronger than he looked and he managed to get his hands up on Nolan's face. He started to gouge out Nolan's remaining eye. Nolan was terrified and instantly felt a rush of adrenaline. The thought of being made blind way out here gave him the extra strength he needed to push the pirate away.

With this action, the knife finally fell out of Zeek's hair. They both dove for it as it started to sink, and in the process, knocked heads violently.

It was almost comical, but Zeek got the worst of it—and this allowed Nolan to grab him around the neck.

He was exhausted, as was Zeek. But Nolan would not be denied.

With his one free hand, he managed to grab the ends of the pirate's two gold chains and twist them under his throat. Zeek began thrashing wildly as he realized what Nolan was doing—but it was too late. Nolan was able to wrap the chains completely around Zeek's neck and yank them tight.

The pirate fought back ferociously, but after a few seconds slowly began to lose strength. Nolan heard him start to gurgle.

He screamed in the pirate's ear: "Do you have any more brothers?"

Zeek started wailing. "No—none!"

That's when Nolan used the last of his strength to pull the gold chains as tight as he could. Zeek battled mightily one last time, but then he could fight no more. A spray of blood came out of his mouth and he went limp.

Nolan hung on, though. He didn't loosen his grip for at least two minutes. Only when he saw Zeek had voided himself did he finally let him go.

Then he watched as the body slowly slipped beneath the waves.

NOLAN COULD BARELY breathe.

He kicked off his boots, took off all his clothing except his shorts, then rolled over on his back, not sure if he could stay conscious. He was cut, he was bleeding, he had water in his lungs, and he felt like he was dying of pure exhaustion. How was he going to get out of this?

Then he thought, what was the point in hanging on? He was out in the middle of the ocean, with no raft, nothing to cling to. The nearest land was at least thirty miles away, probably much more. He couldn't swim it. He could barely move.

So, was *this* how it was going to end? he thought.

Drowning in the Indian Ocean . . .

He lay back, gasping for breath now. The faces of his colleagues flashed before his eyes.

Good-bye, guys. . . .

Then other faces from earlier in his life.

His family. His friends. That girl he should have married.

Good-bye to all . . .

He closed his eyes and began to sink.

But then he heard something pop up right beside him. He looked to his left and was stunned. It was Twitch's Coke bottle, still capped, rising to the surface after escaping from the sinking work copter.

Nolan actually laughed. In low morbid humor, he managed to grab the bottle and uncap it and pretend to pour the air out of it onto himself, appreciating one last time the huge cosmic joke.

That's when he heard a great gushing sound behind him. He turned just in time to see, incredibly, the work copter come roaring back from the depths and dramatically return to the surface.

Nolan couldn't believe it. He stared at the copter for the longest time, bobbing in the waves, trying to make some sense of it. The aircraft was made of lightweight materials. And the closed part of the cockpit held a fair amount of air, he supposed. Plus the fuel tank, one of the biggest things on the copter, was empty, so full of air as well.

But he stopped questioning it at that point and just swam over to it and hung on tight.

It would be his lifeboat.

27

Italy
Three Weeks Later

THE U.S. NAVY hospital at Percino was located in the south of Italy, on a cliff overlooking the warm Mediterranean Sea.

Though it was open to anyone serving in the Navy, it was mostly high-ranking officers who came here to recuperate from combat wounds or other medical issues.

There were six main buildings, all designed in a faux monastery style, fitting in with their lush, scenic surroundings.

There was a large recreation area here, too, featuring swimming pools, handball courts and a professional-size soccer field. On this warm, pleasant afternoon, a team made up of American servicemen was playing a local Italian club.

On a terrace atop the highest building in the hospital complex, a tense meeting was about to take place. A rectangular table had been set up with an umbrella providing shade. Several pitchers of ice water and lemonade were brought out. An ashtray was also provided.

On one side of the table sat Mikos Kilos, owner of Kilos Shipping. Beside him sat his Middle East security manager, Mark Conley, and the Kilos company attorney.

Sitting across from them and already sweating bullets was a rear admiral representing the U.S. Navy's Persian Gulf Fleet, a representative from the Department of Defense, and a high-ranking official from the CIA.

One seat at the table was still empty. The others waited in uncomfortable silence for the seventh person to join them.

Finally he appeared. Dressed in plain blue fatigues, a straw hat and sunglasses, he carried a bottle of wine and a cigarette pack in his right hand. His left arm was in a sling. Protruding from it was a wrap of heavy bandages where the left hand might be. Sticking out of the bandages was a five-inch, bright metal hook.

Batman Bob Graves took his seat at the table. He poured

himself a glass of wine, lit a cigarette that smelled suspiciously like marijuana, and then leaned back in his chair and said, "Ready when you are."

The government representatives were appalled by his appearance and his actions, but said nothing. They were not in control here. No matter how many different ways they looked at it, Graves held all the cards.

The DoD representative began the meeting. He had a two-page document in his hands.

"We have looked over your proposals," he started—but Graves cut him off instantly.

"They are not 'proposals,'" he said. "They are demands."

The DoD man grimaced, but continued.

"We can fulfill most of these," he said. "Even though I'd like to go on record as saying the vast majority of them are outrageous."

Graves took a long drag on his cigarette, then a sip of wine.

"Duly noted," he said. "The DoD thinks the demands are outrageous. Next?"

The Kilos attorney spoke up. "I think it's in everyone's best interests that we go over the . . . well, the list, just to make sure we are all on the same page."

"Sounds good to me," Graves said.

On a helipad on the roof of the next building over sat two brand-new OH-6J helicopters armed to the teeth with 50-caliber machine guns, wing-mounted rockets and a nose-mounted 30mm cannons. Both were painted ghostly black and had decals on their noses identifying them as *Bad Dawg One* and *Bad Dawg Two*.

"Item one," the attorney began, gesturing over his shoulder at the pair of fierce-looking copters. "Mister Graves, those two aircraft now belong to you and your associates."

The three government representatives sank a little lower in their seats.

The attorney next put two photographs on the table. One showed six sniper rifles, of various shapes and sizes, all of them brand new and equipped with classified targeting equipment. The second photo showed an updated version of the

M198 howitzer with a variety of shells on display around it, including satellite-guided ordnance.

"Item two," the attorney said. "The equipment in these photos now belongs to Mr. Graves and his associates. Delivery date to be determined."

Graves picked up his wine glass and pretended to toast the government reps.

"Item three," the attorney went on. "Agent Curt Hush of the ONI will immediately be relieved of his duties, and an independent prosecutor will be appointed to investigate any illegal acts committed by Agent Hush and/or the ONI in or around the Indian Ocean in the past ninety days."

More embarrassed looks from the government's side of the table.

"Item four," the attorney continued. "Any officers and staff assigned to Building 18 at Walter Reed Army Medical Center as of January of last year will be immediately relieved of duty.

"Item five, the DoD will reimburse the owners of the Rijah Saleem shopping mall in Yanbu District, Saudi Arabia, for the price of one slightly used IH-6 work helicopter.

"And item six—the U.S. Navy agrees not to perform any unwarranted searches on vessels belonging to Kilos Shipping or its subsidiaries."

Kilos and Conley did their best to suppress a smile at this.

The attorney flipped over to the second page.

"Now for the items in dispute," he said.

He turned to the Navy admiral.

"The floor is yours," the attorney told him.

The Navy officer looked sternly at Graves for a few moments. In reply, Graves blew a cloud of smoke in his direction.

"Mr. Graves," the admiral began. "Investigating the ONI I can understand, I guess. But you can't really expect me to give you the names of the two pilots who, quite unfortunately, shot at you that night in the Indian Ocean."

"Why not?" Graves asked him.

"Well, because you're not really clear what you want these names for," the officer replied.

"I want to find these guys and fuck them up," Graves said plainly.

"As in physically assault them?"

"Yes."

The Navy officer looked at Graves's left hand. "Are you sure?" he asked.

Graves sent another cloud of smoke his way. "Breathe deep, Admiral," Graves told him.

The lawyer interrupted. "Is this a deal-breaker?" he asked Graves. "It *is* highly unusual."

Graves thought a moment and then just shook his head no. "I'll find out eventually," he said.

The attorney breathed a sigh of relief. "OK, then let's move on."

The DoD official spoke next. "We looked into your next request—or demand, whatever," he began. "And we have to tell you this will be harder than you think."

"Why?" Graves wanted to know.

"Because it is extremely difficult to reverse the decision of a military court," the DoD man said.

"But that was a secret court," Graves told him, getting angry. "And it was a sham. There was no defense attorney present. No right of rebuttal or appeal."

"It was 'the times,'" the DoD official said. "Post-9/11. And it was an order that went all the way up to the person who was at the top of the DoD at the time. And you'll have to believe me, I know Washington politics. The judge, we can make do a back flip on this. But that former top guy? You'll have to wait until he dies before that decision can be reversed. I'm sorry—but that's just the way it is."

There was complete silence around the table. The only noise was coming from the soccer field on the other side of the hospital. The U.S. team had just scored a goal. In celebration, people were chanting, "USA! USA!"

The Kilos attorney looked at Graves and shrugged slightly.

"Deal-breaker?" he asked.

Graves looked at Kilos himself and Conley. Both men knew how passionate Graves felt about this last item.

"OK," Graves finally said. "I want two alternate things as a substitute."

He leaned forward so he was just inches away from the DoD representative.

"I want you to appoint an attorney whose sole job it will be to get this military trial decision overturned," he said. "Not in a backroom or a funeral home, but in the courts, through legal means. I want this guy to have an office, an aide and a secretary. I want him working full time on this until it happens."

The DoD man was stunned. "And your second request?"

Graves leaned back in his chair. "Five million dollars," he said. "Tax-free, in cash."

Those on the government side of the table all looked like they wanted to throttle Graves, one hand or not.

But after a brief discussion, they reluctantly agreed to everything.

"Now it's your turn to come through, to make good," the CIA man said to Graves.

Graves took a long drag of his cigarette and crushed it out. Then he retrieved a notebook from his back pocket. It was the book he'd taken that night while raiding the brothel on Brothel Beach. He put it on the table and pushed it toward the man from the CIA.

"Page fifty-six," Graves said. "It's the only one written in red ink."

THE MEETING BROKE up five minutes later. Graves walked back to the rehab wing of the hospital to find Crash, Twitch and Gunner waiting for him in the lobby.

The team had been here since the action on Calzino Island. The U.S. military agreed to take care of them in return for a briefing on everything that happened in their pursuit of Zeek Kurjan. In particular, the CIA wanted the address book from the brothel and especially the dirt on the Chinese leadership and its sexual peccadilloes.

This was Graves's enormous bargaining chip, and it had pretty much gotten him what he wanted for his teammates—all except for Nolan.

The Team Whiskey leader had been recuperating in his own private suite on the top floor of the rehab wing. After his final battle with Zeek, a Filipino tuna boat had fished him out of the sea, ironic in a way. The Filipino crew contacted the DUS-7, but by the time Nolan had been transferred back to the *Dustboat*, the U.S. Navy, NATO and the Seychelles military had all converged on Calzino Island.

"We'll be back in business in less than a month," Graves told the team members now. "And we'll be richer for it, too."

There were high fives all round, and then Graves said he'd meet them back in his room for some serious drinking. But first he wanted to go talk to Nolan.

He made his way down the corridor and up the stairs, finally arriving outside Nolan's room. There was a long, narrow window on the door, and before knocking, Graves peeked in.

He saw Nolan, standing at the foot of his bed, his back partially turned to him. Oddly, Nolan had a typical household iron in his hand and a small ironing board set up in front of him.

Graves actually scratched his head. What the heck was he doing?

He watched his colleague for a few moments and then realized that Nolan was ironing an American flag. Graves recognized it as the same flag Nolan had given to Twitch to stem his bleeding that night over the Talua Tangs, the same one Nolan had waved from the mast of the DUS-7 to save them from getting sunk by the Navy fighter jets, the same one Nolan had been quietly carrying around with him ever since that fateful day at Tora Bora.

As Graves continued watching, Nolan pressed out the newly washed flag firm and square. Then, putting the iron aside, he meticulously folded the flag into a triangle, and finally sat on the edge of his bed. He started turning the folded flag over and over in his hands, stopping only occasionally to wipe his good eye.

Graves removed his hand from the doorknob and decided not to knock. He quietly walked away.

They could talk some other time.

* * *

A FEW MINUTES later, Nolan carefully laid the flag on the table next to his bed. He walked out on the open balcony of his suite and sat in the padded chair there. From here he could look right out on the Mediterranean.

He could see all kinds of ships passing by: pleasure boats, commercial ships. Some military vessels. The afternoon was warm with only a slight breeze, but out on the water, several fog banks had emerged.

Nolan wiped his moist eye a few more times, then leaned back and eventually fell into a deep sleep, his first in a very long time.

Had he stayed awake, though, he would have seen an unusual vessel passing slowly out of one fog bank.

It was container ship, painted black with a white bridge—and to anyone paying attention, it looked curiously empty.

It was in sight for only a minute or so, before it slipped into another fog bank and vanished again.

TOR

Award-winning authors
Compelling stories

Please join us at the website
below for more information
about this author and other great
Tor selections, and to sign up for
our monthly newsletter!